PENGUIN BOOKS

IRELAND: SELECTED STORIES

William Trevor was born in Mitchelstown, Co. Cork, in 1928, and spent his childhood in provincial Ireland. He attended a number of Irish schools and, later, Trinity College, Dublin. He is a member of the Irish Academy of Letters.

Among his books are *The Old Boys* (1964), winner of the Hawthornden Prize; *The Children of Dynmouth* (1976) and *Fools of Fortune* (1983), both winners of the Whitbread Award; *The Silence in the Garden* (1989), winner of the Yorkshire Post Book of the Year Award; and *Two Lives* (1991; comprising the novellas *Reading Turgenev*, shortlisted for the Booker Prize, and *My House in Umbria*), which was named by *The New York Times* as one of the ten best books of the year. His eight volumes of stories were brought together in *The Collected Stories* (1992), chosen by *The New York Times* as one of the ten best books of the year. Many of his stories have appeared in *The New Yorker* and other magazines. He has also written plays for the stage, and for radio and television. In 1977 William Trevor was named honorary Commander of the British Empire in recognition of his services to literature. His last novel, *Felicia's Journey* (1994), won the Whitbread Book of the Year Award and the Sunday Express prize. It was a national bestseller. His most recent novel, *Death in Summer* (1998), is available from Viking.

William Trevor lives in Devon, England.

IRELAND

Selected Stories

William Trevor

PENGUIN BOOKS

PENGUIN BOOKS

Published by the Penguin Group
Penguin Putnam Inc., 375 Hudson Street,
New York, New York 10014, U.S.A.
Penguin Books Ltd, 27 Wrights Lane,
London W8 5TZ, England
Penguin Books Australia Ltd, Ringwood,
Victoria, Australia
Penguin Books Canada Ltd, 10 Alcorn Avenue,
Toronto, Ontario, Canada M4V 3B2
Penguin Books (N.Z.) Ltd, 182–190 Wairau Road,
Auckland 10, New Zealand
Penguin India, 210 Chiranjiv Tower, 43 Nehru Place,
New Delhi 11009, India

Penguin Books Ltd, Registered Offices:
Harmondsworth, Middlesex, England

First published in Penguin Books (U.K.) 1995
This edition with the stories "The Piano Tuner's Wives" and "Lost Ground"
published in Penguin Books (U.S.A.) 1998

3 5 7 9 10 8 6 4 2

Copyright © William Trevor, 1998
All rights reserved

The stories in this book appeared previously in the periodicals *Grand
Street*, *London* magazine, *The New Yorker*, *The Times* (London),
Woman's Journal and in the following short story collections of Mr.
Trevor, all published by Penguin Books: *After Rain*, *Angels at the Ritz*,
The Ballroom of Romance, *Beyond the Pale*, *Collected Stories*, *Family
Sins*, *Lovers of Their Time*, and *The News from Ireland*.

LIBRARY OF CONGRESS CATALOGING IN PUBLICATION DATA
Trevor, William, 1928–
Ireland: selected stories / William Trevor.
p. cm.— (Penguin classics)
ISBN 0 14 02.7759 5
1. Ireland—Social life and customs—Fiction. I. Title.
II. Series.
PR6070.R4A6   1998
823'.914—dc21   98–15420

Printed in the United States of America
Set in Adobe Garamond
Designed by Virginia Norey

Contents

Contents

Author's Note

This selection of stories has been made from the Viking and Penguin editions of my *Collected Stories* and *After Rain*. It is representative of these collections as a whole rather than being a personal choice of those stories which I consider to be the best.

William Trevor

IRELAND

The Ballroom of Romance

On Sundays, or on Mondays if he couldn't make it and often he couldn't, Sunday being his busy day, Canon O'Connell arrived at the farm in order to hold a private service with Bridie's father, who couldn't get about any more, having had a leg amputated after gangrene had set in. They'd had a pony and cart then and Bridie's mother had been alive: it hadn't been difficult for the two of them to help her father on to the cart in order to make the journey to Mass. But two years later the pony had gone lame and eventually had to be destroyed; not long after that her mother had died. 'Don't worry about it at all,' Canon O'Connell had said, referring to the difficulty of transporting her father to Mass. 'I'll slip up by the week, Bridie.'

The milk lorry called daily for the single churn of milk, Mr Driscoll delivered groceries and meal in his van, and took away the eggs that Bridie had collected during the week. Since Canon O'Connell had made his offer, in 1953, Bridie's father hadn't left the farm.

As well as Mass on Sundays and her weekly visits to a wayside dance-hall Bridie went shopping once every month, cycling to the town early on a Friday afternoon. She bought things for herself, material for a dress, knitting wool, stockings, a newspaper, and paper-backed Wild West novels for her father. She talked in the shops to some of the girls she'd been at school with, girls who had married shop-assistants or shopkeepers, or had become assistants themselves. Most of them had families of their own by now. 'You're lucky to be peaceful in the hills,' they said to Bridie, 'instead of stuck in a hole like this.' They had a tired look, most of them, from pregnancies and their efforts to organize and control their large families.

As she cycled back to the hills on a Friday Bridie often felt that they truly envied her her life, and she found it surprising that they should do so. If it hadn't been for her father she'd have wanted to work in the town also, in the tinned-meat factory maybe, or in a shop. The town had a cinema called the Electric, and a fish-and-chip shop where people met at night, eating chips out of newspaper on the pavement outside. In the evenings, sitting in the farmhouse with her father, she often thought about the town, imagining the shop-windows lit up to display their goods and the sweet-shops still open so that people could purchase chocolates or fruit to take with them to the Electric cinema. But the town was eleven miles away, which was too far to cycle, there and back, for an evening's entertainment.

'It's a terrible thing for you, girl,' her father used to say, genuinely troubled, 'tied up to a one-legged man.' He would sigh heavily, hobbling back from the fields, where he managed as best he could. 'If your mother hadn't died,' he'd say, not finishing the sentence.

If her mother hadn't died her mother could have looked after him and the scant acres he owned, her mother could somehow have lifted the milk-churn on to the collection platform and attended to the few hens and the cows. 'I'd be dead without the girl to assist me,' she'd heard her father saying to Canon O'Connell, and Canon O'Connell replied that he was certainly lucky to have her.

'Amn't I as happy here as anywhere?' she'd say herself, but her father knew she was pretending and was saddened because the weight of circumstances had so harshly interfered with her life.

Although her father still called her a girl, Bridie was thirty-six. She was tall and strong: the skin of her fingers and her palms were stained, and harsh to touch. The labour they'd experienced had found its way into them, as though juices had come out of vegetation and pigment out of soil: since childhood she'd torn away the rough scotch grass that grew each spring among her father's mangolds and sugar beet; since childhood she'd harvested potatoes in

August, her hands daily rooting in the ground she loosened and turned. Wind had toughened the flesh of her face, sun had browned it; her neck and nose were lean, her lips touched with early wrinkles.

But on Saturday nights Bridie forgot the scotch grass and the soil. In different dresses she cycled to the dance-hall, encouraged to make the journey by her father. 'Doesn't it do you good, girl?' he'd say, as though he imagined she begrudged herself the pleasure. 'Why wouldn't you enjoy yourself?' She'd cook him his tea and then he'd settle down with the wireless, or maybe a Wild West novel. In time, while still she danced, he'd stoke the fire up and hobble his way upstairs to bed.

The dance-hall, owned by Mr Justin Dwyer, was miles from anywhere, a lone building by the roadside with treeless boglands all around and a gravel expanse in front of it. On pink pebbled cement its title was painted in an azure blue that matched the depth of the background shade yet stood out well, unfussily proclaiming *The Ballroom of Romance*. Above these letters four coloured bulbs—in red, green, orange and mauve—were lit at appropriate times, an indication that the evening rendezvous was open for business. Only the façade of the building was pink, the other walls being a more ordinary grey. And inside, except for pink swing-doors, everything was blue.

On Saturday nights Mr Justin Dwyer, a small, thin man, unlocked the metal grid that protected his property and drew it back, creating an open mouth from which music would later pour. He helped his wife to carry crates of lemonade and packets of biscuits from their car, and then took up a position in the tiny vestibule between the drawn-back grid and the pink swing-doors. He sat at a card-table, with money and tickets spread out before him. He'd made a fortune, people said: he owned other ballrooms also.

People came on bicycles or in old motor-cars, country people like Bridie from remote hill farms and villages. People who did not often see other people met there, girls and boys, men and women. They paid Mr Dwyer and passed into his dance-hall, where shadows were cast on pale-blue walls and light from a crystal bowl was dim.

The band, known as the Romantic Jazz Band, was composed of clarinet, drums and piano. The drummer sometimes sang.

Bridie had been going to the dance-hall since first she left the Presentation Nuns, before her mother's death. She didn't mind the journey, which was seven miles there and seven back: she'd travelled as far every day to the Presentation Nuns on the same bicycle, which had once been the property of her mother, an old Rudge purchased originally in 1936. On Sundays she cycled six miles to Mass, but she never minded either: she'd grown quite used to all that.

'How're you, Bridie?' inquired Mr Justin Dwyer when she arrived in a new scarlet dress one autumn evening. She said she was all right and in reply to Mr Dwyer's second query she said that her father was all right also. 'I'll go up one of these days,' promised Mr Dwyer, which was a promise he'd been making for twenty years.

She paid the entrance fee and passed through the pink swing-doors. The Romantic Jazz Band was playing a familiar melody of the past, 'The Destiny Waltz'. In spite of the band's title, jazz was not ever played in the ballroom: Mr Dwyer did not personally care for that kind of music, nor had he cared for various dance movements that had come and gone over the years. Jiving, rock and roll, twisting and other such variations had all been resisted by Mr Dwyer, who believed that a ballroom should be, as much as possible, a dignified place. The Romantic Jazz Band consisted of Mr Maloney, Mr Swanton, and Dano Ryan on drums. They were three middle-aged men who drove out from the town in Mr Maloney's car, amateur performers who were employed otherwise by the tinned-meat factory, the Electricity Supply Board and the County Council.

'How're you, Bridie?' inquired Dano Ryan as she passed him on her way to the cloakroom. He was idle for a moment with his drums, 'The Destiny Waltz' not calling for much attention from him.

'I'm all right, Dano,' she said. 'Are you fit yourself? Are the eyes better?' The week before he'd told her that he'd developed a watering of the eyes that must have been some kind of cold or other.

He'd woken up with it in the morning and it had persisted until the afternoon: it was a new experience, he'd told her, adding that he'd never had a day's illness or discomfort in his life.

'I think I need glasses,' he said now, and as she passed into the cloakroom she imagined him in glasses, repairing the roads, as he was employed to do by the County Council. You hardly ever saw a road-mender with glasses, she reflected, and she wondered if all the dust that was inherent in his work had perhaps affected his eyes.

'How're you, Bridie?' a girl called Eenie Mackie said in the cloakroom, a girl who'd left the Presentation Nuns only a year ago.

'That's a lovely dress, Eenie,' Bridie said. 'Is it nylon, that?'

'Tricel actually. Drip-dry.'

Bridie took off her coat and hung it on a hook. There was a small wash-basin in the cloakroom above which hung a discoloured oval mirror. Used tissues and pieces of cotton-wool, cigarette-butts and matches covered the concrete floor. Lengths of green-painted timber partitioned off a lavatory in a corner.

'Jeez, you're looking great, Bridie,' Madge Dowding remarked, waiting for her turn at the mirror. She moved towards it as she spoke, taking off a pair of spectacles before endeavouring to apply make-up to the lashes of her eye. She stared myopically into the oval mirror, humming while the other girls became restive.

'Will you hurry up, for God's sake!' shouted Eenie Mackie. 'We're standing here all night, Madge.'

Madge Dowding was the only one who was older than Bridie. She was thirty-nine, although often she said she was younger. The girls sniggered about that, saying that Madge Dowding should accept her condition—her age and her squint and her poor complexion—and not make herself ridiculous going out after men. What man would be bothered with the like of her anyway? Madge Dowding would do better to give herself over to do Saturday-night work for the Legion of Mary: wasn't Canon O'Connell always looking for aid?

'Is that fellow there?' she asked now, moving away from the mirror. 'The guy with the long arms. Did anyone see him outside?'

'He's dancing with Cat Bolger,' one of the girls replied. 'She has herself glued to him.'

'Lover boy,' remarked Patty Byrne, and everyone laughed because the person referred to was hardly a boy any more, being over fifty it was said, a bachelor who came only occasionally to the dance-hall.

Madge Dowding left the cloakroom rapidly, not bothering to pretend she wasn't anxious about the conjunction of Cat Bolger and the man with the long arms. Two sharp spots of red had come into her cheeks, and when she stumbled in her haste the girls in the cloakroom laughed. A younger girl would have pretended to be casual.

Bridie chatted, waiting for the mirror. Some girls, not wishing to be delayed, used the mirrors of their compacts. Then in twos and threes, occasionally singly, they left the cloakroom and took their places on upright wooden chairs at one end of the dance-hall, waiting to be asked to dance. Mr Maloney, Mr Swanton and Dano Ryan played 'Harvest Moon' and 'I Wonder Who's Kissing Her Now' and 'I'll Be Around'.

Bridie danced. Her father would be falling asleep by the fire; the wireless, tuned in to Radio Eireann, would be murmuring in the background. Already he'd have listened to *Faith and Order* and *Spot the Talent*. His Wild West novel, *Three Rode Fast* by Jake Matall, would have dropped from his single knee on to the flagged floor. He would wake with a jerk as he did every night and, forgetting what night it was, might be surprised not to see her, for usually she was sitting there at the table, mending clothes or washing eggs. 'Is it time for the news?' he'd automatically say.

Dust and cigarette smoke formed a haze beneath the crystal bowl, feet thudded, girls shrieked and laughed, some of them dancing together for want of a male partner. The music was loud, the musicians had taken off their jackets. Vigorously they played a number of tunes from *State Fair* and then, more romantically, 'Just One of Those Things'. The tempo increased for a Paul Jones, after which Bridie found herself with a youth who told her he was saving up to emigrate, the nation in his opinion being finished. 'I'm up in the hills with the uncle,' he said, 'labouring fourteen hours a day. Is it any life for a young fellow?' She knew his uncle, a hill farmer whose stony acres were separated from her father's by one other farm only. 'He has me gutted with work,' the youth told her. 'Is there sense in it at all, Bridie?'

At ten o'clock there was a stir, occasioned by the arrival of three middle-aged bachelors who'd cycled over from Carey's public house. They shouted and whistled, greeting other people across the dancing area. They smelt of stout and sweat and whiskey.

Every Saturday at just this time they arrived, and, having sold them their tickets, Mr Dwyer folded up his card-table and locked the tin box that held the evening's takings: his ballroom was complete.

'How're you, Bridie?' one of the bachelors, known as Bowser Egan, inquired. Another one, Tim Daly, asked Patty Byrne how she was. 'Will we take the floor?' Eyes Horgan suggested to Madge Dowding, already pressing the front of his navy-blue suit against the net of her dress. Bridie danced with Bowser Egan, who said she was looking great.

The bachelors would never marry, the girls of the dance-hall considered: they were wedded already, to stout and whiskey and laziness, to three old mothers somewhere up in the hills. The man with the long arms didn't drink but he was the same in all other ways: he had the same look of a bachelor, a quality in his face.

'Great,' Bowser Egan said, feather-stepping in an inaccurate and inebriated manner. 'You're a great little dancer, Bridie.'

'Will you lay off that!' cried Madge Dowding, her voice shrill above the sound of the music. Eyes Horgan had slipped two fingers into the back of her dress and was now pretending they'd got there by accident. He smiled blearily, his huge red face streaming with perspiration, the eyes which gave him his nickname protuberant and bloodshot.

'Watch your step with that one,' Bowser Egan called out, laughing so that spittle sprayed on to Bridie's face. Eenie Mackie, who was also dancing near the incident, laughed also and winked at Bridie. Dano Ryan left his drums and sang. 'Oh, how I miss your gentle kiss,' he crooned, 'and long to hold you tight.'

Nobody knew the name of the man with the long arms. The only words he'd ever been known to speak in the Ballroom of Romance were the words that formed his invitation to dance. He was a shy man who stood alone when he wasn't performing on the dance-floor. He rode away on his bicycle afterwards, not saying good-night to anyone.

'Cat has your man leppin' tonight,' Tim Daly remarked to Patty Byrne, for the liveliness that Cat Bolger had introduced into foxtrot and waltz was noticeable.

'I think of you only,' sang Dano Ryan. 'Only wishing, wishing you were by my side.'

Dano Ryan would have done, Bridie often thought, because he was a different kind of bachelor: he had a lonely look about him, as if he'd become tired of being on his own. Every week she thought he would have done, and during the week her mind regularly returned to that thought. Dano Ryan would have done because she felt he wouldn't mind coming to live in the farmhouse while her one-legged father was still about the place. Three could live as cheaply as two where Dano Ryan was concerned because giving up the wages he earned as a road-worker would be balanced by the saving made on what he paid for lodgings. Once, at the end of an evening, she'd pretended that there was a puncture in the back wheel of her bicycle and he'd concerned himself with it while Mr Maloney and Mr Swanton waited for him in Mr Maloney's car. He'd blown the tyre up with the car pump and had said he thought it would hold.

It was well known in the dance-hall that she fancied her chances with Dano Ryan. But it was well known also that Dano Ryan had got into a set way of life and had remained in it for quite some years. He lodged with a widow called Mrs Griffin and Mrs Griffin's mentally affected son, in a cottage on the outskirts of the town. He was said to be good to the affected child, buying him sweets and taking him out for rides on the crossbar of his bicycle. He gave an hour or two of his time every week to the Church of Our Lady Queen of Heaven, and he was loyal to Mr Dwyer. He performed in the two other rural dance-halls that Mr Dwyer owned, rejecting advances from the town's more sophisticated dance-hall, even though it was more conveniently situated for him and the fee was more substantial than that paid by Mr Dwyer. But Mr Dwyer had discovered Dano Ryan and Dano had not forgotten it, just as Mr Maloney and Mr Swanton had not forgotten their discovery by Mr Dwyer either.

'Would we take a lemonade?' Bowser Egan suggested. 'And a packet of biscuits, Bridie?'

No alcoholic liquor was ever served in the Ballroom of Romance, the premises not being licensed for this added stimulant. Mr Dwyer in fact had never sought a licence for any of his premises, knowing that romance and alcohol were difficult commodities to mix, especially in a dignified ballroom. Behind where the girls sat on the wooden chairs Mr Dwyer's wife, a small stout woman, served the bottles of lemonade, with straws, and the biscuits, and crisps. She talked busily while doing so, mainly about the turkeys she kept. She'd once told Bridie that she thought of them as children.

'Thanks,' Bridie said, and Bowser Egan led her to the trestle table. Soon it would be the intermission: soon the three members of the band would cross the floor also for refreshment. She thought up questions to ask Dano Ryan.

When first she'd danced in the Ballroom of Romance, when she was just sixteen, Dano Ryan had been there also, four years older than she was, playing the drums for Mr Maloney as he played them now. She'd hardly noticed him then because of his not being one of the dancers: he was part of the ballroom's scenery, like the trestle table and the lemonade bottles, and Mrs Dwyer and Mr Dwyer. The youths who'd danced with her then in their Saturday-night blue suits had later disappeared into the town, or to Dublin or Britain, leaving behind them those who became the middle-aged bachelors of the hills. There'd been a boy called Patrick Grady whom she had loved in those days. Week after week she'd ridden away from the Ballroom of Romance with the image of his face in her mind, a thin face, pale beneath black hair. It had been different, dancing with Patrick Grady, and she'd felt that he found it different dancing with her, although he'd never said so. At night she'd dreamed of him and in the daytime too, while she helped her mother in the kitchen or her father with the cows. Week by week she'd returned to the ballroom, delighting in its pink façade and dancing in the arms of Patrick Grady. Often they'd stood together drinking lemonade, not saying anything, not knowing what to say. She knew he loved her, and she believed then that he would lead her one day from the dim, romantic ballroom, from its blueness and its pinkness and its crystal bowl of light and its music. She believed he would lead her into sunshine, to the town and the Church of Our Lady Queen of Heaven, to marriage and smiling faces. But someone else had got Patrick Grady, a girl from the town who'd never danced in the wayside ballroom. She'd scooped up Patrick Grady when he didn't have a chance.

Bridie had wept, hearing that. By night she'd lain in her bed in the farmhouse, quietly crying, the tears rolling into her hair and making the pillow damp. When she woke in the early morning the thought was still naggingly with her and it remained with her by day, replacing her daytime dreams of happiness. Someone told her later on that he'd crossed to Britain, to Wolverhampton, with the girl he'd married, and she imagined him there, in a place she wasn't able properly to visualize, labouring in a factory, his children being born and acquiring the accent of the area. The Ballroom of Romance wasn't the same without him, and when no one else stood out for her particularly over the years and when no one offered her marriage, she found herself wondering about Dano Ryan. If you couldn't have love, the next best thing was surely a decent man.

Bowser Egan hardly fell into that category, nor did Tim Daly. And it was plain to everyone that Cat Bolger and Madge Dowding were wasting their time over the man with the long arms. Madge Dowding was already a figure of fun in the ballroom, the way she ran after the bachelors; Cat Bolger would end up the same if she wasn't careful. One way or another it wasn't difficult to be a figure of fun in the ballroom, and you didn't have to be as old as Madge Dowding: a girl who'd just left the Presentation Nuns had once asked Eyes Horgan what he had in his trouser pocket and he told her it was a penknife. She'd repeated this afterwards in the cloakroom, how she'd requested Eyes Horgan not to dance so close to her because his penknife was sticking into her. 'Jeez, aren't you the right baby!' Patty Byrne had shouted delightedly; everyone had laughed, knowing that Eyes Horgan only came to the ballroom for stuff like that. He was no use to any girl.

'Two lemonades, Mrs Dwyer,' Bowser Egan said, 'and two packets of Kerry Creams. Is Kerry Creams all right, Bridie?'

She nodded, smiling. Kerry Creams would be fine, she said.

'Well, Bridie, isn't that the great outfit you have!' Mrs Dwyer remarked. 'Doesn't the red suit her, Bowser?'

By the swing-doors stood Mr Dwyer, smoking a cigarette that he held cupped in his left hand. His small eyes noted all developments. He had been aware of Madge Dowding's anxiety when Eyes Horgan had inserted two fingers into the back opening of her dress. He had looked away, not caring for the incident, but had it developed further he would have spoken to Eyes Horgan, as he had on other occasions. Some of the younger lads didn't know any better and would dance very close to their partners, who generally were too embarrassed to do anything about it, being young themselves. But that, in Mr Dwyer's opinion, was a different kettle of fish altogether because they were decent young lads who'd in no time at all be doing a steady line with a girl and would end up as he had himself with Mrs Dwyer, in the same house with her, sleeping in a bed with her, firmly married. It was the middle-aged bachelors who required the watching: they came down from the hills like mountain goats, released from their mammies and from the smell of animals and soil. Mr Dwyer continued to watch Eyes Horgan, wondering how drunk he was.

Dano Ryan's song came to an end, Mr Swanton laid down his

clarinet, Mr Maloney rose from the piano. Dano Ryan wiped sweat from his face and the three men slowly moved towards Mrs Dwyer's trestle table.

'Jeez, you have powerful legs,' Eyes Horgan whispered to Madge Dowding, but Madge Dowding's attention was on the man with the long arms, who had left Cat Bolger's side and was proceeding in the direction of the men's lavatory. He never took refreshments. She moved, herself, towards the men's lavatory, to take up a position outside it, but Eyes Horgan followed her. 'Would you take a lemonade, Madge?' he asked. He had a small bottle of whiskey on him: if they went into a corner they could add a drop of it to the lemonade. She didn't drink spirits, she reminded him, and he went away.

'Excuse me a minute,' Bowser Egan said, putting down his bottle of lemonade. He crossed the floor to the lavatory. He too, Bridie knew, would have a small bottle of whiskey on him. She watched while Dano Ryan, listening to a story Mr Maloney was telling, paused in the centre of the ballroom, his head bent to hear what was being said. He was a big man, heavily made, with black hair that was slightly touched with grey, and big hands. He laughed when Mr Maloney came to the end of his story and then bent his head again, in order to listen to a story told by Mr Swanton.

'Are you on your own, Bridie?' Cat Bolger asked, and Bridie said she was waiting for Bowser Egan. 'I think I'll have a lemonade,' Cat Bolger said.

Younger boys and girls stood with their arms still around one another, queuing up for refreshments. Boys who hadn't danced at all, being nervous because they didn't know any steps, stood in groups, smoking and making jokes. Girls who hadn't been danced with yet talked to one another, their eyes wandering. Some of them sucked at straws in lemonade bottles.

Bridie, still watching Dano Ryan, imagined him wearing the glasses he'd referred to, sitting in the farmhouse kitchen, reading one of her father's Wild West novels. She imagined the three of them eating a meal she'd prepared, fried eggs and rashers and fried potato-cakes, and tea and bread and butter and jam, brown bread and soda and shop bread. She imagined Dano Ryan leaving the kitchen in the morning to go out to the fields in order to weed the mangolds, and her father hobbling off behind him, and the two men working together. She saw hay being cut, Dano Ryan with the scythe that she'd learned to use herself, her father using a rake as best he could. She saw herself, because of the extra help, being able to attend to things in the farmhouse, things she'd never had time for because of the cows and the hens and the fields. There were bedroom curtains that needed repairing where the net had ripped, and wallpaper that had become loose and needed to be stuck up with flour paste. The scullery required white-washing.

The night he'd blown up the tyre of her bicycle she'd thought he was going to kiss her. He'd crouched on the ground in the darkness with his ear to the tyre, listening for escaping air. When he could hear none he'd straightened up and said he thought she'd be all right on the bicycle. His face had been quite close to hers and she'd smiled at him. At that moment, unfortunately, Mr Maloney had blown an impatient blast on the horn of his motor-car.

Often she'd been kissed by Bowser Egan, on the nights when he insisted on riding part of the way home with her. They had to dismount in order to push their bicycles up a hill and the first time he'd accompanied her he'd contrived to fall against her, steadying himself by putting a hand on her shoulder. The next thing she was aware of was the moist quality of his lips and the sound of his bicycle as it clattered noisily on the road. He'd suggested then, regaining his breath, that they should go into a field.

That was nine years ago. In the intervening passage of time she'd been kissed as well, in similar circumstances, by Eyes Horgan and Tim Daly. She'd gone into fields with them and permitted them to put their arms about her while heavily they breathed. At one time or another she had imagined marriage with one or other of them, seeing them in the farmhouse with her father, even though the fantasies were unlikely.

Bridie stood with Cat Bolger, knowing that it would be some

time before Bowser Egan came out of the lavatory. Mr Maloney, Mr Swanton and Dano Ryan approached, Mr Maloney insisting that he would fetch three bottles of lemonade from the trestle table.

'You sang the last one beautifully,' Bridie said to Dano Ryan. 'Isn't it a beautiful song?'

Mr Swanton said it was the finest song ever written, and Cat Bolger said she preferred 'Danny Boy', which in her opinion was the finest song ever written.

'Take a suck of that,' said Mr Maloney, handing Dano Ryan and Mr Swanton bottles of lemonade. 'How's Bridie tonight? Is your father well, Bridie?'

Her father was all right, she said.

'I hear they're starting a cement factory,' said Mr Maloney. 'Did anyone hear talk of that? They're after striking some commodity in the earth that makes good cement. Ten feet down, over at Kilmalough.'

'It'll bring employment,' said Mr Swanton. 'It's employment that's necessary in this area.'

'Canon O'Connell was on about it,' Mr Maloney said. 'There's Yankee money involved.'

'Will the Yanks come over?' inquired Cat Bolger. 'Will they run it themselves, Mr Maloney?'

Mr Maloney, intent on his lemonade, didn't hear the questions and Cat Bolger didn't repeat them.

'There's stuff called Optrex,' Bridie said quietly to Dano Ryan, 'that my father took the time he had a cold in his eyes. Maybe Optrex would settle the watering, Dano.'

'Ah sure, it doesn't worry me that much—'

'It's terrible, anything wrong with the eyes. You wouldn't want to take a chance. You'd get Optrex in a chemist, Dano, and a little bowl with it so that you can bathe the eyes.'

Her father's eyes had become red-rimmed and unsightly to look at. She'd gone into Riordan's Medical Hall in the town and had explained what the trouble was, and Mr Riordan had recommended

Optrex. She told this to Dano Ryan, adding that her father had had no trouble with his eyes since. Dano Ryan nodded.

'Did you hear that, Mrs Dwyer?' Mr Maloney called out. 'A cement factory for Kilmalough.'

Mrs Dwyer wagged her head, placing empty bottles in a crate. She'd heard references to the cement factory, she said: it was the best news for a long time.

'Kilmalough won't know itself,' her husband commented, joining her in her task with the empty lemonade bottles.

'Twill bring prosperity certainly,' said Mr Swanton. 'I was saying just there, Justin, that employment's what's necessary.'

'Sure, won't the Yanks—' began Cat Bolger, but Mr Maloney interrupted her.

'The Yanks'll be in at the top, Cat, or maybe not here at all—maybe only inserting money into it. It'll be local labour entirely.'

'You'll not marry a Yank, Cat,' said Mr Swanton, loudly laughing. 'You can't catch those fellows.'

'Haven't you plenty of homemade bachelors?' suggested Mr Maloney. He laughed also, throwing away the straw he was sucking through and tipping the bottle into his mouth. Cat Bolger told him to get on with himself. She moved towards the men's lavatory and took up a position outside it, not speaking to Madge Dowding, who was still standing there.

'Keep a watch on Eyes Horgan,' Mrs Dwyer warned her husband, which was advice she gave him at this time every Saturday night, knowing that Eyes Horgan was drinking in the lavatory. When he was drunk Eyes Horgan was the most difficult of the bachelors.

'I have a drop of it left, Dano,' Bridie said quietly. 'I could bring it over on Saturday. The eye stuff.'

'Ah, don't worry yourself, Bridie—'

'No trouble at all. Honestly now—'

'Mrs Griffin has me fixed up for a test with Dr Cready. The old eyes are no worry, only when I'm reading the paper or at the pictures. Mrs Griffin says I'm only straining them due to lack of glasses.'

He looked away while he said that, and she knew at once that Mrs Griffin was arranging to marry him. She felt it instinctively: Mrs Griffin was going to marry him because she was afraid that if he moved away from her cottage, to get married to someone else, she'd find it hard to replace him with another lodger who'd be good to her affected son. He'd become a father to Mrs Griffin's affected son, to whom already he was kind. It was a natural outcome, for Mrs Griffin had all the chances, seeing him every night and morning and not having to make do with weekly encounters in a ballroom.

She thought of Patrick Grady, seeing in her mind his pale, thin face. She might be the mother of four of his children now, or seven or eight maybe. She might be living in Wolverhampton, going out to the pictures in the evenings, instead of looking after a one-legged man. If the weight of circumstances hadn't intervened she wouldn't be standing in a wayside ballroom, mourning the marriage of a road-mender she didn't love. For a moment she thought she might cry, standing there thinking of Patrick Grady in Wolverhampton. In her life, on the farm and in the house, there was no place for tears. Tears were a luxury, like flowers would be in the fields where the mangolds grew, or fresh whitewash in the scullery. It wouldn't have been fair ever to have wept in the kitchen while her father sat listening to *Spot the Talent*: her father had more right to weep, having lost a leg. He suffered in a greater way, yet he remained kind and concerned for her.

In the Ballroom of Romance she felt behind her eyes the tears that it would have been improper to release in the presence of her father. She wanted to let them go, to feel them streaming on her cheeks, to receive the sympathy of Dano Ryan and of everyone else. She wanted them all to listen to her while she told them about Patrick Grady who was now in Wolverhampton and about the death of her mother and her own life since. She wanted Dano Ryan to put his arm around her so that she could lean her head against it. She wanted him to look at her in his decent way and to stroke with his road-mender's fingers the backs of her hands. She might wake in a bed with him and imagine for a moment that he was Patrick Grady. She might bathe his eyes and pretend.

'Back to business,' said Mr Maloney, leading his band across the floor to their instruments.

'Tell your father I was asking for him,' Dano Ryan said. She smiled and she promised, as though nothing had happened, that she would tell her father that.

She danced with Tim Daly and then again with the youth who'd said he intended to emigrate. She saw Madge Dowding moving swiftly towards the man with the long arms as he came out of the lavatory, moving faster than Cat Bolger. Eyes Horgan approached Cat Bolger. Dancing with her, he spoke earnestly, attempting to persuade her to permit him to ride part of the way home with her. He was unaware of the jealousy that was coming from her as she watched Madge Dowding holding close to her the man with the long arms while they performed a quickstep. Cat Bolger was in her thirties also.

'Get away out of that,' said Bowser Egan, cutting in on the youth who was dancing with Bridie. 'Go home to your mammy, boy.' He took her into his arms, saying again that she was looking great tonight. 'Did you hear about the cement factory?' he said. 'Isn't it great for Kilmalough?'

She agreed. She said what Mr Swanton and Mr Maloney had said: that the cement factory would bring employment to the neighbourhood.

'Will I ride home with you a bit, Bridie?' Bowser Egan suggested, and she pretended not to hear him. 'Aren't you my girl, Bridie, and always have been?' he said, a statement that made no sense at all.

His voice went on whispering at her, saying he would marry her tomorrow only his mother wouldn't permit another woman in the house. She knew what it was like herself, he reminded her, having a parent to look after: you couldn't leave them to rot, you had to honour your father and your mother.

She danced to 'The Bells Are Ringing', moving her legs in time with Bowser Egan's while over his shoulder she watched Dano Ryan softly striking one of his smaller drums. Mrs Griffin had got him even though she was nearly fifty, with no looks at all, a lumpish woman with lumpish legs and arms. Mrs Griffin had got him just as the girl had got Patrick Grady.

The music ceased, Bowser Egan held her hard against him, trying to touch her face with his. Around them, people whistled and clapped: the evening had come to an end. She walked away from Bowser Egan, knowing that not ever again would she dance in the Ballroom of Romance. She'd been a figure of fun, trying to promote a relationship with a middle-aged County Council labourer, as ridiculous as Madge Dowding dancing on beyond her time.

'I'm waiting outside for you, Cat,' Eyes Horgan called out, lighting a cigarette as he made for the swing-doors.

Already the man with the long arms—made long, so they said, from carrying rocks off his land—had left the ballroom. Others were moving briskly. Mr Dwyer was tidying the chairs.

In the cloakroom the girls put on their coats and said they'd see one another at Mass the next day. Madge Dowding hurried. 'Are you OK, Bridie?' Patty Byrne asked and Bridie said she was. She smiled at little Patty Byrne, wondering if a day would come for the younger girl also, if one day she'd decide that she was a figure of fun in a wayside ballroom.

'Good-night so,' Bridie said, leaving the cloakroom, and the girls who were still chatting there wished her good-night. Outside the cloakroom she paused for a moment. Mr Dwyer was still tidying the chairs, picking up empty lemonade bottles from the floor, setting the chairs in a neat row. His wife was sweeping the floor. 'Good-night, Bridie,' Mr Dwyer said. 'Good-night, Bridie,' his wife said.

Extra lights had been switched on so that the Dwyers could see what they were doing. In the glare the blue walls of the ballroom seemed tatty, marked with hair-oil where men had leaned against them, inscribed with names and initials and hearts with arrows through them. The crystal bowl gave out a light that was ineffective in the glare; the bowl was broken here and there, which wasn't noticeable when the other lights weren't on.

'Good-night so,' Bridie said to the Dwyers. She passed through the swing-doors and descended the three concrete steps on the gravel expanse in front of the ballroom. People were gathered on the gravel, talking in groups, standing with their bicycles. She saw Madge Dowding going off with Tim Daly. A youth rode away with a girl on the crossbar of his bicycle. The engines of motor-cars started.

'Good-night, Bridie,' Dano Ryan said.

'Good-night, Dano,' she said.

She walked across the gravel towards her bicycle, hearing Mr Maloney, somewhere behind her, repeating that no matter how you looked at it the cement factory would be a great thing for Kilmalough. She heard the bang of a car door and knew it was Mr Swanton banging the door of Mr Maloney's car because he always gave it the same loud bang. Two other doors banged as she reached her bicycle and then the engine started up and the headlights went on. She touched the two tyres of the bicycle to make certain she hadn't a puncture. The wheels of Mr Maloney's car traversed the gravel and were silent when they reached the road.

'Good-night, Bridie,' someone called, and she replied, pushing her bicycle towards the road.

'Will I ride a little way with you?' Bowser Egan asked.

They rode together and when they arrived at the hill for which it was necessary to dismount she looked back and saw in the distance the four coloured bulbs that decorated the façade of the Ballroom of Romance. As she watched, the lights went out, and she imagined Mr Dwyer pulling the metal grid across the front of his property and locking the two padlocks that secured it. His wife would be waiting with the evening's takings, sitting in the front of their car.

'D'you know what it is, Bridie,' said Bowser Egan, 'you were never looking better than tonight.' He took from a pocket of his suit the small bottle of whiskey he had. He uncorked it and drank some and then handed it to her. She took it and drank. 'Sure, why wouldn't you?' he said, surprised to see her drinking because she never had in his company before. It was an unpleasant taste, she considered, a taste she'd experienced only twice before, when she'd taken whiskey as a remedy for toothache. 'What harm would it do you?' Bowser Egan said as she raised the bottle again to her lips. He reached out a hand for it, though, suddenly concerned lest she should consume a greater share than he wished her to.

She watched him drinking more expertly than she had. He would always be drinking, she thought. He'd be lazy and useless, sitting in the kitchen with the *Irish Press*. He'd waste money buying a secondhand motor-car in order to drive into the town to go to the public houses on fair-days.

'She's shook these days,' he said, referring to his mother. 'She'll hardly last two years, I'm thinking.' He threw the empty whiskey bottle into the ditch and lit a cigarette. They pushed their bicycles. He said:

'When she goes, Bridie, I'll sell the bloody place up. I'll sell the pigs and the whole damn one and twopence worth.' He paused in order to raise the cigarette to his lips. He drew in smoke and exhaled it. 'With the cash that I'll get I could improve some place else, Bridie.'

They reached a gate on the left-hand side of the road and automatically they pushed their bicycles towards it and leaned them against it. He climbed over the gate into the field and she climbed after him. 'Will we sit down here, Bridie?' he said, offering the suggestion as one that had just occurred to him, as though they'd entered the field for some other purpose.

'We could improve a place like your own one,' he said, putting his right arm around her shoulders. 'Have you a kiss in you, Bridie?' He kissed her, exerting pressure with his teeth. When his mother died he would sell his farm and spend the money in the town. After that he would think of getting married because he'd have nowhere to go, because he'd want a fire to sit at and a woman to cook food for him. He kissed her again, his lips hot, the sweat on his cheeks sticking to her. 'God, you're great at kissing,' he said.

She rose, saying it was time to go, and they climbed over the gate again. 'There's nothing like a Saturday,' he said. 'Good-night to you so, Bridie.'

He mounted his bicycle and rode down the hill, and she pushed hers to the top and then mounted it also. She rode through the night as on Saturday nights for years she had ridden and never would ride again because she'd reached a certain age. She would wait now and in time Bowser Egan would seek her out because his mother would have died. Her father would probably have died also by then. She would marry Bowser Egan because it would be lonesome being by herself in the farmhouse.

The Distant Past

In the town and beyond it they were regarded as harmlessly peculiar. Odd, people said, and in time this reference took on a burnish of affection.

They had always been thin, silent with one another, and similar in appearance: a brother and sister who shared a family face. It was a bony countenance, with pale blue eyes and a sharp, well-shaped nose and high cheekbones. Their father had had it too, but unlike them their father had been an irresponsible and careless man, with red flecks in his cheeks that they didn't have at all. The Middletons of Carraveagh the family had once been known as, but now the brother and sister were just the Middletons, for Carraveagh didn't count any more, except to them.

They owned four Herefords, a number of hens, and the house itself, three miles outside the town. It was a large house, built in the reign of George II, a monument that reflected in its glory and later decay the fortunes of a family. As the brother and sister aged, its roof increasingly ceased to afford protection, rust ate at its gutters, grass thrived in two thick channels all along its avenue. Their father had mortgaged his inherited estate, so local rumour claimed, in order to keep a Catholic Dublin woman in brandy and jewels. When he died, in 1924, his two children discovered that they possessed only a dozen acres. It was locally said also that this adversity hardened their will and that, because of it, they came to love the remains of Carraveagh more than they could ever have loved a husband or a wife. They blamed for their ill-fortune the Catholic Dublin woman whom they'd never met and they blamed as well the new national regime, contriving in their eccentric way to relate the two. In the days of the Union Jack such women would have known their place: wasn't it all part and parcel?

Twice a week, on Fridays and Sundays, the Middletons journeyed into the town, first of all in a trap and later in a Ford Anglia car. In the shops and elsewhere they made, quite gently, no secret of their continuing loyalty to the past. They attended on Sundays St Patrick's Protestant Church, a place that matched their mood, for prayers were still said there for the King whose sovereignty their country had denied. The revolutionary regime would not last, they quietly informed the Reverend Packham: what sense was there in green-painted pillar-boxes and a language that nobody understood?

On Fridays, when they took seven or eight dozen eggs to the town, they dressed in pressed tweeds and were accompanied over the years by a series of red setters, the breed there had always been at Carraveagh. They sold the eggs in Gerrity's grocery and then had a drink with Mrs Gerrity in the part of her shop that was devoted to the consumption of refreshment. Mr Middleton had whiskey and his sister Tio Pepe. They enjoyed the occasion, for they liked Mrs Gerrity and were liked by her in return. Afterwards they shopped, chatting to the shopkeepers about whatever news there was, and then they went to Healy's Hotel for a few more drinks before driving home.

Drink was their pleasure and it was through it that they built up, in spite of their loyalty to the past, such convivial relationships with the people of the town. Fat Cranley, who kept the butcher's shop, used even to joke about the past when he stood with them in Healy's Hotel or stood behind his own counter cutting their slender chops or thinly slicing their liver. 'Will you ever forget it, Mr Middleton? I'd ha' run like a rabbit if you'd lifted a finger at me.' Fat Cranley would laugh then, rocking back on his heels with a glass of stout in his hand or banging their meat on to his weighing-scales. Mr Middleton would smile. 'There was alarm in your eyes, Mr Cranley,' Miss Middleton would murmur, smiling also at the memory of the distant occasion.

Fat Cranley, with a farmer called Maguire and another called Breen, had stood in the hall of Carraveagh, each of them in charge of a shot-gun. The Middletons, children then, had been locked with their mother and father and an aunt into an upstairs room. Nothing else had happened: the expected British soldiers had not, after all, arrived and the men in the hall had eventually relaxed their vigil. 'A massacre they wanted,' the Middletons' father said after they'd gone. 'Damn bloody ruffians.'

The Second World War took place. Two Germans, a man and his wife called Winkelmann who ran a glove factory in the town, were suspected by the Middletons of being spies for the Third Reich. People laughed, for they knew the Winkelmanns well and could lend no credence to the Middletons' latest fantasy: typical of them, they explained to the Winkelmanns, who had been worried. Soon after the War the Reverend Packham died and was replaced by the Reverend Bradshaw, a younger man who laughed also and regarded the Middletons as an anachronism. They protested when prayers were no longer said for the Royal Family in St Patrick's, but the Reverend Bradshaw considered that their protests were as absurd as the prayers themselves had been. Why pray for the monarchy of a neighbouring island when their own island had its chosen President now? The Middletons didn't reply to that argument. In the Reverend Bradshaw's presence they rose to their feet when the BBC played 'God Save the King', and on the day of the coronation of Queen Elizabeth II they drove into the town with a small Union Jack propped up in the back window of their Ford Anglia. 'Bedad, you're a holy terror, Mr Middleton!' Fat Cranley laughingly exclaimed, noticing the flag as he lifted a tray of pork steaks from his display shelf. The Middletons smiled. It was a great day for the Commonwealth of Nations, they replied, a remark which further amused Fat Cranley and which he later repeated in Phelan's public house. 'Her Britannic Majesty,' guffawed his friend Mr Breen.

Situated in a valley that was noted for its beauty and with convenient access to rich rivers and bogs over which game-birds flew, the town benefited from post-war tourism. Healy's Hotel changed its title and became, overnight, the New Ormonde. Shopkeepers had their shop-fronts painted and Mr Healy organized an annual Salmon Festival. Even Canon Cotter, who had at first commented severely on the habits of the tourists, and in particular on the summertime dress of the women, was in the end obliged to confess that the morals of his flock remained unaffected. 'God and good sense', he proclaimed, meaning God and his own teaching. In time he even derived pride from the fact that people with other values came briefly to the town and that the values esteemed by his parishioners were in no way diminished.

The town's grocers now stocked foreign cheeses, brie and camembert and Port Salut, and wines were available to go with them. The plush Cocktail Room of the New Ormonde set a standard: the wife of a solicitor, a Mrs Duggan, began to give six o'clock parties once or twice a year, obliging her husband to mix gin and Martini in glass jugs and herself handing round a selection of nuts and small Japanese crackers. Canon Cotter looked in as a rule and satisfied himself that all was above board. He rejected, though, the mixture in the jugs, retaining his taste for a glass of John Jameson.

From the windows of their convent the Loreto nuns observed the long, sleek cars with GB plates; English and American accents drifted on the breeze to them. Mothers cleaned up their children and sent them to the Golf Club to seek employment as caddies. Sweet-shops sold holiday mementoes. The brown, soda and currant breads of Murphy-Flood's bakery were declared to be delicious. Mr Healy doubled the number of local girls who served as waitresses in his dining-room, and in the winter of 1961 he had the builders in again, working on an extension for which the Munster and Leinster Bank had lent him twenty-two thousand pounds.

But as the town increased its prosperity Carraveagh continued its decline. The Middletons were in their middle-sixties now and were reconciled to a life that became more uncomfortable with every passing year. Together they roved the vast lofts of their house, placing old paint tins and flowerpot saucers beneath the drips from the roof. At night they sat over their thin chops in a dining-room that had once been gracious and which in a way was gracious still, except for the faded appearance of furniture that was dry from lack of polish and of a wallpaper that time had rendered colourless. In the hall their father gazed down at them, framed in ebony and gilt, in the uniform of the Irish Guards. He had conversed with Queen Victoria, and even in their middle-sixties they could still hear him saying that God and Empire and Queen formed a trinity unique in any worthy soldier's heart. In the hall hung the family crest, and on ancient Irish linen the Cross of St George.

The dog that accompanied the Middletons now was called Turloch, an animal whose death they dreaded for they felt they couldn't manage the antics of another pup. Turloch, being thirteen, moved slowly and was blind and a little deaf. He was a reminder to them of their own advancing years and of the effort it had become to tend the Herefords and collect the weekly eggs. More and more they looked forward to Fridays, to the warm companionship of Mrs Gerrity and Mr Healy's chatter in the hotel. They stayed longer now with Mrs Gerrity and in the hotel, and idled longer in the shops, and drove home more slowly. Dimly, but with no less loyalty, they still recalled the distant past and were listened to without ill-feeling when they spoke of it and of Carraveagh as it had been, and of the Queen whose company their careless father had known.

The visitors who came to the town heard about the Middletons and were impressed. It was a pleasant wonder, more than one of them remarked, that old wounds could heal so completely, that the Middletons continued in their loyalty to the past and that, in spite of it, they were respected in the town. When Miss Middleton had been ill with a form of pneumonia in 1958 Canon Cotter had driven out to Carraveagh twice a week with pullets and young ducks that his housekeeper had dressed. 'An upright couple,' was the Canon's public opinion of the Middletons, and he had been known to add that eccentric views would hurt you less than malice. 'We can disagree without guns in this town,' Mr Healy pronounced in his Cocktail Room, and his visitors usually replied that as far as they could see this was the result of living in a Christian country. That the Middletons bought their meat from a man who had once locked them into an upstairs room and had then waited to shoot soldiers in their hall was a fact that amazed the seasonal visitors. You lived and learned, they remarked to Mr Healy.

The Middletons, privately, often considered that they led a strange life. Alone in their two beds at night they now and again wondered why they hadn't just sold Carraveagh forty-eight years ago when their father died: why had the tie been so strong and why had they in perversity encouraged it? They didn't fully know, nor did they attempt to discuss the matter in any way. Instinctively they had remained at Carraveagh, instinctively feeling that it would have been cowardly to go. Yet often it seemed to them now to be no more than a game they played, this worship of the distant past. And at other times it seemed as real and as important as the remaining acres of land, and the house itself.

'Isn't that shocking?' Mr Healy said one day in 1968. 'Did you hear about that, Mr Middleton, blowing up them post offices in Belfast?'

Mr Healy, red-faced and short-haired, spoke casually in his Cocktail Room, making midday conversation. He had commented in much the same way at breakfast-time, looking up from the *Irish Independent*. Everyone in the town had said it too: that the blowing up of sub-post offices in Belfast was a shocking matter.

'A bad business,' Fat Cranley remarked, wrapping the Middletons' meat. 'We don't want that old stuff all over again.'

'We didn't want it in the first place,' Miss Middleton reminded him. He laughed, and she laughed, and so did her brother. Yes, it was a game, she thought: how could any of it be as real or as important as the afflictions and problems of the old butcher himself, his rheumatism and his reluctance to retire? Did her brother, she wondered, privately think so too?

'Come on, old Turloch,' he said, stroking the flank of the red setter with the point of his shoe, and she reflected that you could never tell what he was thinking. Certainly it wasn't the kind of thing you wanted to talk about.

'I've put him in a bit of mince,' Fat Cranley said, which was something he often did these days, pretending the mince would otherwise be thrown away. There'd been a red setter about the place that night when he waited in the hall for the soldiers: Breen and Maguire had pushed it down into a cellar, frightened of it.

'There's a heart of gold in you, Mr Cranley,' Miss Middleton murmured, nodding and smiling at him. He was the same age as she was, sixty-six: he should have shut up shop years ago. He would have, he'd once told them, if there'd been a son to leave the business to. As it was, he'd have to sell it and when it came to the point he found it hard to make the necessary arrangements. 'Like us and Carraveagh,' she'd said, even though on the face of it it didn't seem the same at all.

Every evening they sat in the big old kitchen, hearing the news. It was only in Belfast and Derry, the wireless said; outside Belfast and Derry you wouldn't know anything was happening at all. On Fridays they listened to the talk in Mrs Gerrity's bar and in the hotel. 'Well, thank God it has nothing to do with the South,' Mr Healy said often, usually repeating the statement.

The first British soldiers landed in the North of Ireland, and soon people didn't so often say that outside Belfast and Derry you wouldn't know anything was happening. There were incidents in Fermanagh and Armagh, in Border villages and towns. One Prime Minister resigned and then another one. The troops were unpopular, the newspapers said; internment became part of the machinery of government. In the town, in St Patrick's Protestant Church and in the Church of the Holy Assumption, prayers for peace were offered, but no peace came.

'We're hit, Mr Middleton,' Mr Healy said one Friday morning. 'If there's a dozen visitors this summer it'll be God's own stroke of luck for us.'

'Luck?'

'Sure, who wants to come to a country with all that malarkey in it?'

'But it's only in the North.'

'Tell that to your tourists, Mr Middleton.'

The town's prosperity ebbed. The Border was more than sixty miles away, but over that distance had spread some wisps of the fog of war. As anger rose in the town at the loss of fortune so there rose also the kind of talk there had been in the distant past. There was talk of atrocities and counter-atrocities, and of guns and gelignite and the rights of people. There was bitterness suddenly in Mrs Gerrity's bar because of the lack of trade, and in the empty hotel there was bitterness also.

On Fridays, only sometimes at first, there was a silence when the Middletons appeared. It was as though, going back nearly twenty years, people remembered the Union Jack in the window of their car and saw it now in a different light. It wasn't something to laugh at any more, nor were certain words that the Middletons had gently spoken, nor were they themselves just an old, peculiar couple. Slowly the change crept about, all around them in the town, until Fat Cranley didn't wish it to be remembered that he had ever given them mince for their dog. He had stood with a gun in the enemy's house, waiting for soldiers so that soldiers might be killed: it was better that people should remember that.

One day Canon Cotter looked the other way when he saw the Middletons' car coming and they noticed this movement of his head, although he hadn't wished them to. And on another day Mrs Duggan, who had always been keen to talk to them in the hotel, didn't reply when they addressed her.

The Middletons naturally didn't discuss these rebuffs, but they each of them privately knew that there was no conversation they could have at this time with the people of the town. The stand they had taken and kept to for so many years no longer seemed ridiculous in the town. Had they driven with a Union Jack now they might, astoundingly, have been shot.

'It will never cease.' He spoke disconsolately one night, standing by the dresser where the wireless was.

She washed the dishes they'd eaten from, and the cutlery. 'Not in our time,' she said.

'It is worse than before.'

'Yes, it is worse than before.'

They took from the walls of the hall the portrait of their father in the uniform of the Irish Guards because it seemed wrong to them that at this time it should hang there. They took down also the crest of their family and the Cross of St George, and from a vase on the drawing-room mantel-piece they removed the small Union Jack that had been there since the Coronation of Queen Elizabeth II. They did not remove these articles in fear, but in mourning for the *modus vivendi* that had existed for so long between them and the people of the town. They had given their custom to a butcher who had planned to shoot down soldiers in their hall and he, in turn, had given them mince for their dog. For fifty years they had experienced, after suspicion had seeped away, a tolerance that never again in the years that were left to them would they know.

One November night their dog died and he said to her after he had buried it that they must not be depressed by all that was happening. They would die themselves and the house would become a ruin because there was no one to inherit it, and the distant past would be set to rest. But she disagreed: the *modus vivendi* had been easy for them, she pointed out, because they hadn't really minded the dwindling of their fortunes while the town prospered. It had given them a life, and a kind of dignity: you could take a pride out of living in peace.

He did not say anything and then, because of the emotion that both of them felt over the death of their dog, he said in a rushing way that they could no longer at their age hope to make a living out of the remains of Carraveagh. They must sell the hens and the four Herefords. As he spoke, he watched her nodding, agreeing with the sense of it. Now and again, he thought, he would drive slowly into the town, to buy groceries and meat with the money they had saved, and to face the silence that would sourly thicken as their own two deaths came closer and death increased in another part of their island. She felt him thinking that and she knew that he was right. Because of the distant past they would die friendless. It was worse than being murdered in their beds.

Teresa's Wedding

The remains of the wedding-cake were on top of the piano in Swanton's lounge-bar, beneath a framed advertisement for Power's whiskey. Chas Flynn, the best man, had opened two packets of confetti: it lay thickly on the remains of the wedding-cake, on the surface of the bar and the piano, on the table and the two small chairs that the lounge-bar contained, and on the tattered green-and-red linoleum.

The wedding guests, themselves covered in confetti, stood in groups. Father Hogan, who had conducted the service in the Church of the Immaculate Conception, stood with Mrs Atty, the mother of the bride, and Mrs Cornish, the mother of the bride-groom, and Mrs Tracy, a sister of Mrs Atty's.

Mrs Tracy was the stoutest of the three women, a farmer's widow who lived eight miles from the town. In spite of the jubilant nature of the occasion, she was dressed in black, a colour she had affected since the death of her husband three years ago. Mrs Atty, bespec-tacled, with her grey hair in a bun, wore a flowered dress—small yellow-and-blue blooms that blended easily with the confetti. Mrs Cornish was in pink, with a pink hat. Father Hogan, a big red-complexioned man, held a tumbler containing whiskey and water in equal measures; his companions sipped Winter's Tale sherry.

Artie Cornish, the bridegroom, drank stout with his friends Eddie Boland and Chas Flynn, who worked in the town's bacon factory, and Screw Doyle, so called because he served behind the counter in McQuaid's hardware shop. Artie, who worked in a shop himself—Driscoll's Provisions and Bar—was a freckled man of twenty-eight, six years older than his bride. He was heavily built, his bulk encased now in a suit of navy-blue serge, similar to the suits that all the other men were wearing that morning in Swanton's lounge-bar. In the opinion of Mr Driscoll, his employer, he was a conscientious shopman, with a good memory for where commodities were kept on the shelves. Customers occasionally found him slow.

The fathers of the bride and bridegroom, Mr Atty and Mr Cornish, were talking about greyhounds, keeping close to the bar. They shared a feeling of unease, caused by being in the lounge-bar of Swanton's, with women present, on a Saturday morning. 'Bring us two more big ones,' Mr Cornish requested of Kevin, a youth behind the bar, hoping that this addition to his consumption of whiskey would relax matters. They wore white carnations in the buttonholes of their suits, and stiff white collars which were reddening their necks. Unknown to one another, they shared the same thought: a wish that the bride and groom would soon decide to bring the occasion to an end by going to prepare themselves for their journey to Cork on the half-one bus. Mr Atty and Mr Cornish, bald-headed men of fifty-three and fifty-five, had it in mind to spend the remainder of the day in Swanton's lounge-bar, celebrating in their particular way the union of their children.

The bride, who had been Teresa Atty and was now Teresa Cornish, had a round, pretty face and black, pretty hair, and was a month and a half pregnant. She stood in the corner of the lounge with her friends, Philomena Morrissey and Kitty Roche, both of whom had been bridesmaids. All three of them were attired in their wedding finery, dresses they had feverishly worked on to get finished in time for the wedding. They planned to alter the dresses and have them dyed so that later on they could go to parties in them, even though parties were rare in the town.

'I hope you'll be happy, Teresa,' Kitty Roche whispered. 'I hope you'll be all right.' She couldn't help giggling, even though she didn't want to. She giggled because she'd drunk a glass of gin and Kia-Ora orange, which Screw Doyle had said would steady her. She'd been nervous in the church. She'd tripped twice on the walk down the aisle.

'You'll be marrying yourself one of these days,' Teresa whispered, her cheeks still glowing after the excitement of the ceremony. 'I hope you'll be happy too, Kit.'

But Kitty Roche, who was asthmatic, did not believe she'd ever marry. She'd be like Miss Levis, the Protestant woman on the Cork road, who'd never got married because of tuberculosis. Or old Hannah Flood, who had a bad hip. And it wasn't just that no one would want to be saddled with a diseased wife: there was also the fact that the asthma caused a recurrent skin complaint on her face and neck and hands.

Teresa and Philomena drank glasses of Babycham, and Kitty drank Kia-Ora with water instead of gin in it. They'd known each other all their lives. They'd been to the Presentation Nuns together, they'd taken First Communion together. Even when they'd left the Nuns, when Teresa had gone to work in the Medical Hall and Kitty Roche and Philomena in Keane's drapery, they'd continued to see each other almost every day.

'We'll think of you, Teresa,' Philomena said. 'We'll pray for you.' Philomena, plump and pale-haired, had every hope of marrying and had even planned her dress, in light lemony lace, with a Limerick veil. Twice in the last month she'd gone out with Des Foley the vet, and even if he was a few years older than he might be and had a car that smelt of cattle disinfectant, there was more to be said for Des Foley than for many another.

Teresa's two sisters, much older than Teresa, stood by the piano and the framed Power's advertisement, between the two windows of the lounge-bar. Agnes, in smart powder-blue, was tall and thin, the older of the two; Loretta, in brown, was small. Their own two marriages, eleven and nine years ago, had been consecrated by Father Hogan in the Church of the Immaculate Conception and celebrated afterwards in this same lounge-bar. Loretta had married a man who was no longer mentioned because he'd gone to England and had never come back. Agnes had married George Tobin, who was at present sitting outside the lounge-bar in a Ford Prefect, in charge of his and Agnes's three small children. The Tobins lived in

Cork now, George being the manager of a shoe-shop there. Loretta lived with her parents, like an unmarried daughter again.

'Sickens you,' Agnes said 'She's only a kid, marrying a goop like that. She'll be stuck in this dump of a town for ever.'

Loretta didn't say anything. It was well known that Agnes's own marriage had turned out well: George Tobin was a teetotaller and had no interest in either horses or greyhounds. From where she stood Loretta could see him through the window, sitting patiently in the Ford Prefect, reading a comic to his children. Loretta's marriage had not been consummated.

'Well, though I've said it before I'll say it again,' said Father Hogan. 'It's a great day for a mother.'

Mrs Atty and Mrs Cornish politely agreed, without speaking. Mrs Tracy smiled.

'And for an aunt too, Mrs Tracy. Naturally enough.'

Mrs Tracy smiled again. 'A great day,' she said.

'Ah, I'm happy for Teresa,' Father Hogan said. 'And for Artie, too, Mrs Cornish; naturally enough. Aren't they as fine a couple as ever stepped out of this town?'

'Are they leaving the town?' Mrs Tracy asked, confusion breaking in her face. 'I thought Artie was fixed in Driscoll's.'

'It's a manner of speaking, Mrs Tracy,' Father Hogan explained. 'It's a way of putting the thing. When I was marrying them this morning I looked down at their two faces and I said to myself, "Isn't it great God gave them life?" '

The three women looked across the lounge, at Teresa standing with her friends Philomena Morrissey and Kitty Roche, and then at Artie, with Screw Doyle, Eddie Boland and Chas Flynn.

'He has a great career in front of him in Driscoll's,' Father Hogan pronounced. 'Will Teresa remain on in the Medical Hall, Mrs Atty?'

Mrs Atty replied that her daughter would remain for a while in the Medical Hall. It was Father Hogan who had persuaded Artie of his duty when Artie had hesitated. Mrs Atty and Teresa had gone to him for advice, he'd spoken to Artie and to Mr and Mrs Cornish, and the matter had naturally not been mentioned on either side since.

'Will I get you another glassful, Father?' inquired Mrs Tracy, holding out her hand for the priest's tumbler.

'Well, it isn't every day I'm honoured,' said Father Hogan with his smile, putting the tumbler into Mrs Tracy's hand.

At the bar Mr Atty and Mr Cornish drank steadily on. In their corner Teresa and her bridesmaids talked about weddings that had taken place in the Church of the Immaculate Conception in the past, how they had stood by the railings of the church when they were children, excited by the finery and the men in serge suits. Teresa's sisters whispered, Agnes continuing about the inadequacy of the man Teresa had just married. Loretta whispered without actually forming words. She wished her sister wouldn't go on so because she didn't want to think about any of it, about what had happened to Teresa, and what would happen to her again tonight, in a hotel in Cork. She'd fainted when it had happened to herself, when he'd come at her like a farm animal. She'd fought like a mad thing.

It was noisier in the lounge-bar than it had been. The voices of the bridegroom's friends were raised; behind the bar young Kevin had switched on the wireless. '*Don't get around much anymore,*' cooed a soft male voice.

'Bedad, there'll be no holding you tonight, Artie,' Eddie Boland whispered thickly into the bridegroom's ear. He nudged Artie in the stomach with his elbow, spilling some Guinness. He laughed uproariously.

'We're following you in two cars,' Screw Doyle said. 'We'll be waiting in the double bed for you.' Screw Doyle laughed also, striking the floor repeatedly with his left foot, which was a habit of his when excited. At a late hour the night before he'd told Artie that once, after a dance, he'd spent an hour in a field with the girl whom Artie had agreed to marry. 'I had a great bloody ride of her,' he'd confided.

'I'll have a word with Teresa,' said Father Hogan, moving away from Teresa's mother, her aunt and Mrs Cornish. He did not, however, cross the lounge immediately, but paused by the bar, where Mr Cornish and Mr Atty were. He put his empty tumbler on the bar itself, and Mr Atty pushed it towards young Kevin, who at once refilled it.

'Well, it's a great day for a father,' said Father Hogan. 'Aren't they a tip-top credit to each other?'

'Who's that, Father?' inquired Mr Cornish, his eyes a little bleary, sweat hanging from his cheeks.

Father Hogan laughed. He put his tumbler on the bar again, and Mr Cornish pushed it towards young Kevin for another refill.

In their corner Philomena confided to Teresa and Kitty Roche that she wouldn't mind marrying Des Foley the vet. She'd had four glasses of Babycham. If he asked her this minute, she said, she'd probably say yes. 'Is Chas Flynn nice?' Kitty Roche asked, squinting across at him.

On the wireless Petula Clark was singing 'Downtown'. Eddie Boland was whistling 'Mother Macree'. 'Listen, Screw,' Artie said, keeping his voice low although it wasn't necessary. 'Is that true? Did you go into a field with Teresa?'

Loretta watched while George Tobin in his Ford Prefect turned a page of the comic he was reading to his children. Her sister's voice continued in its abuse of the town and its people, in particular the shopman who had got Teresa pregnant. Agnes hated the town and always had. She'd met George Tobin at a dance in Cork and had said to Loretta that in six months' time she'd be gone from the town for ever. Which was precisely what had happened, except that marriage had made her less nice than she'd been. She'd hated the town in a jolly way once, laughing over it. Now she hardly laughed at all.

'Look at him,' she was saying. 'I doubt he knows how to hold a knife and fork.'

Loretta ceased her observation of her sister's husband through the window and regarded Artie Cornish instead. She looked away from him immediately because his face, so quickly replacing the face of George Tobin, had caused in her mind a double image which now brutally persisted. She felt a sickness in her stomach, and closed her eyes and prayed. But the double image remained: George Tobin and Artie Cornish coming at her sisters like two farmyard animals and her sisters fighting to get away. 'Dear Jesus,' she whispered to herself. 'Dear Jesus, help me.'

'Sure it was only a bit of gas,' Screw Doyle assured Artie. 'Sure there was no harm done, Artie.'

In no way did Teresa love him. She had been aware of that when Father Hogan had arranged the marriage, and even before that, when she'd told her mother that she thought she was pregnant and had then mentioned Artie Cornish's name. Artie Cornish was much the same as his friends: you could be walking along a road with Screw Doyle or Artie Cornish and you could hardly tell the difference. There was nothing special about Artie Cornish, except that he always added up the figures twice when he was serving you in Driscoll's. There was nothing bad about him either, any more than there was anything bad about Eddie Boland or Chas Flynn or even Screw Doyle. She'd said privately to Father Hogan that she didn't love him or feel anything for him one way or the other: Father Hogan had replied that in the circumstances all that line of talk was irrelevant.

When she was at the Presentation Convent Teresa had imagined her wedding, and even the celebration in this very lounge-bar. She had imagined everything that had happened that morning, and the things that were happening still. She had imagined herself standing with her bridesmaids as she was standing now, her mother and her aunt drinking sherry, Agnes and Loretta being there, too, and other people, and music. Only the bridegroom had been mysterious, some faceless, bodiless presence, beyond imagination. From conversations she had had with Philomena and Kitty Roche, and with her sisters, she knew that they had imagined in a similar way. Yet Agnes had settled for George Tobin because George Tobin was employed in Cork and could take her away from the town. Loretta, who had been married for a matter of weeks, was going to become a nun.

Artie ordered more bottles of stout from young Kevin. He didn't want to catch the half-one bus and have to sit beside her all the way to Cork. He didn't want to go to the Lee Hotel when they could just as easily have remained in the town, when he could just as easily have gone in to Driscoll's tomorrow and continued as before. It would have been different if Screw Doyle hadn't said he'd been in a field with her: you could pretend a bit on the bus, and in the hotel, just to make the whole thing go. You could pretend like you'd been pretending ever since Father Hogan had laid down the law, you could make the best of it like Father Hogan had said.

He handed a bottle of stout to Chas Flynn and one to Screw Doyle and another to Eddie Boland. He'd ask her about it on the bus. He'd repeat what Screw Doyle had said and ask her if it was true. For all he knew the child she was carrying was Screw Doyle's child and would be born with Screw Doyle's thin nose, and everyone in the town would know when they looked at it. His mother had told him when he was sixteen never to trust a girl, never to get involved, because he'd be caught in the end. He'd get caught because he was easy-going, because he didn't possess the smartness of Screw Doyle and some of the others. 'Sure, you might as well marry Teresa as anyone else,' his father had said after Father Hogan had called to see them about the matter. His mother had said things would never be the same between them again.

Eddie Boland sat down at the piano and played 'Mother Macree', causing Agnes and Loretta to move to the other side of the lounge-bar. In the motor-car outside the Tobin children asked their father what the music was for.

'God go with you, girl,' Father Hogan said to Teresa, motioning Kitty Roche and Philomena away. 'Isn't it a grand thing that's happened, Teresa?' His red-skinned face, with the shiny false teeth so evenly arrayed in it, was close to hers. For a moment she thought he might kiss her, which of course was ridiculous, Father Hogan kissing anyone, even at a wedding celebration.

'It's a great day for all of us, girl.'

When she'd told her mother, her mother said it made her feel sick in her stomach. Her father hit her on the side of the face. Agnes came down specially from Cork to try and sort the matter out. It was then that Loretta had first mentioned becoming a nun.

'I want to say two words,' said Father Hogan, still standing beside her, but now addressing everyone in the lounge-bar. 'Come over here alongside us, Artie. Is there a drop in everyone's glass?'

Artie moved across the lounge-bar, with his glass of stout. Mr Cornish told young Kevin to pour out a few more measures. Eddie Boland stopped playing the piano.

'It's only this,' said Father Hogan. 'I want us all to lift our glasses to Artie and Teresa. May God go with you, the pair of you,' he said, lifting his own glass.

'Health, wealth and happiness,' proclaimed Mr Cornish from the bar.

'And an early night,' shouted Screw Doyle. 'Don't forget to draw the curtains, Artie.'

They stood awkwardly, not holding hands, not even touching. Teresa watched while her mother drank the remains of her sherry, and while her aunt drank and Mrs Cornish drank. Agnes's face was disdainful, a calculated reply to the coarseness of Screw Doyle's remarks. Loretta was staring ahead of her, concentrating her mind on her novitiate. A quick flush passed over the roughened countenance of Kitty Roche. Philomena laughed, and all the men in the lounge-bar, except Father Hogan, laughed.

'That's sufficient of that talk,' Father Hogan said with contrived severity. 'May you meet happiness halfway,' he added, suitably altering his intonation. 'The pair of you, Artie and Teresa.'

Noise broke out again after that. Father Hogan shook hands with Teresa and then with Artie. He had a funeral at half past two, he said: he'd better go and get his dinner inside him.

'Goodbye, Father,' Artie said. 'Thanks for doing the job.'

'God bless the pair of you,' said Father Hogan, and went away.

'We should be going for the bus,' Artie said to her. 'It wouldn't do to miss the old bus.'

'No, it wouldn't.'

'I'll see you down there. You'll have to change your clothes.'

'Yes.'

'I'll come the way I am.'

'You're fine the way you are, Artie.'

He looked at the stout in his glass and didn't raise his eyes from it when he spoke again. 'Did Screw Doyle take you into a field, Teresa?'

He hadn't meant to say it then. It was wrong to come out with it like that, in the lounge-bar, with the wedding-cake still there on the piano, and Teresa still in her wedding-dress, and confetti everywhere. He knew it was wrong even before the words came out; he knew that the stout had angered and befuddled him.

'Sorry,' he said. 'Sorry, Teresa.'

She shook her head. It didn't matter: it was only to be expected that a man you didn't love and who didn't love you would ask a question like that at your wedding celebration.

'Yes,' she said. 'Yes, he did.'

'He told me. I thought he was codding. I wanted to know.'

'It's your baby, Artie. The other thing was years ago.'

He looked at her. Her face was flushed, her eyes had tears in them.

'I had too much stout,' he said.

They stood where Father Hogan had left them, drawn away from their wedding guests. Not knowing where else to look, they looked together at Father Hogan's black back as he left the lounge-bar, and then at the perspiring, naked heads of Mr Cornish and Mr Atty by the bar.

At least they had no illusions, she thought. Nothing worse could happen than what had happened already, after Father Hogan had laid down the law. She wasn't going to get a shock like Loretta had got. She wasn't going to go sour like Agnes had gone when she'd discovered that it wasn't enough just to marry a man for a purpose, in order to escape from a town. Philomena was convincing herself that she'd fallen in love with an elderly vet, and if she got any encouragement Kitty Roche would convince herself that she was mad about anyone at all.

For a moment as Teresa stood there, the last moment before she left the lounge-bar, she felt that she and Artie might make some kind of marriage together because there was nothing that could be destroyed, no magic or anything else. He could ask her the question he had asked, while she stood there in her wedding-dress: he could ask her and she could truthfully reply, because there was nothing special about the occasion, or the lounge-bar all covered in confetti.

Death in Jerusalem

'Till then,' Father Paul said, leaning out of the train window. 'Till Jerusalem, Francis.'

'Please God, Paul.' As he spoke the Dublin train began to move and his brother waved from the window and he waved back, a modest figure on the platform. Everyone said Francis might have been a priest as well, meaning that Francis's quietness and meditative disposition had an air of the cloister about them. But Francis contented himself with the running of Conary's hardware business, which his mother had run until she was too old for it. 'Are we game for the Holy Land next year?' Father Paul had asked that July. 'Will we go together, Francis?' He had brushed aside all Francis's protestations, all attempts to explain that the shop could not be left, that their mother would be confused by the absence of Francis from the house. Rumbustiously he'd pointed out that there was their sister Kitty, who was in charge of the household of which Francis and their mother were part and whose husband, Myles, could surely be trusted to look after the shop for a single fortnight. For thirty years, ever since he was seven, Francis had wanted to go to the Holy Land. He had savings which he'd never spent a penny of: you couldn't take them with you, Father Paul had more than once stated that July.

On the platform Francis watched until the train could no longer be seen, his thoughts still with his brother. The priest's ruddy countenance smiled again behind cigarette smoke; his bulk remained impressive in his clerical clothes, the collar pinching the flesh of his neck, his black shoes scrupulously polished. There were freckles on the backs of his large, strong hands; he had a fine head of hair, grey and crinkly. In an hour and a half's time the train would creep into Dublin, and he'd take a taxi. He'd spend a night in the Gresham Hotel, probably falling in with another priest, having a drink or two, maybe playing a game of bridge after his meal. That was his brother's way and always had been—an extravagant, easy kind of way, full of smiles and good humour. It was what had taken him to America and made him successful there. In order to raise money for the church that he and Father Steigmuller intended to build before 1980 he took parties of the well-to-do from San Francisco to Rome and Florence, to Chartres and Seville and the Holy Land. He was good at raising money, not just for the church but for the boys' home of which he was president, and for the Hospital of Our Saviour, and for St Mary's Old People's Home on the west side of the city. But every July he flew back to Ireland, to the town in Co. Tipperary where his mother and brother and sister still lived. He stayed in the house above the shop which he might have inherited himself on the death of his father, which he'd rejected in favour of the religious life. Mrs Conary was eighty now. In the shop she sat silently behind the counter, in a corner by the chicken-wire, wearing only clothes that were black. In the evenings she sat with Francis in the lace-curtained sitting-room, while the rest of the family occupied the kitchen. It was for her sake most of all that Father Paul made the journey every summer, considering it his duty.

Walking back to the town from the station, Francis was aware that he was missing his brother. Father Paul was fourteen years older and in childhood had often taken the place of their father, who had died when Francis was five. His brother had possessed an envied strength and knowledge; he'd been a hero, quite often worshipped, an example of success. In later life he had become an example of generosity as well: ten years ago he'd taken their mother to Rome, and their sister Kitty and her husband two years later; he'd paid the expenses when their sister Edna had gone to Canada; he'd assisted two nephews to make a start in America. In childhood Francis hadn't possessed his brother's healthy freckled face, just as in middle age he didn't have his ruddy complexion and his stoutness and his easiness with people. Francis was slight, his sandy hair receding, his face rather pale. His breathing was sometimes laboured because of wheeziness in the chest. In the ironmonger's shop he wore a brown cotton coat.

'Hullo, Mr Conary,' a woman said to him in the main street of the town. 'Father Paul's gone off, has he?'

'Yes, he's gone again.'

'I'll pray for his journey so,' the woman promised, and Francis thanked her.

A year went by. In San Francisco another wing of the boys' home was completed, another target was reached in Father Paul and Father Steigmuller's fund for the church they planned to have built by 1980. In the town in Co. Tipperary there were baptisms and burial services and First Communions. Old Loughlin, a farmer from Bansha, died in McSharry's grocery and bar, having gone there to celebrate a good price he'd got for a heifer. Clancy, from behind the counter in Doran's drapery, married Maureen Talbot; Mr Nolan's plasterer married Miss Carron; Johneen Meagher married Seamus in the chip-shop, under pressure from her family to do so. A local horse, from the stables on the Limerick road, was said to be an entry for the Fairyhouse Grand National, but it turned out not to be true. Every evening of that year Francis sat with his mother in the lace-curtained sitting-room above the shop. Every weekday she sat in her corner by the chicken-wire, watching while he counted out screws and weighed staples, or advised about yard brushes or tap-washers. Occasionally, on a Saturday, he visited the three Christian Brothers who lodged with Mrs Shea and afterwards he'd tell his mother about how the authority was slipping these days from the nuns and the Christian Brothers, and how Mrs Shea's elderly maid, Ita, couldn't see to cook the food any more. His mother would nod and hardly ever speak. When he told a joke— what young Hogan had said when he'd found a nail in his egg or how Ita had put mint sauce into a jug with milk in it—she never laughed, and looked at him in surprise when he laughed himself. But Dr Foran said it was best to keep her cheered up.

All during that year Francis talked to her about his forthcoming visit to the Holy Land, endeavouring to make her understand that for a fortnight next spring he would be away from the house and the shop. He'd been away before for odd days, but that was when she'd been younger. He used to visit an aunt in Tralee, but three years ago the aunt had died and he hadn't left the town since.

Francis and his mother had always been close. Before his birth two daughters had died in infancy, and his very survival had often struck Mrs Conary as a gift. He had always been her favourite, the one among her children whom she often considered least able to stand on his own two feet. It was just like Paul to have gone blustering off to San Francisco instead of remaining in Co. Tipperary. It was just like Kitty to have married a useless man. 'There's not a girl in the town who'd touch him,' she'd said to her daughter at the time, but Kitty had been headstrong and adamant, and there was Myles now, doing nothing whatsoever except cleaning other people's windows for a pittance and placing bets in Donovan's the turf accountant's. It was the shop and the arrangement Kitty had with Francis and her mother that kept her and the children going, three of whom had already left the town, which in Mrs Conary's opinion they mightn't have done if they'd had a better type of father. Mrs Conary often wondered what her own two babies who'd died might have grown up into, and imagined they might have been like Francis, about whom she'd never had a moment's worry. Not in a million years would he give you the feeling that he was too big for his boots, like Paul sometimes did with his lavishness and his big talk of America. He wasn't silly like Kitty, or so sinful you couldn't forgive him, the way you couldn't forgive Edna, even though she was dead and buried in Toronto.

Francis understood how his mother felt about the family. She'd had a hard life, left a widow early on, trying to do the best she could for everyone. In turn he did his best to compensate for the struggles and disappointments she'd suffered, cheering her in the evenings while Kitty and Myles and the youngest of their children watched the television in the kitchen. His mother had ignored the existence of Myles for ten years, ever since the day he'd taken money out of the till to pick up the odds on Gusty Spirit at Phoenix Park. And although Francis got on well enough with Myles he quite understood that there should be a long aftermath to that day. There'd been a terrible row in the kitchen, Kitty screaming at Myles and Myles telling lies and Francis trying to keep them calm, saying they'd give the old woman a heart attack.

She didn't like upsets of any kind, so all during the year before he was to visit the Holy Land Francis read the New Testament to her in order to prepare her. He talked to her about Bethlehem and Nazareth and the miracle of the loaves and fishes and all the other miracles. She kept nodding, but he often wondered if she didn't assume he was just casually referring to episodes in the Bible. As a child he had listened to such talk himself, with awe and fascination, imagining the walking on the water and the temptation in the wilderness. He had imagined the cross carried to Calvary, and the rock rolled back from the tomb, and the rising from the dead on the third day. That he was now to walk in such places seemed extraordinary to him, and he wished his mother was younger so that she could appreciate his good fortune and share it with him when she received the postcards he intended, every day, to send her. But her eyes seemed always to tell him that he was making a mistake, that somehow he was making a fool of himself by doing such a showy thing as going to the Holy Land. *I have the entire itinerary mapped out,* his brother wrote from San Francisco. *There's nothing we'll miss.*

It was the first time Francis had been in an aeroplane. He flew by Aer Lingus from Dublin to London and then changed to an El Al flight to Tel Aviv. He was nervous and he found it exhausting. All the time he seemed to be eating, and it was strange being among so many people he didn't know. 'You will taste honey such as never before,' an Israeli businessman in the seat next to his assured him. 'And Galilean figs. Make certain to taste Galilean figs.' Make certain too, the businessman went on, to experience Jerusalem by night and in the early dawn. He urged Francis to see places he had never heard of, Yad Va-Shem, the treasures of the Shrine of the Book. He urged him to honour the martyrs of Masada and to learn a few words of Hebrew as a token of respect. He told him of a shop where he could buy mementoes and warned him against Arab street traders.

'The hard man, how are you?' Father Paul said at Tel Aviv airport, having flown in from San Francisco the day before. Father Paul had had a drink or two and he suggested another when they arrived at the Plaza Hotel in Jerusalem. It was half past nine in the evening. 'A quick little nightcap,' Father Paul insisted, 'and then hop into bed with you, Francis.' They sat in an enormous open lounge with low, round tables and square modern armchairs. Father Paul said it was the bar.

They had said what had to be said in the car from Tel Aviv to Jerusalem. Father Paul had asked about their mother, and Kitty and Myles. He'd asked about other people in the town, old Canon Mahon and Sergeant Murray. He and Father Steigmuller had had a great year of it, he reported: as well as everything else, the boys' home had turned out two tip-top footballers. 'We'll start on a tour at half-nine in the morning,' he said. 'I'll be sitting having breakfast at eight.'

Francis went to bed and Father Paul ordered another whisky, with ice. To his great disappointment there was no Irish whiskey in the hotel so he'd had to content himself with Haig. He fell into conversation with an American couple, making them promise that if they were ever in Ireland they wouldn't miss out Co. Tipperary. At eleven o'clock the barman said he was wanted at the reception desk and when Father Paul went there and announced himself he was given a message in an envelope. It was a telegram that had come, the girl said in poor English. Then she shook her head, saying it was a telex. He opened the envelope and learnt that Mrs Conary had died.

Francis fell asleep immediately and dreamed that he was a boy again, out fishing with a friend whom he couldn't now identify.

On the telephone Father Paul ordered whisky and ice to be brought to his room. Before drinking it he took his jacket off and knelt by his bed to pray for his mother's salvation. When he'd completed the prayers he walked slowly up and down the length of the room, occasionally sipping at his whisky. He argued with himself and finally arrived at a decision.

For breakfast they had scrambled eggs that looked like yellow ice-cream, and orange juice that was delicious. Francis wondered about bacon, but Father Paul explained that bacon was not readily available in Israel.

'Did you sleep all right?' Father Paul inquired. 'Did you have the jet-lag?'

'Jet-lag?'

'A tiredness you get after jet flights. It'd knock you out for days.'

'Ah, I slept great, Paul.'

'Good man.'

They lingered over breakfast. Father Paul reported a little more of what had happened in his parish during the year, in particular about the two young footballers from the boys' home. Francis told about the decline in the cooking at Mrs Shea's boarding-house, as related to him by the three Christian Brothers. 'I have a car laid on,' Father Paul said, and twenty minutes later they walked out into the Jerusalem sunshine.

The hired car stopped on the way to the walls of the Old City. It drew into a lay-by at Father Paul's request and the two men got out and looked across a wide valley dotted with houses and olive trees. A road curled along the distant slope opposite. 'The Mount of Olives,' Father Paul said. 'And that's the road to Jericho.' He pointed more particularly. 'You see that group of eight big olives? Just off the road, where the church is?'

Francis thought he did, but was not sure. There were so many olive trees, and more than one church. He glanced at his brother's pointing finger and followed its direction with his glance.

'The Garden of Gethsemane,' Father Paul said.

Francis did not say anything. He continued to gaze at the distant church, with the clump of olive trees beside it. Wild flowers were profuse on the slopes of the valley, smears of orange and blue on land that looked poor. Two Arab women herded goats.

'Could we see it closer?' he asked, and his brother said that definitely they would. They returned to the waiting car and Father Paul ordered it to the Gate of St Stephen.

Tourists heavy with cameras thronged the Via Dolorosa. Brown, barefoot children asked for alms. Stall-keepers pressed their different wares: cotton dresses, metal-ware, mementoes, sacred goods. 'Get out of the way,' Father Paul kept saying to them, genially laughing to show he wasn't being abrupt. Francis wanted to stand still and close his eyes, to visualize for a moment the carrying of the Cross. But the ceremony of the Stations, familiar to him for as long as he could remember, was unreal. Try as he would, Christ's journey refused to enter his imagination, and his own plain church seemed closer to the heart of the matter than the noisy lane he was now being jostled on. 'God damn it, of course it's genuine,' an angry American voice proclaimed, in reply to a shriller voice which insisted that cheating had taken place. The voices argued about a piece of wood, neat beneath plastic in a little box, a sample or not of the Cross that had been carried.

They arrived at the Church of the Holy Sepulchre, and at the Chapel of the Nailing to the Cross, where they prayed. They passed through the Chapel of the Angel, to the tomb of Christ. Nobody spoke in the marble cell, but when they left the church Francis overheard a quiet man with spectacles saying it was unlikely that a body would have been buried within the walls of the city. They walked to Hezekiah's Pool and out of the Old City at the Jaffa Gate, where their hired car was waiting for them. 'Are you peckish?' Father Paul asked, and although Francis said he wasn't they returned to the hotel.

Delay funeral till Monday was the telegram Father Paul had sent. There was an early flight on Sunday, in time for an afternoon one from London to Dublin. With luck there'd be a late train on Sunday evening and if there wasn't they'd have to fix a car. Today was Tuesday. It would give them four and a half days. *Funeral eleven Monday* the telegram at the reception desk now confirmed. 'Ah, isn't that great?' he said to himself, bundling the telegram up.

'Will we have a small one?' he suggested in the open area that was the bar. 'Or better still a big one.' He laughed. He was in good spirits in spite of the death that had taken place. He gestured at the barman, wagging his head and smiling jovially.

His face had reddened in the morning sun; there were specks of sweat on his forehead and his nose. 'Bethlehem this afternoon,' he laid down. 'Unless the jet-lag . . . ?'

'I haven't got the jet-lag.'

In the Nativity Boutique Francis bought for his mother a small metal plate with a fish on it. He had stood for a moment, scarcely able to believe it, on the spot where the manger had been, in the Church of the Nativity. As in the Via Dolorosa it had been difficult to clear his mind of the surroundings that now were present: the exotic Greek Orthodox trappings, the foreign-looking priests, the oriental smell. Gold, frankincense and myrrh, he'd kept thinking, for somehow the church seemed more the church of the kings than of Joseph and Mary and their child. Afterwards they returned to Jerusalem, to the Tomb of the Virgin and the Garden of Gethsemane. 'It could have been anywhere,' he heard the quiet, bespectacled sceptic remarking in Gethsemane. 'They're only guessing.'

Father Paul rested in the late afternoon, lying down on his bed with his jacket off. He slept from half past five until a quarter past seven and awoke refreshed. He picked up the telephone and asked for whisky and ice to be brought up and when it arrived he undressed and had a bath, relaxing in the warm water with the drink on a ledge in the tiled wall beside him. There would be time to take in Nazareth and Galilee. He was particularly keen that his brother should see Galilee because Galilee had atmosphere and was beautiful. There wasn't, in his own opinion, very much to Nazareth but it would be a pity to miss it all the same. It was at the Sea of Galilee that he intended to tell his brother of their mother's death.

We've had a great day, Francis wrote on a postcard that showed an aerial view of Jerusalem. *The Church of the Holy Sepulchre, where Our Lord's tomb is, and Gethsemane and Bethlehem. Paul's in great form.* He addressed it to his mother, and then wrote other cards, to Kitty and Myles and to the three Christian Brothers in Mrs Shea's, and to Canon Mahon. He gave thanks that he was privileged to be in Jerusalem. He read St Mark and some of St Matthew. He said his rosary.

'Will we chance the wine?' Father Paul said at dinner, not that wine was something he went in for, but a waiter had come up and put a large padded wine-list into his hand.

'Ah, no, no,' Francis protested, but already Father Paul was running his eye down the listed bottles.

'Have you local wine?' he inquired of the waiter. 'A nice red one?'

The waiter nodded and hurried away, and Francis hoped he wouldn't get drunk, the red wine on top of the whisky he'd had in the bar before the meal. He'd only had the one whisky, not being much used to it, making it last through his brother's three.

'I heard some gurriers in the bar,' Father Paul said, 'making a great song and dance about the local red wine.'

Wine made Francis think of the Holy Communion, but he didn't say so. He said the soup was delicious and he drew his brother's attention to the custom there was in the hotel of a porter ringing a bell and walking about with a person's name chalked on a little blackboard on the end of a rod.

'It's a way of paging you,' Father Paul explained. 'Isn't it nicer than bellowing out some fellow's name?' He smiled his easy smile, his eyes beginning to water as a result of the few drinks he'd had. He was beginning to feel the strain: he kept thinking of their mother lying there, of what she'd say if she knew what he'd done, how she'd savagely upbraid him for keeping the fact from Francis. Out of duty and humanity he had returned each year to see her because, after all, you only had the one mother. But he had never cared for her.

Francis went for a walk after dinner. There were young soldiers with what seemed to be toy guns on the streets, but he knew the guns were real. In the shop windows there were television sets for sale, and furniture and clothes, just like anywhere else. There were advertisements for some film or other, two writhing women without a stitch on them, the kind of thing you wouldn't see in Co. Tipperary. 'You want something, sir?' a girl said, smiling at him with broken front teeth. The siren of a police car or an ambulance shrilled urgently near by. He shook his head at the girl. 'No, I don't want anything,' he said, and then realized what she had meant. She was small and very dark, no more than a child. He hurried on, praying for her.

When he returned to the hotel he found his brother in the lounge with other people, two men and two women. Father Paul was ordering a round of drinks and called out to the barman to bring another whisky. 'Ah, no, no,' Francis protested, anxious to go to his room and to think about the day, to read the New Testament and perhaps to write a few more postcards. Music was playing, coming from speakers that could not be seen.

'My brother Francis,' Father Paul said to the people he was with, and the people all gave their names, adding that they came from New York. 'I was telling them about Tipp,' Father Paul said to his brother, offering his packet of cigarettes around.

'You like Jerusalem, Francis?' one of the American women asked him, and he replied that he hadn't been able to take it in yet. Then, feeling that didn't sound enthusiastic enough, he added that being there was the experience of a lifetime.

Father Paul went on talking about Co. Tipperary and then spoke of his parish in San Francisco, the boys' home and the two promising footballers, the plans for the new church. The Americans listened and in a moment the conversation drifted on to the subject of their travels in England, their visit to Istanbul and Athens, an argument they'd had with the Customs at Tel Aviv. 'Well, I think I'll hit the hay,' one of the men announced eventually, standing up.

The others stood up too and so did Francis. Father Paul remained where he was, gesturing again in the direction of the barman. 'Sit down for a nightcap,' he urged his brother.

'Ah, no, no—' Francis began.

'Bring us two more of those,' the priest ordered with a sudden abruptness, and the barman hurried away. 'Listen,' said Father Paul. 'I've something to tell you.'

After dinner, while Francis had been out on his walk, before he'd dropped into conversation with the Americans, Father Paul had said to himself that he couldn't stand the strain. It was the old woman stretched out above the hardware shop, as stiff as a board already, with the little lights burning in her room: he kept seeing all that, as if she wanted him to, as if she was trying to haunt him. Nice as the idea was, he didn't think he could continue with what he'd planned, with waiting until they got up to Galilee.

Francis didn't want to drink any more. He hadn't wanted the whisky his brother had ordered him earlier, nor the one the Americans had ordered for him. He didn't want the one that the barman now brought. He thought he'd just leave it there, hoping his brother wouldn't see it. He lifted the glass to his lips, but he managed not to drink any.

'A bad thing has happened,' Father Paul said.

'Bad? How d'you mean, Paul?'

'Are you ready for it?' He paused. Then he said, 'She died.'

Francis didn't know what he was talking about. He didn't know who was meant to be dead, or why his brother was behaving in an odd manner. He didn't like to think it but he had to: his brother wasn't fully sober.

'Our mother died,' Father Paul said. 'I'm after getting a telegram.'

The huge area that was the lounge of the Plaza Hotel, the endless tables and people sitting at them, the swiftly moving waiters and barmen, seemed suddenly a dream. Francis had a feeling that he was not where he appeared to be, that he wasn't sitting with his brother, who was wiping his lips with a handkerchief. For a moment he appeared in his confusion to be struggling his way up the Via Dolorosa again, and then in the Nativity Boutique.

'Take it easy, boy,' his brother was saying. 'Take a mouthful of whisky.'

Francis didn't obey that injunction. He asked his brother to repeat what he had said, and Father Paul repeated that their mother had died.

Francis closed his eyes and tried as well to shut away the sounds around them. He prayed for the salvation of his mother's soul. 'Blessed Virgin, intercede,' his own voice said in his mind. 'Dear Mary, let her few small sins be forgiven.'

Having rid himself of his secret, Father Paul felt instant relief. With the best of intentions, it had been a foolish idea to think he could maintain the secret until they arrived in a place that was perhaps the most suitable in the world to hear about the death of a person who'd been close to you. He took a gulp of his whisky and wiped his mouth with his handkerchief again. He watched his brother, waiting for his eyes to open.

'When did it happen?' Francis asked eventually.

'Yesterday.'

'And the telegram only came—'

'It came last night, Francis. I wanted to save you the pain.'

'Save me? How could you save me? I sent her a postcard, Paul.'

'Listen to me, Francis—'

'How could you save me the pain?'

'I wanted to tell you when we got up to Galilee.'

Again Francis felt he was caught in the middle of a dream. He couldn't understand his brother: he couldn't understand what he meant by saying a telegram had come last night, why at a moment like this he was talking about Galilee. He didn't know why he was sitting in this noisy place when he should be back in Ireland.

'I fixed the funeral for Monday,' Father Paul said.

Francis nodded, not grasping the significance of this arrangement. 'We'll be back there this time tomorrow,' he said.

'No need for that, Francis. Sunday morning's time enough.'

'But she's dead—'

'We'll be there in time for the funeral.'

'We can't stay here if she's dead.'

It was this, Father Paul realized, he'd been afraid of when he'd argued with himself and made his plan. If he had knocked on Francis's door the night before, Francis would have wanted to return immediately without seeing a single stone of the land he had come so far to be moved by.

'We could go straight up to Galilee in the morning,' Father Paul said quietly. 'You'll find comfort in Galilee, Francis.'

But Francis shook his head. 'I want to be with her,' he said.

Father Paul lit another cigarette. He nodded at a hovering waiter, indicating his need of another drink. He said to himself that he must keep his cool, an expression he was fond of.

'Take it easy, Francis,' he said.

'Is there a plane out in the morning? Can we make arrangements now?' He looked about him as if for a member of the hotel staff who might be helpful.

'No good'll be done by tearing off home, Francis. What's wrong with Sunday?'

'I want to be with her.'

Anger swelled within Father Paul. If he began to argue his words would become slurred: he knew that from experience. He must keep his cool and speak slowly and clearly, making a few simple points. It was typical of her, he thought, to die inconveniently.

'You've come all this way,' he said as slowly as he could without sounding peculiar. 'Why cut it any shorter than we need? We'll be losing a week anyway. She wouldn't want us to go back.'

'I think she would.'

He was right in that. Her possessiveness in her lifetime would have reached out across a dozen continents for Francis. She'd known what she was doing by dying when she had.

'I shouldn't have come,' Francis said. 'She didn't want me to come.'

'You're thirty-seven years of age, Francis.'

'I did wrong to come.'

'You did no such thing.'

The time he'd taken her to Rome she'd been difficult for the whole week, complaining about the food, saying everywhere was dirty. Whenever he'd spent anything she'd disapprove. All his life, Father Paul felt, he'd done his best for her. He had told her before anyone else when he'd decided to enter the priesthood, certain that she'd be pleased. 'I thought you'd take over the shop,' she'd said instead.

'What difference could it make to wait, Francis?'

'There's nothing to wait for.'

As long as he lived Francis knew he would never forgive himself. As long as he lived he would say to himself that he hadn't been able to wait a few years, until she'd passed quietly on. He might even have been in the room with her when it happened.

'It was a terrible thing not to tell me,' he said. 'I sat down and wrote her a postcard, Paul. I bought her a plate.'

'So you said.'

'You're drinking too much of that whisky.'

'Now, Francis, don't be silly.'

'You're half drunk and she's lying there.'

'She can't be brought back no matter what we do.'

'She never hurt anyone,' Francis said.

Father Paul didn't deny that, although it wasn't true. She had hurt their sister Kitty, constantly reproaching her for marrying the man she had, long after Kitty was aware she'd made a mistake. She'd driven Edna to Canada after Edna, still unmarried, had had a miscarriage that only the family knew about. She had made a

shadow out of Francis although Francis didn't know
hold on to her other children, she had grasped her you
as if she had borne him to destroy him.

'It'll be you who'll say a Mass for her?' Francis said
'Yes, of course it will.'

'You should have told me.'

Francis realized why, all day, he'd been disappointed. From the
moment when the hired car had pulled into the lay-by and his
brother had pointed across the valley at the Garden of Gethsemane
he'd been disappointed and had not admitted it. He'd been disappointed in the Via Dolorosa and in the Church of the Holy
Sepulchre and in Bethlehem. He remembered the bespectacled man
who'd kept saying that you couldn't be sure about anything. All
the people with cameras made it impossible to think, all the jostling
and pushing was distracting. When he'd said there'd been too much
to take in he'd meant something different.

'Her death got in the way,' he said.

'What d'you mean, Francis?'

'It didn't feel like Jerusalem, it didn't feel like Bethlehem.'

'But it is, Francis, it is.'

'There are soldiers with guns all over the place. And a girl came
up to me on the street. There was that man with a bit of the Cross.
There's you, drinking and smoking in this place—'

'Now, listen to me, Francis—'

'Nazareth would be a disappointment. And the Sea of Galilee.
And the Church of the Loaves and Fishes.' His voice had risen. He
lowered it again. 'I couldn't believe in the Stations this morning. I
couldn't see it happening the way I do at home.'

'That's nothing to do with her death, Francis. You've got a bit
of jet-lag, you'll settle yourself up in Galilee. There's an atmosphere
in Galilee that nobody misses.'

'I'm not going near Galilee.' He struck the surface of the table,
and Father Paul told him to contain himself. People turned their
heads, aware that anger had erupted in the pale-faced man with the
priest.

'Quieten up,' Father Paul commanded sharply, but Francis didn't.

'She knew I'd be better at home,' he shouted, his voice shrill and reedy. 'She knew I was making a fool of myself, a man out of a shop trying to be big—'

'Will you keep your voice down? Of course you're not making a fool of yourself.'

'Will you find out about planes tomorrow morning?'

Father Paul sat for a moment longer, not saying anything, hoping his brother would say he was sorry. Naturally it was a shock, naturally he'd be emotional and feel guilty, in a moment it would be better. But it wasn't, and Francis didn't say he was sorry. Instead he began to weep.

'Let's go up to your room,' Father Paul said, 'and I'll fix about the plane.'

Francis nodded but did not move. His sobbing ceased, and then he said, 'I'll always hate the Holy Land now.'

'No need for that, Francis.'

But Francis felt there was and he felt he would hate, as well, the brother he had admired for as long as he could remember. In the lounge of the Plaza Hotel he felt mockery surfacing everywhere. His brother's deceit, and the endless whisky in his brother's glass, and his casualness after a death seemed like the scorning of a Church which honoured so steadfastly the mother of its founder. Vivid in his mind, his own mother's eyes reminded him that they'd told him he was making a mistake, and upbraided him for not heeding her. Of course there was mockery everywhere, in the splinter of wood beneath plastic, and in the soldiers with guns that were not toys, and the writhing nakedness in the Holy City. He'd become part of it himself, sending postcards to the dead. Not speaking again to his brother, he went to his room to pray.

'Eight a.m., sir,' the girl at the reception desk said, and Father Paul asked that arrangements should be made to book two seats on the plane, explaining that it was an emergency, that a death had occurred. 'It will be all right, sir,' the girl promised.

He went slowly downstairs to the bar. He sat in a corner and lit a cigarette and ordered two whiskys and ice, as if expecting a companion. He drank them both himself and ordered more. Francis would return to Co. Tipperary and after the funeral he would take up again the life she had ordained for him. In his brown cotton coat he would serve customers with nails and hinges and wire. He would regularly go to Mass and to Confession and to Men's Confraternity. He would sit alone in the lace-curtained sitting-room, lonely for the woman who had made him what he was, married forever to her memory.

Father Paul lit a fresh cigarette from the butt of the last one. He continued to order whisky in two glasses. Already he could sense the hatred that Francis had earlier felt taking root in himself. He wondered if he would ever again return in July to Co. Tipperary, and imagined he would not.

At midnight he rose to make the journey to bed and found himself unsteady on his feet. People looked at him, thinking it disgraceful for a priest to be drunk in Jerusalem, with cigarette ash all over his clerical clothes.

Downstairs at Fitzgerald's

Cecilia's father would sit there, slowly eating oysters. Cecilia would tell him about school and about her half-brothers, and of course she'd have to mention her mother because it was impossible to have a conversation without doing that. She'd mention Ronan also, but because of her father's attitude to her stepfather this was never an embarrassment.

'Aren't they good today?' Tom, the waiter at Fitzgerald's, would remark, always at the same moment, when placing in front of Cecilia's father his second pint of stout.

'Great, Tom,' her father would unhesitatingly reply, and then Tom would ask Cecilia how her bit of steak was and if the chips were crisp. He'd mention the name of a racehorse and Cecilia's father would give his opinion of it, drawing a swift breath of disapproval or thoughtfully pursing his lips.

These occasions in Fitzgerald's Oyster Bar—downstairs at the counter—were like a thread of similar beads that ran through Cecilia's childhood, never afterwards to be forgotten. Dublin in the 1940s was a different city from the city it later became; she'd been different herself. Cecilia was five when her father first took her to Fitzgerald's, the year after her parents were divorced.

'And tell me,' he said some time later, when she was growing up a bit, 'have you an idea at all about what you'll do with yourself?'

'When I leave school, d'you mean?'

'Well, there's no hurry, I'm not saying there is. Still and all, you're nearly thirteen these days.'

'In June.'

'Ah, I know it's June, Cecilia.' He laughed, with his glass halfway to his lips. He looked at her over the rim, his light-blue eyes twinkling in a way she was fond of. He was a burly man with a brown bald head and freckles on the back of his hands and all over his forehead and his nose.

'I don't know what I'll do,' she said.

'Some fellow'll snap you up. Don't worry about that.' He swallowed another oyster and wiped his mouth with his napkin. 'How's your mother?'

'She's fine.'

He never spoke disparagingly of her mother, nor she of him. When Cecilia was younger he used to drive up the short avenue of the house in Chapelizod in his old sloping-backed Morris, and Cecilia would always be ready for him. Her mother would say hullo to him and they'd have a little chat, and if Ronan opened the door or happened to be in the garden her father would ask him how he was, as though nothing untoward had ever occurred between them. Cecilia couldn't understand any of it, but mistily there was the memory of her father living in the house in Chapelizod, and fragments from that time had lodged in her recollection. By the fire in the dining-room he read her a story she had now forgotten. 'Your jersey's inside out,' he said to her mother and then he laughed because it was April Fools' Day. Her father and Ronan had run a furniture-making business together, two large workshops in Chapelizod, not far from the house.

'Lucky,' he said in Fitzgerald's. 'Any fellow you'd accept.'

She blushed. At school a few of her friends talked of getting married, but in a way that wasn't serious. Maureen Finnegan was in love with James Stewart, Betsy Bloom with a boy called George O'Malley: silly, really, it all was.

'The hard case,' a man in a thick overcoat said to her father, pausing on his way to the other end of the bar. 'Would I chance money on Persian Gulf?'

Cecilia's father shook his head and the man, accepting this verdict, nodded his. He winked at Cecilia in the way her father's friends sometimes did after such an exchange, an acknowledgement of her father's race-track wisdom. When he had gone her father told her that he was a very decent person who had come down in the world due to heavy drinking. Her father often had such titbits to impart and when he did so his tone was matter-of-fact, neither malicious nor pitying. In return, Cecilia would relate another fact or two about school, about Miss O'Shaughnessy or Mr Horan or the way Maureen Finnegan went on about James Stewart. Her father always listened attentively.

He hadn't married again. He lived on his own in a flat in Waterloo Road, his income accumulating from a variety of sources, several of them to do with horse-racing. He'd explained that to her when she'd asked him once about this, wondering if he went to an office every day. She had never been to his flat, but he had described it to her because she'd wondered about that too.

'We'll take the trifle?' he suggested, the only alternative offered by Fitzgerald's being something called Bonanza Cream, over which Tom the waiter had years ago strenuously shaken his head.

'Yes, please,' she said.

When they'd finished it her father had a glass of whiskey and Cecilia another orange soda, and then he lit the third of his afternoon's cigarettes. They never had lunch upstairs at Fitzgerald's, where the restaurant proper was. 'Now come and I'll show you,' her father had offered a year or so ago, and they had stared through a glass door that had the word *Fitzgerald's* in elaborate letters running diagonally across it. Men and women sat at tables covered with pink tablecloths and with scarlet-shaded electric lamps on them, the lamps alight even though it was the afternoon. 'Ah no, it's nicer downstairs,' her father had insisted, but Cecilia hadn't entirely agreed, for downstairs in Fitzgerald's possessed none of that cosiness. There were green tiles instead of the pink peacock wallpaper of the upper room, and stark rows of gin and whiskey bottles, and a workmanlike mahogany foodlift that banged up and down loaded with plates of oysters. Tom the waiter was really a barman, and the customers were all men. Cecilia had never seen a woman downstairs in Fitzgerald's.

'Bedad, isn't her ladyship growing up,' Tom said when her father had finished his whiskey and they both stood up. 'Sure, it's hardly a day ago she was a chiseler.'

'Hardly a day,' Cecilia's father agreed, and Cecilia blushed again, glancing down at her wrists because she didn't know where else to look. She didn't like her wrists. They were the thinnest in Class Three, which was a fact she knew because a week ago one of the boys had measured everyone's wrists with a piece of string. She didn't like the black hair that hung down on either side of her face because it wasn't curly like her mother's. She didn't like her eyes and she didn't like the shape of her mouth, but the boy who had measured her wrists said she was the prettiest girl in Class Three. Other people said that too.

'She's a credit to yourself, sir,' Tom said, scooping up notes and coins from the bar. 'Thanks very much.'

Her father held her coat for her, taking it from a peg by the door. It and the hat he handed her were part of her school uniform, both of them green, the hat with a pale blue band. He didn't put on his own overcoat, saying that the afternoon wasn't chilly. He never wore a hat.

They walked past Christ Church Cathedral, towards Grafton Street. Their lunchtime encounters always took place on a Saturday, and sometimes in the middle of one Cecilia's father would reveal that he had tickets for a rugby international at Lansdowne Road, or a taxi-driver would arrive in Fitzgerald's to take them to the races at Phoenix Park. Sometimes they'd walk over to the Museum or the National Gallery. Cecilia's father no longer drove a car.

'Will we go to the pictures?' he said today. '*Reap the Wild Wind* at the Grafton?'

He didn't wait for an answer because he knew she'd want to go. He walked a little ahead of her, tidy in his darkish suit, his overcoat over his arm. On the steps of the cinema he gave her some money to go up to Noblett's to buy chocolate and when she returned he was waiting with the tickets in his hand. She smiled at him, thanking him. She often wondered if he was lonely in his flat, and at the back of her mind she had an idea that what she'd like best when she left school would be to look after him there. It gave her a warm feeling in her stomach when she imagined the flat he had described and thought about cooking meals for him in its tiny kitchen.

After the cinema they had tea in Roberts' and then he walked with her to the bus stop in the centre of the city. On the way he told her about an elderly couple in the café who'd addressed him by name, people who lived out in Greystones and bred Great Danes. 'Till next time then,' he said as the bus drew in, and kissed her shyly, in the manner of someone not used to kissing people.

She waved to him from her seat by the window and watched him turn and become lost in the crowded street. He would call in at a few public houses on his way back to the flat in Waterloo Road, places he often referred to by name, Toner's and O'Donoghue's and the upstairs lounge of Mooney's, places where he met his friends and talked about racing. She imagined him there, with men like the man who'd asked if he should chance his money on Persian Gulf. But again she wondered if he was lonely.

It was already dark and had begun to rain by the time Cecilia reached the white house in Chapelizod where her father had once lived but which was occupied now by her mother and Ronan, and by Cecilia and her two half-brothers. A stove, with baskets of logs on either side of it, burned in the square, lofty hall where she took her coat and hat off. The brass doorplates and handles gleamed in the electric light. From the drawing-room came the sound of the wireless. 'Ah, the wanderer's returned,' Ronan murmured when she entered, smiling, making her welcome.

Her half-brothers were constructing a windmill out of Meccano on the floor. Her mother and Ronan were sitting close together, he in an armchair, she on the hearthrug. They were going out that night, Cecilia could tell because her mother's face was already made up: cerise lipstick and mascara, smudges of shadow beneath her eyes that accentuated their brownness, the same brown as her own. Her mother was petite and dark-haired—like Claudette Colbert, as Maureen Finnegan had once said.

'Hullo,' her mother said. 'Nice time?'

'Yes, thanks.'

She didn't say anything else because they were listening to the wireless. Her father would be drinking more stout, she thought, his overcoat on a chair beside him, a fresh cigarette in his mouth. There wasn't a public house between Stephen's Green and Waterloo Road in which he wouldn't know somebody. Of course he wasn't lonely.

The voices on the wireless told jokes, a girl sang a song about a nightingale. Cecilia glanced at her mother and Ronan, she snuggling against his legs, his hand on her shoulder. Ronan was very thin, with a craggy face and a smile that came languidly on to his lips and died away languidly also. He was never cross: in the family, anger didn't play the part it did in the households of several of Cecilia's school friends, where there was fear of a father or a mother. Every Sunday she went with Ronan to the workshops where the furniture was made and he showed her what had been begun or completed during the week. She loved the smell of wood-shavings and glue and French polish.

When the programme on the wireless came to an end her mother rose to go upstairs, to finish getting ready. Ronan muttered lazily that he supposed he'd have to get himself into a suit. He stacked logs on to the fire and set the fireguard in place. 'Your tweed one's ironed,' Cecilia's mother reminded him sternly before she left the room. He grimaced at the boys, who were showing him their completed windmill. Then he grimaced at Cecilia. It was a joke in the family that Ronan never wanted to put on a suit.

Cecilia went to a school across the city from Chapelizod, in Ranelagh. It was an unusual place in the Dublin of that time, catering for both boys and girls, for Catholics and Protestants and Jews, and for Mohammedans when that rare need arose. Overflowing from a large suburban house into the huts and prefabricated buildings that served as extra classrooms, it was run by a headmaster, assisted by a staff of both sexes. There were sixty-eight pupils.

In spite of the superficially exotic nature of this establishment

Cecilia was the only child whose parents had been divorced, and in the kind of conversations she began to have when she was twelve the details of that were increasingly a subject of curiosity. Divorce had a whiff of Hollywood and wickedness. Betsy Bloom claimed to have observed her parents naked on their bed, engaged in the act of love; Enid Healy's father had run amok with a sofa leg. What had happened within the privacy of Cecilia's family belonged in that same realm, and Cecilia was questioned closely. Even though her parents' divorce had had to be obtained in England owing to the shortcomings of the Irish law, the events leading up to it must clearly have occurred in Chapelizod. Had Cecilia ever walked into a room and found her mother and her stepfather up to something? Was it true that her mother and her stepfather used to meet for cocktails in the Gresham Hotel? What exactly *were* cocktails? Had detectives been involved? Her mother and Ronan were glanced at with interest on the very few occasions when they put in an appearance at a school function, and it was agreed that they lived up to the roles they had been cast in. The clothes her mother wore were not like the all-purpose garments of Mrs O'Reilly-Hamilton or Kitty Benson's mother. 'Sophisticated,' Maureen Finnegan had pronounced. 'Chic.'

But in the end Cecilia was aware of her schoolfellows' disappointment. There had been no detectives that she could recall, and she didn't know if there had been meetings in the Gresham Hotel. She had never walked into a room to find something untoward taking place and she could remember no quarrels—nothing that was even faintly in the same category as Enid Healy's father brandishing a sofa leg. In America, so the newspapers said, kidnappings occasionally took place when the estranged couples of divorce could not accept the dictates of the law where their children were concerned. 'Your daddy never try that?' Maureen Finnegan hopefully prompted, and Cecilia had to laugh at the absurdity of it. A satisfactory arrangement had been made, she explained for the umpteenth time, knowing it sounded dreary: everyone was content.

The headmaster of the school once spoke to her of the divorce also, though only in passing. He was a massively proportioned man known as the Bull, who shambled about the huts and prefabricated buildings calling out names in the middle of a lesson, ticking his way down the columns of his enormous roll-book. Often he would pause as if he had forgotten what he was about and for a moment or two would whistle through his breath 'The British Grenadiers', the marching song of the regiment in which he had once served with distinction. The only tasks he had ever been known to perform were the calling out of names and the issuing of an occasional vague announcement at the morning assemblies which were conducted by Mr Horan. Otherwise he remained lodged in his own cloudlands, a faint, blue-suited presence, benignly unaware of the feuds that stormed among his staff or the nature of the sixty-eight children whose immediate destinies had been placed in his care.

To Cecilia's considerable surprise the Bull sent for her one morning, the summons interrupting one of Miss O'Shaughnessy's science periods. Miss O'Shaughnessy was displaying how a piece of litmus paper had impressively changed colour, and when Mickey, the odd-job boy, entered the classroom and said that the headmaster wanted Cecilia an immediate whispering broke out. The substance of this was that a death must have taken place.

'Ah,' the Bull said when Cecilia entered the study where he ate all his meals, read the *Irish Times* and interviewed prospective parents. His breakfast tray was still on his desk, a paper-backed Sexton Blake adventure story beside it. 'Ah,' he said again, and did not continue. His bachelor existence was nicely expressed by the bleak furnishings of the room, the row of pipes above a damply smouldering fire, the insignia of the Grenadier Guards scattered on darkly panelled walls.

'Is anything the matter, sir?' Cecilia eventually inquired, for the suggestion that a death might have occurred still echoed as she stood there.

The headmaster regarded her without severity. The breathy whistling of the marching song began as he reached for a pipe and slowly filled it with tobacco. The whistling ceased. He said:

'The fees are sometimes a little tardy. The circumstances are unusual, since you are not regularly in touch with your father. But I
would be obliged, when next you see him, if you would just say
that the fees have of late been tardy.'

A match was struck, the tobacco ignited. Cecilia was not formally
dismissed, but the headmaster's immense hand seized the Sexton
Blake adventure story, indicating that the interview was over. It had
never occurred to her before that it was her father, not her mother
and Ronan, who paid her school fees. Her father had never in his
life visited the school, as her mother and Ronan had. It was strange
that he should be responsible for the fees, and Cecilia resolved to
thank him when next she saw him. It was also embarrassing that
they were sometimes late.

'Ah,' the Bull said when she had reached the door. 'You're—
ah—all right, are you? The—ah—family trouble . . . ?'

'Oh, that's all over, sir.'

'So it is. So it is. And everything . . . ?'

'Everything's fine, sir.'

'Good. Good.'

Interest in the divorce had dwindled and might even have dissipated entirely had not the odd behaviour of a boy called Abrahamson begun. Quite out of the blue, about a month after the
Saturday on which Cecilia and her father had gone to see *Reap the
Wild Wind*, Abrahamson began to stare at her.

In the big classroom where Mr Horan's morning assemblies were
held his eyes repeatedly darted over her features, and whenever they
met in a corridor or by the tennis courts he would glance at her
sharply and then glance away again, trying to do so before she
noticed. Abrahamson's father was the solicitor to the furniture-
making business and because of that Abrahamson occasionally
turned up in the house in Chapelizod. No one else from the school
did so, Chapelizod being too distant from the neighbourhoods
where most of the school's sixty-eight pupils lived. Abrahamson was
younger than Cecilia, a small olive-skinned boy whom Cecilia had

many times entertained in the nursery while his parents sat downstairs, having a drink. He was an only child, self-effacing and anxious not to be a nuisance: when he came to Chapelizod now he obligingly played with Cecilia's half-brothers, humping them about the garden on his back or acting the unimportant parts in the playlets they composed.

At school he was always called by his surname and was famous for his brains. He was neither popular nor unpopular, content to remain on the perimeter of things. Because of this, Cecilia found it difficult to approach him about his staring, and the cleverness that was reflected in the liquid depths of his eyes induced a certain apprehension. But since his interest in her showed no sign of diminishing she decided she'd have to point out that she found it discomfiting. One showery afternoon, on the way down the shrubbed avenue of the school, she questioned him.

Being taller than the boy and his voice being softly pitched, Cecilia had to bend over him to catch his replies. He had a way of smiling when he spoke—a smile, so everyone said, that had to do with his thoughts rather than with any conversation he happened to be having at the time.

'I'm sorry,' he said. 'I'm really sorry, Cecilia. I didn't know I was doing it.'

'You've been doing it for weeks, Abrahamson.'

He nodded, obligingly accepting the truth of the accusation. And since an explanation was required, he obligingly offered one.

'It's just that when you reach a certain age the features of your face aren't those of a child any more. I read it in a book: a child's face disguises its real features, but at a certain age the disguise falls off. D'you understand, Cecilia?'

'No, I don't. And I don't know why you've picked on me just because of something you read in a book.'

'It happens to everyone, Cecilia.'

'You don't go round staring at everyone.'

'I'm sorry. I'm terribly sorry, Cecilia.'

Abrahamson stopped and opened the black case in which he carried his school-books. Cecilia thought that in some clever way he was going to produce from it an explanation that made more sense. She waited without pressing the matter. On the avenue boys kicked each other, throwing caps about. Miss O'Shaughnessy passed on her motorized bicycle. Mr Horan strode by with his violin.

'Like one?' Abrahamson had taken from his case a carton containing two small, garishly iced cakes. 'Go on, really.'

She took the raspberry-coloured one, after which Abrahamson meticulously closed the carton and returned it to his case. Every day he came to school with two of these cakes, supplied by his mother for consumption during the eleven o'clock break. He sold them to anyone who had a few pence to spare, and if he didn't sell them at school he did so to a girl in a newsagent's shop which he passed on his journey home.

'I don't want to tell you,' he said as they walked on. 'I'm sorry you noticed.'

'I couldn't help noticing.'

'Call it quits now, will we?' There was the slightest of gestures towards the remains of the cake, sticky in Cecilia's hand. Abrahamson's tone was softer than ever, his distant smile an echo from his private world. It was said that he played chess games in his head.

'I'd like to know, Abrahamson.'

His thin shoulders just perceptibly shifted up and down. He appeared to be stating that Cecilia was foolish to insist, and to be stating as well that if she continued to insist he did not intend to waste time and energy in argument. They had passed through the gates of the school and were standing on the street, waiting for a number 11 bus.

'It's odd,' he said, 'if you want to know. Your father and all that.'

'Odd?'

The bus drew up. They mounted to the upper deck. When they sat down Abrahamson stared out of the window. It was as if he had already said everything that was necessary, as if Cecilia should effortlessly be able to deduce the rest. She had to nudge him with her elbow, and then—politely and very swiftly—he glanced at her, silently apologizing for her inability to understand the obvious. A pity, his small face declared, a shame to have to carry this burden of stupidity.

'When people get divorced,' he said, carefully spacing the words, 'there's always a reason. You'll observe that in films. Or if you read in the paper about the divorce of, say, William Powell and Carole Lombard. They don't actually bother with divorce if they only dislike one another.'

The conductor came to take their fares. Again the conversation appeared to have reached its termination.

'But what on earth's that got to do with what we're talking about, Abrahamson?'

'Wouldn't there have been a reason why your parents got divorced? Wouldn't the reason be the man your mother married?'

She nodded vehemently, feeling hot and silly. Abrahamson said:

'They'd have had a love affair while your father was still around. In the end there would have been the divorce.'

'I know all that, Abrahamson.'

'Well, then.'

Impatiently, she began to protest again but broke off in the middle of a sentence and instead sat there frowning. She sensed that the last two words her companion had uttered contained some further declaration, but was unable to grasp it.

'Excuse me,' Abrahamson said, politely, before he went.

'Aren't you hungry?' her mother asked, looking across the lace-trimmed white cloth on the dining-room table. 'You haven't been gorging yourself, have you?'

Cecilia shook her head, and the hair she didn't like swung about. Her half-brothers giggled, a habit they had recently developed. They were years younger than Cecilia, yet the briskness in her mother's voice placed her in a category with them, and she suddenly wondered if her mother could somehow guess what had come into her mind and was telling her not to be silly. Her mother was wearing a green dress and her fingernails had been freshly tinted. Her black bobbed hair gleamed healthily in watery afternoon sunshine, her dimples came and went.

'How was the Latin?'

'All right.'

'Did you get the passive right?'

'More or less.'

'Why're you so grumpy, Cecilia?'

'I'm not.'

'Well, I think I'd disagree with that.'

Cecilia's cheeks had begun to burn, which caused her half-brothers to giggle again. She knew they were kicking one another beneath the table and to avoid their scrutiny she stared through the french windows, out into the garden. She'd slept in a pram beneath the apple tree and once had crawled about among the flowerbeds: she could just remember that, she could remember her father laughing as he picked her up.

Cecilia finished her cup of tea and rose, leaving half a piece of coffee-cake on her plate. Her mother called after her when she reached the door.

'I'm going to do my homework,' Cecilia said.

'But you haven't eaten your cake.'

'I don't want it.'

'That's rude, you know.'

She didn't say anything. She opened the door and closed it softly behind her. Locked in the bathroom, she examined in the looking-glass the features Abrahamson had spoken of. She made herself smile. She squinted, trying to see her profile. She didn't want to think about any of it, yet she couldn't help herself. She hated being here, with the door locked at five o'clock in the evening, yet she couldn't help that either. She stared at herself for minutes on end, performing further contortions, glancing and grimacing, catching herself unawares. But she couldn't see anywhere a look of her stepfather.

'Well, you wouldn't,' Abrahamson explained. 'It's difficult to analyse your own face.'

They walked together slowly, on the cinder-track that ran around the tennis courts and the school's single hockey pitch. She was wearing her summer uniform, a green-and-blue dress, short white socks. Abrahamson wore flannel shorts and the elaborate school blazer.

'Other people would have noticed, Abrahamson.'

He shook his head. Other people weren't so interested in things like that, he said. And other people weren't so familiar with her family.

'It isn't a likeness or anything, Cecilia. Not a strong resemblance, nothing startling. It's only a hint, Cecilia, an inkling you could call it.'

'I wish you hadn't told me.'

'You wanted me to.'

'Yes, I know.'

They had reached the end of the cinder-track. They turned and walked back towards the school buildings in silence. Girls were playing tennis. 'Love, forty,' called the elderly English master, No-teeth Carroll he was known as.

'I've looked and looked,' Cecilia said. 'I spend hours in the bathroom.'

'Even if I hadn't read about the development of the features I think I'd have stumbled on it for myself. "Now, what on earth is it about that girl?" I kept saying to myself. "Why's her face so interesting all of a sudden?" '

'I think you're imagining it.'

'Well, maybe I am.'

They watched the tennis-players. He wasn't someone who made mistakes, or made things up; he wasn't like that at all. She wished she had her father's freckles, just a couple, anywhere, on her forehead or her nose. 'Deuce,' No-teeth Carroll called. 'No, it's definitely deuce,' he insisted, but an argument continued. The poor old fellow was on a term's notice, Abrahamson said.

They walked on. She'd heard it too, she agreed, about the term's notice. Pity, because he wasn't bad, the way he let you do anything you liked provided you were quiet.

'Would you buy one of my cakes today?' Abrahamson asked.

'Please don't tell anyone, Abrahamson.'

'You could buy them *every* day, you know. I never eat them myself.'

A little time went by. On the 15th of June Cecilia became thirteen. A great fuss was made of the occasion, as was usual in the family whenever there was a birthday. Ronan gave her *A Tale of Two Cities*, her mother a dress which she had made herself, with rosebuds on it, and her half-brothers gave her a red bangle. There was chicken for her birthday lunch, with roast potatoes and peas, and then lemon meringue pie. All of them were favourites of hers.

'Happy birthday, darling,' Ronan whispered, finding a special moment to say it when everyone else was occupied. She knew he was fond of her, she knew that he enjoyed their Sunday mornings in the workshops. She liked him too. She'd never thought of not liking him.

'*Really* happy birthday,' he said and it was then, as he smiled and turned away, that something occurred to her which she hadn't thought of before, and which Abrahamson clearly hadn't thought of either: when you'd lived for most of your life in a house with the man whom your mother had married you could easily pick up some of his ways. You could pick them up without knowing it, like catching a cold, his smile or some other hint of himself. You might laugh the way he did, or say things with his voice. You'd never guess you were doing it.

'Oh, of course,' Abrahamson obligingly agreed when she put it to him. 'Of course, Cecilia.'

'But wouldn't that be it then? I mean, mightn't that account—'

'Indeed it might.'

His busy, unassuming eyes looked up into hers and then at the distant figure of No-teeth Carroll, who was standing dismally by the long-jump pit.

'Indeed,' Abrahamson said again.

'I'm *certain* that's it. I mean, I still can't see anything myself in my looks—'

'Oh, there's definitely something.' He interrupted sharply, his tone suggesting that it was illogical and ridiculous to question what had already been agreed upon. 'It's very interesting, what you're saying about growing like someone you live with and quite like. It's perfectly possible, just as the other is perfectly possible. If you asked your mother, Cecilia, she probably wouldn't know what's what any more than anyone else does. On account of the circumstances.'

He was bored by the subject. He had acceded to her request about not telling anyone. It was best to let the subject go.

'Chocolate and strawberry today,' he said, smiling again as he passed over the two small cakes.

There was another rendezvous in Fitzgerald's Oyster Bar. Cecilia wore her new rosebud dress and her red bangle. On her birthday a ten-shilling note had arrived from her father, which she now thanked him for.

'When I was thirteen myself,' he said, pulling the cellophane from a packet of Sweet Afton, 'I didn't know whether I was coming or going.'

Cecilia kept her head averted. At least the light wasn't strong. There was a certain amount of stained glass in the windows and only weak bulbs burned in the globe-topped brass lamps that were set at intervals along the mahogany bar. She tried not to smile in case the inkling in her face had something to do with that.

'Well, I see your man's going up in front of the stewards,' Tom the waiter remarked. 'Sure, isn't it time they laid down the law on that fellow?'

'Oh, a terrible chancer that fellow, Tom.'

Their order was taken, and shouted down the lift-shaft.

'We might indulge in a drop of wine, Tom. On account of her ladyship's birthday.'

'I have a great little French one, sir. Mâcon, sir.'

'That'll suit us fine, Tom.'

It was early, the bar was almost empty. Two men in camel-coloured coats were talking in low voices by the door. Cecilia had seen them before. They were bookies, her father had told her.

'Are you all right?' he inquired. 'You haven't got the toothache or anything?'

'No, I'm all right, thanks.'

The bar filled up. Men stopped to speak to her father and then sat at the small tables behind them or on stools by the bar itself. Her father lit another cigarette.

'I didn't realize you paid the fees,' she said.

'What fees do you mean?'

She told him in order to thank him, because she thought they could laugh over the business of the fees being late every term. But her father received the reprimand solemnly. He was at fault, he confessed: the headmaster was quite right, and must be apologized to on his behalf.

'He's not someone you talk to,' Cecilia explained, realizing that although she'd so often spoken about school to her father she'd never properly described the place, the huts and prefabricated buildings that were its classrooms, the Bull going round every morning with his huge roll-book.

She watched Tom drawing the cork from the bottle of red wine. She said that only yesterday Miss O'Shaughnessy's motorized bicycle had given up the ghost and she repeated the rumour that poor old No-teeth Carroll was on a term's notice. She couldn't say that she'd struck a silent bargain with a boy called Abrahamson, who brought to the school each day two dainty little cakes in a carton. She'd have liked just to tell about the cakes because her father would have appreciated the oddity of it. It was strange that she hadn't done so before.

'Now,' said Tom, placing the oysters in front of her father and her steak in front of her. He filled up their wine-glasses and drew a surplus of foam from the surface of someone else's stout.

'Is your mother well, Cecilia?'

'Oh, yes.'

'And everyone in Chapelizod?'

'They're all well.'

He looked at her. He had an oyster on the way to his mouth and he glanced at her and then he ate the oyster. He took a mouthful of wine to wash it down.

'Well, that's great,' he said.

Slowly he continued to consume his oysters. 'If we felt like it,' he said, 'we could catch the races at the Park.'

He had been through all of it, just as she had. Ever since the divorce he must have wondered, looking at her as he had looked at her just now, for tell-tale signs. 'They'd have had a love affair while your father was still around,' came the echo of Abrahamson's confident voice, out of place in the oyster bar. Her father had seen Abrahamson's inkling and had felt as miserable as she had. He had probably even comforted himself with the theory about two people in the same house, she picking up her stepfather's characteristics. He had probably said all that to himself over and over again but the doubt had lingered, as it had lingered with her. Married to one man, her mother had performed with another the same act of passion which Betty Bloom had witnessed in her parents' bedroom. As Abrahamson had fairly pointed out, in confused circumstances such as these no one would ever know what was what.

'We'll take the trifle, will we?' her father said.

'Two trifle,' Tom shouted down the lift-shaft.

'You're getting prettier all the time, girl.'

'I don't like my looks at all.'

'Nonsense, girl. You're lovely.'

His eyes, pinched a bit because he was laughing, twinkled. He was much older than her mother, Cecilia suddenly realized, something which had never struck her before.

Were the fees not paid on time because he didn't always have the money? Was that why he had sold his car?

'Will we settle for the races, or something else? You're the birthday lady today.'

'The races would be lovely.'

'Could you ever put that on for me, sir?' Tom requested in a whisper, passing a pound note across the bar. 'Amazon Girl, the last race.'

'I will of course, Tom.'

His voice betrayed nothing of the pain which Cecilia now knew must mark these Saturday occasions for him. The car that was due to collect them was late, he said, and as he spoke the taxi man entered.

'Step on it,' her father said, 'like a good man.'

He gave her money and advised her which horses to gamble on. He led her by the hand when they went to find a good place to watch from. It was a clear, sunny day, the sky without a cloud in it, and in the noise and bustle no one seemed unhappy.

'There's a boy at school,' she said, 'who brings two little cakes for the eleven o'clock lunch. He sells them to me every day.'

He wagged his head and smiled. But in a serious voice he said he hoped she didn't pay too much for the cakes, and she explained that she didn't.

It was odd the way Maureen Finnegan and all the others, even the Bull, had suspected the tidy settlement there'd been. It would be ridiculous now, ever to look after him in his flat.

'I hate to lose poor Tom's money for him.'

'Won't Amazon Girl win?'

'Never a hope.'

Women in brightly coloured dresses passed by as Cecilia's father paused for a moment by a bookmaker's stand to examine the offered odds. He ran a hand over his jaw, considering. A woman with red hair and sunglasses came up. She said it was good to see him and then passed on.

'We'll take a small little flutter on Gillian's Choice,' he finally said. 'D'you like the sound of that, Cecilia?'

She said she did. She put some of the money he had given her on the horse and waited for him while he transacted with another bookmaker. He approached a third one with Tom's pound for Amazon Girl. It was a habit of his to bet with different bookmakers.

'That red-haired woman's from Carlow,' he said as they set off to their vantage point. 'The widow of the county surveyor.'

'Yes,' she said, not caring much about the red-haired woman.

'Gillian's Choice is the one with the golden hoops,' he said. 'Poor Tom's old nag is the grey one.'

The horses went under starter's orders and then, abruptly, were off. In the usual surprisingly short space of time the race was over.

'What did I tell you?' He laughed down at her as they went to collect the winnings from their two different bookmakers. He had won more than three hundred pounds, she fourteen and sixpence. They always counted at the end; they never lost when they went together. He said she brought him luck, but she knew it was the other way round.

'You'll find your way to the bus, Cecilia?'

'Yes, I will. Thanks very much.'

He nodded. He kissed her in his awkward way and then disappeared into the crowd, as he always seemed to do when they parted. It was standing about in the sun, she thought, that caused him to have so many freckles. She imagined him at other race-courses, idling between races without her, sunning himself while considering a race-card. She imagined him in his flat in Waterloo Road and wondered if he ever cried.

She walked slowly away, the money clenched in her hand because the rosebud dress had no pockets. He did cry, she thought: on the Saturdays when they met, when he was on his own again. It was easy to imagine him because she wanted to cry herself, because on all their occasions in the future there would be the doubt. Neither of them would ever really know what being together meant, downstairs at Fitzgerald's or anywhere else.

Beyond the Pale

We always went to Ireland in June.

Ever since the four of us began to go on holidays together, in 1965 it must have been, we had spent the first fortnight of the month at Glencorn Lodge in Co. Antrim. Perfection, as Dekko put it once, and none of us disagreed. It's a Georgian house by the sea, not far from the village of Ardbeag. It's quite majestic in its rather elegant way, a garden running to the very edge of a cliff, a long rhododendron drive—or avenue, as they say in Ireland. The English couple who bought the house in the early sixties, the Malseeds, have had to build on quite a bit but it's all been discreetly done, the Georgian style preserved throughout. Figs grow in the sheltered gardens, and apricots, and peaches in the greenhouses which old Mr Saxton presides over. He's Mrs Malseed's father actually. They brought him with them from Surrey, and their Dalmatians, Charger and Snooze.

It was Strafe who found Glencorn for us. He'd come across an advertisement in the *Lady* in the days when the Malseeds still felt the need to advertise. 'How about this?' he said one evening at the end of the second rubber, and then read out the details. We had gone away together the summer before, to a hotel that had been recommended on the Costa del Sol, but it hadn't been a success because the food was so appalling. 'We could try this Irish one,' Dekko suggested cautiously, which is what eventually we did.

The four of us have been playing bridge together for ages, Dekko, Strafe, Cynthia and myself. They call me Milly, though strictly speaking my name is Dorothy Milson. Dekko picked up his nickname at school, Dekko Deakin sounding rather good, I dare say. He and Strafe were in fact at school together, which must be why we all call Strafe by his surname: Major R.B. Strafe he is, the initials standing for Robert Buchanan. We're of an age, the four of us, all in the early fifties: the prime of life, so Dekko insists. We live quite close to Leatherhead, where the Malseeds were before they decided to make the change from Surrey to Co. Antrim. Quite a coincidence, we always think.

'How *very* nice,' Mrs Malseed said, smiling her welcome again this year. Some instinct seems to tell her when guests are about to arrive, for she's rarely not waiting in the large, low-ceilinged hall that always smells of flowers. She dresses beautifully, differently every day, and changing of course in the evening. Her blouse on this occasion was scarlet and silver, in stripes, her skirt black. This choice gave her a brisk look, which was fitting because being so busy she often has to be a little on the brisk side. She has smooth grey hair which she once told me she entirely looks after herself, and she almost always wears a black velvet band in it. Her face is well made up, and for one who arranges so many vases of flowers and otherwise has to use her hands she manages to keep them marvellously in condition. Her fingernails are varnished a soft pink, and a small gold bangle always adorns her right wrist, a wedding present from her husband.

'Arthur, take the party's luggage,' she commanded the old porter, who doubles as odd-job man. 'Rose, Geranium, Hydrangea, Fuchsia.' She referred to the titles of the rooms reserved for us: in winter, when no one much comes to Glencorn Lodge, pleasant little details like that are seen to. Mrs Malseed herself painted the flower-plaques that are attached to the doors of the hotel instead of numbers; her husband sees to redecoration and repairs.

'Well, well, well,' Mr Malseed said now, entering the hall through the door that leads to the kitchen regions. 'A hundred thousand welcomes,' he greeted us in the Irish manner. He's rather shorter than Mrs Malseed, who's handsomely tall. He wears Donegal tweed suits and is brown as a berry, including his head, which is bald. His dark brown eyes twinkle at you, making you feel rather more than just another hotel guest. They run the place like a country house, really.

'Good trip?' Mr Malseed inquired.

'Super,' Dekko said. 'Not a worry all the way.'

'Splendid.'

'The wretched boat sailed an hour early one day last week,' Mrs Malseed said. 'Quite a little band were left stranded at Stranraer.'

Strafe laughed. Typical of that steamship company, he said. 'Catching the tide, I dare say?'

'They caught a rocket from me,' Mrs Malseed replied good-humouredly. 'A couple of old dears were due with us on Tuesday and had to spend the night in some awful Scottish lodging-house. It nearly finished them.'

Everyone laughed, and I could feel the others thinking that our holiday had truly begun. Nothing had changed at Glencorn Lodge, all was well with its Irish world. Kitty from the dining-room came out to greet us, spotless in her uniform. 'Ach, you're looking younger,' she said, paying the compliment to all four of us, causing everyone in the hall to laugh again. Kitty's a bit of a card.

Arthur led the way to the rooms called Rose, Geranium, Hydrangea and Fuchsia, carrying as much of our luggage as he could manage and returning for the remainder. Arthur has a beaten, fisherman's face and short grey hair. He wears a green baize apron, and a white shirt with an imitation-silk scarf tucked into it at the neck. The scarf, in different swirling greens which blend nicely with the green of his apron, is an idea of Mrs Malseed's and one appreciates the effort, if not at a uniform, at least at tidiness.

'Thank you very much,' I said to Arthur in my room, smiling and finding him a coin.

We played a couple of rubbers after dinner as usual, but not of course going on for as long as we might have because we were still quite tired after the journey. In the lounge there was a French family, two girls and their parents, and a honeymoon couple—or so we had speculated during dinner—and a man on his own. There had been other people at dinner of course, because in June Glencorn Lodge is always full: from where we sat in the window we could see some of them strolling about the lawns, a few taking the cliff path down to the seashore. In the morning we'd do the same: we'd walk along the sands to Ardbeag and have coffee in the hotel there, back in time for lunch. In the afternoon we'd drive somewhere.

I knew all that because over the years this kind of pattern had developed. We had our walks and our drives, tweed to buy in Cushendall, Strafe's and Dekko's fishing day when Cynthia and I just sat on the beach, our visit to the Giant's Causeway and one to Donegal perhaps, though that meant an early start and taking pot-luck for dinner somewhere. We'd come to adore Co. Antrim, its glens and coastline, Rathlin Island and Tievebulliagh. Since first we got to know it, in 1965, we'd all four fallen hopelessly in love with every variation of this remarkable landscape. People in England thought us mad of course: they see so much of the troubles on television that it's naturally difficult for them to realize that most places are just as they've always been. Yet coming as we did, taking the road along the coast, dawdling through Ballygally, it was impossible to believe that somewhere else the unpleasantness was going on. We'd never seen a thing, nor even heard people talking about incidents that might have taken place. It's true that after a particularly nasty carry-on a few winters ago we did consider finding somewhere else, in Scotland perhaps, or Wales. But as Strafe put it at the time, we felt we owed a certain loyalty to the Malseeds and indeed to everyone we'd come to know round about, people who'd always been glad to welcome us back. It seemed silly to lose our heads, and when we returned the following summer we knew immediately we'd been right. Dekko said that nothing could be further away from all the violence than Glencorn Lodge, and though his remark could hardly be taken literally I think we all knew what he meant.

'Cynthia's tired,' I said because she'd been stifling yawns. 'I think we should call it a day.'

'Oh, not at all,' Cynthia protested. 'No, please.'

But Dekko agreed with me that she was tired, and Strafe said he didn't mind stopping now. He suggested a nightcap, as he always does, and as we always do also, Cynthia and I declined. Dekko said he'd like a Cointreau.

The conversation drifted about. Dekko told us an Irish joke about a drunk who couldn't find his way out of a telephone box, and then Strafe remembered an incident at school concerning his and Dekko's housemaster, A.D. Cowley-Stubbs, and the house wag, Thrive Major. A.D. Cowley-Stubbs had been known as Cows and often featured in our after-bridge reminiscing. So did Thrive Major.

'Perhaps I *am* sleepy,' Cynthia said. 'I don't think I closed my eyes once last night.'

She never does on a sea crossing. Personally I'm out like a light the moment my head touches the pillow; I often think it must be the salt in the air because normally I'm an uneasy sleeper at the best of times.

'You run along, old girl,' Strafe advised.

'Brekky at nine,' Dekko said.

Cynthia said good-night and went, and we didn't remark on her tiredness because as a kind of unwritten rule we never comment on one another. We're four people who play bridge. The companionship it offers, and the holidays we have together, are all part of that. We share everything: the cost of petrol, the cups of coffee or drinks we have; we even each make a contribution towards the use of Strafe's car because it's always his we go on holiday in, a Rover it was on this occasion.

'Funny, being here on your own,' Strafe said, glancing across what the Malseeds call the After-Dinner Lounge at the man who didn't have a companion. He was a red-haired man of about thirty, not wearing a tie, his collar open at the neck and folded back over the jacket of his blue serge suit. He was uncouth-looking, though it's a hard thing to say, not at all the kind of person one usually sees at Glencorn Lodge. He sat in the After-Dinner Lounge as he had in the dining-room, lost in some concentration of his own, as if calculating sums in his mind. There had been a folded newspaper on his table in the dining-room. It now reposed tidily on the arm of his chair, still unopened.

'Commercial gent,' Dekko said. 'Fertilizers.'

'Good heavens, never. You wouldn't get a rep in here.'

I took no part in the argument. The lone man didn't much interest me, but I felt that Strafe was probably right: if there was anything dubious about the man's credentials he might have found it difficult to secure a room. In the hall of Glencorn Lodge there's a notice which reads: *We prefer not to feature in hotel guides, and we would be grateful to our guests if they did not seek to include Glencorn Lodge in the Good Food Guide, the Good Hotel Guide, the Michelin, Egon Ronay or any others. We have not advertised Glencorn since our early days, and prefer our recommendations to be by word of mouth.*

'Ah, thank you,' Strafe said when Kitty brought his whisky and Dekko's Cointreau. 'Sure you won't have something?' he said to me, although he knew I never did.

Strafe is on the stout side, I suppose you could say, with a gingery moustache and gingery hair, hardly touched at all by grey. He left the Army years ago, I suppose because of me in a sense, because he didn't want to be posted abroad again. He's in the Ministry of Defence now.

I'm still quite pretty in my way, though nothing like as striking as Mrs Malseed, for I've never been that kind of woman. I've put on weight, and wouldn't have allowed myself to do so if Strafe hadn't kept saying he can't stand a bag of bones. I'm careful about my hair and, unlike Mrs Malseed, I have it very regularly seen to because if I don't it gets a salt-and-pepper look, which I hate. My husband, Terence, who died of food-poisoning when we were still quite young, used to say I wouldn't lose a single look in middle age, and to some extent that's true. We were still putting off having children when he died, which is why I haven't any. Then I met Strafe, which meant I didn't marry again.

Strafe is married himself, to Cynthia. She's small and ineffectual, I suppose you'd say without being untruthful or unkind. Not that Cynthia and I don't get on or anything like that, in fact we get on extremely well. It's Strafe and Cynthia who don't seem quite to hit it off, and I often think how much happier all round it would have been if Cynthia had married someone completely different, someone like Dekko in a way, except that that mightn't quite have worked out either. The Strafes have two sons, both very like their father, both of them in the Army. And the very sad thing is they think nothing of poor Cynthia.

'Who's that chap?' Dekko asked Mr Malseed, who'd come over to wish us good-night.

'Awfully sorry about that, Mr Deakin. My fault entirely, a booking that came over the phone.'

'Good heavens, not at all,' Strafe protested, and Dekko looked horrified in case it should be thought he was objecting to the locals. 'Splendid-looking fellow,' he said, overdoing it.

Mr Malseed murmured that the man had only booked in for a single night, and I smiled the whole thing away, reassuring him with a nod. It's one of the pleasantest of the traditions at Glencorn Lodge that every evening Mr Malseed makes the rounds of his guests just to say good-night. It's because of little touches like that that I, too, wished Dekko hadn't questioned Mr Malseed about the man because it's the kind of thing one doesn't do at Glencorn Lodge. But Dekko is a law unto himself, very tall and gangling, always immaculately suited, a beaky face beneath mousy hair in which flecks of grey add a certain distinction. Dekko has money of his own and though he takes out girls who are half his age he has never managed to get around to marriage. The uncharitable might say he has a rather gormless laugh; certainly it's sometimes on the loud side.

We watched while Mr Malseed bade the lone man good-night. The man didn't respond, but just sat gazing. It was ill-mannered, but this lack of courtesy didn't appear to be intentional: the man was clearly in a mood of some kind, miles away.

'Well, I'll go up,' I said. 'Good-night, you two.'

'Cheery-bye, Milly,' Dekko said. 'Brekky at nine, remember.'

'Good-night, Milly,' Strafe said.

The Strafes always occupy different rooms on holidays, and at home also. This time he was in Geranium and she in Fuchsia. I was in Rose, and in a little while Strafe would come to see me. He stays with her out of kindness, because he fears for her on her own. He's a sentimental, good-hearted man, easily moved to tears: he simply cannot bear the thought of Cynthia with no one to talk to in the evenings, with no one to make her life around. 'And besides,' he often says when he's being jocular, 'it would break up our bridge four.' Naturally we never discuss her shortcomings or in any way analyse the marriage. The unwritten rule that exists among the four of us seems to extend as far as that.

He slipped into my room after he'd had another drink or two, and I was waiting for him as he likes me to wait, in bed but not quite undressed. He has never said so, but I know that that is something Cynthia would not understand in him, or even attempt to comply with. Terence, of course, would not have understood either; poor old Terence would have been shocked. Actually it's all rather sweet, Strafe and his little ways.

'I love you, dear,' I whispered to him in the darkness, but just then he didn't wish to speak of love and referred instead to my body.

If Cynthia hadn't decided to remain in the hotel the next morning instead of accompanying us on our walk to Ardbeag everything might have been different. As it happened, when she said at breakfast she thought she'd just potter about the garden and sit with her book out of the wind somewhere, I can't say I was displeased. For a moment I hoped Dekko might say he'd stay with her, allowing Strafe and myself to go off on our own, but Dekko—who doesn't go in for saying what you want him to say—didn't. 'Poor old sausage,' he said instead, examining Cynthia with a solicitude that suggested she was close to the grave, rather than just a little lowered by the change of life or whatever it was.

'I'll be perfectly all right,' Cynthia assured him. 'Honestly.'

'Cynthia likes to mooch, you know,' Strafe pointed out, which of course is only the truth. She reads too much, I always think. You often see her putting down a book with the most melancholy look in her eyes, which can't be good for her. She's an imaginative woman, I suppose you would say, and of course her habit of reading so much is often useful on our holidays: over the years she has read her way through dozens of Irish guidebooks. 'That's where the garrison pushed the natives over the cliffs,' she once remarked on a drive. 'Those rocks are known as the Maidens,' she remarked on another occasion. She has led us to places of interest which we had no idea existed: Garron Tower on Garron Point, the mausoleum at Bonamargy, the Devil's Backbone. As well as which, Cynthia is extremely knowledgeable about all matters relating to Irish history. Again she has read endlessly: biographies and autobiographies, long accounts of the centuries of battling and politics there've been. There's hardly a town or village we ever pass through that hasn't some significance for Cynthia, although I'm afraid her impressive fund of information doesn't always receive the attention it deserves. Not that Cynthia ever minds; it doesn't seem to worry her when no one listens. My own opinion is that she'd have made a much better job of her relationship with Strafe and her sons if she could have somehow developed a bit more character.

We left her in the garden and proceeded down the cliff path to the shingle beneath. I was wearing slacks and a blouse, with the arms of a cardigan looped round my neck in case it turned chilly: the outfit was new, specially bought for the holiday, in shades of tangerine. Strafe never cares how he dresses and of course she doesn't keep him up to the mark: that morning, as far as I remember, he wore rather shapeless corduroy trousers, the kind men sometimes garden in, and a navy-blue fisherman's jersey. Dekko as usual was a fashion plate: a pale-green linen suit with pleated jacket pockets, a maroon shirt open at the neck, revealing a medallion on a fine gold chain. We didn't converse as we crossed the rather difficult shingle, but when we reached the sand Dekko began to talk about some girl or other, someone called Juliet who had apparently proposed marriage to him just before we'd left Surrey. He'd told her, so he said, that he'd think about it while on holiday and he wondered now about dispatching a telegram from Ardbeag saying, *Still thinking*. Strafe, who has a simple sense of humour, considered this hugely funny and spent most of the walk persuading Dekko that the telegram must certainly be sent, and other telegrams later on, all with the same message. Dekko kept laughing, throwing his head back in a way that always reminds me of an Australian bird I once saw in a nature film on television. I could see this was going to become one of those jokes that would accompany us all through the holiday, a man's thing really, but of course I didn't mind. The girl called Juliet was nearly thirty years younger than Dekko. I supposed she knew what she was doing.

Since the subject of telegrams had come up, Strafe recalled the occasion when Thrive Major had sent one to A.D. Cowley-Stubbs: *Darling regret three months gone love Beulah*. Carefully timed, it had arrived during one of Cows' Thursday evening coffee sessions. Beulah was a maid who had been sacked the previous term, and old Cows had something of a reputation as a misogynist. When he read the message he apparently went white and collapsed into an armchair. Warrington P.J. managed to read it too, and after that the fat was in the fire. The consequences went on rather, but I never minded listening when Strafe and Dekko drifted back to their school-days. I just wish I'd known Strafe then, before either of us had gone and got married.

We had our coffee at Ardbeag, the telegram was sent off, and then Strafe and Dekko wanted to see a man called Henry O'Reilly whom we'd met on previous holidays, who organizes mackerel-fishing trips. I waited on my own, picking out postcards in the village shop that sells almost everything, and then I wandered down towards the shore. I knew that they would be having a drink with the boatman because a year had passed since they'd seen him last. They joined me after about twenty minutes, Dekko apologizing but Strafe not seeming to be aware that I'd had to wait because Strafe is not a man who notices little things. It was almost one o'clock when we reached Glencorn Lodge and were told by Mr Malseed that Cynthia needed looking after.

The hotel, in fact, was in a turmoil. I have never seen anyone as ashen-faced as Mr Malseed; his wife, in a forget-me-not dress, was limp. It wasn't explained to us immediately what had happened, because in the middle of telling us that Cynthia needed looking after Mr Malseed was summoned to the telephone. I could see through the half-open door of their little office a glass of whiskey or brandy on the desk and Mrs Malseed's bangled arm reaching out for it. Not for ages did we realize that it all had to do with the lone man whom we'd speculated about the night before.

'He just wanted to talk to me,' Cynthia kept repeating hysterically in the hall. 'He sat with me by the magnolias.'

I made her lie down. Strafe and I stood on either side of her bed as she lay there with her shoes off, her rather unattractively cut plain pink dress crumpled and actually damp from her tears. I wanted to make her take it off and to slip under the bedclothes in her petticoat but somehow it seemed all wrong, in the circumstances, for Strafe's wife to do anything so intimate in my presence.

'I couldn't stop him,' Cynthia said, the rims of her eyes crimson by now, her nose beginning to run again. 'From half past ten till well after twelve. He had to talk to someone, he said.'

I could sense that Strafe was thinking precisely the same as I was: that the red-haired man had insinuated himself into Cynthia's company by talking about himself and had then put a hand on her knee. Instead of simply standing up and going away Cynthia would have stayed where she was, embarrassed or tongue-tied, at any rate unable to cope. And when the moment came she would have turned hysterical. I could picture her screaming in the garden, running across the lawn to the hotel, and then the pandemonium in the hall. I could sense Strafe picturing that also.

'My God, it's terrible,' Cynthia said.

'I think she should sleep,' I said quietly to Strafe. 'Try to sleep, dear,' I said to her, but she shook her head, tossing her jumble of hair about on the pillow.

'Milly's right,' Strafe urged. 'You'll feel much better after a little rest. We'll bring you a cup of tea later on.'

'My God!' she cried again. 'My God, how could I sleep?'

I went away to borrow a couple of mild sleeping pills from Dekko, who is never without them, relying on the things too much in my opinion. He was tidying himself in his room, but found the pills immediately. Strangely enough, Dekko's always sound in a crisis.

I gave them to her with water and she took them without asking what they were. She was in a kind of daze, one moment making a fuss and weeping, the next just peering ahead of her, as if frightened. In a way she was like someone who'd just had a bad nightmare and hadn't yet completely returned to reality. I remarked as much to Strafe while we made our way down to lunch, and he said he quite agreed.

'Poor old Cynth!' Dekko said when we'd all ordered lobster bisque and entrecôte béarnaise. 'Poor old sausage.'

You could see that the little waitress, a new girl this year, was bubbling over with excitement; but Kitty, serving the other half of the dining-room, was grim, which was most unusual. Everyone was talking in hushed tones and when Dekko said, 'Poor old Cynth!' a couple of heads were turned in our direction because he can never keep his voice down. The little vases of roses with which Mrs Malseed must have decorated each table before the fracas had occurred seemed strangely out of place in the atmosphere which had developed.

The waitress had just taken away our soup plates when Mr Malseed hurried into the dining-room and came straight to our table. The lobster bisque surprisingly hadn't been quite up to scratch, and in passing I couldn't help wondering if the fuss had caused the kitchen to go to pieces also.

'I wonder if I might have a word, Major Strafe,' Mr Malseed said, and Strafe rose at once and accompanied him from the dining-room. A total silence had fallen, everyone in the dining-room pretending to be intent on eating. I had an odd feeling that we had perhaps got it all wrong, that because we'd been out for our walk when it had happened all the other guests knew more of the details than Strafe and Dekko and I did. I began to wonder if poor Cynthia had been raped.

Afterwards Strafe told us what occurred in the Malseeds' office, how Mrs Malseed had been sitting there, slumped, as he put it, and how two policemen had questioned him. 'Look, what on earth's all this about?' he had demanded rather sharply.

'It concerns this incident that's taken place, sir,' one of the policemen explained in an unhurried voice. 'On account of your wife—'

'My wife's lying down. She must not be questioned or in any way disturbed.'

'Ach, we'd never do that, sir.'

Strafe does a good Co. Antrim brogue and in relating all this to us he couldn't resist making full use of it. The two policemen were in uniform and their natural slowness of intellect was rendered more noticeable by the lugubrious air the tragedy had inspired in the hotel. For tragedy was what it was: after talking to Cynthia for nearly two hours the lone man had walked down to the rocks and been drowned.

When Strafe finished speaking I placed my knife and fork together on my plate, unable to eat another mouthful. The facts appeared to be that the man, having left Cynthia by the magnolias, had clambered down the cliff to a place no one ever went to, on the other side of the hotel from the sands we had walked along to

Ardbeag. No one had seen him except Cynthia, who from the cliff-top had apparently witnessed his battering by the treacherous waves. The tide had been coming in, but by the time old Arthur and Mr Malseed reached the rocks it had begun to turn, leaving behind it the fully dressed corpse. Mr Malseed's impression was that the man had lost his footing on the seaweed and accidentally stumbled into the depths, for the rocks were so slippery it was difficult to carry the corpse more than a matter of yards. But at least it had been placed out of view, while Mr Malseed hurried back to the hotel to telephone for assistance. He told Strafe that Cynthia had been most confused, insisting that the man had walked out among the rocks and then into the sea, knowing what he was doing.

Listening to it all, I no longer felt sorry for Cynthia. It was typical of her that she should so sillily have involved us in all this. Why on earth had she sat in the garden with a man of that kind instead of standing up and making a fuss the moment he'd begun to paw her? If she'd acted intelligently the whole unfortunate episode could clearly have been avoided. Since it hadn't, there was no point what-soever in insisting that the man had committed suicide when at that distance no one could possibly be sure.

'It really does astonish me,' I said at the lunch table, unable to prevent myself from breaking our unwritten rule. 'Whatever came over her?'

'It can't be good for the hotel,' Dekko commented, and I was glad to see Strafe giving him a little glance of irritation.

'It's hardly the point,' I said coolly.

'What I meant was, hotels occasionally hush things like this up.'

'Well, they haven't this time.' It seemed an age since I had waited for them in Ardbeag, since we had been so happily laughing over the effect of Dekko's telegram. He'd included his address in it so that the girl could send a message back, and as we'd returned to the hotel along the seashore there'd been much speculation between the two men about the form this would take.

'I suppose what Cynthia's thinking,' Strafe said, 'is that after he'd tried something on with her he became depressed.'

'Oh, but he could just as easily have lost his footing. He'd have been on edge anyway, worried in case she reported him.'

'Dreadful kind of death,' Dekko said. His tone suggested that that was that, that the subject should now be closed, and so it was.

After lunch we went to our rooms, as we always do at Glencorn Lodge, to rest for an hour. I took my slacks and blouse off, hoping that Strafe would knock on my door, but he didn't and of course that was understandable. Oddly enough I found myself thinking of Dekko, picturing his long form stretched out in the room called Hydrangea, his beaky face in profile on his pillow. The precise nature of Dekko's relationship with these girls he picks up has always privately intrigued me: was it really possible that somewhere in London there was a girl called Juliet who was prepared to marry him for his not inconsiderable money?

I slept and briefly dreamed. Thrive Major and Warrington P.J. were running the post office in Ardbeag, sending telegrams to everyone they could think of, including Dekko's friend Juliet. Cynthia had been found dead beside the magnolias and people were waiting for Hercule Poirot to arrive. 'Promise me you didn't do it,' I whispered to Strafe, but when Strafe replied it was to say that Cynthia's body reminded him of a bag of old chicken bones.

Strafe and Dekko and I met for tea in the tea-lounge. Strafe had looked in to see if Cynthia had woken, but apparently she hadn't. The police officers had left the hotel, Dekko said, because he'd noticed their car wasn't parked at the front any more. None of the three of us said, but I think we presumed, that the man's body had been removed from the rocks during the quietness of the afternoon. From where we sat I caught a glimpse of Mrs Malseed passing quite briskly through the hall, seeming almost herself again. Certainly our holiday would be affected, but it might not be totally ruined. All that remained to hope for was Cynthia's recovery, and then everyone could set about forgetting the unpleasantness. The nicest thing would be if a jolly young couple turned up and occupied the man's room, exorcising the incident, as newcomers would.

The family from France—the two little girls and their parents —were chattering away in the tea-lounge, and an elderly trio who'd arrived that morning were speaking in American accents. The honeymoon couple appeared, looking rather shy, and began to whisper and giggle in a corner. People who occupied the table next to ours in the dining-room, a Wing-Commander Orfell and his wife, from Guildford, nodded and smiled as they passed. Everyone was making an effort, and I knew it would help matters further if Cynthia felt up to a rubber or two before dinner. That life should continue as normally as possible was essential for Glencorn Lodge, the example already set by Mrs Malseed.

Because of our interrupted lunch I felt quite hungry, and the Malseeds pride themselves on their teas. The chef, Mr McBride, whom of course we've met, has the lightest touch I know with sponge-cakes and little currant scones. I was, in fact, buttering a scone when Strafe said:

'Here she is.'

And there indeed she was. By the look of her she had simply pushed herself off her bed and come straight down. Her pink dress was even more crumpled than it had been. She hadn't so much as run a comb through her hair, her face was puffy and unpowdered. For a moment I really thought she was walking in her sleep.

Strafe and Dekko stood up. 'Feeling better, dear?' Strafe said, but she didn't answer.

'Sit down, Cynth,' Dekko urged, pushing back a chair to make room for her.

'He told me a story I can never forget. I've dreamed about it all over again.' Cynthia swayed in front of us, not even attempting to sit down. To tell the truth, she sounded inane.

'Story, dear?' Strafe inquired, humouring her.

She said it was the story of two children who had apparently ridden bicycles through the streets of Belfast, out into Co. Antrim. The bicycles were dilapidated, she said; she didn't know if they were stolen or not. She didn't know about the children's homes because the man hadn't spoken of them, but she claimed to know instinctively that they had ridden away from poverty and unhappiness. 'From the clatter and the quarrelling,' Cynthia said. 'Two children who later fell in love.'

'Horrid old dream,' Strafe said. 'Horrid for you, dear.'

She shook her head, and then sat down. I poured another cup of tea. 'I had the oddest dream myself,' I said. 'Thrive Major was running the post office in Ardbeag.'

Strafe smiled and Dekko gave his laugh, but Cynthia didn't in any way acknowledge what I'd said.

'A fragile thing the girl was, with depths of mystery in her wide brown eyes. Red-haired of course he was himself, thin as a rake in those days. Glencorn Lodge was derelict then.'

'You've had a bit of a shock, old thing,' Dekko said.

Strafe agreed, kindly adding, 'Look, dear, if the chap actually interfered with you—'

'Why on earth should he do that?' Her voice was shrill in the tea-lounge, edged with a note of hysteria. I glanced at Strafe, who was frowning into his teacup. Dekko began to say something, but broke off before his meaning emerged. Rather more calmly Cynthia said:

'It was summer when they came here. Honeysuckle he described. And mother of thyme. He didn't know the name of either.'

No one attempted any kind of reply, not that it was necessary, for Cynthia just continued.

'At school there were the facts of geography and arithmetic. And the legends of scholars and of heroes, of Queen Maeve and Finn MacCool. There was the coming of St Patrick to a heathen people. History was full of kings and high-kings, and Silken Thomas and Wolfe Tone, the Flight of the Earls, the Siege of Limerick.'

When Cynthia said that, it was impossible not to believe that the unfortunate events of the morning had touched her with some kind of madness. It seemed astonishing that she had walked into the tea-lounge without having combed her hair, and that she'd stood there swaying before sitting down, that out of the blue she had started on about two children. None of it made an iota of sense, and surely she could see that the nasty experience she'd suffered should not be dwelt upon? I offered her the plate of scones, hoping that if she began to eat she would stop talking, but she took no notice of my gesture.

'Look, dear,' Strafe said, 'there's not one of us who knows what you're talking about.'

'I'm talking about a children's story, I'm talking about a girl and a boy who visited this place we visit also. He hadn't been here for years, but he returned last night, making one final effort to understand. And then he walked out into the sea.'

She had taken a piece of her dress and was agitatedly crumpling it between the finger and thumb of her left hand. It was dreadful really, having her so grubby-looking. For some odd reason I suddenly thought of her cooking, how she wasn't in the least interested in it or in anything about the house. She certainly hadn't succeeded in making a home for Strafe.

'They rode those worn-out bicycles through a hot afternoon. Can you feel all that? A newly surfaced road, the snap of chippings beneath their tyres, the smell of tar? Dust from a passing car, the city they left behind?'

'Cynthia dear,' I said, 'drink your tea, and why not have a scone?'

'They swam and sunbathed on the beach you walked along today. They went to a spring for water. There were no magnolias then. There was no garden, no neat little cliff paths to the beach. Surely you can see it clearly?'

'No,' Strafe said. 'No, we really cannot, dear.'

'This place that is an idyll for us was an idyll for them too: the trees, the ferns, the wild roses near the water spring, the very sea and sun they shared. There was a cottage lost in the middle of the woods: they sometimes looked for that. They played a game, a kind of hide-and-seek. People in a white farmhouse gave them milk.'

For the second time I offered Cynthia the plate of scones and for the second time she pointedly ignored me. Her cup of tea hadn't been touched. Dekko took a scone and cheerfully said:

'All's well that's over.'

But Cynthia appeared to have drifted back into a daze, and I wondered again if it could really be possible that the experience had unhinged her. Unable to help myself, I saw her being led away from the hotel, helped into the back of a blue van, something like an ambulance. She was talking about the children again, how they had planned to marry and keep a sweetshop.

'Take it easy, dear,' Strafe said, which I followed up by suggesting for the second time that she should make an effort to drink her tea.

'Has it to do with the streets they came from? Or the history they learnt, he from his Christian Brothers, she from her nuns? History is unfinished in this island; long since it has come to a stop in Surrey.'

Dekko said, and I really had to hand it to him:

'Cynth, we have to put it behind us.'

It didn't do any good. Cynthia just went rambling on, speaking again of the girl being taught by nuns, and the boy by Christian Brothers. She began to recite the history they might have learnt, the way she sometimes did when we were driving through an area that had historical connections. 'Can you imagine,' she embarrassingly asked, 'our very favourite places bitter with disaffection, with plotting and revenge? Can you imagine the treacherous murder of Shane O'Neill the Proud?'

Dekko made a little sideways gesture of his head, politely marvelling. Strafe seemed about to say something, but changed his mind. Confusion ran through Irish history, Cynthia said, like convolvulus in a hedgerow. On 24 May 1487, a boy of ten called Lambert Simnel, brought to Dublin by a priest from Oxford, was declared Edward VI of all England and Ireland, crowned with a golden circlet taken from a statue of the Virgin Mary. On 24 May 1798, here in Antrim, Presbyterian farmers fought for a common cause with their Catholic labourers. She paused and looked at Strafe. Chaos and contradiction, she informed him, were hidden everywhere beneath nice-sounding names. 'The Battle of the Yellow Ford,' she suddenly chanted in a singsong way that sounded thoroughly peculiar, 'the Statutes of Kilkenny. The Battle of Glenmama, the Convention of Drumceat. The Act of Settlement, the Renunciation Act. The Act of Union, the Toleration Act. Just so much history it sounds like now, yet people starved or died while other people watched. A language was lost, a faith forbidden. Famine followed revolt, plantation followed that. But it was people who were struck into the soil of other people's land, not forests of new trees; and it was greed and treachery that spread as a disease among them all. No wonder unease clings to these shreds of history and shots ring out in answer to the mockery of drums. No wonder the air is nervy with suspicion.'

There was an extremely awkward silence when she ceased to speak. Dekko nodded, doing his best to be companionable. Strafe nodded also. I simply examined the pattern of roses on our teatime china, not knowing what else to do. Eventually Dekko said: 'What an awful lot you know, Cynth!'

'Cynthia's always been interested,' Strafe said. 'Always had a first-rate memory.'

'Those children of the streets are part of the battles and the Acts,' she went on, seeming quite unaware that her talk was literally almost crazy. 'They're part of the blood that flowed around those nice-sounding names.' She paused, and for a moment seemed disinclined to continue. Then she said:

'The second time they came here the house was being rebuilt. There were concrete-mixers, and lorries drawn up on the grass, noise and scaffolding everywhere. They watched all through another afternoon and then they went their different ways: their childhood was over, lost with their idyll. He became a dockyard clerk. She went to London, to work in a betting shop.'

'My dear,' Strafe said very gently, 'it's interesting, everything you say, but it really hardly concerns us.'

'No, of course not.' Quite emphatically Cynthia shook her head, appearing wholly to agree. 'They were degenerate, awful creatures. They must have been.'

'No one's saying that, my dear.'

'Their story should have ended there, he in the docklands of Belfast, she recording bets. Their complicated childhood love should just have dissipated, as such love often does. But somehow nothing was as neat as that.'

Dekko, in an effort to lighten the conversation, mentioned a boy called Gollsol who'd been at school with Strafe and himself, who'd formed a romantic attachment for the daughter of one of the groundsmen and had later actually married her. There was a silence for a moment, then Cynthia, without emotion, said:

'You none of you care. You sit there not caring that two people are dead.'

'Two people, Cynthia?' I said.

'For God's sake, I'm telling you!' she cried. 'That girl was murdered in a room in Maida Vale.'

Although there is something between Strafe and myself, I do try my best to be at peace about it. I go to church and take communion, and I know Strafe occasionally does too, though not as often as perhaps he might. Cynthia has no interest in that side of life, and it rankled with me now to hear her blaspheming so casually, and so casually speaking about death in Maida Vale on top of all this stuff about history and children. Strafe was shaking his head, clearly believing that Cynthia didn't know what she was talking about.

'Cynthia dear,' I began, 'are you sure you're not muddling something up here? You've been upset, you've had a nightmare: don't you think your imagination, or something you've been reading—'

'Bombs don't go off on their own. Death doesn't just happen to occur in Derry and Belfast, in London and Amsterdam and Dublin, in Berlin and Jerusalem. There are people who are murderers: that is what this children's story is about.'

A silence fell, no one knowing what to say. It didn't matter of course because without any prompting Cynthia continued.

'We drink our gin with Angostura bitters, there's lamb or chicken Kiev. Old Kitty's kind to us in the dining-room and old Arthur in the hall. Flowers are everywhere, we have our special table.'

'Please let us take you to your room now,' Strafe begged, and as he spoke I reached out a hand in friendship and placed it on her arm. 'Come on, old thing,' Dekko said.

'The limbless are left on the streets, blood spatters the car-parks. *Brits Out* it says on a rockface, but we know it doesn't mean us.'

I spoke quietly then, measuring my words, measuring the pause between each so that its effect might be registered. I felt the statement had to be made, whether it was my place to make it or not. I said:

'You are very confused, Cynthia.'

The French family left the tea-lounge. The two Dalmatians, Charger and Snooze, ambled in and sniffed and went away again. Kitty came to clear the French family's tea things. I could hear her speaking to the honeymoon couple, saying the weather forecast was good.

'Cynthia,' Strafe said, standing up, 'we've been very patient with you but this is now becoming silly.'

I nodded just a little. 'I really think,' I softly said, but Cynthia didn't permit me to go on.

'Someone told him about her. Someone mentioned her name, and he couldn't believe it. She sat alone in Maida Vale, putting together the mechanisms of her bombs: this girl who had laughed on the seashore, whom he had loved.'

'Cynthia,' Strafe began, but he wasn't permitted to continue either. Hopelessly, he just sat down again.

'Whenever he heard of bombs exploding he thought of her, and couldn't understand. He wept when he said that; her violence haunted him, he said. He couldn't work, he couldn't sleep at night. His mind filled up with images of her, their awkward childhood kisses, her fingers working neatly now. He saw her with a carrier-bag, hurrying it through a crowd, leaving it where it could cause most death. In front of the mouldering old house that had once been Glencorn Lodge they'd made a fire and cooked their food. They'd lain for ages on the grass. They'd cycled home to their city streets.'

It suddenly dawned on me that Cynthia was knitting this whole fantasy out of nothing. It all worked backwards from the moment when she'd had the misfortune to witness the man's death in the sea. A few minutes before he'd been chatting quite normally to her, he'd probably even mentioned a holiday in his childhood and some girl there'd been: all of it would have been natural in the circumstances, possibly even the holiday had taken place at Glencorn. He'd said goodbye and then unfortunately he'd had his accident. Watching from the cliff edge, something had cracked in poor Cynthia's brain, she having always been a prey to melancholy. I suppose it must be hard having two sons who don't think much of you, and a marriage not offering you a great deal, bridge and holidays probably the best part of it. For some odd reason of her own she'd created her fantasy about a child turning into a terrorist. The violence of the man's death had clearly filled her imagination with Irish violence, so regularly seen on television. If we'd been on holiday in Suffolk I wondered how it would have seemed to the poor creature.

I could feel Strafe and Dekko beginning to put all that together also, beginning to realize that the whole story of the red-haired man and the girl was clearly Cynthia's invention. 'Poor creature,' I wanted to say, but did not do so.

'For months he searched for her, pushing his way among the people of London, the people who were her victims. When he found her she just looked at him, as if the past hadn't even existed. She didn't smile, as if incapable of smiling. He wanted to take her away, back to where they came from, but she didn't reply when he suggested that. Bitterness was like a disease in her, and when he left her he felt the bitterness in himself.'

Again Strafe and Dekko nodded, and I could feel Strafe thinking that there really was no point in protesting further. All we could hope for was that the end of the saga was in sight.

'He remained in London, working on the railways. But in the same way as before he was haunted by the person she'd become, and the haunting was more awful now. He bought a gun from a man he'd been told about and kept it hidden in a shoe-box in his rented room. Now and again he took it out and looked at it, then put it back. He hated the violence that possessed her, yet he was full of it himself: he knew he couldn't betray her with anything but death. Humanity had left both of them when he visited her again in Maida Vale.'

To my enormous relief and, I could feel, to Strafe's and Dekko's too, Mr and Mrs Malseed appeared beside us. Like his wife, Mr Malseed had considerably recovered. He spoke in an even voice, clearly wishing to dispose of the matter. It was just the diversion we needed.

'I must apologize, Mrs Strafe,' he said. 'I cannot say how sorry we are that you were bothered by that man.'

'My wife is still a little dicky,' Strafe explained, 'but after a decent night's rest I think we can say she'll be as right as rain again.'

'I only wish, Mrs Strafe, you had made contact with my wife or myself when he first approached you.' There was a spark of irritation in Mr Malseed's eyes, but his voice was still controlled. 'I mean, the unpleasantness you suffered might just have been averted.'

'Nothing would have been averted, Mr Malseed, and certainly not the horror we are left with. Can you see her as the girl she became, seated at a chipped white table, her wires and fuses spread around her? What were her thoughts in that room, Mr Malseed? What happens in the mind of anyone who wishes to destroy? In a back street he bought his gun for too much money. When did it first occur to him to kill her?'

'We really are a bit at sea,' Mr Malseed replied without the slightest hesitation. He humoured Cynthia by displaying no surprise, by speaking very quietly.

'All I am saying, Mr Malseed, is that we should root our heads out of the sand and wonder about two people who are beyond the pale.'

'My dear,' Strafe said, 'Mr Malseed is a busy man.'

Still quietly, still perfectly in control of every intonation, without a single glance around the tea-lounge to ascertain where his guests' attention was, Mr Malseed said:

'There is unrest here, Mrs Strafe, but we do our best to live with it.'

'All I am saying is that perhaps there can be regret when two children end like this.'

Mr Malseed did not reply. His wife did her best to smile away the awkwardness. Strafe murmured privately to Cynthia, no doubt beseeching her to come to her senses. Again I imagined a blue van drawn up in front of Glencorn Lodge, for it was quite understandable now that an imaginative woman should go mad, affected by the ugliness of death. The garbled speculation about the man and the girl, the jumble in the poor thing's mind—a children's story as she called it—all somehow hung together when you realized they didn't have to make any sense whatsoever.

'Murderers are beyond the pale, Mr Malseed, and England has always had its pales. The one in Ireland began in 1395.'

'Dear,' I said, 'what has happened has nothing whatsoever to do with calling people murderers and placing them beyond some pale or other. You witnessed a most unpleasant accident, dear, and it's only to be expected that you've become just a little lost. The man had a chat with you when you were sitting by the magnolias and then the shock of seeing him slip on the seaweed—'

'He didn't slip on the seaweed,' she suddenly screamed. 'My God, he didn't slip on the seaweed.'

Strafe closed his eyes. The other guests in the tea-lounge had fallen silent ages ago, openly listening. Arthur was standing near the door and was listening also. Kitty was waiting to clear away our tea things, but didn't like to because of what was happening.

'I must request you to take Mrs Strafe to her room, Major,' Mr Malseed said. 'And I must make it clear that we cannot tolerate further upset in Glencorn Lodge.'

Strafe reached for her arm, but Cynthia took no notice.

'An Irish joke,' she said, and then she stared at Mr and Mrs

Malseed, her eyes passing over each feature of their faces. She stared at Dekko and Strafe, and last of all at me. She said eventually:

'An Irish joke, an unbecoming tale: of course it can't be true. Ridiculous, that a man returned here. Ridiculous, that he walked again by the seashore and through the woods, hoping to understand where a woman's cruelty had come from.'

'This talk is most offensive,' Mr Malseed protested, his calmness slipping just a little. The ashen look that had earlier been in his face returned. I could see he was beside himself with rage. 'You are trying to bring something to our doorstep which most certainly does not belong there.'

'On your doorstep they talked about a sweetshop: Cadbury's bars and different-flavoured creams, nut-milk toffee, Aero and Crunchie.'

'For God's sake pull yourself together,' I clearly heard Strafe whispering, and Mrs Malseed attempted to smile. 'Come along now, Mrs Strafe,' she said, making a gesture. 'Just to please us, dear. Kitty wants to clear away the dishes. Kitty!' she called out, endeavouring to bring matters down to earth.

Kitty crossed the lounge with her tray and gathered up the cups and saucers. The Malseeds, naturally still anxious, hovered. No one was surprised when Cynthia began all over again, by crazily asking Kitty what she thought of us.

'I think, dear,' Mrs Malseed began, 'Kitty's quite busy really.'

'Stop this at once,' Strafe quietly ordered.

'For fourteen years, Kitty, you've served us with food and cleared away the teacups we've drunk from. For fourteen years we've played our bridge and walked about the garden. We've gone for drives, we've bought our tweed, we've bathed as those children did.'

'Stop it,' Strafe said again, a little louder. Bewildered and getting red in the face, Kitty hastily bundled china on to her tray. I made a sign at Strafe because for some reason I felt that the end was really in sight. I wanted him to retain his patience, but what Cynthia said next was almost unbelievable.

'In Surrey we while away the time, we clip our hedges. On a

bridge night there's coffee at nine o'clock, with macaroons or *petits fours*. Last thing of all we watch the late-night News, packing away our cards and scoring-pads, our sharpened pencils. There's been an incident in Armagh, one soldier's had his head shot off, another's run amok. Our lovely Glens of Antrim, we all four think, our coastal drives: we hope that nothing disturbs the peace. We think of Mr Malseed, still busy in Glencorn Lodge, and Mrs Malseed finishing her flower-plaques for the rooms of the completed annexe.'

'Will you for God's sake shut up?' Strafe suddenly shouted. I could see him struggling with himself, but it didn't do any good. He called Cynthia a bloody spectacle, sitting there talking rubbish. I don't believe she even heard him.

'Through honey-tinted glasses we love you and we love your island, Kitty. We love the lilt of your racy history, we love your earls and heroes. Yet we made a sensible pale here once, as civilized people create a garden, pretty as a picture.'

Strafe's outburst had been quite noisy and I could sense him being ashamed of it. He muttered that he was sorry, but Cynthia simply took advantage of his generosity, continuing about a pale.

'Beyond it lie the bleak untouchables, best kept as dots on the horizon, too terrible to contemplate. How can we be blamed if we make neither head nor tail of anything, Kitty, your past and your present, those battles and Acts of Parliament? We people of Surrey: how can we know? Yet I stupidly thought, you see, that the tragedy of two children could at least be understood. He didn't discover where her cruelty had come from because perhaps you never can: evil breeds evil in a mysterious way. That's the story the red-haired stranger passed on to me, the story you huddle away from.'

Poor Strafe was pulling at Cynthia, pleading with her, still saying he was sorry.

'Mrs Strafe,' Mr Malseed tried to say, but got no further. To my horror Cynthia abruptly pointed at me.

'That woman,' she said, 'is my husband's mistress, a fact I am supposed to be unaware of, Kitty.'

'My God!' Strafe said.

'My husband is perverted in his sexual desires. His friend, who shared his schooldays, has never quite recovered from that time. I myself am a pathetic creature who has closed her eyes to a husband's infidelity and his mistress's viciousness. I am dragged into the days of Thrive Major and A.D. Cowley-Stubbs: mechanically I smile. I hardly exist, Kitty.'

There was a most unpleasant silence, and then Strafe said:

'None of that's true. For God's sake, Cynthia,' he suddenly shouted, 'go and lie down.'

Cynthia shook her head and continued to address the waitress. She'd had a rest, she told her. 'But it didn't do any good, Kitty, because hell has invaded the paradise of Glencorn, as so often it has invaded your island. And we, who have so often brought it, pretend it isn't there. Who cares about children made into murderers?'

Strafe shouted again. 'You fleshless ugly bitch!' he cried. 'You bloody old fool!' He was on his feet, trying to get her on to hers. The blood was thumping in his bronzed face, his eyes had a fury in them I'd never seen before. 'Fleshless!' he shouted at her, not caring that so many people were listening. He closed his eyes in misery and in shame again, and I wanted to reach out and take his hand but of course I could not. You could see the Malseeds didn't blame him, you could see them thinking that everything was ruined for us. I wanted to shout at Cynthia too, to batter the silliness out of her, but of course I could not do that. I could feel the tears behind my eyes, and I couldn't help noticing that Dekko's hands were shaking. He's quite sensitive behind his joky manner, and had quite obviously taken to heart her statement that he had never recovered from his schooldays. Nor had it been pleasant, hearing myself described as vicious.

'No one cares,' Cynthia said in the same unbalanced way, as if she hadn't just been called ugly and a bitch. 'No one cares, and on our journey home we shall all four be silent. Yet is the truth about ourselves at least a beginning? Will we wonder in the end about the hell that frightens us?'

Strafe still looked wretched, his face deliberately turned away from us. Mrs Malseed gave a little sigh and raised the fingers of her left hand to her cheek, as if something tickled it. Her husband breathed heavily. Dekko seemed on the point of tears.

Cynthia stumbled off, leaving a silence behind her. Before it was broken I knew she was right when she said we would just go home, away from this country we had come to love. And I knew as well that neither here nor at home would she be led to a blue van that was not quite an ambulance. Strafe would stay with her because Strafe is made like that, honourable in his own particular way. I felt a pain where perhaps my heart is, and again I wanted to cry. Why couldn't it have been she who had gone down to the rocks and slipped on the seaweed or just walked into the sea, it didn't matter which? Her awful rigmarole hung about us as the last of the tea things were gathered up—the earls who'd fled, the famine and the people planted. The children were there too, grown up into murdering riff-raff.

An Evening with
John Joe Dempsey

In Keogh's one evening Mr Lynch talked about the Piccadilly tarts, and John Joe Dempsey on his fifteenth birthday closed his eyes and travelled into a world he did not know. 'Big and little,' said Mr Lynch, 'winking their eyes at you and enticing you up to them. Wetting their lips,' said Mr Lynch, 'with the ends of their tongues.'

John Joe Dempsey had walked through the small town that darkening autumn evening, from the far end of North Street where he and his mother lived, past the cement building that was the Coliseum cinema, past Kelly's Atlantic Hotel and a number of shops that were now closed for the day. 'Go to Keogh's like a good boy,' his mother had requested, for as well as refreshments and stimulants Keogh's public house sold a variety of groceries: it was for a pound of rashers that Mrs Dempsey had sent her son.

'Who is there?' Mr Lynch had called out from the licensed area of the premises, hearing John Joe rapping with a coin to draw attention to his presence. A wooden partition with panes of glass in the top half of it rose to a height of eight feet between the grocery and the bar. 'I'm here for rashers,' John Joe explained through the pebbly glass. 'Isn't it a stormy evening, Mr Lynch? I'm fifteen today, Mr Lynch.'

There was a silence before a door in the partition opened and Mr Lynch appeared. 'Fifteen?' he said. 'Step in here, boy, and have a bottle of stout.'

John Joe protested that he was too young to drink a bottle of stout and then said that his mother required the rashers immediately. 'Mrs Keogh's gone out to Confession,' Mr Lynch said. 'I'm in charge till her ladyship returns.'

John Joe, knowing that Mr Lynch would not be prepared to set the bacon machine in action, stepped into the bar to await the return of Mrs Keogh, and Mr Lynch darted behind the counter for two bottles of stout. Having opened and poured them, he began about the Piccadilly tarts.

'You've got to an age,' Mr Lynch said, 'when you would have to be advised. Did you ever think in terms of emigration to England?'

'I did not, Mr Lynch.'

'I would say you were right to leave it alone, John Joe. Is that the first bottle of stout you ever had?'

'It is, Mr Lynch.'

'A bottle of stout is an acquired taste. You have to have had a dozen bottles or maybe more before you do get an urge for it. With the other matter it's different.'

Mr Lynch, now a large, fresh-faced man of fifty-five who was never seen without a brown hat on his head, had fought for the British Army during the Second World War, which was why one day in 1947 he had found himself, with companions, in Piccadilly Circus. As he listened, John Joe recalled that he'd heard boys at the Christian Brothers' referring to some special story that Mr Lynch confidentially told to those whom he believed would benefit from it. He had heard boys sniggering over this story, but he had never sought to discover its content, not knowing it had to do with Piccadilly tarts.

'There was a fellow by the name of Baker,' said Mr Lynch, 'who'd been telling us that he knew the ropes. Baker was a London man. He knew the places, he was saying, where he could find the glory girls, but when it came to the point of the matter, John Joe, we hardly needed a guide.'

Because, explained Mr Lynch, the tarts were everywhere. They stood in the doorways of shops showing off the stature of their legs. Some would speak to you, Mr Lynch said, addressing you fondly and stating their availability. Some had their bosoms cocked out so that maybe they'd strike a passing soldier and entice him away from his companions. 'I'm telling you this, John Joe, on account of your daddy being dead. Are you fancying that stout?'

John Joe nodded his head. Thirteen years ago his father had fallen to his death from a scaffold, having been by trade a builder. John Joe could not remember him, although he knew what he had looked like from a photograph that was always on view on the kitchen dresser. He had often wondered what it would be like to have that bulky man about the house, and more often still he listened to his mother talking about him. But John Joe didn't think about his father now, in spite of Mr Lynch's reference to him: keen to hear more about the women of Piccadilly, he asked what had happened when Mr Lynch and his companions finished examining them in the doorways.

'I saw terrible things in Belgium,' replied Mr Lynch meditatively. 'I saw a Belgian woman held down on the floor while four men satisfied themselves on her. No woman could be the same after that. Combat brings out the brute in a man.'

'Isn't it shocking what they'd do, Mr Lynch? Wouldn't it make you sick?'

'If your daddy was alive today, he would be telling you a thing or two in order to prepare you for your manhood and the temptations in another country. Your mother wouldn't know how to tackle a matter like that, nor would Father Ryan, nor the Christian Brothers. Your daddy might have sat you down in this bar and given you your first bottle of stout. He might have told you about the facts of life.'

'Did one of the glory girls entice yourself, Mr Lynch?'

'Listen to me, John Joe.' Mr Lynch regarded his companion through small blue eyes, both of which were slightly bloodshot. He lit a cigarette and drew on it before continuing. Then he said: 'Baker had the soldiers worked up with his talk of the glory girls taking off their togs. He used to describe the motion of their haunches. He used to lie there at night in the dug-out describing the private areas of the women's bodies. When the time came we went out with Baker and Baker went up to the third one he saw and said could the six of us make arrangements with her? He was keen to strike a bargain because we had only limited means on account of having remained in a public house for four hours. Myself included, we were in an intoxicated condition.'

'What happened, Mr Lynch?'

'I would not have agreed to an arrangement like that if it hadn't been for drink. I was a virgin boy, John Joe. Like yourself.'

'I'm that way, certainly, Mr Lynch.'

'We marched in behind the glory girl, down a side street. "Bedad, you're fine men," she said. We had bottles of beer in our pockets. "We'll drink that first," she said, "before we get down to business." '

John Joe laughed. He lifted the glass of stout to his lips and took a mouthful in a nonchalant manner, as though he'd been drinking stout for half a lifetime and couldn't do without it.

'Aren't you the hard man, Mr Lynch!' he said.

'You've got the wrong end of the stick,' replied Mr Lynch sharply. 'What happened was, I had a vision on the street. Amn't I saying to you those girls are no good to any man? I had a vision of the Virgin when we were walking along.'

'How d'you mean, Mr Lynch?'

'There was a little statue of the Holy Mother in my bedroom at home, a little special one my mother gave me at the occasion of my First Communion. It came into my mind, John Joe, when the six of us were with the glory girl. As soon as the glory girl said we'd drink the beer before we got down to business I saw the statue of the Holy Mother, as clear as if it was in front of me.'

John Joe, who had been anticipating an account of the soldiers' pleasuring, displayed disappointment. Mr Lynch shook his head at him.

'I was telling you a moral story,' he said reprovingly. 'The facts of life is one thing, John Joe, but keep away from dirty women.'

John Joe was a slight youth, pale of visage, as his father had been, and with large, awkward hands that bulged in his trouser pockets. He had no friends at the Christian Brothers' School he attended, being regarded there, because of his private nature and lack of interest in either scholastic or sporting matters, as something of an oddity—an opinion that was strengthened by his association with an old, simple-minded dwarf called Quigley, with whom he was regularly to be seen collecting minnows in a jam jar or walking along the country roads. In class at the Christian Brothers' John Joe would drift into a meditative state and could not easily be reached. 'Where've you gone, boy?' Brother Leahy would whisper, standing above him. His fingers would reach out for a twist of John Joe's scalp, and John Joe would rise from the ground with the Brother's thumb and forefinger tightening the short hairs of his neck, yet seeming not to feel the pain. It was only when the other hand of Brother Leahy gripped one of his ears that he would return to the classroom with a cry of anguish, and the boys and Brother Leahy would laugh. 'What'll we make of you?' Brother Leahy would murmur, returning to the blackboard while John Joe rubbed his head and his ear.

'There is many a time in the years afterwards,' said Mr Lynch ponderously, 'when I have gone through in my mind that moment in my life. I was tempted in bad company: I was two minutes off damnation.'

'I see what you mean, Mr Lynch.'

'When I came back to West Cork my mother asked me was I all right. Well, I was, I said. "I had a bad dream about you," my mother said. "I had a dream one night your legs were on fire." She looked at my legs, John Joe, and to tell you the truth of it she made me slip down my britches. "There's no harm there," she said. 'Twas only afterwards I worked it out: she had that dream in the very minute I was standing on the street seeing the vision in my brain. What my mother dreamed, John Joe, was that I was licked by the flames of Hell. She was warned that time, and from her dream she sent out a message that I was to receive a visit from the little statue. I'm an older man now, John Joe, but that's an account I tell to every boy in this town that hasn't got a father. That little story is an introduction to life and manhood. Did you enjoy the stout?'

'The stout's great stuff, Mr Lynch.'

'No drink you can take, John Joe, will injure you the way a dirty woman would. You might go to twenty million Confessions and you wouldn't relieve your heart and soul of a dirty woman. I didn't marry myself, out of shame for the memory of listening to Baker making that bargain. Will we have another bottle?'

John Joe, wishing to hear in further detail the bargain that Baker had made, said he could do with another drop. Mr Lynch directed him to a crate behind the counter. 'You're acquiring the taste,' he said.

John Joe opened and poured the bottles. Mr Lynch offered him a cigarette, which he accepted. In the Coliseum cinema he had seen Piccadilly Circus, and in one particular film there had been Piccadilly tarts, just as Mr Lynch described, loitering in doorways provocatively. As always, coming out of the Coliseum, it had been a little strange to find himself again among small shops that sold clothes and hardware and meat, among vegetable shops and tiny confectioners' and tobacconists' and public houses. For a few minutes after the Coliseum's programme was over the three streets of the town were busy with people going home, walking or riding on bicycles, or driving cars to distant farms, or going towards the chip-shop. When he was alone, John Joe usually leaned against the window of a shop to watch the activity before returning home himself; when his mother accompanied him to the pictures they naturally went home at once, his mother chatting on about the film they'd seen.

'The simple thing is, John Joe, keep a certain type of thought out of your mind.'

'Thought, Mr Lynch?'

'Of a certain order.'

'Ah, yes. Ah, definitely, Mr Lynch. A young fellow has no time for that class of thing.'

'Live a healthy life.'

'That's what I'm saying, Mr Lynch.'

'If I hadn't had a certain type of thought I wouldn't have found myself on the street that night. It was Baker who called them the glory girls. It's a peculiar way of referring to the sort they are.'

'Excuse me, Mr Lynch, but what kind of an age would they be?'

'They were all ages, boy. There were nippers and a few more of them had wrinkles on the flesh of their faces. There were some who must have weighed fourteen stone and others you could put in your pocket.'

'And was the one Baker made the bargain with a big one or a little one?'

'She was medium-sized, boy.'

'And had she black hair, Mr Lynch?'

'As black as your boot. She had a hat on her head that was a disgrace to the nation, and black gloves on her hands. She was carrying a little umbrella.'

'And, Mr Lynch, when your comrades met up with you again, did they tell you a thing at all?'

Mr Lynch lifted the glass to his lips. He filled his mouth with stout and savoured the liquid before allowing it to pass into his stomach. He turned his small eyes on the youth and regarded him in silence.

'You have pimples on your chin,' said Mr Lynch in the end. 'I hope you're living a clean life, now.'

'A healthy life, Mr Lynch.'

'It is a question your daddy would ask you. You know what I mean? There's some lads can't leave it alone.'

'They go mad in the end, Mr Lynch.'

'There was fellows in the British Army that couldn't leave it alone.'

'They're a heathen crowd, Mr Lynch. Isn't there terrible reports in the British papers?'

'The body is God-given. There's no need to abuse it.'

'I've never done that thing, Mr Lynch.'

'I couldn't repeat,' said Mr Lynch, 'what the glory girl said when I walked away.'

John Joe, whose classroom meditations led him towards the naked bodies of women whom he had seen only clothed and whose conversations with the town's idiot, Quigley, were of an obscene nature, said it was understandable that Mr Lynch could not repeat what the girl had said to him. A girl like that, he added, wasn't fit to be encountered by a decent man.

'Go behind the counter,' said Mr Lynch, 'and lift out two more bottles.'

John Joe walked to the crate of stout bottles. 'I looked in at a window one time,' Quigley had said to him, 'and I saw Mrs Nugent resisting her husband. Nugent took no notice of her at all; he had the clothes from her body like you'd shell a pod of peas.'

'I don't think Baker lived,' said Mr Lynch. 'He'd be dead of disease.'

'I feel sick to think of Baker, Mr Lynch.'

'He was like an animal.'

All the women of the town—and most especially Mrs Taggart, the wife of a postman—John Joe had kept company with in his imagination. Mrs Taggart was a well-built woman, a foot taller than himself, a woman with whom he had seen himself walking in the fields on the Ballydehob road. She had found him alone and had said that she was crossing the fields to where her husband had fallen into a bog-hole, and would he be able to come with her? She had a heavy, chunky face and a wide neck on which the fat lay in encircling folds, like a fleshy necklace. Her hair was grey and black, done up in hairpins. 'I was only codding you,' she said when they reached the side of a secluded hillock. 'You're a good-looking fellow, Dempsey.' On the side of the hillock, beneath a tree, Mrs Taggart commenced to rid herself of her outer garments, remarking that it was hot. 'Slip out of that little jersey,' she urged. 'Wouldn't it bake you today?' Sitting beside him in her underclothes, Mrs Taggart asked him if he liked sunbathing. She drew her petticoat up so that the sun might reach the tops of her legs. She asked him to put his hand on one of her legs so that he could feel the muscles; she was a strong woman, she said, and added that the strongest muscles she possessed were the muscles of her stomach. 'Wait till I show you,' said Mrs Taggart.

On other occasions he found himself placed differently with Mrs Taggart: once, his mother had sent him round to her house to inquire if she had any eggs for sale and after she had put a dozen eggs in a basket Mrs Taggart asked him if he'd take a look at a thorn in the back of her leg. Another time he was passing her house and he heard her crying out for help. When he went inside he discovered that she had jammed the door of the bathroom and couldn't get out. He managed to release the door and when he entered the bathroom he discovered that Mrs Taggart was standing up in the bath, seeming to have forgotten that she hadn't her clothes on.

Mrs Keefe, the wife of a railway official, another statuesque woman, featured as regularly in John Joe's imagination, as did a Mrs O'Brien, a Mrs Summers, and a Mrs Power. Mrs Power kept a bread-shop, and a very pleasant way of passing the time when Brother Leahy was talking was to walk into Mrs Power's shop and hear her saying that she'd have to slip into the bakery for a small pan loaf and would he like to accompany her? Mrs Power wore a green overall with a belt that was tied in a knot at the front. In the bakery, while they were chatting, she would attempt to untie the belt but always found it difficult. 'Can you aid me?' Mrs Power would ask and John Joe would endeavour to loose the knot that lay tight against Mrs Power's stout stomach. 'Where've you gone, boy?' Brother Leahy's voice would whisper over and over again like a familiar incantation and John Joe would suddenly shout, realizing he was in pain.

'It was the end of the war,' said Mr Lynch. 'The following morning myself and a gang of the other lads got a train up to Liverpool, and then we crossed back to Dublin. There was a priest on the train and I spoke to him about the whole thing. Every man was made like that, he said to me, only I was lucky to be rescued in the nick of time. If I'd have taken his name I'd have sent him the information about my mother's dream. I think that would have interested him, John Joe. Wouldn't you think so?'

'Ah, it would of course.'

'Isn't it a great story, John Joe?'

'It is, Mr Lynch.'

'Don't forget it ever, boy. No man is clear of temptations. You don't have to go to Britain to get temptations.'

'I understand you, Mr Lynch.'

Quigley had said that one night he looked through a window and saw the Protestant clergyman, the Reverend Johnson, lying on the floor with his wife. There was another time, he said, that he observed Hickey the chemist being coaxed from an armchair by certain activities on the part of Mrs Hickey. Quigley had climbed up on the roof of a shed and had seen Mrs Sweeney being helped out of her stockings by Sweeney, the builder and decorator. Quigley's voice might continue for an hour and a half, for there was hardly a man and his wife in the town whom he didn't claim to have observed in intimate circumstances. John Joe did not ever ask how, when there was no convenient shed to climb on to, the dwarf managed to make his way to so many exposed upstairs windows. Such a question would have been wholly irrelevant.

At Mass, when John Joe saw the calves of women's legs stuck out from the kneeling position, he experienced an excitement that later bred new fantasies within him. 'That Mrs Moore,' he would say to the old dwarf, and the dwarf would reply that one night in February he had observed Mrs Moore preparing herself for the return of her husband from a County Council meeting in Cork. From the powdered body of Mrs Moore, as described by Quigley, John Joe would move to an image that included himself. He saw himself pushing open the hall door of the Moores' house, having been sent to the house with a message from his mother, and hearing Mrs Moore's voice calling out, asking him to come upstairs. He stood on a landing and Mrs Moore came to him with a red coat wrapped round her to cover herself up. He could smell the powder on her body; the coat kept slipping from her shoulders. 'I have some magazines for your mother,' she said. 'They're inside the bedroom.' He went and sat on the bed while she collected a pile of magazines. She sat beside him then, drawing his attention to a story here and there that might be of particular interest to his mother. Her knee was pressed against his, and in a moment she put her arm round his shoulders and said he was a good-looking lad. The red coat fell back on to the bed when Mrs Moore took one of John Joe's large hands and placed it on her stomach. She then suggested, the evening being hot, that he should take off his jersey and his shirt.

Mrs Keogh, the owner of the public house, had featured also in John Joe's imagination and in the conversation of the old dwarf. Quigley had seen her, he said, a week before her husband died, hitting her husband with a length of wire because he would not oblige her with his attentions. 'Come down to the cellar,' said Mrs Keogh while Brother Leahy scribbled on the blackboard. 'Come down to the cellar, John Joe, and help me with a barrel.' He descended the cellar steps in front of her and when he looked back he saw her legs under her dark mourning skirt. 'I'm lost these days,' she said, 'since Mr Keogh went on.' They moved the barrel together and then Mrs Keogh said it was hot work and it would be better if they took off their jerseys. 'Haven't you the lovely arms!' she said as they rolled the barrel from one corner of the cellar to another. 'Will we lie down here for a rest?'

'We'll chance another bottle,' suggested Mr Lynch. 'Is it going down you all right?'

'My mother'll be waiting for the rashers, Mr Lynch.'

'No rasher can be cut, boy, till Mrs Keogh returns. You could slice your hand off on an old machine like that.'

'We'll have one more so.'

At the Christian Brothers', jokes were passed about that concerned grisly developments in the beds of freshly wedded couples, or centered around heroes who carried by chance strings of sausages in their pockets and committed unfortunate errors when it came to cutting one off for the pan. Such yarns, succeeding generally, failed with John Joe, for they seemed to him to be lacking in quality.

'How's your mammy?' Mr Lynch asked, watching John Joe pouring the stout.

'Ah, she's all right. I'm only worried she's waiting on the rashers—'

'There's honour due to a mother.'

John Joe nodded. He held the glass at an angle to receive the dark, foaming liquid, as Mr Lynch had shown him. Mr Lynch's mother, now seventy-nine, was still alive. They lived together in a house which Mr Lynch left every morning in order to work in the office of a meal business and which he left every evening in order to drink bottles of stout in Keogh's. The bachelor state of Mr Lynch was one which John Joe wondered if he himself would one day share. Certainly, he saw little attraction in the notion of marriage, apart from the immediate physical advantage. Yet Mr Lynch's life did not seem enviable either. Often on Sunday afternoons he observed the meal clerk walking slowly with his mother on his arm, seeming as lost in gloom as the married men who walked beside women pushing prams. Quigley, a bachelor also, was a happier man than Mr Lynch. He lived in what amounted to a shed at the bottom of his niece's garden. Food was carried to him, but there were few, with the exception of John Joe, who lingered in his company. On Sundays, a day which John Joe, like Mr Lynch, spent with his mother, Quigley walked alone.

'When'll you be leaving the Brothers?' Mr Lynch asked.

'In June.'

'And you'll be looking out for employment, John Joe?'

'I was thinking I'd go into the sawmills.'

Mr Lynch nodded approvingly. 'There's a good future in the sawmills,' he said. 'Is the job fixed up?'

'Not yet, Mr Lynch. They might give me a trial.'

Mr Lynch nodded again, and for a moment the two sat in silence. John Joe could see from the thoughtful way Mr Lynch was regarding his stout that there was something on his mind. Hoping to hear more about the Piccadilly tarts, John Joe patiently waited.

'If your daddy was alive,' said Mr Lynch eventually, 'he might mention this to you, boy.'

He drank more stout and wiped the foam from his lips with the back of his hand. 'I often see you out with Quigley. Is it a good thing to be spending your hours with a performer like that? Quigley's away in the head.'

'You'd be sorry for the poor creature, Mr Lynch.'

Mr Lynch said there was no need to feel sorry for Quigley, since that was the way Quigley was made. He lit another cigarette. He said:

'Maybe they would say to themselves up at the sawmills that you were the same way as Quigley. If he keeps company with Quigley, they might say, aren't they two of a kind?'

'Ah, I don't think they'd bother themselves, Mr Lynch. Sure, if you do the work well what would they have to complain of?'

'Has the manager up there seen you out with Quigley and the jam jars?'

'I don't know, Mr Lynch.'

'Everything I'm saying to you is for your own good in the future. Do you understand that? If I were in your shoes I'd let Quigley look after himself.'

For years his mother had been saying the same to him. Brother Leahy had drawn him aside one day and had pointed out that an elderly dwarf wasn't a suitable companion for a young lad, especially since the dwarf was not sane. 'I see you took no notice of me,' Brother Leahy said six months later. 'Tell me this, young fellow-me-lad, what kind of a conversation do you have with old Quigley?' They talked, John Joe said, about trees and the flowers in the hedge-rows. He liked to listen to Quigley, he said, because Quigley had acquired a knowledge of such matters. 'Don't tell me lies,' snapped Brother Leahy, and did not say anything else.

Mrs Keogh returned from Confession. She came breathlessly into the bar, with pink cheeks, her ungloved hands the colour of meat.

She was a woman of advanced middle age, a rotund woman who approached the proportions that John Joe most admired. She wore spectacles and had grey hair that was now a bit windswept. Her hat had blown off on the street, she said: she'd nearly gone mad trying to catch it. 'Glory be to God,' she cried when she saw John Joe. 'What's that fellow doing with a bottle of stout?'

'We had a man-to-man talk,' explained Mr Lynch. 'I started him off on the pleasures of the bottle.'

'Are you mad?' shouted Mrs Keogh with a loud laugh. 'He's under age.'

'I came for rashers,' said John Joe. 'A pound of green rashers, Mrs Keogh. The middle cut.'

'You're a shocking man,' said Mrs Keogh to Mr Lynch. She threw off her coat and hat. 'Will you pour me a bottle,' she asked, 'while I attend to this lad? Finish up that now, Mr Dempsey.'

She laughed again. She went away and they heard from the grocery the sound of the bacon machine.

John Joe finished his stout and stood up.

'Good-night, Mr Lynch.'

'Remember about Quigley like a good fellow. When the day will come that you'll want to find a girl to marry, she might be saying you were the same type as Quigley. D'you understand me, John Joe?'

'I do, Mr Lynch.'

He passed through the door in the partition and watched Mrs Keogh slicing the bacon. He imagined her, as Quigley had said he'd seen her, belabouring her late husband with a length of wire. He imagined her as he had seen her himself, taking off her jersey because it was hot in the cellar, and then unzipping her green tweed skirt.

'I've sliced it thin,' she said. 'It tastes better thin, I think.'

'It does surely, Mrs Keogh.'

'Are you better after your stout? Don't go telling your mammy now.' Mrs Keogh laughed again, revealing long, crowded teeth. She weighed the bacon and wrapped it, munching a small piece of lean. 'If there's parsley in your mammy's garden,' she advised, 'chew a bit to get the smell of the stout away, in case she'd be cross with Mr Lynch. Or a teaspoon of tea-leaves.'

'There's no parsley, Mrs Keogh.'

'Wait till I get you the tea then.'

She opened a packet of tea and poured some on to the palm of his hand. She told him to chew it slowly and thoroughly and to let the leaves get into all the crevices of his mouth. She fastened the packet again, saying that no one would miss the little she'd taken from it. 'Four and two for the rashers,' she said.

He paid the money, with his mouth full of dry tea-leaves. He imagined Mrs Keogh leaning on her elbows on the counter and asking him if he had a kiss for her at all, calling him Mr Dempsey. He imagined her face stuck out towards his and her mouth open, displaying the big teeth, and her tongue damping her lips as the tongues of the Piccadilly tarts did, according to Mr Lynch. With the dryness in his own mouth and a gathering uneasiness in his stomach, his lips would go out to hers and he would taste her saliva.

'Good-night so, Mrs Keogh.'

'Good-night, Mr Dempsey. Tell your mother I was asking for her.'

He left the public house. The wind which had dislodged Mrs Keogh's hat felt fresh and cold on his face. The pink wash on a house across the street seemed pinker than it had seemed before, the ground moved beneath his feet, the street lighting seemed brighter. Youths and girls stood outside the illuminated windows of the small sweetshops, waiting for the Coliseum to open. Four farmers left Regan's public house and mounted four bicycles and rode away, talking loudly. *Your Murphy Dealer* announced a large coloured sign in the window of a radio shop. Two boys he had known at school came out of a shop eating biscuits from a paper bag. 'How're you, John Joe?' one of them said. 'How's Quigley these days?' They had left the school now: one of them worked in Kilmartin's the hardware's, the other in the Courthouse. They were wearing blue serge suits; their hair had been combed with care, and greased to remain tidy. They would go to the Coliseum, John Joe guessed, and sit behind two girls, giggling and whispering during the programme. Afterwards they would follow the girls for a little while, pretending to have no interest in them; they would buy chips in the chip-shop before they went home.

Thursday, Friday, Saturday, announced the sign outside the Coliseum: *His Girl Friday.* As John Joe read them, the heavy black letters shifted, moving about on green paper that flapped in the wind, fixed with drawing-pins to an unpainted board. Mr Dunne, the owner of the grey Coliseum, arrived on his bicycle and unlocked his property. *Sunday Only: Spencer Tracy in Boom Town.* In spite of the sickness in his stomach and the unpleasant taste of tea-leaves in his mouth, John Joe felt happy and was aware of an inclination to loiter for a long time outside the cinema instead of returning to his mother.

'It's great tonight, John Joe,' Mr Dunne said. 'Are you coming in?'

John Joe shook his head. 'I have to bring rashers home to my mother,' he said. He saw Mrs Dunne approaching with a torch, for the small cinema was a family business. Every night and twice on Sundays, Mr Dunne sold the tickets while his wife showed the customers to their seats. 'I looked in a window one time,' Quigley had said, 'and she was trying to put on her underclothes. Dunne was standing in his socks.'

A man and a girl came out of a sweet-shop next to the cinema, the girl with a box of Urney chocolates in her hand. She was thanking the man for them, saying they were lovely. 'It's a great show tonight, John Joe,' Mrs Dunne said, repeating the statement of her husband, repeating what she and he said every day of their lives. John Joe wagged his head at her. It looked a great show definitely, he said. He imagined her putting on her underclothes. He imagined her one night, unable because of a cold to show the customers to their seats, remaining at home in bed while her husband managed as best he could. 'I made a bit of bread for Mrs Dunne,' his mother said. 'Will you carry it down to her, John Joe?' He rang the bell and waited until she came to the door with a coat over her night-dress. He handed her the bread wrapped in creased brown paper and she asked him to step into the hall out of the wind. 'Will you take a bottle, John Joe?' Mrs Dunne said. He followed her into the kitchen, where she poured them each a glass of stout. 'Isn't it shock-ing hot in here?' she said. She took off her coat and sat at the kitchen table in her night-dress. 'You're a fine young fellow,' she said, touching his hand with her fingers.

John Joe walked on, past Blackburn's the draper's and Kelly's Atlantic Hotel. A number of men were idling outside the entrance to the bar, smoking cigarettes, one of them leaning on a bicycle. 'There's a dance in Clonakilty,' a tall man said. 'Will we drive over to that?' The others took no notice of this suggestion. They were talking about the price of turkeys.

'How're you, John Joe?' shouted a red-haired youth who worked in the sawmills. 'Quigley was looking for you.'

'I was up in Keogh's for my mother.'

'You're a decent man,' said the youth from the sawmills, going into the bar of Kelly's Hotel.

At the far end of North Street, near the small house where he lived with his mother, he saw Quigley waiting for him. Once he had gone to the Coliseum with Quigley, telling his mother he was going with Kinsella, the boy who occupied the desk next to his at the Christian Brothers'. The occasion, the first and only time that Quigley had visited the Coliseum, had not been a success. Quigley hadn't understood what was happening and had become frightened. He'd begun to mutter and kick the seats in front of him. 'Take him off out of here,' Mr Dunne had whispered, flashing his wife's torch. 'He'll bring the house down.' They had left the cinema after only a few minutes and had gone instead to the chip-shop.

'I looked in a window last night,' said Quigley now, hurrying to his friend's side, 'and, God, I saw a great thing.'

'I was drinking stout with Mr Lynch in Keogh's,' said John Joe. He might tell Quigley about the glory girls that Mr Lynch had advised him against, and about Baker who had struck a bargain with one of them, but it wouldn't be any use because Quigley never listened. No one held a conversation with Quigley: Quigley just talked.

'It was one o'clock in the morning,' said Quigley. His voice continued while John Joe opened the door of his mother's house and closed it behind him. Quigley would wait for him in the street and later on they'd perhaps go down to the chip-shop together.

'John Joe, where've you been?' demanded his mother, coming into the narrow hall from the kitchen. Her face was red from sitting too close to the range, her eyes had anger in them. 'What kept you, John Joe?'

'Mrs Keogh was at Confession.'

'What's that on your teeth?'

'What?'

'You've got dirt on your teeth.'

'I'll brush them then.'

He handed her the rashers. They went together to the kitchen, which was a small, low room with a flagged floor and a dresser that reached to the ceiling. On this, among plates and dishes, was the framed photograph of John Joe's father.

'Were you out with Quigley?' she asked, not believing that Mrs Keogh had kept him waiting for more than an hour.

He shook his head, brushing his teeth at the sink. His back was to her, and he imagined her distrustfully regarding him, her dark eyes gleaming with a kind of jealousy, her small wiry body poised as if to spring on any lie he should utter. Often he felt when he spoke to her that for her the words came physically from his lips, that they were things she could examine after he'd ejected them, in order to assess their truth.

'I talked to Mr Lynch,' he said. 'He was looking after the shop.'

'Is his mother well?'

'He didn't say.'

'He's very good to her.'

She unwrapped the bacon and dropped four rashers on to a pan that was warming on the range. John Joe sat down at the kitchen table. The feeling of euphoria that had possessed him outside the Coliseum was with him no longer; the floor was steady beneath his chair.

'They're good rashers,' his mother said.

'Mrs Keogh cut them thin.'

'They're best thin. They have a nicer taste.'

'Mrs Keogh said that.'

'What did Mr Lynch say to you? Didn't he mention the old mother?'

'He was talking about the war he was in.'

'It nearly broke her heart when he went to join it.'

'It was funny all right.'

'We were a neutral country.'

Mr Lynch would be still sitting in the bar of Keogh's. Every night of his life he sat there with his hat on his head, drinking bottles of stout. Other men would come into the bar and he would discuss matters with them and with Mrs Keogh. He would be drunk at the end of the evening. John Joe wondered if he chewed tea so that the smell of the stout would not be detected by his mother when he returned to her. He would return and tell her some lies about where he had been. He had joined the British Army in order to get away from her for a time, only she'd reached out to him from a dream.

'Lay the table, John Joe.'

He put a knife and a fork for each of them on the table, and found butter and salt and pepper. His mother cut four pieces of griddle bread and placed them to fry on the pan. 'I looked in a window one time,' said the voice of Quigley, 'and Mrs Sullivan was caressing Sullivan's legs.'

'We're hours late with the tea,' his mother said. 'Are you starving, pet?'

'Ah, I am, definitely.'

'I have nice fresh eggs for you.'

It was difficult for her sometimes to make ends meet. He knew it was, yet neither of them had ever said anything. When he went to work in the sawmills it would naturally be easier, with a sum each week to add to the pension.

She fried the eggs, two for him and one for herself. He watched her basting them in her expert way, intent upon what she was doing. Her anger was gone, now that he was safely in the kitchen, waiting for the food she cooked. Mr Lynch would have had his tea earlier in the evening, before he went down to Keogh's. 'I'm going out for a long walk,' he probably said to his mother, every evening after he'd wiped the egg from around his mouth.

'Did he tell you an experience he had in the war?' his mother asked, placing the plate of rashers, eggs and fried bread in front of him. She poured boiling water into a brown enamel teapot and left it on the range to draw.

'He told me about a time they were attacked by the Germans,' John Joe said. 'Mr Lynch was nearly killed.'

'She thought he'd never come back.'

'Oh, he came back all right.'

'He's very good to her now.'

When Brother Leahy twisted the short hairs on his neck and asked him what he'd been dreaming about he usually said he'd been working something out in his mind, like a long-division sum. Once he said he'd been trying to translate a sentence into Irish, and another time he'd said he'd been solving a puzzle that had appeared in the *Sunday Independent*. Recalling Brother Leahy's face, he ate the fried food. His mother repeated that the eggs were fresh. She poured him a cup of tea.

'Have you homework to do?'

He shook his head, silently registering that lie, knowing that there was homework to be done, but wishing instead to accompany Quigley to the chip-shop.

'Then we can listen to the wireless,' she said.

'I thought maybe I'd go out for a walk.'

Again the anger appeared in her eyes. Her mouth tightened, she laid down her knife and fork.

'I thought you'd stop in, John Joe,' she said, 'on your birthday.'

'Ah, well now—'

'I have a little surprise for you.'

She was telling him lies, he thought, just as he had told her lies. She began to eat again, and he could see in her face a reflection of the busyness that had developed in her mind. What could she find to produce as a surprise? She had given him that morning a green shirt that she knew he'd like because he liked the colour. There was a cake that she'd made, some of which they'd have when they'd eaten what was in front of them now. He knew about this birthday cake because he had watched her decorating it with hundreds and thousands: she couldn't suddenly say it was a surprise.

'When I've washed the dishes,' she said, 'we'll listen to the wireless and we'll look at that little thing I have.'

'All right,' he said.

He buttered bread and put a little sugar on the butter, which was a mixture he liked. She brought the cake to the table and cut them each a slice. She said she thought the margarine you got nowadays was not as good as margarine in the past. She turned the wireless on. A woman was singing.

'Try the cake now,' she said. 'You're growing up, John Joe.'

'Fifteen.'

'I know, pet.'

Only Quigley told the truth, he thought. Only Quigley was honest and straightforward and said what was in his mind. Other people told Quigley to keep that kind of talk to himself because they knew it was the truth, because they knew they wanted to think the thoughts that Quigley thought. 'I looked in a window,' Quigley had said to him when he was nine years old, the first time he had spoken to him, 'I saw a man and woman without their clothes on.' Brother Leahy would wish to imagine as Quigley imagined, and as John Joe imagined too. And what did Mr Lynch think about when he walked in gloom with his mother on a Sunday? Did he dream of the medium-sized glory girl he had turned away from because his mother had sent him a Virgin Mary from her dreams? Mr Lynch was not an honest man. It was a lie when he said that shame had kept him from marrying. It was his mother who prevented that, with her dreams of legs on fire and her First Communion statues. Mr Lynch had chosen the easiest course: bachelors might be gloomy on occasion, but they were untroubled men in some respects, just as men who kept away from the glory girls were.

'Isn't it nice cake?'

'Yes,' he said.

'This time next year you'll be in the sawmills.'

'I will.'

'It's good there's work for you.'

'Yes.'

They ate the two pieces of cake and then she cleared away the dishes and put them in the sink. He sat on a chair by the range. The men who'd been loitering outside Kelly's Hotel might have driven over to Clonakilty by now, he thought. They'd be dancing with girls and later they'd go back to their wives and say they'd been somewhere else, playing cards together in Kelly's maybe. Within the grey cement of the Coliseum the girl who'd been given the box of chocolates would be eating them, and the man who was with her would be wanting to put his hands on her.

Why couldn't he say to his mother that he'd drunk three bottles of stout in Keogh's? Why couldn't he say he could see the naked body of Mrs Taggart? Why hadn't he said to Mr Lynch that he should tell the truth about what was in his mind, like Quigley told the truth? Mr Lynch spent his life returning to the scenes that obsessed him, to the Belgian woman on the ground and the tarts of Piccadilly Circus. Yet he spoke of them only to fatherless boys, because it was the only excuse for mentioning them that he'd been able to think up.

'I have this for you,' she said.

She held towards him an old fountain pen that had belonged to his father, a pen he had seen before. She had taken it from a drawer of the dresser, where it was always kept.

'I thought you could have it on your fifteenth birthday,' she said.

He took it from her, a black-and-white pen that hadn't been filled with ink for thirteen years. In the drawer of the dresser there was a pipe of his father's, and a tie-pin and a bunch of keys and a pair of bicycle clips. She had washed and dried the dishes, he guessed, racking her mind to think of something she might offer him as the surprise she'd invented. The pen was the most suitable thing; she could hardly offer him the bicycle clips.

'Wait till I get you the ink,' she said, 'and you can try it out.' From the wireless came the voice of a man advertising household products. 'Ryan's Towel Soap', urged the voice gently. 'No better cleanser.'

He filled the pen from the bottle of ink she handed him. He sat down at the kitchen table again and tried the nib out on the piece of brown paper that Mrs Keogh had wrapped round the rashers and which his mother had neatly folded away for further use.

'Isn't it great it works still?' she said. 'It must be a good pen.'

It's hot in here, he wrote. *Wouldn't you take off your jersey?*

'That's a funny thing to write,' his mother said.

'It came into my head.'

They didn't like him being with Quigley because they knew what Quigley talked about when he spoke the truth. They were jealous because there was no pretence between Quigley and himself. Even though it was only Quigley who talked, there was an understanding between them: being with Quigley was like being alone.

'I want you to promise me a thing,' she said, 'now that you're fifteen.'

He put the cap on the pen and bundled up the paper that had contained the rashers. He opened the top of the range and dropped the paper into it. She would ask him to promise not to hang about with the town's idiot any more. He was a big boy now, he was big enough to own his father's fountain pen, and it wasn't right that he should be going out getting minnows in a jam jar with an elderly affected creature. It would go against his chances in the sawmills.

He listened to her saying what he had anticipated she would say. She went on talking, telling him about his father and the goodness there had been in his father before he fell from the scaffold. She took from the dresser the framed photograph that was so familiar to him and she put it into his hands, telling him to look closely at it. It would have made no difference, he thought, if his father had lived. His father would have been like the others; if ever he'd have dared to mention the nakedness of Mrs Taggart his father would have beaten him with a belt.

'I am asking you for his sake,' she said, 'as much as for my own and for yours, John Joe.'

He didn't understand what she meant by that, and he didn't inquire. He would say what she wished to hear him say, and he would keep his promise to her because it would be the easiest thing to do. Quigley wasn't hard to push away, you could tell him to get away like you'd tell a dog. It was funny that they should think that it would make much difference to him now, at this stage, not having Quigley to listen to.

'All right,' he said.

'You're a good boy, John Joe. Do you like the pen?'

'It's a lovely pen.'

'You might write better with that one.'

She turned up the volume of the wireless and together they sat by the range, listening to the music. To live in a shed like Quigley did would not be too bad: to have his food carried down through a garden by a niece, to go about the town in that special way, alone with his thoughts. Quigley did not have to pretend to the niece who fed him. He didn't have to say he'd been for a walk when he'd been drinking in Keogh's, or that he'd been playing cards with men when he'd been dancing in Clonakilty. Quigley didn't have to chew tea and keep quiet. Quigley talked; he said the words he wanted to say. Quigley was lucky being how he was.

'I will go to bed now,' he said eventually.

They said good-night to one another, and he climbed the stairs to his room. She would rouse him in good time, she called after him. 'Have a good sleep,' she said.

He closed the door of his room and looked with affection at his bed, for in the end there was only that. It was a bed that, sagging, held him in its centre and wrapped him warmly. There was ornamental brass-work at the head but not at the foot, and on the web of interlocking wire the hair mattress was thin. John Joe shed his clothes, shedding also the small town and his mother and Mr Lynch and the fact that he, on his fifteenth birthday, had drunk his first stout and had chewed tea. He entered his iron bed and the face of Mr Lynch passed from his mind and the voices of boys telling stories about freshly married couples faded away also. No one said to him now that he must not keep company with a crazed dwarf. In his iron bed, staring into the darkness, he made of the town what he wished to make of it, knowing that he would not be drawn away from his dreams by the tormenting fingers of a Christian Brother. In his iron bed he heard again only the voice of the town's idiot and then that voice, too, was there no more. He travelled alone, visiting in his way the women of the town, adored and adoring, more alive in his bed than ever he was at the Christian Brothers' School, or in the grey Coliseum, or in the chip-shop, or Keogh's public house, or his mother's kitchen, more alive than ever he would be at the sawmills. In his bed he entered a paradise: it was grand being alone.

Autumn Sunshine

The rectory was in County Wexford, eight miles from Enniscorthy. It was a handsome eighteenth-century house, with Virginia creeper covering three sides and a tangled garden full of buddleia and struggling japonica which had always been too much for its incumbents. It stood alone, seeming lonely even, approximately at the centre of the country parish it served. Its church—St Michael's Church of Ireland—was two miles away, in the village of Boharbawn.

For twenty-six years the Morans had lived there, not wishing to live anywhere else. Canon Moran had never been an ambitious man; his wife, Frances, had found contentment easy to attain in her lifetime. Their four girls had been born in the rectory, and had become a happy family there. They were grown up now, Frances's death was still recent: like the rectory itself, its remaining occupant was alone in the countryside. The death had occurred in the spring of the year, and the summer had somehow been bearable. The clergyman's eldest daughter had spent May and part of June at the rectory with her children. Another one had brought her family for most of August, and a third was to bring her newly married husband in the winter. At Christmas nearly all of them would gather at the rectory and some would come at Easter. But that September, as the days drew in, the season was melancholy.

Then, one Tuesday morning, Slattery brought a letter from Canon Moran's youngest daughter. There were two other letters as well, in unsealed buff envelopes which meant that they were either bills or receipts. Frail and grey-haired in his elderliness, Canon Moran had been wondering if he should give the lawn in front of the house a last cut when he heard the approach of Slattery's van. The lawn-mower was the kind that had to be pushed, and in the spring the job was always easier if the grass had been cropped close at the end of the previous summer.

'Isn't that a great bit of weather, Canon?' Slattery remarked, winding down the window of the van and passing out the three envelopes. 'We're set for a while, would you say?'

'I hope so, certainly.'

'Ah, we surely are, sir.'

The conversation continued for a few moments longer, as it did whenever Slattery came to the rectory. The postman was young and easy-going, not long the successor to old Mr O'Brien, who'd been making the round on a bicycle when the Morans first came to the rectory in 1952. Mr O'Brien used to talk about his garden; Slattery talked about fishing, and often brought a share of his catch to the rectory.

'It's a great time of year for it,' he said now, 'except for the darkness coming in.'

Canon Moran smiled and nodded; the van turned round on the gravel, dust rising behind it as it moved swiftly down the avenue to the road. Everyone said Slattery drove too fast.

He carried the letters to a wooden seat on the edge of the lawn he'd been wondering about cutting. Deirdre's handwriting hadn't changed since she'd been a child; it was round and neat, not at all a reflection of the girl she was. The blue English stamp, the Queen in profile blotched a bit by the London postmark, wasn't on its side or half upside down, as you might possibly expect with Deirdre. Of all the Moran children, she'd grown up to be the only difficult one. She hadn't come to the funeral and hadn't written about her mother's death. She hadn't been to the rectory for three years.

I'm sorry, she wrote now. *I couldn't stop crying actually. I've never known anyone as nice or as generous as she was. For ages I didn't even want to believe she was dead. I went on imagining her in the rectory and doing the flowers in church and shopping in Enniscorthy.*

Deirdre was twenty-one now. He and Frances had hoped she'd go to Trinity and settle down, but although at school she'd seemed to be the cleverest of their children she'd had no desire to become a student. She'd taken the Rosslare boat to Fishguard one night, having said she was going to spend a week with her friend Maeve Coles in Cork. They hadn't known she'd gone to England until they received a picture postcard from London telling them not to worry, saying she'd found work in an egg-packing factory.

Well, I'm coming back for a little while now, she wrote, *if you could put up with me and if you wouldn't find it too much. I'll cross over to Rosslare on the 29th, the morning crossing, and then I'll come on to Enniscorthy on the bus. I don't know what time it will be but there's a pub just by where the bus drops you so could we meet in the small bar there at six o'clock and then I won't have to lug my cases too far? I hope you won't mind going into such a place. If you can't make it, or don't want to see me, it's understandable, so if you don't turn up by half six I'll see if I can get a bus on up to Dublin. Only I need to get back to Ireland for a while.*

It was, as he and Slattery had agreed, a lovely autumn. Gentle sunshine mellowed the old garden, casting an extra sheen of gold on leaves that were gold already. Roses that had been ebullient in June and July bloomed modestly now. Michaelmas daisies were just beginning to bud. Already the crab-apples were falling, hydrangeas had a forgotten look. Canon Moran carried the letter from his daughter into the walled vegetable garden and leaned against the side of the greenhouse, half sitting on a protruding ledge, reading the letter again. Panes of glass were broken in the greenhouse, white paint and putty needed to be renewed, but inside a vine still thrived, and was heavy now with black ripe fruit. Later that morning he would pick some and drive into Enniscorthy, to sell the grapes to Mrs Neary in Slaney Street.

Love, Deirdre: the letter was marvellous. Beyond the rectory the fields of wheat had been harvested, and the remaining stubble had the same tinge of gold in the autumn light; the beech trees and the chestnuts were triumphantly magnificent. But decay and rotting were only weeks away, and the letter from Deirdre was full of life.

'*Love, Deirdre*' were words more beautiful than all the season's glories. He prayed as he leaned against the sunny greenhouse, thanking God for this salvation.

For all the years of their marriage Frances had been a help. As a younger man, Canon Moran hadn't known quite what to do. He'd been at a loss among his parishioners, hesitating in the face of this weakness or that: the pregnancy of Alice Pratt in 1954, the argument about grazing rights between Mr Willoughby and Eugene Dunlevy in 1960, the theft of an altar cloth from St Michael's and reports that Mrs Tobin had been seen wearing it as a skirt. Alice Pratt had been going out with a Catholic boy, one of Father Gowan's flock, which made the matter more difficult than ever. Eugene Dunlevy was one of Father Gowan's also, and so was Mrs Tobin.

'Father Gowan and I had a chat,' Frances had said, and she'd had a chat as well with Alice Pratt's mother. A month later Alice Pratt married the Catholic boy, but to this day attended St Michael's every Sunday, the children going to Father Gowan. Mrs Tobin was given Hail Marys to say by the priest; Mr Willoughby agreed that his father had years ago granted Eugene Dunlevy the grazing rights. Everything, in these cases and in many others, had come out all right in the end: order emerged from the confusion that Canon Moran so disliked, and it was Frances who had always begun the process, though no one ever said in the rectory that she understood the mystery of people as well as he understood the teachings of the New Testament. She'd been a freckle-faced girl when he'd married her, pretty in her way. He was the one with the brains.

Frances had seen human frailty everywhere: it was weakness in people, she said, that made them what they were as much as strength did. And she herself had her own share of such frailty, falling short in all sorts of ways of the God's image her husband preached about. With the small amount of housekeeping money she could be allowed she was a spendthrift, and she said she was lazy. She loved clothes and often overreached herself on visits to Dublin; she sat in the sun while the rectory gathered dust and the garden became rank; it was only where people were concerned that she was practical. But for what she was her husband had loved her with unobtrusive passion for fifty years, appreciating her conversation and the help she'd given him because she could so easily sense the truth. When he'd found her dead in the garden one morning he'd felt he had lost some part of himself.

Though many months had passed since then, the trouble was that Frances hadn't yet become a ghost. Her being alive was still too recent, the shock of her death too raw. He couldn't distance himself; the past refused to be the past. Often he thought that her fingerprints were still in the rectory, and when he picked the grapes or cut the grass of the lawn it was impossible not to pause and remember other years. Autumn had been her favourite time.

'Of course I'd come,' he said. 'Of course, dear. Of course.'

'I haven't treated you very well.'

'It's over and done with, Deirdre.'

She smiled, and it was nice to see her smile again, although it was strange to be sitting in the back bar of a public house in Enniscorthy. He saw her looking at him, her eyes passing over his clerical collar and black clothes, and his quiet face. He could feel her thinking that he had aged, and putting it down to the death of the wife he'd been so fond of.

'I'm sorry I didn't write,' she said.

'You explained in your letter, Deirdre.'

'It was ages before I knew about it. That was an old address you wrote to.'

'I guessed.'

In turn he examined her. Years ago she'd had her long hair cut. It was short now, like a black cap on her head. And her face had lost its chubbiness; hollows where her cheeks had been made her eyes more dominant, pools of seaweed green. He remembered her child's stocky body, and the uneasy adolescence that had spoilt the family's serenity. Her voice had lost its Irish intonation.

'I'd have met you off the boat, you know.'

'I didn't want to bother you with that.'

'Oh, now, it isn't far, Deirdre.'

She drank Irish whiskey, and smoked a brand of cigarettes called Three Castles. He'd asked for a mineral himself, and the woman serving them had brought him a bottle of something that looked like water but which fizzed up when she'd poured it. A kind of lemonade he imagined it was, and didn't much care for it.

'I have grapes for Mrs Neary,' he said.

'Who's that?'

'She has a shop in Slaney Street. We always sold her the grapes. You remember?'

She didn't, and he reminded her of the vine in the greenhouse. A shop surely wouldn't be open at this hour of the evening, she said, forgetting that in a country town of course it would be. She asked if the cinema was still the same in Enniscorthy, a cement building halfway up a hill. She said she remembered bicycling home from it at night with her sisters, not being able to keep up with them. She asked after her sisters and he told her about the two marriages that had taken place since she'd left: she had in-laws she'd never met, and nephews and a niece.

They left the bar, and he drove his dusty black Vauxhall straight to the small shop he'd spoken of. She remained in the car while he carried into the shop two large chip-baskets full of grapes. Afterwards Mrs Neary came to the door with him.

'Well, is that Deirdre?' she said as Deirdre wound down the window of the car. 'I'd never know you, Deirdre.'

'She's come back for a little while,' Canon Moran explained, raising his voice a little because he was walking round the car to the driver's seat as he spoke.

'Well, isn't that grand?' said Mrs Neary.

Everyone in Enniscorthy knew Deirdre had just gone off, but it didn't matter now. Mrs Neary's husband, who was a red-cheeked man with a cap, much smaller than his wife, appeared beside her in the shop doorway. He inclined his head in greeting, and Deirdre smiled and waved at both of them. Canon Moran thought it was pleasant when she went on waving while he drove off.

In the rectory he lay wakeful that night, his mind excited by Deirdre's presence. He would have loved Frances to know, and guessed that she probably did. He fell asleep at half past two and dreamed that he and Frances were young again, that Deirdre was still a baby. The freckles on Frances's face were out in profusion, for they were sitting in the sunshine in the garden, tea things spread about them, the children playing some game among the shrubs. It was autumn then also, the last of the September heat. But because he was younger in his dream he didn't feel part of the season himself, or sense its melancholy.

A week went by. The time passed slowly because a lot was happening, or so it seemed. Deirdre insisted on cooking all the meals and on doing the shopping in Boharbawn's single shop or in Enniscorthy. She still smoked her endless cigarettes, but the peakiness there had been in her face when she'd first arrived wasn't quite so pronounced—or perhaps, he thought, he'd become used to it. She told him about the different jobs she'd had in London and the different places she'd lived in, because on the postcards she'd occasionally sent there hadn't been room to go into detail. In the rectory they had always hoped she'd managed to get a training of some sort, though guessing she hadn't. In fact, her jobs had been of the most rudimentary kind: as well as her spell in the egg-packing factory, there'd been a factory that made plastic earphones, a cleaning job in a hotel near Euston, and a year working for the Use-Us Office Cleansing Service. 'But you can't have liked any of that work, Deirdre?' he suggested, and she agreed she hadn't.

From the way she spoke he felt that that period of her life was over: adolescence was done with, she had steadied and taken stock. He didn't suggest to her that any of this might be so, not wishing to seem either too anxious or too pleased, but he felt she had returned to the rectory in a very different frame of mind from the one in which she'd left it. He imagined she would remain for quite a while, still taking stock, and in a sense occupying her mother's place. He thought he recognized in her a loneliness that matched his own, and he wondered if it was a feeling that their loneliness might be shared which had brought her back at this particular time. Sitting in the drawing-room while she cooked or washed up, or gathering grapes in the greenhouse while she did the shopping, he warmed delightedly to this theme. It seemed like an act of God that their circumstances should interlace this autumn. By Christmas she would know what she wanted to do with her life, and in the spring that followed she would perhaps be ready to set forth again. A year would have passed since the death of Frances.

'I have a friend,' Deirdre said when they were having a cup of coffee together in the middle of one morning. 'Someone who's been good to me.'

She had carried a tray to where he was composing next week's sermon, sitting on the wooden seat by the lawn at the front of the house. He laid aside his exercise book, and a pencil and a rubber. 'Who's that?' he inquired.

'Someone called Harold.'

He nodded, stirring sugar into his coffee.

'I want to tell you about Harold, Father. I want you to meet him.'

'Yes, of course.'

She lit a cigarette. She said, 'We have a lot in common. I mean, he's the only person . . .'

She faltered and then hesitated. She lifted her cigarette to her lips and drew on it.

He said, 'Are you fond of him, Deirdre?'

'Yes, I am.'

Another silence gathered. She smoked and drank her coffee. He added more sugar to his.

'Of course I'd like to meet him,' he said.

'Could he come to stay with us, Father? Would you mind? Would it be all right?'

'Of course I wouldn't mind. I'd be delighted.'

Harold was summoned, and arrived at Rosslare a few days later. In the meantime Deirdre had explained to her father that her friend was an electrician by trade and had let it fall that he was an intellectual kind of person. She borrowed the old Vauxhall and drove it to Rosslare to meet him, returning to the rectory in the early evening.

'How d'you do?' Canon Moran said, stretching out a hand in the direction of an angular youth with a birthmark on his face. His dark hair was cut very short, cropped almost. He was wearing a black leather jacket.

'I'm fine,' Harold said.

'You've had a good journey?'

'Lousy, 'smatter of fact, Mr Moran.'

Harold's voice was strongly Cockney, and Canon Moran wondered if Deirdre had perhaps picked up some of her English vowel sounds from it. But then he realized that most people in London would speak like that, as people did on the television and the wireless. It was just a little surprising that Harold and Deirdre should have so much in common, as they clearly had from the affectionate way they held one another's hand. None of the other Moran girls had gone in so much for holding hands in front of the family.

He was to sit in the drawing-room, they insisted, while they made supper in the kitchen, so he picked up the *Irish Times* and did as he was bidden. Half an hour later Harold appeared and said that the meal was ready: fried eggs and sausages and bacon, and some tinned beans. Canon Moran said grace.

Having stated that County Wexford looked great, Harold didn't say much else. He didn't smile much, either. His afflicted face bore an edgy look, as if he'd never become wholly reconciled to his birthmark. It was like a scarlet map on his left cheek, a shape that reminded Canon Moran of the toe of Italy. Poor fellow, he thought.

And yet a birthmark was so much less to bear than other afflictions there could be.

'Harold's fascinated actually,' Deirdre said, 'by Ireland.'

Her friend didn't add anything to that remark for a moment, even though Canon Moran smiled and nodded interestedly. Eventually Harold said, 'The struggle of the Irish people.'

'I didn't know a thing about Irish history,' Deirdre said. 'I mean, not anything that made sense.'

The conversation lapsed at this point, leaving Canon Moran greatly puzzled. He began to say that Irish history had always been of considerable interest to him also, that it had a good story to it, its tragedy uncomplicated. But the other two didn't appear to understand what he was talking about and so he changed the subject. It was a particularly splendid autumn, he pointed out.

'Harold doesn't go in for anything like that,' Deirdre replied.

During the days that followed Harold began to talk more, surprising Canon Moran with almost everything he said. Deirdre had been right to say he was fascinated by Ireland, and it wasn't just a tourist's fascination. Harold had read widely: he spoke of ancient battles, and of the plantations of James I and Elizabeth, of Robert Emmet and the Mitchelstown martyrs, of Pearse and de Valera. 'The struggle of the Irish people' was the expression he most regularly employed. It seemed to Canon Moran that the relationship between Harold and Deirdre had a lot to do with Harold's fascination, as though his interest in Deirdre's native land had somehow caused him to become interested in Deirdre herself.

There was something else as well. Fascinated by Ireland, Harold hated his own country. A sneer whispered through his voice when he spoke of England: a degenerate place, he called it, destroyed by class-consciousness and the unjust distribution of wealth. He described in detail the city of Nottingham, to which he appeared to have a particular aversion. He spoke of unnecessary motorways and the stupidity of bureaucracy, the stifling presence of a Royal family. 'You could keep an Indian village,' he claimed, 'on what those corgis eat. You could house five hundred homeless in Buckingham

Palace.' There was brainwashing by television and the newspaper barons. No ordinary person had a chance because pap was fed to the ordinary person, a deliberate policy going back into Victorian times when education and religion had been geared to the enslavement of minds. The English people had brought it on themselves, having lost their spunk, settling instead for consumer durables. 'What better can you expect,' Harold demanded, 'after the hypocrisy of that empire the bosses ran?'

Deirdre didn't appear to find anything specious in this line of talk, which surprised her father. 'Oh, I wonder about that,' he said himself from time to time, but he said it mildly, not wishing to cause an argument, and in any case his interjections were not acknowledged. Quite a few of the criticisms Harold levelled at his own country could be levelled at Ireland also and, Canon Moran guessed, at many countries throughout the world. It was strange that the two neighbouring islands had been so picked out, although once Germany was mentioned and the point made that developments beneath the surface there were a hopeful sign, that a big upset was on the way.

'We're taking a walk,' Harold said one afternoon. 'She's going to show me Kinsella's Barn.'

Canon Moran nodded, saying to himself that he disliked Harold. It was the first time he had admitted it, but the feeling was familiar. The less generous side of his nature had always emerged when his daughters brought to the rectory the men they'd become friendly with or even proposed to marry. Emma, the eldest girl, had brought several before settling in the end for Thomas. Linda had brought only John, already engaged to him. Una had married Carley not long after the death, and Carley had not yet visited the rectory: Canon Moran had met him in Dublin, where the wedding had taken place, for in the circumstances Una had not been married from home. Carley was an older man, an importer of tea and wine, stout and flushed, certainly not someone Canon Moran would have chosen for his second-youngest daughter. But, then, he had thought the same about Emma's Thomas and about Linda's John.

Thomas was a farmer, sharing a sizeable acreage with his father in Co. Meath. He always brought to mind the sarcasm of an old schoolmaster who in Canon Moran's distant schooldays used to refer to a gang of boys at the back of the classroom as 'farmers' sons', meaning that not much could be expected of them. It was an inaccurate assumption but even now, whenever Canon Moran found himself in the company of Thomas, he couldn't help recalling it. Thomas was mostly silent, with a good-natured smile that came slowly and lingered too long. According to his father, and there was no reason to doubt the claim, he was a good judge of beef cattle.

Linda's John was the opposite. Wiry and suave, he was making his way in the Bank of Ireland, at present stationed in Waterford. He had a tiny orange-coloured moustache and was good at golf. Linda's ambition for him was that he should become the Bank of Ireland's manager in Limerick or Galway, where the insurances that went with the position were particularly lucrative. Unlike Thomas, John talked all the time, telling jokes and stories about the Bank of Ireland's customers.

'Nothing is perfect,' Frances used to say, chiding her husband for an uncharitableness he did his best to combat. He disliked being so particular about the men his daughters chose, and he was aware that other people saw them differently: Thomas would do anything for you, John was fun, the middle-aged Carley laid his success at Una's feet. But whoever the husbands of his daughters had been, Canon Moran knew he'd have felt the same. He was jealous of the husbands because ever since his daughters had been born he had loved them unstintingly. When he had prayed after Frances's death he'd felt jealous of God, who had taken her from him.

'There's nothing much to see,' he pointed out when Harold announced that Deirdre was going to show him Kinsella's Barn. 'Just the ruin of a wall is all that's left.'

'Harold's interested, Father.'

They set off on their walk, leaving the old clergyman ashamed that he could not like Harold more. It wasn't just his griminess: there was something sinister about Harold, something furtive about the way he looked at you, peering at you cruelly out of his afflicted face, not meeting your eye. Why was he so fascinated about a country that wasn't his own? Why did he refer so often to 'Ireland's struggle' as if that struggle particularly concerned him? He hated walking, he had said, yet he'd just set out to walk six miles through woods and fields to examine a ruined wall.

Canon Moran had wondered as suspiciously about Thomas and John and Carley, privately questioning every statement they made, finding hidden motives everywhere. He'd hated the thought of his daughters being embraced or even touched, and had forced himself not to think about that. He'd prayed, ashamed of himself then, too. 'It's just a frailty in you,' Frances had said, her favourite way of cutting things down to size.

He sat for a while in the afternoon sunshine, letting all of it hang in his mind. It would be nice if they quarrelled on their walk. It would be nice if they didn't speak when they returned, if Harold simply went away. But that wouldn't happen, because they had come to the rectory with a purpose. He didn't know why he thought that, but he knew it was true: they had come for a reason, something that was all tied up with Harold's fascination and with the kind of person Harold was, with his cold eyes and his afflicted face.

In March 1798 an incident had taken place in Kinsella's Barn, which at that time had just been a barn. Twelve men and women, accused of harbouring insurgents, had been tied together with ropes at the command of a Sergeant James. They had been led through the village of Boharbawn, the Sergeant's soldiers on horseback on either side of the procession, the Sergeant himself bringing up the rear. Designed as an act of education, an example to the inhabitants of Boharbawn and the country people around, the twelve had been herded into a barn owned by a farmer called Kinsella and there burned to death. Kinsella, who had played no part either in the harbouring of insurgents or in the execution of the twelve, was afterwards murdered by his own farm labourers.

'Sergeant James was a Nottingham man,' Harold said that evening at supper. 'A soldier of fortune who didn't care what he did. Did you know he acquired great wealth, Mr Moran?'

'No, I wasn't at all aware of that,' Canon Moran replied.

'Harold found out about him,' Deirdre said.

'He used to boast he was responsible for the death of a thousand Irish people. It was in Boharbawn he reached the thousand. They rewarded him well for that.'

'Not much is known about Sergeant James locally. Just the legend of Kinsella's Barn.'

'No way it's a legend.'

Deirdre nodded; Canon Moran did not say anything. They were eating cooked ham and salad. On the table there was a cake which Deirdre had bought in McGovern's in Enniscorthy, and a pot of tea. There were several bunches of grapes from the greenhouse, and a plate of wafer biscuits. Harold was fond of salad cream, Canon Moran had noticed; he had a way of hitting the base of the jar with his hand, causing large dollops to spurt all over his ham. He didn't place his knife and fork together on the plate when he'd finished, but just left them anyhow. His fingernails were edged with black.

'You'd feel sick,' he was saying now, working the salad cream again. 'You'd stand there looking at that wall and you'd feel a revulsion in your stomach.'

'What I meant,' Canon Moran said, 'is that it has passed into local legend. No one doubts it took place; there's no question about that. But two centuries have almost passed.'

'And nothing has changed,' Harold interjected. 'The Irish people still share their bondage with the twelve in Kinsella's Barn.'

'Round here of course—'

'It's not round here that matters, Mr Moran. The struggle's world-wide; the sickness is everywhere actually.'

Again Deirdre nodded. She was like a zombie, her father thought. She was being used because she was an Irish girl; she was Harold's Irish connection, and in some almost frightening way she believed herself in love with him. Frances had once said they'd made a mistake with her. She had wondered if Deirdre had perhaps found all the love they'd offered her too much to bear. They were quite old when Deirdre was a child, the last expression of their own love. She was special because of that.

'At least Kinsella got his chips,' Harold pursued, his voice relentless. 'At least that's something.'

Canon Moran protested. The owner of the barn had been an innocent man, he pointed out. The barn had simply been a convenient one, large enough for the purpose, with heavy stones near it that could be piled up against the door before the conflagration. Kinsella, that day, had been miles away, ditching a field.

'It's too long ago to say where he was,' Harold retorted swiftly. 'And if he was keeping a low profile in a ditch it would have been by arrangement with the imperial forces.'

When Harold said that, there occurred in Canon Moran's mind a flash of what appeared to be the simple truth. Harold was an Englishman who had espoused a cause because it was one through which the status quo in his own country might be damaged. Similar such Englishmen, read about in newspapers, stirred in the clergyman's mind: men from Ealing and Liverpool and Wolverhampton who had changed their names to Irish names, who had even learned the Irish language, in order to ingratiate themselves with the new Irish revolutionaries. Such men dealt out death and chaos, announcing that their conscience insisted on it.

'Well, we'd better wash the dishes,' Deirdre said, and Harold rose obediently to help her.

The walk to Kinsella's Barn had taken place on a Saturday afternoon. The following morning Canon Moran conducted his services in St Michael's, addressing his small Protestant congregation, twelve at Holy Communion, eighteen at morning service. He had prepared a sermon about repentance, taking as his text St Luke, 15:32: . . . *for this thy brother was dead, and is alive again; and was lost, and is found.* But at the last moment he changed his mind and spoke instead of the incident in Kinsella's Barn nearly two centuries ago.

He tried to make the point that one horror should not fuel another, that passing time contained its own forgiveness. Deirdre and Harold were naturally not in the church, but they'd been present at breakfast, Harold frying eggs on the kitchen stove, Deirdre pouring tea. He had looked at them and tried to think of them as two young people on holiday. He had tried to tell himself they'd come to the rectory for a rest and for his blessing, that he should be grateful instead of fanciful. It was for his blessing that Emma had brought Thomas to the rectory, that Linda had brought John. Una would bring Carley in November. 'Now, don't be silly,' Frances would have said.

'The man Kinsella was innocent of everything,' he heard his voice insisting in his church. 'He should never have been murdered also.'

Harold would have delighted in the vengeance exacted on an innocent man. Harold wanted to inflict pain, to cause suffering and destruction. The end justified the means for Harold, even if the end was an artificial one, a pettiness grandly dressed up. In his sermon Canon Moran spoke of such matters without mentioning Harold's name. He spoke of how evil drained people of their humour and compassion, how people pretended even to themselves. It was worse than Frances's death, he thought as his voice continued in the church: it was worse that Deirdre should be part of wickedness.

He could tell that his parishioners found his sermon odd, and he didn't blame them. He was confused, and naturally distressed. In the rectory Deirdre and Harold would be waiting for him. They would all sit down to Sunday lunch while plans for atrocities filled Harold's mind, while Deirdre loved him.

'Are you well again, Mrs Davis?' he inquired at the church door of a woman who suffered from asthma.

'Not too bad, Canon. Not too bad, thank you.'

He spoke to all the others, inquiring about health, remarking on the beautiful autumn. They were farmers mostly and displayed a farmer's gratitude for the satisfactory season. He wondered suddenly who'd replace him among them when he retired or died. Father Gowan had had to give up a year ago. The young man, Father White, was always in a hurry.

'Goodbye so, Canon,' Mr Willoughby said, shaking hands as he always did, every Sunday. It was a long time since there'd been the trouble about Eugene Dunlevy's grazing rights; three years ago Mr Willoughby had been left a widower himself. 'You're managing all right, Canon?' he asked, as he also always did.

'Yes, I'm all right, thank you, Mr Willoughby.'

Someone else inquired if Deirdre was still at the rectory, and he said she was. Heads nodded, the unspoken thought being that that was nice for him, his youngest daughter at home again after all these years. There was forgiveness in several faces, forgiveness of Deirdre, who had been thoughtless to go off to an egg-packing factory. There was the feeling, also unexpressed, that the young were a bit like that.

'Goodbye,' he said in a general way. Car doors banged, engines started. In the vestry he removed his surplice and his cassock and hung them in a cupboard.

'We'll probably go tomorrow,' Deirdre said during lunch.

'Go?'

'We'll probably take the Dublin bus.'

'I'd like to see Dublin,' Harold said.

'And then you're returning to London?'

'We're easy about that,' Harold interjected before Deirdre could reply. 'I'm a tradesman, Mr Moran, an electrician.'

'I know you're an electrician, Harold.'

'What I mean is, I'm on my own; I'm not answerable to the bosses. There's always a bob or two waiting in London.'

For some reason Canon Moran felt that Harold was lying. There was a quickness about the way he'd said they were easy about their plans, and it didn't seem quite to make sense, the logic of not being answerable to bosses and a bob or two always waiting for him.

Harold was being evasive about their movements, hiding the fact that they would probably remain in Dublin for longer than he implied, meeting other people like himself.

'It was good of you to have us,' Deirdre said that evening, all three of them sitting around the fire in the drawing-room because the evenings had just begun to get chilly. Harold was reading a book about Che Guevara and hadn't spoken for several hours. 'We've enjoyed it, Father.'

'It's been nice having you, Deirdre.'

'I'll write to you from London.'

It was safe to say that: he knew she wouldn't because she hadn't before, until she'd wanted something. She wouldn't write to thank him for the rectory's hospitality, and that would be quite in keeping. Harold was the same kind of man as Sergeant James had been: it didn't matter that they were on different sides. Sergeant James had maybe borne an affliction also, a humped back or a withered arm. He had ravaged a country that existed then for its spoils, and his most celebrated crime was neatly at hand so that another Englishman could make matters worse by attempting to make amends. In Harold's view the trouble had always been that these acts of war and murder died beneath the weight of print in history books, and were forgotten. But history could be rewritten, and for that Kinsella's Barn was an inspiration: Harold had journeyed to it as people make journeys to holy places.

'Yes?' Deirdre said, for while these reflections had passed through his mind he had spoken her name, wanting to ask her to tell him the truth about her friend.

He shook his head. 'I wish you could have seen your mother again,' he said instead. 'I wish she were here now.'

The faces of his three sons-in-law irrelevantly appeared in his mind: Carley's flushed cheeks, Thomas's slow good-natured smile, John's little moustache. It astonished him that he'd ever felt suspicious of their natures, for they would never let his daughters down. But Deirdre had turned her back on the rectory, and what could be expected when she came back with a man? She had never been like Emma or Linda or Una, none of whom smoked Three Castles cigarettes and wore clothes that didn't seem quite clean. It was impossible to imagine any of them becoming involved with a revolutionary, a man who wanted to commit atrocities.

'He was just a farmer, you know,' he heard himself saying. 'Kinsella.'

Surprise showed in Deirdre's face. 'It was Mother we were talking about,' she reminded him, and he could see her trying to connect her mother with a farmer who had died two hundred years ago, and not being able to. Elderliness, he could see her thinking. 'Only time he wandered,' she would probably say to her friend.

'It was good of you to come, Deirdre.'

He looked at her, far into her eyes, admitting to himself that she had always been his favourite. When the other girls were busily growing up she had still wanted to sit on his knee. She'd had a way of interrupting him no matter what he was doing, arriving beside him with a book she wanted him to read to her.

'Goodbye, Father,' she said the next morning while they waited in Enniscorthy for the Dublin bus. 'Thank you for everything.'

'Yeah, thanks a ton, Mr Moran,' Harold said.

'Goodbye, Harold. Goodbye, my dear.'

He watched them finding their seats when the bus arrived and then he drove the old Vauxhall back to Boharbawn, meeting Slattery in his postman's van and returning his salute. There was shopping he should have done, meat and potatoes, and tins of things to keep him going. But his mind was full of Harold's afflicted face and his black-rimmed fingernails, and Deirdre's hand in his. And then flames burst from the straw that had been packed around living people in Kinsella's Barn. They burned through the wood of the barn itself, revealing the writhing bodies. On his horse the man called Sergeant James laughed.

Canon Moran drove the car into the rectory's ramshackle garage, and walked around the house to the wooden seat on the front lawn. Frances should come now with two cups of coffee, appearing at the front door with the tray and then crossing the gravel and the lawn.

He saw her as she had been when first they came to the rectory, when only Emma had been born; but the grey-haired Frances was somehow there as well, shadowing her youth. 'Funny little Deirdre,' she said, placing the tray on the seat between them.

It seemed to him that everything that had just happened in the rectory had to do with Frances, with meeting her for the first time when she was eighteen, with loving her and marrying her. He knew it was a trick of the autumn sunshine that again she crossed the gravel and the lawn, no more than pretence that she handed him a cup and saucer. 'Harold's just a talker,' she said. 'Not at all like Sergeant James.'

He sat for a while longer on the wooden seat, clinging to these words, knowing they were true. Of course it was cowardice that ran through Harold, inspiring the whisper of his sneer when he spoke of the England he hated so. In the presence of a befuddled girl and an old Irish clergyman England was an easy target, and Ireland's troubles a kind of target also.

Frances laughed, and for the first time her death seemed far away, as her life did too. In the rectory the visitors had blurred her fingerprints to nothing, and had made of her a ghost that could come back. The sunshine warmed him as he sat there, the garden was less melancholy than it had been.

The Paradise Lounge

On her high stool by the bar the old woman was as still as a statue. Perhaps her face is expressionless, Beatrice thought, because in repose it does not betray the extent of her years. The face itself was lavishly made up, eyes and mouth, rouge softening the wrinkles, a dusting of perfumed powder. The chin was held more than a little high, at an angle that tightened the loops of flesh beneath it. Grey hair was short beneath a black cloche hat that suggested a fashion of the past, as did the tight black skirt and black velvet coat. Eighty she'd be, Beatrice deduced, or eighty-two or -three.

'We can surely enjoy ourselves,' Beatrice's friend said, interrupting her scrutiny of the old woman. 'Surely we can, Bea?'

She turned her head. The closeness of his brick-coloured flesh and of the smile in his eyes caused her lips to tremble. She appeared to smile also, but what might have been taken for pleasure was a checking of her tears.

'Yes,' she said. 'Of course.'

They were married, though not to one another. Beatrice's friend, casually dressed for a summer weekend, was in early middle age, no longer slim yet far from bulky. Beatrice was thirty-two, petite and black-haired in a blue denim dress. Sunglasses disguised her deep-rust eyes, which was how—a long time ago now—her father had described them. She had wanted to be an actress then.

'It's best,' her friend said, repeating the brief statement for what might have been the hundredth time since they had settled into his car earlier that afternoon. The affair was over, the threat to their families averted. They had come away to say goodbye.

'Yes, I know it's best,' she said, a repetition also.

At the bar the old woman slowly raised a hand to her hat and touched it delicately with her fingers. Slowly the hand descended, and then lifted her cocktail glass. Her scarlet mouth was not quite misshapen, but age had harshly scored what once had been a perfect outline, lips pressed together like a rosebud on its side. Failure, Beatrice thought as casually she observed all this: in the end the affair was a failure. She didn't even love him any more, and long ago he'd ceased to love her. It was euphemism to call it saying goodbye: they were having a dirty weekend, there was nothing left to lift it higher than that.

'I'm sorry we couldn't manage longer,' he said. 'I'm sorry about Glengarriff.'

'It doesn't matter.'

'Even so.'

She ceased to watch the old woman at the bar. She smiled at him, again disguising tears but also wanting him to know that there were no hard feelings, for why on earth should there be?

'After all, we've been to Glengarriff,' she said, a joke because on the one occasion they'd visited the place they had nearly been discovered in their deceptions. She'd used her sister as an excuse for her absences from home: for a long time now her sister had been genuinely unwell in a farmhouse in Co. Meath, a house that fortunately for Beatrice's purpose didn't have a telephone.

'I'll never forget you,' he said, his large tanned hand suddenly on one of hers, the vein throbbing in his forehead. A line of freckles ran down beside the vein, five smudges on the redbrick skin. In winter you hardly noticed them.

'Nor I you.'

'Darling old Bea,' he said, as if they were back at the beginning.

The bar was a dim, square lounge with a scattering of small tables, one of which they occupied. Ashtrays advertised Guinness, beer-mats Heineken. Sunlight touched the darkened glass in one of two windows, drawing from it a glow that was not unlike the amber gleam of whiskey. Behind the bar itself the rows of bottles, spirits upside down above their global measures, glittered pleasantly as a centrepiece, their reflections gaudy in a cluttered mirror. The floor had a patterned carpet, further patterned with cigarette burns and a diversity of stains. The Paradise Lounge the bar had been titled in a moment of hyperbole by the grandfather of the present proprietor, a sign still proclaiming as much on the door that opened from the hotel's mahogany hall. Beatrice's friend had hesitated, for the place seemed hardly promising: Keegan's Railway Hotel in a town neither of them knew. They might have driven on, but he was tired and the sun had been in his eyes. 'It's all right,' she had reassured him.

He took their glasses to the bar and had to ring a bell because the man in charge had disappeared ten minutes ago. 'Nice evening,' he said to the old woman on the bar-stool, and she managed to indicate agreement without moving a muscle of her carefully held head. 'We'll have the same again,' he said to the barman, who apologized for his absence, saying he'd been mending a tap.

Left on her own, Beatrice sighed a little and took off her sunglasses. There was no need for this farewell, no need to see him for the last time in his pyjamas or to sit across a table from him at dinner and at breakfast, making conversation that once had come naturally. 'A final fling', he'd put it, and she'd thought of someone beating a cracked drum, trying to extract a sound that wasn't there any more. How could it have come to this? The Paradise Lounge of Keegan's Railway Hotel, Saturday night in a hilly provincial town, litter caught in the railings of the Christian Brothers': how *could* this be the end of what they once had had? Saying goodbye to her, he was just somebody else's husband: the lover had slipped away.

'Well, it's a terrible bloody tap we have,' the barman was saying. 'Come hell or high water, I can't get a washer into it.'

'It can be a difficult job.'

'You could come in and say that to the wife for me, sir.'

The drinks were paid for, the transaction terminated. Further gin and Martini were poured into the old woman's glass, and Beatrice watched again while like a zombie the old woman lit a cigarette.

Miss Doheny her name was: though beautiful once, she had never married. Every Saturday evening she met the Meldrums in the Paradise Lounge, where they spent a few hours going through the week that had passed, exchanging gossip and commenting on the world. Miss Doheny was always early and would sit up at the bar for twenty minutes on her own, having the extra couple of drinks that, for her, were always necessary. Before the Meldrums arrived she would make her way to a table in a corner, for that was where Mrs Meldrum liked to be.

It wasn't usual that other people were in the bar then. Occasionally it filled up later but at six o'clock, before her friends arrived, she nearly always had it to herself. Francis Keegan—the hotel's inheritor, who also acted as barman—spent a lot of time out in the back somewhere, attending to this or that. It didn't matter because after their initial greeting of one another, and a few remarks about the weather, there wasn't much conversation that Miss Doheny and he had to exchange. She enjoyed sitting up at the bar on her own, glancing at the reflections in the long mirror behind the bottles, provided the reflections were never of herself. On the other hand it was a pleasant enough diversion, having visitors.

Miss Doheny, who had looked twice at Beatrice and once at her companion, guessed at their wrong-doing. Tail-ends of conversation had drifted across the lounge, no effort being made to lower voices since more often than not the old turn out to be deaf. They were people from Dublin whose relationship was not that recorded in Francis Keegan's register in the hall. Without much comment, modern life permitted their sin; the light-brown motor-car parked in front of the hotel made their self-indulgence a simple matter.

How different it had been, Miss Doheny reflected, in 1933! Correctly she estimated that that would have been the year when she herself was the age the dark-haired girl was now. In 1933 adultery and divorce and light-brown motor-cars had belonged more in

America and England, read about and alien to what already was being called the Irish way of life. 'Catholic Ireland,' Father Cully used to say. 'Decent Catholic Ireland.' The term was vague and yet had meaning: the emergent nation, seeking pillars on which to build itself, had plumped for holiness and the Irish language—natural choices in the circumstances. 'A certain class of woman,' old Father Cully used to say, 'constitutes an abhorrence.' The painted women of Clancy's Picture House—sound introduced in 1936—were creatures who carried a terrible warning. Jezebel women, Father Cully called them, adding that the picture house should never have been permitted to exist. In his grave for a quarter of a century, he would hardly have believed his senses if he'd walked into the Paradise Lounge in Keegan's Railway Hotel to discover two adulterers, and one of his flock who had failed to heed his castigation of painted women. Yet for thirty-five years Miss Doheny had strolled through the town on Saturday evenings to this same lounge, past the statue of the 1798 rebel, down the sharp incline of Castle Street. On Sundays she covered the same ground again, on the way to and from Mass. Neither rain nor cold prevented her from making the journey to the Church of the Resurrection or to the hotel, and illness did not often afflict her. That she had become more painted as the years piled up seemed to Miss Doheny to be natural in the circumstances.

In the Paradise Lounge she felt particularly at home. In spring and summer the Meldrums brought plants for her, or bunches of chives or parsley, sometimes flowers. Not because she wished to balance the gesture with one of her own but because it simply pleased her to do so she brought for them a pot of jam if she had just made some, or pieces of shortbread. At Christmas, more formally, they exchanged gifts of a different kind. At Christmas the lounge was decorated by Francis Keegan, as was the hall of the hotel and the dining-room. Once a year, in April, a dance was held in the dining-room, in connection with a local point-to-point, and it was said in the town that Francis Keegan made enough in the bar during the course of that long night to last him for the next twelve months. The hotel ticked over from April to April, the Paradise Lounge becoming quite brisk with business when an occasional function was held in the dining-room, though never achieving the abandoned spending that distinguished the night of the point-to-point. Commercial travellers sometimes stayed briefly, taking pot-luck with Mrs Keegan's cooking, which at the best of times was modest in ambition and achievement. After dinner these men would sit on one of the high stools in the Paradise Lounge, conversing with Francis Keegan and drinking bottles of stout. Mrs Keegan would sometimes put in a late appearance and sip a glass of gin and water. She was a woman of slatternly appearance, with loose grey hair and slippers. Her husband complemented her in style and manner, his purplish complexion reflecting a dedication to the wares he traded in across his bar. They were an undemanding couple, charitable in their opinions, regarded as unfortunate in the town since their union had not produced children. Because of that, Keegan's Railway Hotel was nearing the end of its days as a family concern and in a sense it was fitting that that should be so, for the railway that gave it its title had been closed in 1951.

How I envy her! Miss Doheny thought. How fortunate she is to find herself in these easy times, not condemned because she loves a man! It seemed right to Miss Doheny that a real love affair was taking place in the Paradise Lounge and that no one questioned it. Francis Keegan knew perfectly well that the couple were not man and wife: the strictures of old Father Cully were as fusty by now as neglected mice droppings. The holiness that had accompanied the birth of a nation had at last begun to shed its first tight skin: liberation, Miss Doheny said to herself, marvelling over the word.

They walked about the town because it was too soon for dinner. Many shops were still open, greengrocers anxious to rid themselves of cabbage that had been limp for days and could not yet again be offered for sale after the weekend, chemists and sweetshops. Kevin Croady, Your Best for Hi-Fi, had arranged a loudspeaker in a window above his premises: Saturday-night music blared forth, punk harmonies and a tenor rendering of 'Kelly the Boy from Killann'. All tastes were catered for.

The streets were narrow, the traffic congested. Women picked over the greengrocers' offerings, having waited until this hour because prices would be reduced. Newly shaved men slipped into the public houses, youths and girls loitered outside Redmond's Café and on the steps of the 1798 statue. Two dogs half-heartedly fought outside the Bank of Ireland.

The visitors to the town inquired where the castle was, and then made their way up Castle Hill. 'Opposite Castle Motors,' the child they'd asked had said, and there it was: an ivy-covered ruin, more like the remains of a cowshed. Corrugated iron sealed off an archway, its torn bill-posters advertising Calor Gas and a rock group, Duffy's Circus and Fine Gael, and the annual point-to-point that kept Keegan's Railway Hotel going. Houses had been demolished in this deserted area, concrete replacements only just begun. The graveyard of the Protestant church was unkempt; *New Premises in Wolfe Tone Street*, said a placard in the window of Castle Motors. Litter was everywhere.

'Not exactly camera fodder,' he said with his easy laugh. 'A bloody disgrace, some of these towns are.'

'The people don't notice, I suppose.'

'They should maybe wake themselves up.'

The first time he'd seen her, he'd afterwards said, he had heard himself whispering that it was she he should have married. They'd sat together, talking over after-dinner coffee in someone else's house. He'd told her, lightly, that he was in the Irish rope business, almost making a joke of it because that was his way. A week later his car had drawn up beside her in Rathgar Road, where she'd lived since her marriage. 'I thought I recognized you,' he said, afterwards confessing that he'd looked up her husband's name in the telephone directory. 'Come in for a drink,' she invited, and of course he had. Her two children had been there, her husband had come in.

They made their way back to the town, she taking his arm as they descended the steep hill they'd climbed. A wind had gathered, cooling the evening air.

'It feels so long ago,' she said. 'The greater part of my life appears to have occurred since that day when you first came to the house.'

'I know, Bea.'

He'd seemed extraordinary and nice, and once when he'd smiled at her she'd found herself looking away. She wasn't unhappy in her marriage, only bored by the monotony of preparing food and seeing to the house and the children. She had, as well, a reluctant feeling that she wasn't appreciated, that she hadn't been properly loved for years.

'You don't regret it happened?' he said, stepping out into the street because the pavement was still crowded outside Redmond's Café.

She pitched her voice low so that he wouldn't hear her saying she wasn't sure. She didn't want to tell a lie, she wasn't certain of the truth.

He nodded, assuming her reassurance. Once, of course, he would never have let a mumbled reply slip by.

Miss Doheny had moved from the bar and was sitting at a table with the Meldrums when Beatrice and her friend returned to the Paradise Lounge after dinner. Mrs Meldrum was telling all about the visit last Sunday afternoon of her niece, Kathleen. 'Stones she's put on,' she reported, and then recalled that Kathleen's newly acquired husband had sat there for three hours hardly saying a word. Making a fortune he was, in the dry-goods business, dull but good-hearted.

Miss Doheny listened. Strangely, her mind was still on the visitors who had returned to the lounge. She'd heard the girl saying that a walk about the town would be nice, and as the Meldrums had entered the lounge an hour or so ago she'd heard the man's voice in the hall and had guessed they were then on their way to the dining-room. The dinner would not have been good, for Miss

Doheny had often heard complaints about the nature of Mrs Keegan's cooking. And yet the dinner, naturally, would not have mattered in the least.

Mrs Meldrum's voice continued: Kathleen's four children by her first marriage were all grown up and off her hands, she was lucky to have married so late in life into a prosperous dry-goods business. Mr Meldrum inclined his head or nodded, but from time to time he would also issue a mild contradiction, setting the facts straight, regulating his wife's memory. He was a grey-haired man in a tweed jacket, very spare and stooped, his face as sharp as a blade, his grey moustache well cared-for. He smoked while he drank, allowing a precise ten minutes to elapse between the end of one cigarette and the lighting of the next. Mrs Meldrum was smaller than her companions by quite some inches, round and plump, with glasses and a black hat.

The strangers were drinking Drambuie now, Miss Doheny noticed. The man made a joke, probably about the food they'd eaten; the girl smiled. It was difficult to understand why it was that they were so clearly not man and wife. There was a wistfulness in the girl's face, but the wistfulness said nothing very much. In a surprising way Miss Doheny imagined herself crossing the lounge to where they were. 'You're lucky, you know,' she heard herself saying. 'Honestly, you're lucky, child.' She glanced again in the girl's direction and for a moment caught her eye. She almost mouthed the words, but changed her mind because as much as possible she liked to keep her face in repose.

Beatrice listened to her companion's efforts to cheer the occasion up. The town and the hotel—especially the meal they'd just consumed—combined to reflect the mood that the end of the affair had already generated. They were here, Beatrice informed herself again, not really to say goodbye to one another but to commit adultery for the last time. They would enjoy it as they always had, but the enjoyment would not be the same as that inspired by the love there had been. They might not have come, they might more elegantly have said goodbye, yet their presence in a bar ridiculously named the Paradise Lounge seemed suddenly apt. The bedroom where acts of mechanical passion would take place had a dingy wallpaper, its flattened pink soap already used by someone else. Dirty weekend, Beatrice thought again, for stripped of love all that was left was the mess of deception and lies there had been, of theft and this remaining, too ordinary desire. Her sister, slowly dying in the farmhouse, had been a bitter confidante and would never forgive her now. Tonight in a provincial bedroom a manufacturer of rope would have his way with her and she would have her way with him. There would be their nakedness and their mingled sweat.

'I thought that steak would walk away,' he spiritedly was continuing now. 'Being somebody's shoe-leather.'

She suddenly felt drunk, and wanted to be drunker. She held her glass toward him. 'Let's just drink,' she said.

She caught the eye of the old woman at the other table and for a moment sensed Miss Doheny's desire to communicate with her. It puzzled her that an elderly woman whom she did not know should wish to say something, yet she strongly felt that this was so. Then Miss Doheny returned her attention to what the other old woman was saying.

When they'd finished the drinks that Beatrice's companion had just fetched they moved from the table they were at and sat on two bar-stools, listening to Francis Keegan telling them about the annual liveliness in the hotel on the night of the April point-to-point. Mrs Keegan appeared at his side and recalled an occasion when Willie Kincart had ridden the horse he'd won the last race on into the hall of the hotel and how old Packy Briscoe had imagined he'd caught the d.t.'s when he looked down from the top of the stairs. And there was the story—before Mrs Keegan's time, as she was swift to point out—when Jack Doyle and Movita had stayed in Keegan's, when just for the hell of it Jack Doyle had chased a honeymoon couple up Castle Hill, half naked from their bed. After several further drinks, Beatrice began to laugh. She felt much less forlorn now that the faces of Francis Keegan and his wife were beginning to float agreeably in her vision. When she looked at the elderly trio in the corner, the only other people in the lounge, their faces floated also.

The thin old man came to the bar for more drinks and cigarettes. He nodded and smiled at Beatrice; he remarked upon the weather. 'Mr Meldrum,' said Francis Keegan by way of introduction. 'How d'you do,' Beatrice said.

Her companion yawned and appeared to be suggesting that they should go to bed. Beatrice took no notice. She pushed her glass at Francis Keegan, reaching for her handbag and announcing that it was her round. 'A drink for everyone,' she said, aware that when she gestured towards the Keegans and the elderly trio she almost lost her balance. She giggled. 'Definitely my round,' she slurred, giggling again.

Mrs Keegan told another story, about a commercial traveller called Artie Logan who had become drunk in his room and had sent down for so many trays of tea and buttered bread that every cup and saucer in the hotel had been carried up to him. 'They said to thank you,' her husband passed on, returning from the elderly trio's table. Beatrice turned her head. All three of them were looking at her, their faces still slipping about a bit. Their glasses were raised in her direction. 'Good luck,' the old man called out.

It was then that Beatrice realized. She looked from face to face, making herself smile to acknowledge the good wishes she was being offered, the truth she sensed seeming to emerge from a blur of features and clothes and three raised glasses. She nodded, and saw the heads turn away again. It had remained unstated: the love that was there had never in any way been exposed. In this claustrophobic town, in this very lounge, there had been the endless lingering of a silent passion, startlingly different from the instant requiting of her own.

Through the muzziness of inebriation Beatrice glanced again across the bar. Behind her the Keegans were laughing, and the man she'd once so intensely loved was loudly laughing also. She heard the sound of the laughter strangely, as if it echoed from a distance, and she thought for a moment that it did not belong in the Paradise Lounge, that only the two old women and the old man belonged there. He was loved, and in silence he returned that love. His plump, bespectacled wife had never had reason to feel betrayed; no shame nor guilt attached. In all the years a sister's dying had never been made use of. Nor had there been hasty afternoons in Rathgar Road, blinds drawn against neighbours who might guess, a bedroom set to rights before children came in from school. There hadn't been a single embrace.

Yet the love that had continued for so long would go on now until the grave: without even thinking, Beatrice knew that that was so. The old woman paraded for a purpose the remnants of her beauty, the man was elegant in his tweed. How lovely that was! Beatrice thought, still muzzily surveying the people at the table, the wife who had not been deceived quite contentedly chatting, the two who belonged together occupying their magic worlds.

How lovely that nothing had been destroyed: Beatrice wanted to tell someone that, but there was no one to tell. In Rathgar Road her children would be watching the television, their father sitting with them. Her sister would die before the year was finished. What cruelty there seemed to be, and more sharply now she recalled the afternoon bedroom set to rights and her sister's wasted face. She wanted to run away, to go backwards into time so that she might shake her head at her lover on the night they'd first met.

Miss Doheny passed through the darkened town, a familiar figure on a Saturday night. It had been the same as always, sitting there, close to him, the smoke drifting from the cigarette that lolled between his fingers. The girl by now would be close in a different way to the man who was somebody else's husband also. As in a film, their clothes would be scattered about the room that had been hired for love, their murmurs would break a silence. Tears ran through Miss Doheny's meticulous make-up, as often they did when she walked away from the Paradise Lounge on a Saturday night. It was difficult sometimes not to weep when she thought about the easy times that had come about in her lifetime, mocking the agony of her stifled love.

Two More Gallants

You will not, I believe, find either Lenehan or Corley still parading the streets of Dublin, but often in the early evening a man called Heffernan may be found raising a glass of Paddy in Toner's public house; and FitzPatrick, on his bicycle, every working day makes the journey across the city, from Ranelagh to the offices of McGibbon, Tait & FitzPatrick, solicitors and commissioners for oaths. It is on his doctor's advice that he employs this mode of transport. It is against the advice of *his* that Heffernan continues to indulge himself in Toner's. The two men no longer know one another. They do not meet and, in order to avoid a confrontation, each has been known to cross a street.

Thirty or so years ago, when I first knew Heffernan and Fitz-Patrick, the relationship was different. The pair were closely attached, Heffernan the mentor, FitzPatrick ready with a laugh. All three of us were students, but Heffernan, a Kilkenny man, was different in the sense that he had been a student for as long as anyone could remember. The College porters said they recalled his presence over fifteen years and, though given to exaggeration, they may well have been accurate in that: certainly Heffernan was well over thirty, a small ferrety man, swift to take offence.

FitzPatrick was bigger and more amiable. An easy smile perpetually creased the bland ham of his face, causing people to believe, quite incorrectly, that he was stupid. His mouse-coloured hair was kept short enough not to require a parting, his eyes reflected so profound a degree of laziness that people occasionally professed surprise to find them open. Heffernan favoured pin-striped suits, FitzPatrick a commodious blue blazer. They drank in Kehoe's in Anne Street.

'He is one of those chancers,' Heffernan said, 'we could do without.'

'Oh, a right old bollocks,' agreed FitzPatrick.

' "Well, Mr Heffernan," ' he says, ' "I see you are still with us." '

'As though you might be dead.'

'If he had his way.'

In the snug of Kehoe's they spoke of Heffernan's *bête noire,* the aged Professor Flacks, a man from the North of Ireland.

' "I see you are still with us," ' Heffernan repeated. 'Did you ever hear the beat of that?'

'Sure, Flacks is senile.'

'The mots in the lecture giggle when he says it.'

'Oh, an ignorant bloody crowd.'

Heffernan became meditative. Slowly he lit a Sweet Afton. He was supported in his continuing studentship by the legacy left to him for that purpose by an uncle in Kilkenny, funds which would cease when he was a student no longer. He kept that tragedy at bay by regularly failing the Littlego examination, a test of proficiency in general studies to which all students were obliged to submit themselves.

'A fellow came up to me this morning,' he said now, 'a right eejit from Monasterevin. Was I looking for grinds in Little-go Logic? Five shillings an hour.'

FitzPatrick laughed. He lifted his glass of stout and drank from it, imposing on his upper lip a moustache of foam which was permitted to remain there.

'A minion of Flacks',' Heffernan continued. 'A Flacks boy and no mistake, I said to myself.'

'You can tell them a mile off.'

' "I know your father," I said to him. "Doesn't he deliver milk?" Well, he went the colour of a sunset. "Avoid conversation with Flacks," I told him. "He drove a wife and two sisters insane." '

'Did your man say anything?'

'Nothing, only "Cripes".'

'Oh, Flacks is definitely peculiar,' FitzPatrick agreed.

In point of fact, at that time FitzPatrick had never met Professor Flacks. It was his laziness that caused him to converse in a manner which suggested he had, and it was his laziness also which prevented him from noticing the intensity of Heffernan's grievance. Heffernan hated Professor Flacks with a fervour, but in his vague and unquestioning way FitzPatrick assumed that the old professor was no more than a passing thorn in his friend's flesh, a nuisance that could be exorcised by means of complaint and abuse. Heffernan's pride did not at that time appear to play a part; and FitzPatrick, who knew his friend as well as anyone did, would not have designated him as a possessor of that quality to an unusual degree. The opposite was rather implied by the nature of his upkeep and his efforts not to succeed in the Littlego examination. But pride, since its presence might indeed be questioned by these facts, came to its own support: when the story is told in Dublin today it is never forgotten that it has roots in Professor Flacks's causing girls to giggle because he repeatedly made a joke at Heffernan's expense.

Employed by the University to instruct in certain aspects of literature, Professor Flacks concentrated his attention on the writings of James Joyce. Shakespeare, Tennyson, Shelley, Coleridge, Wilde, Swift, Dickens, Eliot, Trollope, and many another familiar name were all bundled away in favour of a Joycean scholarship that thirty or so years ago was second to none in Irish university life. Professor Flacks could tell you whom Joyce had described as a terrified YMCA man, and the date of the day on which he had written that his soul was full of decayed ambitions. He spoke knowledgeably of the stale smell of incense, like foul flowerwater; and of flushed eaves and stubble geese.

'Inane bloody show-off,' Heffernan said nastily in Kehoe's.

'You'll see him out, Heff.'

'A bogs like that would last for ever.'

Twelve months later, after he and Heffernan had parted company, FitzPatrick repeated all that to me. I didn't know either of them well, but was curious because a notable friendship had so abruptly come to an end. FitzPatrick, on his own, was inclined to talk to anyone.

We sat in College Park, watching the cricket while he endeavoured to remember the order of subsequent events. It was Heffernan who'd had the idea, as naturally it would be, since FitzPatrick still knew Professor Flacks only by repute and had not suffered the sarcasm which Heffernan found so offensive. But FitzPatrick played a vital part in the events which followed, because the elderly woman who played the main part of all was a general maid in FitzPatrick's digs.

'Has that one her slates on?' Heffernan inquired one night as they passed her by in the hall.

'Ah, she's only a bit quiet.'

'She has a docile expression all right.'

'She wouldn't damage a fly.'

Soon after that Heffernan took to calling in at FitzPatrick's digs in Donnybrook more often than he had in the past. Sometimes he was there when FitzPatrick arrived back in the evening, sitting in the kitchen while the elderly maid pricked sausages or cut up bread for the meal that would shortly be served. Mrs Maginn, the landlady, liked to lie down for a while at that time of day, so Heffernan and the maid had the kitchen to themselves. But finding him present on several occasions when she came downstairs, Mrs Maginn in passing mentioned the fact to her lodger. FitzPatrick, who didn't himself understand what Heffernan's interest in the general maid was, replied that his friend liked to await his return in the kitchen because it was warm. Being an easy-going woman, Mrs Maginn was appeased.

'There's no doubt in my mind at all,' Heffernan stated in Kehoe's after a few weeks of this behaviour. 'If old Flacks could hear it he'd have a tortoise's pup.'

FitzPatrick wagged his head, knowing that an explanation was in the air. Heffernan said: 'She's an interesting old lassie.'

He then told FitzPatrick a story which FitzPatrick had never heard before. It concerned a man called Corley who had persuaded a maid in a house in Baggot Street to do a small service for him. It concerned, as well, Corley's friend, Lenehan, who was something of a wit. At first FitzPatrick was confused by the story, imagining it to be about a couple of fellow-students whom he couldn't place.

'The pen of Jimmy Joyce,' Heffernan explained. 'That yarn is Flacks's favourite of the lot.'

'Well, I'd say there wasn't much to it. Sure, a skivvy never would.'

'She was gone on Corley.'

'But would she steal for him?'

'You're no romantic, Fitz.'

FitzPatrick laughed, agreeable to accepting this opinion. Then, to his astonishment, Heffernan said: 'It's the same skivvy Mrs Maginn has above in your digs.'

FitzPatrick shook his head. He told Heffernan to go on with himself, but Heffernan insisted.

'She told me the full story herself one night I was waiting for you—maybe the first night I ever addressed a word to her. "Come into the kitchen outa the cold, Mr Heffernan," she says. D'you remember the occasion it was? Late after tea, and you didn't turn up at all. She fried me an egg.'

'But, holy Christ, man—'

'It was the same night you did well with the nurse from Dundrum.'

FitzPatrick guffawed. A great girl, he said. He repeated a few details, but Heffernan didn't seem interested.

'I was told the whole works in the kitchen, like Jimmy Joyce had it out of her when she was still in her teens. A little gold sovereign was what she fecked for your man.'

'But the poor old creature is as honest as the day's long.'

'Oh, she took it all right and she still thinks Corley was top of the bill.'

'But Corley never existed—'

'Of course he did. Wasn't he for ever entertaining that fine little tart with the witticisms of Master Lenehan?'

The next thing that happened, according to FitzPatrick, was that a bizarre meeting took place. Heffernan approached Professor Flacks with the information that the model for the ill-used girl in Joyce's story 'Two Gallants' had come to light in a house in Donnybrook. The Professor displayed considerable excitement, and on a night when Mrs Maginn was safely at the pictures he was met by Heffernan at the bus stop and led to the kitchen.

He was a frail man in a tweed suit, not at all as FitzPatrick had imagined him. Mrs Maginn's servant, a woman of about the same age, was slightly deaf and moved slowly owing to rheumatism. Heffernan had bought half a pound of fig-roll biscuits which he arranged on a plate. The old woman poured tea.

Professor Flacks plied her with questions. He asked them gently, with courtesy and diplomacy, without any hint of the tetchiness described so often by Heffernan. It was a polite occasion in the kitchen, Heffernan handing round the fig-rolls, the maid appearing to delight in recalling a romance in her past.

'And later you told Mr Joyce about this?' prompted Professor Flacks.

'He used come to the house when I worked in North Frederick Street, sir. A dentist by the name of O'Riordan.'

'Mr Joyce came to get his teeth done?'

'He did, sir.'

'And you'd talk to him in the waiting-room, is that it?'

'I'd be lonesome, sir. I'd open the hall door when the bell rang and then there'd be a wait for maybe an hour before it'd ring again, sir. I recollect Mr Joyce well, sir.'

'He was interested in your—ah—association with the fellow you mentioned, was he?'

'It was only just after happening, sir. I was turned out of the place in Baggot Street on account of the bit of trouble. I was upset at the time I knew Mr Joyce, sir.'

'That's most understandable.'

'I'd often tell a patient what had happened to me.'

'But you've no hard feelings today? You were badly used by the fellow, yet—'

'Ah, it's long ago now, sir.'

Heffernan and FitzPatrick saw the Professor on to a bus and, according to FitzPatrick, he was quivering with pleasure. He clambered into a seat, delightedly talking to himself, not noticing when they waved from the pavement. They entered a convenient public house and ordered pints of stout.

'Did you put her up to it?' FitzPatrick inquired.

'The thing about that one, she'd do anything for a scrap of the ready. Didn't you ever notice that about her? She's a right old miser.'

It was that that Heffernan had recognized when first he'd paid a visit to Mrs Maginn's kitchen: the old maid was possessed of a meanness that had become obsessional with her. She spent no money whatsoever, and was clearly keen to add to what she had greedily accumulated. He had paid her a pound to repeat the story he had instructed her in.

'Didn't she say it well? Oh, top of the bill, I'd say she was.'

'You'd be sorry for old Flacks.'

'Oh, the devil take bloody Mr Flacks.'

Some months went by. Heffernan no longer visited the kitchen in Donnybrook, and he spoke hardly at all of Professor Flacks. In his lazy way FitzPatrick assumed that the falsehoods which had been perpetrated were the be-all and end-all of the affair, that Heffernan's pride—now clearly revealed to him—had somehow been satisfied. But then, one summer's afternoon while the two idled in Stephen's Green in the hope of picking up girls, Heffernan said: 'There's a thing on we might go to next Friday.'

'What's that?'

'Mr Flacks performing. The Society of the Friends of James Joyce.'

It was a public lecture, one of several that were to be delivered during a week devoted by the Society to the life and work of the author who was its *raison d'être*. The Society's members came from far afield: from the United States, Germany, Finland, Italy, Australia, France, England and Turkey. Learned academics mingled with less learned enthusiasts. Mr James Duffy's Chapelizod was visited, and Mr Power's Dublin Castle. Capel Street and Ely Place were investigated, visits were made to the renowned Martello Tower, to Howth and to Pim's. Betty Bellezza was mentioned, and Val from Skibbereen. The talk was all Joyce talk. For a lively week Joyce reigned in Dublin.

On the appointed evening FitzPatrick accompanied his friend to Professor Flacks's lecture, his premonitions suggesting that the occasion was certain to be tedious. He had no idea what Heffernan was up to, and wasn't prepared to devote energy to speculating. With a bit of luck, he hoped, he'd be able to have a sleep.

Before the main event a woman from the University of Washington spoke briefly about Joyce's use of misprints; a bearded German read a version of 'The Holy Office' that had only recently been discovered. Then the tweeded figure of Professor Flacks rose. He sipped at a tumbler of water, and spoke for almost an hour about the model for the servant girl in the story, 'Two Gallants'. His discovery of that same elderly servant, now employed in a house in Donnybrook, engendered in his audience a whisper of excitement that remained alive while he spoke, and exploded into applause when he finished. A light flush enlivened the paleness of his face as he sat down. It was, as Heffernan remarked to his dozy companion, the old man's finest hour.

It was then that FitzPatrick first became uneasy. The packed lecture-hall had accepted as fact all that had been stated, yet none of it was true. Notes had been taken, questions were now being asked. A voice just behind the two students exclaimed that this remarkable discovery was worth coming two thousand miles to hear about. Mental pictures of James Joyce in a dentist's waiting-room flashed about the hall. North Frederick Street would be visited tomorrow, if not tonight.

'I'd only like to ask,' Heffernan shouted above the hubbub, 'if I may, a simple little question.' He was on his feet. He had caught the attention of Professor Flacks, who was smiling benignly at him. 'I'd only like to inquire,' Heffernan continued, 'if that whole thing couldn't be a lot of baloney.'

'Baloney?' a foreign voice repeated.

'Baloney?' said Professor Flacks.

The buzz of interest hadn't died down. Nobody was much interested in the questions that were being asked except the people who were asking them. A woman near to FitzPatrick said it was extraordinarily moving that the ill-used servant girl, who had been so tellingly presented as an off-stage character by Joyce, should bear no grudge all these years later.

'What I mean, Professor Flacks,' said Heffernan, 'is I don't think James Joyce ever attended a dentist in North Frederick Street. What I'm suggesting to you, sir, is that the source of your information was only looking for a bit of limelight.'

FitzPatrick later described to me the expression that entered Professor Flacks's eyes. 'A lost kind of look,' he said, 'as though someone had poked the living daylights out of him.' The old man stared at Heffernan, frowning, not comprehending at first. His relationship with this student had been quite different since the night of the visit to Mrs Maginn's kitchen: it had been distinguished by a new friendliness, and what had seemed like mutual respect.

'Professor Flacks and myself,' continued Heffernan, 'heard the old lady together. Only I formed the impression that she was making the entire matter up. I thought, sir, you'd formed that opinion also.'

'Oh, but surely now, Mr Heffernan, the woman wouldn't do that.'

'There was never a dentist by the name of O'Riordan that practised in North Frederick Street, sir. That's a fact that can easily be checked.'

Heffernan sat down. An uneasy silence gripped the lecture-hall. Eyes turned upon Professor Flacks. Weakly, with a hoarseness in his voice, he said: 'But why, Mr Heffernan, would she have made all that up? A woman of that class would hardly have read the story, she'd hardly have known—'

'It's an unfortunate thing, sir,' interrupted Heffernan, standing up again, 'but that old one would do anything for a single pound note. She's of a miserly nature. I think what has happened,' he went on, his tone changing as he addressed the assembly, 'is that a student the Professor failed in an examination took a chance to get his own back. Our friend Jas Joyce,' he added, 'would definitely have relished that.'

In misery Professor Flacks lifted the tumbler of water to his lips, his eyes cast down. You could sense him thinking, FitzPatrick reported, that he was a fool and he had been shown to be a fool. You could sense him thinking that he suddenly appeared to be unreliable, asinine and ridiculous. In front of the people who mattered to him most of all he had been exposed as a fraud he did not feel himself to be. Never again could he hold his head up among the Friends of James Joyce. Within twenty-four hours his students would know what had occurred.

An embarrassed shuffling broke out in the lecture-hall. People murmured and began to make their way into the aisles. FitzPatrick recalled the occasion in Mrs Maginn's kitchen, the two elderly puppets on the end of Heffernan's string, the fig-rolls and the tea. He recalled the maid's voice retailing the story that he, because he knew Heffernan so well, had doubted with each word that was uttered. He felt guilty that he hadn't sought the old man out and told him it wasn't true. He glanced through the throng in the lecture-hall at the lone figure in porridgy tweeds, and unhappily reflected that suicide had been known to follow such wretched disgrace. Outside the lecture-hall he told Heffernan to go to hell when a drink in Anne Street was suggested—a remark for which Heffernan never forgave him.

'I mean,' FitzPatrick said as we sat in College Park a long time later, 'how could anyone be as petty? When all the poor old fellow ever said to him was "I see you are still with us?"'

I made some kind of reply. Professor Flacks had died a natural death a year after the delivery of his lecture on 'Two Gallants'. Earlier in his life he had not, as Heffernan had claimed, driven a wife and two sisters mad: he'd been an only child, the obituary said in the *Irish Times*, and a bachelor. It was an awkward kind of obituary, for the gaffe he'd made had become quite famous and was still fresh in Dubliners' minds.

We went on talking about him, FitzPatrick and I, as we watched the cricket in College Park. We spoke of his playful sarcasm and how so vehemently it had affected Heffernan's pride. We marvelled over the love that had caused a girl in a story to steal, and over the miserliness that had persuaded an old woman to be party to a trick. FitzPatrick touched upon his own inordinate laziness, finding a place for that also in our cobweb of human frailty.

The News from Ireland

Poor Irish Protestants is what the Fogartys are: butler and cook. They have church connections, and conversing with Miss Fogarty people are occasionally left with the impression that their father was a rural dean who suffered some misfortune: in fact he was a sexton. Fogarty is the younger and the smaller of the pair, brought up by Miss Fogarty, their mother dying young. His life was saved by his sister's nursing the time he caught scarlatina, when he was only eight.

Dapper in his butler's clothes, a slight and unimposing man with a hazelnut face, Fogarty is at present fascinated by the newly arrived governess: Anna Maria Heddoe, from somewhere in England, a young woman of principle and sensibility, stranger and visitor to Ireland. Fogarty is an educated man, and thinks of other visitors there have been: the Celts, whose ramshackle gypsy empire expired in this same landscape, St Patrick with his holy shamrock, the outrageous Vikings preceding the wily Normans, the adventurers of the Virgin Queen. His present employers arrived here also, eight years ago, in 1839. The Pulvertafts of Ipswich, as Fogarty thinks of them, and wishes they had not bothered to make the journey after old Hugh Pulvertaft died. House and estate fell away under the old man, and in Fogarty's opinion it is a pity the process didn't continue until everything was driven back into the clay it came from. Instead of which along had come the Pulvertafts of Ipswich, taking on more staff, clearing the brambles from the garden in their endeavour to make the place what it had been in the past, long before the old man's time. The Pulvertafts of Ipswich belong here now. They make allowances for the natives, they come to terms, they learn to live with things. Fogarty has watched surprise and dismay fade from their faces. He has watched these people becoming important locally, and calling the place they have come to 'home'. Serving them in the dining-room, holding for them a plate of chops or hurrying to them a gravy dish, he wishes he might speak the truth as it appears to him: that their fresh, decent blood is the blood of the invader though they are not themselves invaders, that they perpetrate theft without being thieves. He does not dislike the Pulvertafts of Ipswich, he has nothing against them beyond the fact that they did not stay where they were. He and his sister might alone have attended the mouldering of the place, urging it back to the clay.

The governess is interesting to Fogarty because she is another of the strangers whom the new Pulvertafts have gathered around them in their advent. Such visitors, in the present and in the past, obsess the butler. He observes Miss Heddoe daily; he studies her closely and from a distance, but he does not reveal his obsession to his sister, who would consider it peculiar. He carries Miss Heddoe's meals to her room when normally this duty would be Cready's or Brigid's; he reads the letters she receives, and the diary she intermittently keeps.

October 15th, 1847. I look out of the window of my attic room, and in the early morning the men are already labouring on the road that is to encircle the estate. The estate manager, the one-armed Mr Erskine, oversees them from his horse. Mr Pulvertaft rides up, gesturing about some immediate necessity—how a particular shrub must be avoided, so his gestures suggest, or where best to construct a bridge. The estate manager listens and assents, his men do not cease in their work. Beyond the trees, beyond the high stone walls of the estate, women and children die of the hunger that God has seen fit to visit upon them. In my prayers I ask for mercy.

October 17th, 1847. Fogarty came in with my dinner on a tray and said that the marks of the stigmata had been discovered on a child.

'Is the child alive?' I demanded when he returned a half-hour later for the tray.

'Oh yes, miss. No doubt on that. The living child was brought to Father Horan.'

I was amazed but he seemed hardly surprised. I questioned him but he was vague; and the conversation continuing because he lingered, I told him the Legend of the True Cross, with which he was unfamiliar. He was delighted to hear of its elaborations, and said he would recount these in the kitchen. The stigmata on the child have been revealed on feet and hands only, but the priest has said that other parts of the body must be watched. The priest has cautiously given an opinion: that so clearly marked a stigma has never before been known in Ireland. The people consider it a miracle, a sign from God in these distressful times.

October 20th, 1847. I am not happy here. I do not understand this household, neither the family nor the servants. This is the middle of my third week, yet I am still in all ways at a loss. Yesterday, in the afternoon, I was for the first time summoned to the drawing-room to hear Adelaide play her pieces, and George Arthur's lessons being over for the day he sat by me, as naturally he should. Charlotte and her mother occupied the sofa, Emily a chair in a recess. Mr Pulvertaft stood toasting his back at the fire, his riding-crop tapping time on the side of his polished boot. They made a handsome family picture—Emily beautiful, Charlotte petite and pretty, the plump motherliness of Mrs Pulvertaft, her husband's ruddy presence. I could not see George Arthur's features, for he was a little in front of me, but I knew them well from the hours I have surveyed them across our lessons-table. He is bright-faced, and dark like all the family except Mrs Pulvertaft, whose hair I would guess was red before becoming grey. Only Adelaide, bespectacled and seeming heavy for her age, does not share the family's gift of grace. Poor Adelaide is cumbersome; her movements are awkward at the piano and she really plays it most inelegantly.

Yet in the drawing-room no frown or wince betrayed the listeners' ennui. As though engrossed in a performance given by a fine musician, Mr Pulvertaft slightly raised and dropped his riding-crop, as he might a baton; similarly expressing absorption, his wife's lips were parted, the hurry and worry of her nature laid aside, her little eyes delighted. And Emily and Charlotte sat as girls more graciously endowed than a plain sister should, neither pouting nor otherwise recoiling from the halting cacophony. I too—I hope successfully— forced delight into an expression that constantly sought to betray me, while surreptitiously examining my surroundings. (I cannot be certain of what passed, or did not pass, over George Arthur's features: in the nursery, certainly, he is not slow to display displeasure.)

The drawing-room is lofty and more than usually spacious, with pleasant recesses, and french windows curving along a single wall. Two smaller windows flank the fireplace, which is of white marble that reflects, both in colour and in the pattern of its carving, the white plasterwork of the ceiling. Walls are of an apricot shade, crowded with landscape scenes and portraits of the Pulvertafts who belong to the past. Silks and velvets are mainly green; escritoires and occasional tables are cluttered with ornaments and porcelain pieces—too many for my own taste, but these are family heir-looms which it would be impolite to hide away. So Mrs Pulvertaft has explained, for the same degree of overcrowding obtains in the hall and dining-room, and on the day of my arrival she remarked upon it.

'*Most* charmingly rendered,' her husband pronounced when the music ceased. 'What fingers Adelaide is blessed with!'

Hands in the drawing-room were delicately clapped. Mr Pulver-taft applauded with his riding-crop. I pursed my lips at the back of George Arthur's head, for he was perhaps a little rumbustious in his response.

'Is not Adelaide talented, Miss Heddoe?' Mrs Pulvertaft sug-gested.

'Indeed, ma'am.'

Two maids, Cready and Brigid, brought in tea. I rose to go, imagining my visit to the drawing-room must surely now be con-cluded. But Mrs Pulvertaft begged me to remain.

'We must get to know you, Miss Heddoe,' she insisted in her bustling manner. (It is from his mother, I believe, that George Arthur inherits his occasional boisterousness.) 'And you,' she added, 'us.'

I felt, to tell the truth, that I knew the Pulvertafts fairly well already. I was not long here before I observed that families and events are often seen historically in Ireland—more so, for some reason, than in England. It surprised me when Mrs Pulvertaft went into details soon after I arrived, informing me that on the death of a distant relative Mr Pulvertaft had found himself the inheritor of this overseas estate. Though at first he had apparently resisted the move to another country, he ended by feeling it his bounden duty to accept the responsibility. 'It was a change of circumstances for us, I can tell you that,' Mrs Pulvertaft confessed. 'But had we remained in Ipswich these many acres would have continued to lose heart. There have been Pulvertafts here, you know, since Queen Elizabeth granted them the land.' I thought, but did not remark, that when Mr Pulvertaft first looked upon drawings of the house and gardens his unexpected inheritance must have seemed like a gift from heaven, which in a sense it was, for the distant relative had been by all accounts a good man.

'Much undergrowth has yet to be cleared and burnt,' Mr Pulvertaft was saying now, with reference to the estate road that was being built. 'The merry fires along the route will continue for a while to come. Next, stones must be chipped and laid, and by the lakeside the ground raised and strengthened. Here and there we must have ornamental seats.'

Cake was offered to us by Cready and by Brigid. It was not my place in the drawing-room to check the manners of George Arthur, but they do leave much to be desired. Old Miss Larvey, who was my predecessor and governess to all four children, had clearly become slack before her death. I smiled a little at George Arthur, and was unable to resist moving my fingers slightly in his direction, a gesture to indicate that a more delicate consuming of the cake would not be amiss. He pretended, mischievously, not to notice.

'Will the road go round Bright Purple Hill?' Emily inquired. 'It would be beautiful if it did.'

It could be made to do so, her father agreed. Yes, certainly it could go round the northern slopes at least. He would speak to Erskine.

'Now, what could be nicer,' he resumed, 'than a picnic of lunch by the lake, then a drive through the silver birches, another pause by the abbey, continuing by the river for a mile, and home by Bright Purple Hill? This road, Miss Heddoe, has become my pride.'

I smiled and nodded, acknowledging this attention in silence. I knew that there was more to the road than that: its construction was an act of charity, a way of employing the men for miles around, since the failure of their potato crops had again reduced them to poverty and idleness. In years to come the road would stand as a memorial to this awful time, and Mr Pulvertaft's magnanimity would be recalled with gratitude.

'Might copper beech trees mark the route?' suggested Adelaide, her dumpling countenance freshened by the excitement this thought induced. Her eyes bulged behind her spectacles and I noticed that her mother, in glancing at her, resisted the impulse to sigh.

'Beech trees indeed! Quite splendid!' enthused Mr Pulvertaft. 'And in future Pulvertaft generations they shall arch a roof, shading our road when need be. Yes, indeed there must be copper beech trees.'

The maids had left the drawing-room and returned now with lamps. They fastened the shutters and drew the curtains over. The velvets and silks changed colour in the lamplight, the faces of the portraits became as they truly were, the faces of ghosts.

A silence gathered after the talk of beech trees, and I found myself surprised at no one mentioning the wonder Fogarty had told me of, the marks of Christ on a peasant child. It seemed so strange and so remarkable, an occurrence of such import and magnitude, that I would hardly have believed it possible that any conversation could take place in the house without some astonished reference to it. Yet none had been made, and the faces and the voices in the drawing-room seemed as untouched by this visitation of the miraculous as they had been by Adelaide's labouring on the piano. In the silence I excused myself and left, taking George Arthur with me, for my time to do so had come.

October 23rd, 1847. I am homesick, I make no bones about it. I cannot help dwelling on all that I have left behind, on familiar sounds and places. First thing when I awake I still imagine I am in England: reality comes most harshly then.

While I write, Emily and George Arthur are conversing in a corner of the nursery. She has come here, as she does from time to time, to persuade him against a military career. I wish she would not do so in this manner, wandering in and standing by the window to await the end of a lesson. It is distracting for George Arthur, and after all this is my domain.

'What I mean, George Arthur, is that it is an uncomfortable life in a general sort of way.'

'Captain Coleborne does not seem uncomfortable. When you look at him he doesn't give that impression in the least.'

'Captain Coleborne hasn't lived in a barracks in India. That leaves a mark, so people say.'

'I should not mind a barracks. And India I should love.'

'I doubt it, actually. Flies carry disease in India, the water you drink is putrid. And you would mind a barracks because they're rough and ready places.'

'You'd drink something else if the water was putrid. You'd keep well away from the flies.'

'You cannot in India. No, George Arthur, I assure you you enjoy your creature comforts. You'd find the uniform rough on your skin and the food unappetizing. Besides, you have a family duty here.'

The nursery is a long, low-ceilinged room, with a fire at one end, close to which I sit as I write, for the weather has turned bitter. The big, square lessons-table occupies the centre of the room, and when Fogarty brings my tray he places it on the smaller table at which I'm writing now. There are pictures on the walls which I must say I find drab: one, in shades of brown, of St George and the Dragon; another of a tower; others of farmyard scenes. The nursery's two armchairs, occupied now by George Arthur and Emily, are at the other end with a rug between them. The floor is otherwise of polished board.

'Well, the truth is, George Arthur, I cannot bear the thought of your being killed.'

With that, Emily left the nursery. She smiled in her graceful manner at me, her head a little to one side, her dark, coiled hair gleaming for a moment in a shaft of afternoon sun. I had not thought a governess's position was difficult in a household, but somehow I am finding it so. I belong neither with the family nor the servants. Fogarty, in spite of calling me 'miss', addresses me more casually than he does the Pulvertafts; his sister is scarcely civil.

'Do they eat their babies, like in the South Seas?' George Arthur startled me by asking. He had crossed to where I sat and in a manner reminiscent of his father stood with his back to the fire, thereby blocking its warmth from me.

'Do who eat their babies, George Arthur?'

'The poor people.'

'Of course they don't.'

'But they are hungry. They have been hungry for ever so long. My mother and sisters give out soup at the back gate-lodge.'

'Hungry people do not eat their babies. And I think, you know, it's enemies, not babies, who are eaten in the South Seas.'

'But suppose a family's baby *did* die and suppose the family was hungry—'

'No, George Arthur, you must not talk like that.'

'Fogarty says he would not be surprised.'

'Well, she has settled down, I think,' Mrs Pulvertaft remarks to her husband in their bedroom, and when he asks her whom she refers to she says the governess.

'Pleasant enough, she seems,' he replies. 'I do prefer, you know, an English governess.'

'Oh yes, indeed.'

George Arthur's sisters have developed no thoughts about Miss Heddoe. They neither like nor dislike her; they do not know her; their days of assessing governesses are over.

But George Arthur's aren't. She is not as pretty as Emily or Charlotte, George Arthur considers, and she is very serious. When she smiles her smile is serious. The way she eats her food is serious, carefully cutting everything, carefully and slowly chewing. Often he comes into the nursery to find her eating from the tray that Fogarty carries up the back staircase for her, sitting all alone on one side of the fireplace, seeming very serious indeed. Miss Larvey had been different somehow, although she'd eaten her meals in much the same position, seated at the very same table, by the fire. Miss Larvey was untidy, her grey hair often working loose from its coils, her whole face untidy sometimes, her tray untidily left.

'Now it is transcription time,' Miss Heddoe says, interrupting these reflections. 'Carefully and slowly, please.'

Fogarty thinks about the governess, but hides such thoughts from his sister. Miss Heddoe will surely make a scene, exclaiming and protesting, saying to the Pulvertafts all the things a butler cannot. She will stand in the drawing-room or the hall, smacking out the truth at them, putting in a nutshell all that must be said. She will bring up the matter of the stigmata found on the child, and the useless folly of the road, and the wisdom of old Hugh Pulvertaft. She will be the voice of reason. Fogarty dwells upon these thoughts while conversing with his sister, adept at dividing his mind. His faith is in the governess.

'Declare to God,' remarks Miss Fogarty, 'Brigid'll be the death of me. Did you ever know a stupider girl?'

'There was a girl we had once who was stupider,' Fogarty replies. 'Fidelma was she called?'

They sit at the wide wooden table that is the pivot of kitchen activities. The preparation of food, the polishing of brass and silver, the stacking of dishes, the disposal of remains, the eating and drinking, all card-playing and ironing, all cutting out of patterns and cloth, the trimming of lamps: the table has as many uses as the people of the kitchen can devise. Tears have soaked into its grain, and blood from meat and accidents; the grease of generations polishes it, not quite scrubbed out by the efforts made, twice every day, with soap and water.

The Fogartys sit with their chairs turned a little away from the table, so that they partly face the range and in anticipation of the benefit they will shortly receive from the glow of dampened slack. It is their early evening pose, daily the same from October to May. In summer the sunlight penetrates to the kitchen in a way that at first seems alien but later is welcomed. It spreads over the surface of the table, drying it out. It warms the Fogartys, who move their chairs to catch its rays when they rest in the early evening.

'You would not credit,' remarks Miss Fogarty, 'that Brigid has been three years in this kitchen. More like three seconds.'

'There are some that are untrainable.' His teeth are less well preserved than his sister's. She is the thinner of the two, razorlike in face and figure.

'I said at the time I would prefer a man. A man is more trainable in my opinion. A man would be more use to yourself.'

'Ah, Cready knows the dining-room by now. I wouldn't want a change made there.'

'It's Cready we have to thank for Brigid. Wasn't it Cready who had you blackguarded until you took her on?'

'We had to take someone. To give Cready her due she said we'd find her slow.'

'I'll tell you this: Cready's no racehorse herself.'

'The slowness is in that family.'

'Whatever He did He forgot to put brains in them.'

'We live with His mistakes.'

Miss Fogarty frowns. She does not care for that remark. Her

brother is sometimes indiscreet in his speech. It is his nature, it is part of his cleverness; but whenever she feels uneasy she draws his attention to the source of her uneasiness, as she does now. It is a dangerous remark, she says, better it had not been made.

Fogarty nods, knowing the nod will soothe her. He has no wish to have her flurried.

'The road is going great guns,' he says, deeming a change of subject wise. 'They were on about it in the dining-room.'

'Did they mention the ground rice pudding?'

'They ate it. Isn't it extraordinary, a road that goes round in a circle, not leading anywhere?'

'Heddoe left her ground rice. A pudding's good enough for the dining-room but not for Madam.'

'Was there an egg in it? Her stomach can't accept eggs.'

'Don't I know the woman can't take eggs? Isn't she on about it the entire time? There were four good turkey eggs in that pudding, and what harm did a turkey egg do anyone? Did eggs harm Larvey?'

'Oh true enough, Larvey ate anything. If you'd took a gate off its hinges she'd have ate it while you'd wink.'

'Larvey was a saint from heaven.'

Again Fogarty nods. In his wish not to cause flurry in his sister he refrains from saying that once upon a time Miss Larvey had been condemned as roundly as Miss Heddoe is now. When she'd been cold in her room she'd sent down to the kitchen for hot-water jars, a request that had not been popular. But when she died, as if to compensate for all this troublesomeness, Miss Larvey left the Fogartys a remembrance in her will.

'A while back I told Heddoe about that child. To see what she'd say for herself.'

Miss Fogarty's peaked face registers interest. Her eyes have narrowed into the slits that all his life have reminded Fogarty of cracks in a plate or a teacup.

'And what did the woman say?'

'She was struck silent, then she asked me questions. After that she told me an extraordinary thing: the Legend of the True Cross.'

As Fogarty speaks, the two maids enter the kitchen. Miss Fogarty regards them with asperity, telling Brigid she looks disgraceful and Cready that her cap is dirty. 'Get down to your work,' she snappishly commands. 'Brigid, push that kettle over the heat and stir a saucepan of milk for me.'

She is badly out of sorts because of Heddoe and the ground rice, Fogarty says to himself, and thinks to ease the atmosphere by relating the legend the governess has told him.

'Listen to me, girls,' he says, 'while I tell you the Legend of the True Cross.'

Cready, who is not a girl, appreciates the euphemism and displays appropriate pleasure as she sets to at the sink, washing parsnips. She is a woman of sixty-one, carelessly stout. Brigid, distantly related to her and thirty or so years younger, is of the same proportions.

'The Legend of the True Cross,' says Fogarty, 'has to do with a seed falling into Adam's mouth, some say his ear. It lay there until he died, and when the body decomposed a tree grew from the seed, which in time was felled to give timber for the beams of a bridge.'

'Well, I never heard that,' exclaims Cready in a loud, shrill voice, so fascinated by the revelation that she cannot continue with the parsnips.

'The Queen of Sheba crossed that bridge in her majesty. Later —well, you can guess—the Cross to which Our Lord was fastened was constructed from those very beams.'

'Is it true, Mr Fogarty?' cries Cready, her voice becoming still shriller in her excitement, her mouth hanging open.

'Control yourself, Cready,' Miss Fogarty admonishes her. 'You look ridiculous.'

'It's only I was never told it before, miss. I never knew the Cross grew out of Adam's ear. Did ever you hear it, Brigid?'

'I did not.'

'It's a legend,' Fogarty explains. 'It illustrates the truth. It does not tell it, Miss Fogarty and myself would say. Your own religion might take it differently.'

'Don't you live and learn?' says Cready.

There is a silence for some moments in the kitchen. Then Brigid, stirring the saucepan of milk on the range as Miss Fogarty has instructed her, says:

'I wonder does Father Horan know that?'

'God, I'd say he would all right.' Cready wags her head, lending emphasis to this opinion. There isn't much relating to theological matters that eludes Father Horan, she says.

'Oh, right enough,' agrees Fogarty. 'The priests will run this country yet. If it's not one crowd it's another.' He explains to the maids that the Legend of the True Cross has come into the house by way of the governess. It is a typical thing, he says, that a Protestant Englishwoman would pass the like of that on. Old Hugh wouldn't have considered it suitable; and the present Pulvertafts have been long enough away from England to consider it unsuitable also. He'd guess they have anyway; he'd consider that true.

Miss Fogarty, still idle in her chair by the range, nods her agreement. She states that, legend or not, she does not care for stuff like that. In lower tones, and privately to her brother, she says she is surprised that he repeated it.

'It's of interest to the girls,' he apologizes. 'To tell the truth, you could have knocked me down when she told me in the nursery.'

'The boulders from the ridge may be used for walls and chipping?' inquires Mr Pulvertaft of his estate manager.

'It is a distance to carry boulders, sir.'

'So it is, but we must continue to occupy these men, Erskine. Time is standing still for them.'

'Yes, sir.'

The two men pace together on a lawn in front of the house, walking from one circular rose-bed to the next, then turning and reversing the procedure. It is here that Mr Pulvertaft likes to discuss the estate with Erskine, strolling on the short grass in the mid-morning. When it rains or is too bitterly cold they converse instead in the great open porch of the house, both of them gazing out into the garden. The eyes of Mr Pulvertaft and Erksine never meet, as if by unspoken agreement. Mr Pulvertaft, though speaking warmly of Erskine's virtues, fears him; and Erskine does not trust his eye to meet his master's in case that conjunction, however brief, should reveal too much. Mr Pulvertaft has been a painless inheritor, in Erskine's view; his life has been without hardship, he takes too easily for granted the good fortune that came his way.

'The road,' he is saying now, seeming to Erskine to make his point for him, 'is our generation's contribution to the estate. You understand me, Erskine? A Pulvertaft planted Abbey Wood, another laid out these gardens. Swift came here, did you know that, Erskine? The Mad Dean assisted in the planning of all these lawns and shrubberies.'

'So you told me, sir.'

It is Erskine's left arm that is missing but he considers the loss as serious as if it had been his right. He is an Englishman, stoutly made and once of renowned strength, still in his middle age. His temper is short, his disposition unsentimental, his soldier's manner abrupt; nor is there, beneath that vigorous exterior, a gentler core. Leading nowhere, without a real purpose, the estate road is unnecessary and absurd, but he accepts his part in its creation. It is ill fortune that people have starved because a law of nature has failed them, it is ill fortune that he has lost a limb and seen a military career destroyed: all that must be accepted also. To be the manager of an estate of such size and importance is hardly recompense for the glories that might have been. He has ended up in a country that is not his own, employing men whose speech he at first found difficult to understand, collecting rents from tenants he does not trust, as he feels he might trust the people of Worcestershire or Durham. The Pulvertaft family—with the exception of Mr Pulvertaft himself—rarely seek to hold with him any kind of conversation beyond the formalities of greeting and leave-taking. Stoically he occupies his position, ashamed because he is a one-armed man, yet never indulging in melancholy, for this he would condemn as weakness.

'There is something concerning the men, sir.'

'Poor fellows, there is indeed.'

'Something other, sir. They have turned ungrateful, sir.'

'Ungrateful?'

'As well to keep an eye open for disaffection, sir.'

'Good God, those men are hardly fit for that.'

'They bite the hand that feeds them, sir. They're reared on it.'

He speaks in a matter-of-fact voice. It is the truth as he recognizes it; he sees no point in dissembling for politeness' sake. He watches while Mr Pulvertaft nods his reluctant agreement. He does not need to remind himself that this is a landowner who would have his estate a realm of heaven, who would have his family and his servants, his tenants and all who work for him, angels of goodness. This is a landowner who expects his own generosity of spirit to beget such generosity in others, his unstinted patronage to find a reflection in unstinted gratitude. But reality, as Erskine daily experiences, keeps shattering the dream, and may shatter it irrevocably in the end.

They speak of other matters, of immediate practicalities. Expert and informed on all the subjects raised, Erskine gives the conversation only part of his attention, devoting the greater part to the recently arrived governess. He has examined her in church on the four occasions there have been since she joined the household. Twenty-five or -six years old, he reckons, not pretty yet not as plain as the plain one among the Pulvertaft girls. Hair too severely done, features too nervous, clothes too dowdy; but all that might be altered. The hands that hold the hymn book open before her are pale as marble, the fingers slender; the lips that open and close have a hint of voluptuousness kept in check; the breast that rises and falls has caused him, once or twice, briefly to close his eyes. He would marry her if she would have him, and why should she not, despite the absence of an arm? As the estate manager's wife she would have a more significant life than as a governess for ever.

'Well, I must not detain you longer,' Mr Pulvertaft says. 'The men are simple people, remember, rough in their ways. They may find gratitude difficult and, you know, I do not expect it. I only wish to do what can be done.'

Erskine, who intends to permit no nonsense, does not say so. He strides off to where his horse is tethered in the paddocks, wondering again about the governess.

Stout and round, Mrs Pulvertaft lies on her bed with her eyes closed. She feels a familiar discomfort low down in her stomach, on the left side, a touch of indigestion. It is very slight, something she has become used to, arriving as it does every day in the afternoon and then going away.

Charlotte will accept Captain Coleborne; Adelaide will not marry; Emily wishes to travel. Perhaps if she travels she will meet someone suitable; she is most particular. Mrs Pulvertaft cannot understand her eldest daughter's desire to visit France and Austria and Italy. They are dangerous places, where war is waged when offence is taken. Only England is not like that: dear, safe, uncomplicated England, thinks Mrs Pulvertaft, and for a moment is nostalgic.

The afternoon discomfort departs from her stomach, but she does not notice because gradually it has become scarcely anything at all. George Arthur must learn the ways of the estate so that he can sensibly inherit when his own time comes. Emily is right: it would be far better if he did not seek a commission. After all, except to satisfy his romantic inclination, there is no need.

Mrs Pulvertaft sighs. She hopes Charlotte will be sensible. An officer's wife commands a considerable position when allied with means, and she has been assured that Captain Coleborne's family, established for generations in Meath, leave nothing whatsoever to be desired socially. It is most unlikely that Charlotte will be silly since everything between her and Captain Coleborne appears to be going swimmingly, but then you never know: girls, being girls, are naturally inexperienced.

Mrs Pulvertaft dozes, and wakes a moment later. The faces of the women who beg on Sundays have haunted a brief dream. She has heard the chiming of the church bell and in some confused way the Reverend Poole's cherub face was among the women's, his surplice flapping in the wind. She stepped from the carriage and went towards the church. 'Give something to the beggars,' her husband's voice commanded, as it does every Sunday while the bell still rings. The bell ceases only when the family are in their pew, with Mr Erskine in the Pulvertaft pew behind them and the Fogartys and Miss Heddoe in the estate pew in the south transept.

It is nobody's fault, Mrs Pulvertaft reflects, that for the second season the potatoes have rotted in the ground. No one can be blamed. It is a horror that so many families have died, that so many bloated, poisoned bodies are piled into the shared graves. But what more can be done than is already being done? Soup is given away in the yard of the gate-lodge; the estate road gives work; the Distress Board is greatly pleased. Just and sensible laws prevent the wholesale distribution of corn, for to flood the country with corn would have consequences as disastrous as the hunger itself: that has been explained to her. Every Sunday, led by the Reverend Poole, they repeat the prayer that takes precedence over all other prayers: that God's love should extend to the hungry at this time, that His wrath may be lifted.

Again Mrs Pulvertaft drifts into a doze. She dreams that she runs through unfamiliar landscape, although she has not run anywhere for many years. There are sand dunes and a flat expanse which is empty, except for tiny white shells, crackling beneath her feet. She seems to be naked, which is alarming, and worries her in her dream. Then everything changes and she is in the drawing-room, listening to Adelaide playing her pieces. Tea is brought in, and there is ordinary conversation.

Emily, alone, walks among the abbey ruins on the lake-shore. It is her favourite place. She imagines the chanting of the monks once upon a time and the simple life they led, transcribing Latin and worshipping God. They built where the landscape was beautiful; their view of Bright Purple Hill had been perfect.

There is a stillness among the ruins, the air is mild for late October. The monks would have fished from the shore, they would have cultivated a garden and induced bees to make honey for them. For many generations they would have buried their dead here, but their graveyards have been lost in the time that has passed.

Evening sun bronzes the heathery purple of the hill. In the spring, Emily reflects, she will begin her journeys. She will stay with her Aunt Margaret in Bath and her Aunt Tabby in Ipswich. Already she has persuaded her Aunt Margaret that it would be beneficial to both of them to visit Florence, and Vienna and Paris. She has persuaded her father that the expense of all the journeys would be money profitably spent, an education that would extend the education he has expended money on already. Emily believes this to be true; she is not prevaricating. She believes that after she has seen again the architecture of England—which she can scarcely remember—and visited the great cities of Europe, some anxious spirit within her will be assuaged. She will return to Ireland and accept a husband, as Charlotte is about to do; or not accept a husband and be content to live her life in her brother's house, as Adelaide's fate seems certainly to be. She will bear children; or walk among the abbey ruins a spinster, composing verse about the ancient times and the monks who fished in the lake.

A bird swoops over the water and comes to rest on the pebbled shore, not far from where Emily stands. It rises on spindly legs, stretches out its wings and pecks at itself. Then it staggers uncomfortably on the pebbles before settling into an attitude that pleases it, head drawn into its body, wings wrapped around like a cloak. Such creatures would not have changed since the time of the monks, and Emily imagines a cowled and roughly bearded figure admiring the bird from a window of the once gracious abbey. He whispers as he does so and Emily remembers enough from her lessons with Miss Larvey to know that the language he speaks is not known to her.

It is a pleasant fancy, one for verse or drawing, to be stored away and one day in the future dwelt upon, and in one way or the other transcribed to paper. She turns her back on the lake and walks slowly through the ruins, past the posts which mark the route of the estate road, by the birchwood and over the stone bridge where Jonathan Swift is said to have stood and ordered the felling of three elms that obscured the panorama which has the great house as its centre. In the far distance she can see the line of men labouring on the road, and the figure of Erskine on his horse. She passes on, following a track that is familiar to her, which skirts the estate beneath its high boundary wall. Beyond the wall lie the Pulvertaft acres of farmland, but they have no interest for Emily, being for the most part flat, a territory that is tediously passed over every Sunday on the journey to and from church.

She reaches the yard of a gate-lodge and speaks to the woman who lives there, reminding her that soup and bread will be brought again tomorrow, that the utensils left last week must be ready by eleven o'clock on the trestle tables. Everything will be waiting, the woman promises, and a high fire alight in the kitchen.

October 31st, 1847. Fogarty told me. He stood beside me while I ate my dinner by the fire: stew and rice, with cabbage; a baked apple, and sago pudding. The child with the stigmata has died and been buried.

'And who will know now,' he questioned, himself as much as me, 'exactly what was what?'

There is a kind of cunning in Fogarty's nutlike face. The eyes narrow, and the lips narrow, and he then looks like his sister. But he is more intelligent, I would say.

'And what *is* what, Mr Fogarty?' I inquired.

'The people are edgy, miss. At the soup canteen they are edgy, I'm to understand. And likewise on the road. There is a feeling among them that the child should not have died. It is unpleasant superstition, of course, but there is a feeling that Our Lord has been crucified again.'

'But that's ridiculous!'

'I am saying so, miss. Coolly ridiculous, everything back to front. The trouble is that starvation causes a lightness in the head.'

'Do the Pulvertafts know of this? No one but you has mentioned this child to me.'

'I heard the matter mentioned at the dinner table. Mr Pulvertaft said that Mr Erskine had passed on to him the news that there was some superstition about. "D'you know its nature, Fogarty?" Mr Pulvertaft said, and I replied that it was to do with the marks of Our Lord's stigmata being noticed on the feet and hands of a child.'

'And what did anyone say then?'

' "Well, what's the secret of it, Fogarty?" Mr Pulvertaft said, and I passed on to him the opinion of Miss Fogarty and myself: that the markings were inflicted at the time of birth. They had all of them reached that conclusion also: Mrs Pulvertaft and Miss Emily and Miss Charlotte and Miss Adelaide, even Master George Arthur, no doubt, although he was not present then. As soon as ever they heard the news they had come to that assumption. Same with Mr Erskine.'

I stared, astonished, at the butler. I could not believe what he was telling me: that all these people had independently dismissed, so calmly and so finally, what the people who were closer to the event took to be a miracle. I had known, from the manner in which Fogarty spoke after his introduction of the subject, that he was in some way dubious. But I had concluded that he doubted the existence of the marks, that he doubted the reliability of the priest. I had never seen Father Horan, so did not know what kind of man he was even in appearance, or what age. Fogarty had told me he'd never seen him either, but from what he gathered through the maids the priest was of advanced years. Fogarty said now:

'My sister and I only decided that that was the truth of it after Cready and Brigid had gone on about the thing for a long time, how the priest was giving out sermons on it, how the bishop had come on a special journey and how a letter had been sent to Rome. Our first view was that the old priest had been presented with the child after he'd had a good couple of glasses. And then oiled up again and shown the child a second time. He's half blind, I've heard it said, and if enough people raved over marks that didn't exist, sure wouldn't he agree instead of admitting he was drunk and couldn't see properly? But as soon as Miss Fogarty and myself heard that the bishop had stirred his stumps and a letter had gone to Rome we realized the affair was wearing a different pair of shoes. They're as wily as cockroaches, these old priests, and there isn't one among them who'd run a chance of showing himself up by giving out sermons and summoning his bishop. He'd have let the matter rest, he'd have kept it local if he was flummoxed. "No doubt at all," Miss Fogarty said. "They've put marks on the baby." '

I couldn't eat. I shivered even though I was warm from the fire. I found it difficult to speak, but in the end I said:

'But why on earth would this cruel and blasphemous thing be done? Surely it could have been real, truly there, as stigmata have occurred in the past?'

'I would doubt that, miss. And hunger would give cruelty and blasphemy a different look. That's all I'd say. Seven other children have been buried in that family, and the two sets of grandparents. There was only the father and the mother with the baby left. "Sure didn't they see the way things was turning?" was how Miss Fogarty put it. "Didn't they see an RIP all ready for them, and wouldn't they be a holy family with the baby the way they'd made it, and wouldn't they be sure of preservation because of it?" '

In his dark butler's clothes, the excitement that enlivened his small face lending him a faintly sinister look, Fogarty smiled at me. The smile was grisly; I did not forgive it, and from that moment I liked the butler as little as I liked his sister. His smile, revealing sharp, discoloured teeth, was related to the tragedy of a peasant family that had been almost extinguished, as, one by one, lamps are in a house at night. It was related to the desperation of survival, to an act so barbarous that one could not pass it by.

'A nine days' wonder,' Fogarty said. 'I'd say it wasn't a bad thing the child was buried. Imagine walking round with a lie like that on you for all your mortal days.'

He took the tray and went away. I heard him in the lavatory off the nursery landing, depositing the food I hadn't eaten down the

WC so that he wouldn't have to listen to his sister's abuse of me. I sat until the fire sank low, without the heart to put more coal on it even though the coal was there. I kept seeing that faceless couple and their just-born child, the woman exhausted, in pain, tormented by hunger, with no milk to give her baby. Had they touched the tiny feet and hands with a hot coal? Had they torn the skin open, as Christ's had been on the Cross? Had either of them in that moment been even faintly sane? I saw the old priest, gazing in wonder at what they later showed him. I saw the Pulvertafts in their dining-room, accepting what had occurred as part of their existence in this house. Must not life go on lest all life cease? A confusion ran wildly in my head, a jumble without a pattern, all sense befogged. In a civilized manner nobody protested at the cacophony in the drawing-room when the piano was played, and nobody spoke to me of the stigmata because the subject was too terrible for conversation.

I wept before I went to bed. I wept again when I lay there, hating more than ever the place I am in, where people are driven back to savagery.

'The men have not arrived this morning,' Erskine reports. 'I suspected they might not from their demeanour last evening. They attach some omen to this death.'

'But surely to heavens they see the whole thing was a fraud?'

'They do not think so, sir. Any more than they believe that the worship of the Virgin Mary is a fraud perpetrated by the priests. Or that the Body and the Blood is. Fraud is grist to their mill.'

Mr Pulvertaft thanks Erskine for reporting the development to him. The men will return to their senses in time, the estate manager assures him. What has happened is only a little thing. Hunger is the master.

Emily packs for her travels, and vows she will not forget the lake, or the shadows and echoes of the monks. In Bath and Florence, in Vienna and Paris she will keep faith with her special corner, where the spirit of a gentler age lingers.

Mrs Pulvertaft dreams that the Reverend Poole ascends to the pulpit with a bath towel over his shoulder. From this day forth we must all carry bath towels wherever we go, and the feet of Jesus must be dried as well as washed. 'And the woman anointed the feet,' proclaims the Reverend Poole, 'and Jesus thanked her and blessed her and went upon his way.' But Mrs Pulvertaft is unhappy because she does not know which of the men is Jesus. They work with shovels on the estate road, and when she asks them they tell her, in a most unlikely manner, to go away.

Alone in front of the drawing-room piano, Adelaide sits stiffly upright, not wishing to play because she is not in the mood. Again, only minutes ago, Captain Coleborne has not noticed her. He did not notice her at lunch; he did not address a single word to her, he evaded her glance as if he could not bear to catch it. Charlotte thinks him dull; she has said so, yet she never spurns his attentions. And he isn't dull. His handsome face, surmounting his sturdily handsome body, twinkles with vigour and with life. He has done so much and when he talks about the places he has been he is so interesting she could listen to him for ages.

Adelaide's spectacles have misted. She takes them off and wipes them with her handkerchief. She must not go red when he comes again, or when his name is mentioned. Going red will give away her secret and Emily and Charlotte will guess and feel sorry for her, which she could not bear.

'Very well,' Charlotte says by the sundial in the fuchsia garden.

Captain Coleborne blinks his eyes in an ecstasy of delight, and Charlotte thinks that yes, it probably will be nice, knowing devotion like this for ever.

'Heddoe's gone broody,' Fogarty reports in the kitchen.

'Not sickness in the house! One thing you could say about Larvey, she was never sick for an hour.'

'I think Heddoe'll maybe leave.' Fogarty speaks with satisfaction. The governess might leave because she finds it too much that such a thing should happen to a baby, and that her employers do not remark on it because they expect no better of these people. Erskine might be knocked from his horse by the men in a fit of anger because the death has not been honoured in the house or by the family. Erskine might lie dead himself on the day of the governess's departure, and the two events, combining, would cause these Pulvertafts of Ipswich to see the error of their ways and return to their native land.

The china rattles on the tea-trays which the maids carry to the draining boards, and Fogarty lights the lamps which he has arrayed on the table, as he does every afternoon at this time in winter. He inspects each flame before satisfying himself that the trimming of the wick is precisely right, then one after another places the glasses in their brass supports and finally adjusts each light.

The maids unburden the trays at the sink, Miss Fogarty places a damp cloth around a fruitcake and lays aside sandwiches and scones, later to be eaten in the kitchen. Then the maids take the lamps that are ready and begin another journey through the house.

In the nursery Miss Heddoe reads from the history book Miss Larvey has used before her: 'In this manner the monasteries were lawfully dissolved, for the King believed they harboured vile and treacherous plots and were the breeding grounds for future disaffection. The King was privy, through counsellors and advisers, of the vengeance that was daily planned, but was wise and bade his time.'

George Arthur does not listen. He is thinking about the savages of the South Sea islands who eat their enemies. He has always thought it was their babies they ate, and wonders if he has misunderstood something Miss Larvey said on the subject. He wonders then if Emily could possibly be right in what she says about the discomfort of the regimental life. It is true that he enjoys being close to the fire, and likes the cosiness of the nursery in the evenings;

and it is true that he doesn't much care for rough material next to his skin. He knows that in spite of what Emily says officers like Captain Coleborne would not be made to drink putrid water, and that flies can't kill you, but the real thing is that he is expected to stay here because he is the only son, because somebody will have to look after the place when his father isn't able to any more. 'Duty', Emily says, and it is that in the end that will steal from him his dream of military glory. Itchy and uneasy, like the bite of an insect, this duty already nags him.

January 12th, 1848. Today it snowed. The fall began after breakfast and continued until it was almost dark. Great drifts have piled up in the garden, and from my window the scene is beautiful. George Arthur has a cold and so remained in bed; he is too feverish for lessons.

January 18th, 1848. The snow is high on the ground. In the garden we break the ice on pools and urns so that the birds may drink. Scraps are thrown out of the scullery doors for them.

February 4th, 1848. It is five months since I arrived here, and all that I have learnt is distressing. There is nothing that is not so. Last night I could not sleep again. I lay there thinking of the starvation, of the faces of the silent women when they come to the gate-lodge for food. There is a yellow-greyness in the flesh of their faces, they are themselves like obedient animals. Their babies die when they feed them grass and roots; in their arms at the gate-lodge the babies who survive are silent also, too weak to cry until the sustenance they receive revives them. Last night I lay thinking of the men who are turned away from the work on the road because they have not the strength that is necessary. I thought of the darkness in the cottages, of dawn bringing with it the glaring eyes of death. I thought of the graves again clawed open, the earth still loose, another carcass pushed on to the rotting heap. I thought of an infant tortured with Our Saviour's wounds.

The famine-fever descends like a rain of further retribution, and I wonder—for I cannot help it—what in His name these people have done to displease God so? It is true they have not been an easy people to govern; they have not abided by the laws which the rest of us must observe; their superstitious worship is a sin. But God is a forgiving God. I pray to understand His will.

February 5th, 1848. Charlotte Pulvertaft is not to be married until her sister's return. 'Will you still be with us for the wedding?' Fogarty impertinently inquired last night, for he knows the age of George Arthur and unless I am dismissed I must of course still be here. The work continues on the road, it having been abandoned during the period of snow.

March 6th, 1848. A singular thing has happened. Walking alone in the grounds, I was hailed by Mr Erskine from his horse. I paused, and watched while he dismounted. I thought he had some message for me from the house, but in this I was wrong. Mr Erskine walked beside me, his horse ambling obediently behind. He spoke of the sunshine we were enjoying, and of the estate road. Beyond saluting me at church on Sundays he has never before paid me any attention whatsoever. My surprise must have shown in my face, for he laughed at something that was displayed there. 'I have always liked you, Miss Heddoe,' he said to my astonishment.

I reddened, as any girl would, and felt extremely awkward. I made no attempt at a reply.

'And have you settled, Miss Heddoe?' he next inquired. 'Do you care for it here?'

No one has asked me that before: why should they? My inclination was to smile and with vague politeness to nod. I did so, for to have said that I did not care for this place would have seemed ill-mannered and offensive. Mr Erskine, after all, is part of it.

'Well, that is good.' He paused and then resumed: 'If ever on your walks, Miss Heddoe, you pass near my house you would be welcome to stroll about the garden.'

I thanked him.

'It is the house at the southernmost point of the estate. The only large house there is, nearly hidden in summer by sycamore trees.'

'That is very kind of you, Mr Erskine.'

'I reclaimed the little garden, as the estate was reclaimed.'

'I see.'

The subject of conversation changed. We spoke again of the time of year and the progress that was being achieved on the estate road. Mr Erskine told me something of his history, how a military career had been cut short before it had properly begun. In return, and because the subjects seemed related, I passed on the ambition George Arthur had had in this direction.

'He is reconciled now,' I said, and soon after that the estate manager and I parted company, he riding back along the way we'd walked, I turning toward the house.

The estate road is completed on June 9th, 1848. Soon after that a letter arrives for Mr Pulvertaft from the Distress Board, thanking him for supplying so many months of work for the impoverished men. Since the beginning of the year the families of the area— some of them tenants of Mr Pulvertaft, some not—have been moving away to the harbour towns, to fill the exile ships bound for America. At least, Fogarty overhears Mr Pulvertaft remark in the dining-room, there is somewhere for them to go.

In August of that year there is champagne at Charlotte's wedding. Guests arrive from miles around. Emily, returned from her travels, is a bridesmaid.

At the celebrations, which take place in the hall and the drawing-room and the dining-room, and spill over into the garden, Fogarty watches Miss Heddoe, even though he is constantly busy. She wears a dress he has not seen before, in light-blue material, with lace at the collar and the wrists, and little pearl buttons. Wherever she is, she is in the company of George Arthur in his sailor suit. They whisper together and seem, as always nowadays, to be the best of friends. Occasionally Miss Heddoe chides him because an observation he has made oversteps the mark or is delivered indiscreetly. When Mr Erskine arrives he goes straight to where they are.

September 24th, 1848. I have been here a year. The potatoes are not good this year but at least the crop has not failed as completely as hitherto. I have not given Mr Erskine his answer, but he is kind and displays no impatience. I am very silly in the matter, I know I am, but sometimes I lie awake at night and pretend I am already his wife. I repeat the name and title; I say it aloud. I think of the house, hidden among the sycamores. I think of sitting with him in church, in the pew behind the Pulvertafts, not at the side with the Fogartys.

September 25th, 1848. A Mr Ogilvie comes regularly to take tea, and often strolls with Emily to the ruined abbey. Emily has made some drawings of it, which show it as it used to be. 'Well?' Mr Erskine said quietly this afternoon, riding up when I was out on my walk. But I begged, again, for more time to consider.

November 1st, 1848. All Saints' Day. Fogarty frightened me to-night. He leaned against the mantelpiece and said:

'I would advise you not to take the step you are considering, miss.'

'What step, Fogarty?'

'To marry or not to marry Mr Erskine.'

I was flabbergasted at this. I felt myself colouring and stammered when I spoke, asking him what he meant.

'I mean only what I say, miss. I would say to you not to marry him.'

'Are you drunk, Fogarty?'

'No, miss. I am not drunk. Or if I am it is only slight. You have been going through in your mind whether or not to marry Mr Erskine. A while ago you said you could never settle in this troubled place. You said that to yourself, miss. You could not become, as the saying goes, more Irish than the Irish.'

'Fogarty—'

'I thought you would go. When I told you about the child I thought you would pack your bags. There is wickedness here: I thought you sensed it, miss.'

'I cannot have you speaking to me like this, Fogarty.'

'Because I am a servant? Well, you are right, of course. In the evenings, miss, I have always indulged myself with port: that has always been my way. I have enjoyed our conversations, but I am disappointed now.'

'You have been reading my diary.'

'I have, miss. I have been reading your diary and your letters, and I have been observing you. Since they came here I have observed the Pulvertafts of Ipswich also, and Mr Erskine, who has done such wonders all around. I have watched his big square head going about its business; I have listened when I could.'

'You had no right to read what was private. If I mentioned this to Mr Pulvertaft—'

'If you did, miss, my sister and I would be sent packing. Mr Pulvertaft is a fair and decent man and it is only just that disloyal servants should be dismissed. But you would have it on your conscience. I had hoped we might keep a secret between us.'

'I have no wish to share secrets with you, Fogarty.'

'A blind eye was turned, miss, you know that. The hunger was a plague: what use a few spoonfuls of soup, and a road that leads nowhere and only insults the pride of the men who built it? The hunger might have been halted, miss, you know that. The people were allowed to die: you said that to yourself. A man and his wife were driven to commit a barbarous act of cruelty: blasphemy you called it, miss.'

'What I called it is my own affair. I should be grateful, Fogarty, if you left me now.'

'If the estate had continued in its honest decline, if these Pulvertafts had not arrived, the people outside the walls would have travelled here from miles around. They would have eaten the wild raspberries and the apples from the trees, the peaches that still thrived on the brick-lined walls, the grapes and plums and greengages, the blackberries and mulberries. They would have fished the lake and snared the rabbits on Bright Purple Hill. There is pheasant and woodcock grown tame in the old man's time. There was his little herd of cows they might have had. I am not putting forth an argument, miss; I am not a humanitarian; I am only telling you.'

'You are taking liberties, Fogarty. If you do not go now I will most certainly mention this.'

'That was the picture, miss, that might have been. Instead we had to hear of Charlotte's marrying and of Emily's travelling, and of George Arthur's brave decision to follow in the footsteps of his father. Adelaide sulks in the drawing-room and is jealous of her sisters. Mrs Pulvertaft, good soul, lies harmlessly down in the afternoon, and you have put it well in calling her husband a fair and decent man.'

'I did not call him that.'

'You thought it long before I said it.'

'You are drunker than you think, Fogarty.'

'No, miss, I am not. The wickedness here is not intentional, miss. Well, you know about the wickedness, for you have acutely sensed it. So did Mr Pulvertaft at first, so did his wife. Charlotte did not, nor Adelaide, nor did the boy. Emily sensed it until a while ago. Emily would linger down by the old abbey, knowing that the men who lie dead there have never been dispossessed by all the visitors and the strangers there have been since. But now the old abbey is a lady's folly, a pretty ruin that pleases and amuses. Well, of course you know all this.'

'I know nothing of the sort. I would ask you to leave me now.'

'You have thought it would be better for the boy to have his military life, to perish for Queen and empire, and so extinguish this line. Listening to talk of the boy's romance, you have thought that would not be bad. So many perish anyway, all about us.'

'That is a wicked thing to say,' I cried, made furious by this. 'And it is quite untrue.'

'It is wicked, miss, but not untrue. It is wicked because it comes from wickedness, you know that. Your sharp fresh eye has needled all that out.'

'I do not know these things.' My voice was quieter now, even, and empty of emotion. 'I would ask you to leave this room at once.'

But Fogarty went on talking until I thought in the end he must surely be insane. He spoke again of Charlotte's marriage to Captain Coleborne, of Emily and Adelaide, of George Arthur taking the place of his father. He spoke again of the hungry passing without hindrance through the gates of the estate, to feed off what its trees and bushes offered. He spoke of his sister and himself left after the old man's death, he glad to see the decay continue, his sister persuaded that they must always remain.

'The past would have withered away, miss. Instead of which it is the future that's withering now.'

Did he mean the hunger and the endless death, the exile ships of those who had survived? I did not ask him. He frightened me more than ever, standing there, his eyes as dead as ice. He was no humanitarian, he repeated, he was no scholar. All he said came from a feeling he had, a servant's feeling which he'd always had in this house during the years the old man had let everything decline. Poor Protestants as they were, he and his sister belonged neither outside the estate gates with the people who had starved nor with a family as renowned as the Pulvertafts. They were servants in their very bones.

'You have felt you have no place either, miss. You can see more clearly for that.'

'Please go, Fogarty.'

He told me of a dream he'd had the night before or last week, I was too upset to note which. The descendants of the people who had been hungry were in the dream, and the son of George Arthur Pulvertaft was shot in the hall of the house, and no Pulvertaft lived in the place again. The road that had been laid in charity was overgrown through neglect, and the gardens were as they had been at the time of old Hugh Pulvertaft, their beauty strangled as they returned to wildness. Fogarty's voice quivered as his rigmarole ridiculously rambled on; an institution for corrected girls the house became, without carpets on the floors. The bones of the dogs that generations of Pulvertafts had buried in the grounds were dug up by the corrected girls when they were ordered by a Mother Superior to make vegetable beds. They threw the bones about, pretending to be frightened by them, pretending they were the bones of people.

'I don't wish to hear your dreams, Fogarty.'

'I have told you only the one, miss. It is a single dream I had. The house of the estate manager was burnt to the ground, and people burnt with it. The stone walls of the estate were broken down, pulled apart in places by the ivy that was let grow. In a continuation of the dream I was standing here talking to you like I'm talking now. I said to you not to perpetuate what has troubled you.'

He took my tray from me and went away. A moment later I heard him in the lavatory, depositing the food I had not eaten.

'Not a bad soul,' Miss Fogarty remarks, 'when you come to know her.'

'Her father was a solicitor's clerk.'

'Oh granted, there's not a pennyworth of background to the creature. But I'd hardly say she wasn't good enough for Erskine.'

Fogarty does not comment. His sister resumes:

'I would expect to be invited to the house for late tea. I would expect her to say: "Why not walk over on Wednesday, Miss Fogarty, if you have a fancy for it?" I would expect the both of us to walk over for cards with the Erskines of an evening.'

'She has pulled herself up by marrying him. She is hardly going to drop down again by playing cards with servants.'

'Friends,' corrects Miss Fogarty. 'I would prefer to say friends.'

'When a bit of time goes by they'll dine with the Pulvertafts, she and Erskine. You'll cook the food at the range, I'll serve it at the table.'

'Oh, I hardly believe that'll be the order of it.'

Fogarty considers it unwise to pursue his argument and so is silent. Anna Maria Heddoe, he thinks, who was outraged when two guileful peasants tried on a trick. Well, he did his best. It is she, not he, who is the scholar and humanitarian. It is she, not he, who came from England and was distressed. She has wept into her pillow, she has been sick at heart. Stranger and visitor, she has written in her diary the news from Ireland. Stranger and visitor, she has learnt to live with things.

The Third Party

The two men met by arrangement in Buswell's Hotel. The time and place had been suggested by the man who was slightly the older of the two; his companion had agreed without seeking an adjustment. Half past eleven in the bar: 'I think we'll probably spot one another all right,' the older man had said. 'Well, she'll have told you what I look like.'

He was tall, acquiring bulkiness, a pinkish-brown sunburn darkening his face, fair curly hair that was turning grey. The man he met was thinner, with spectacles and a smooth black overcoat, a smaller man considerably. Lairdman this smaller man was called; the other's name was Boland. Both were in their early forties.

'Well, we're neither of us late,' Boland said in greeting, the more nervous of the two. 'Fergus Boland. How are you?'

They shook hands. Boland pulled out his wallet. 'I'll have a Jameson myself. What'll I get you?'

'Oh, only a mineral. This time of day, Fergus. A lemonade.'

'A Jameson and a lemonade,' Boland ordered.

'Sure,' the barman said.

They stood by the bar. Boland held out a packet of cigarettes. 'D'you smoke?'

Lairdman shook his head. He cocked an elbow on to the bar, arranging himself tidily. 'Sorry about this,' he said.

They were alone except for the barman, who set their two glasses in front of them. They weren't going to sit down; there was no move to do so. 'A pound and tenpence,' the barman said, and Boland paid him. Boland's clothes—tweed jacket and corduroy trousers—were wrinkled: he'd driven more than a hundred miles that morning.

'I mean I'm really sorry,' Lairdman went on, 'doing this to anyone.'

'Good luck.' Boland raised his glass. He had softened the colour of the whiskey by adding twice as much water. 'You never drink this early in the day, I suppose?' he said, constrainedly polite. 'Well, very wise. That's very sensible: I always say it.'

'I thought it mightn't be a drinking occasion.'

'I couldn't face you without a drink in, Lairdman.'

'I'm sorry about that.'

'You've lifted my wife off me. That isn't an everyday occurrence, you know.'

'I'm sorry—'

'It would be better if you didn't keep saying that.'

Lairdman, who was in the timber business, acknowledged the rebuke with a sideways wag of his head. The whole thing was awkward, he confessed, he hadn't slept a wink the night before.

'You're a Dubliner, she tells me,' Boland said, the same politeness to the fore. 'You make blockboard: there's money in that, no doubt about it.'

Lairdman was offended. She'd described her husband as clumsy but had added that he wouldn't hurt a fly. Already, five minutes into the difficult encounter, Lairdman wasn't so sure about that.

'I don't like Dublin,' Boland continued. 'I'll be frank about it. I never have. I'm a small-town man, but of course you'll know.'

He imagined his wife feeding her lover with information about his provincialism. She liked to tell people things; she talked a great deal. Boland had inherited a bakery in the town he had referred to, one that was quite unconnected with the more renowned Dublin bakery of the same name. A few years ago it had been suggested to him that he should consider retitling his, calling it Ideal Bread and Cakes, or Ovenfresh, in order to avoid confusion, but he saw no need for that, believing, indeed, that if a change should come about it should be made by the Dublin firm.

'I want to thank you,' Lairdman said, 'for taking this so well. Annabella has told me.'

'I doubt I have an option.'

Lairdman's lips were notably thin, his mouth a narrow streak that smiled without apparent effort. He smiled a little now, but shook his head to dispel any misconception: he was not gloating, he was not agreeing that his mistress's husband had no option. Boland was surprised that he didn't have a little chopped-off moustache, as so many Dublin men had.

'I thought when we met you might hit me,' Lairdman said. 'I remarked that to Annabella, but she said that wasn't you at all.'

'No, it isn't me.'

'That's what I mean by taking it well.'

'All I want to know is what you have in mind. She doesn't seem to know herself.'

'In mind?'

'I'm not protesting at your intentions where my wife is concerned, only asking if you're thinking of marrying her, only asking if you have some kind of programme. I mean, have you a place up here that's suitable for her? You're not a married man, I understand? I'll have another J.J.,' Boland called out to the barman.

'No, I'm not a married man. What we were hoping was that—if you're agreeable—Annabella could move herself into my place more or less at once. It's suitable accommodation all right, a seven-room flat in Wellington Road. But in time we'll get a house.'

'Thanks,' Boland said to the barman, paying him more money.

'That was my turn,' Lairdman protested, just a little late.

She wouldn't care for meanness, Boland thought. She'd notice when it began to impinge on her, which in time it would: these things never mattered at first.

'But marriage?' he said. 'It isn't easy, you know, to marry another man's wife in Ireland.'

'Annabella and I would naturally like to be married one day.'

'That's what I wanted to put to you. How are you suggesting that a divorce is fixed? You're not a Catholic, I'm to understand?'

'No.'

'No more am I. No more is Annabella. But that hardly matters, one way or another. She's very vague on divorce. We talked about it for a long time.'

'I appreciate that. And I appreciated your suggestion that we should meet.'

'I have grounds for divorce, Lairdman, but a damn bit of use they are to me. A divorce'll take an age.'

'It could be hurried up if you had an address in England. If the whole thing could be filed over there we'd be home and dry in no time.'

'But I haven't an address in England.'

'It's only a thought, Fergus.'

'So she wasn't exaggerating when she said you wanted to marry her?'

'I don't think I've ever known Annabella to exaggerate,' Lairdman replied stiffly.

Then you don't know the most important thing about her, Boland confidently reflected—that being that she can't help telling lies, which you and I would politely refer to as exaggerations. He believed that his wife actually disliked the truth, a rare enough attribute, he imagined, in any human being.

'I'm surprised you never got married,' he said, genuinely surprised because in his experience cocky little men like this very often had a glamorous woman in tow. He wondered if his wife's lover could possibly be a widower: naturally Annabella would not have been reliable about that.

'I've known your wife a long time,' Lairdman retorted softly, and Boland saw him trying not to let his smile show. 'As soon as I laid eyes on Annabella I knew she was the only woman who would make sense for me in marriage.'

Boland gazed into his whiskey. He had to be careful about what he said. If he became angry for a moment he was quite likely to ruin everything. The last thing he wanted was that the man should change his mind. He lit a cigarette, again offering the packet to Lairdman, who again shook his head. Conversationally, friendlily, Boland said:

'Lairdman's an interesting name—I thought that when she told me.'

'It's not Irish. Huguenot maybe, or part of it anyway.'

'I thought Jewish when she told me.'

'Oh, undoubtedly a hint of that.'

'You know the way you're interested when you're told about a relationship like that? "What's his name?" It's not important, it doesn't matter in the least. But still you ask it.'

'I'm sure. I appreciate that.'

When she'd said his name was Lairdman, Boland had remembered the name from his schooldays. Vaguely, he'd guessed that the man she was telling him about was a boy he couldn't quite place. But knowing the name, he'd recognized in Buswell's bar the adult features immediately.

' "Where did you meet him?" That doesn't matter either. And yet you ask it.'

'Annabella and I—'

'I know, I know.'

At school Lairdman had been notorious for an unexpected reason: his head had been held down a lavatory while his hair was scrubbed with a lavatory brush. Roche and Dead Smith had done it, the kind of thing they tended to do if they suspected uppitiness. Roche and Dead Smith were the bullies of their time, doling out admonitions to new boys who arrived at the school in the summer or winter terms rather than the autumn one, or to boys whose faces they found irritating. Lairdman's head had been scrubbed with the lavatory brush because he kept his hair tidy with perfumed oil that was offensive to Dead Smith.

'I think we were at school together,' Boland said.

Lairdman almost gave a jump, and it was Boland, this time, who disguised his smile. His wife would not have remembered the name of the school in question, not being in the least interested: the coincidence had clearly not been established.

'I don't recollect a Boland,' Lairdman said.

'I'd have been a little senior to yourself.' Deliberately, Boland sounded apologetic. 'But when she said your name I wondered. I was one of the boarders. Up from the country, you know. Terrible bloody place.'

Thirteen boarders there'd been, among nearly a hundred day boys. The day boys used to come noisily up the short, suburban avenue on their bicycles, and later ride noisily away. They were envied because they were returning to warmth and comfort and decent food, because after the weekends they'd talk about how they'd been to the Savoy or the Adelphi or even to the Crystal Ballroom. The boarders in winter would crouch around a radiator in one of the classrooms; in summer they'd walk in twos and threes around the playing-fields. The school matron, a Mrs Porter, was also the cook, but regularly burnt both the breakfast porridge and the barley soup she was given to producing as the main source of sustenance in the evening. An old boy of the school, occupying an attic at the top of a flight of uncarpeted stairs that led out of one of the dormitories, was the junior master, but he appeared to have acquired neither privilege nor distinction through that role: he, too, sat by the radiator in the classroom and dreaded the cooking of Mrs Porter. The bachelor headmaster, a boxer in his time—reputed to have been known in ringside circles as the Belted Earl, an obscurely acquired sobriquet that had remained with him—was a Savonarola-like figure in a green suit, sadistically inclined.

'Oh, I quite liked the place,' Lairdman said.

'You were a day boy.'

'I suppose it made a difference.'

'Of course it did.'

For the first time Boland felt annoyed. Not only was the man she'd become involved with mean, he was stupid as well. All this stuff about an address in England, all this stuff about giving up a seven-room flat, when if he had an iota of common sense he'd realize you didn't go buying houses for the likes of Annabella because in no way whatsoever could you rely on her doing what she said she was going to do.

'I've always thought, actually, it supplied a sound education,' Lairdman was saying.

The awful little Frenchman who couldn't make himself understood. O'Reilly-Flood, whose method of teaching history was to give the class the textbook to read while he wrote letters. The mathematics man who couldn't solve the problems he set. The Belted Earl in his foul laboratory, prodding at your ears with the sharp end of a tweezers until you cried out in pain.

'Oh, a great place,' Boland agreed. 'A fine academy.'

'We'd probably send our children there. If we have boys.'

'Your children?'

'You'd have no objection? Lord no, why should you? I'm sorry, that's a silly thing to say.'

'I'll have another,' Boland requested of the barman. 'How about your mineral?'

'No, I'm OK, thanks.'

This time he did not mention, even too late, that he should pay. Instead he looked away, as if wishing to dissociate himself from an over-indulgence in whiskey on an occasion such as this, before it was yet midday. Boland lit another cigarette. So she hadn't told him? She'd let this poor devil imagine that in no time at all the seven-room flat in Wellington Road wouldn't be spacious enough to contain the family that would naturally come trotting along once she'd rid herself of her provincial husband. Of course there'd have to be a divorce, and of course it would have to be hurried up: no one wanted a litter of little bastards in a seven-room flat or anywhere else.

'Good man, yourself,' he said to the barman when his whiskey came. If he ended up having too much to drink, as indeed might happen, he'd spend the night in the hotel rather than drive back. But it was early yet, and it was surprising what a heavy lunch could do.

'I'm sorry about that,' Lairdman repeated, referring again to his slip of the tongue. 'I wasn't thinking.'

'Ah, for heaven's sake, man!'

Boland briefly touched him, a reassuring tap on the shoulder. He could hear her telling him that the reason for their childless marriage had long ago been established. 'Poor old fellow,' she'd probably said, that being her kind of expression. She'd known before their marriage that she couldn't have children; in a quarrel long after it she'd confessed that she'd known and hadn't said.

'Naturally,' Lairdman blandly continued, 'we'd like to have a family.'

'You would of course.'

'I'm sorry that side of things didn't go right for you.'

'I was sorry myself.'

'The thing is, Fergus, is it OK about the divorce?'

'Are you saying I should agree to be the guilty party?'

'It's the done thing, as a matter of fact.'

'The done thing?'

'If you find it distasteful—'

'Not at all, of course not. I'll agree to be the guilty party and we'll work it out from there.'

'You're being great, Fergus.'

The way he was talking, Boland thought, he might have been drinking. There were people who became easy-going, who adopted that same kind of tone, even if they'd only been with someone else who was drinking: he'd often heard that but he'd never believed it. A sniff of someone else's glass, he'd heard, a vapour in the air.

'D'you remember the cokeman they used to have there? McArdle?'

'Where was that, Fergus?'

'At school.'

Lairdman shook his head. He didn't remember McArdle, he said. He doubted that he'd ever known anyone of that name. 'A cokeman?' he repeated. 'What kind of a cokeman? I don't think I know the word.'

'He looked after the furnace. We called him the cokeman.'

'I never knew that person at all.'

Other people came into the bar. A tall man in a gaberdine over-

coat who opened an *Irish Times* and was poured a glass of stout
without having to order it. An elderly woman and two men who
appeared to be her sons. A priest who looked around the bar and
went away again.

'You wouldn't have noticed McArdle because you weren't a
boarder,' Boland said. 'When you're weekends in a place you notice
more.'

'I'm sorry I don't remember you.'

'I wouldn't expect you to.'

She'd be imagining this conversation, Boland suddenly realized.
It was she who had suggested this bar for their meeting, speaking
as if she knew it and considered it suitable. 'I think I'll go up and
see Phyllis,' she used to say, saying it more often as time went by.
Phyllis was a friend she had in Terenure, whose own marriage had
ended on the rocks and who was suffering from an internal complaint besides. But of course Phyllis had just been a name she'd
used, a stalwart friend who would cover up for her if she needed
it. For all he knew, Phyllis might never have been married, her
internal system might be like iron. 'Phone me,' he used to say, and
obediently and agreeably his wife would. She'd tell him how Dublin
looked and how Phyllis was bearing up. No doubt she'd been sitting
on the edge of a bed in the seven-room flat in Wellington Road.

'It's really good of you to come all this way,' Lairdman said with
a hint of finality in his voice, an indication that quite soon now
the encounter should be brought to an end. 'I really appreciate it.
I'll ring Annabella this afternoon and tell her we know where we
stand. You won't mind that, Fergus?'

'Not at all.'

Boland had often interrupted such a telephone conversation. He
would walk into the hall and there she'd be, knees drawn up, on
the second step of the stairs, the receiver strung through the banisters. She'd be talking quite normally in her slightly high-pitched
voice, but when he stepped through the hall door she'd wave a
greeting and begin to whisper, the hand that had waved to him
now cupped around the mouthpiece. He'd often wondered what

she imagined he thought, or if she achieved some tremor of satisfaction from the hushed twilight of this semi-surreptitious carry-on. The trouble with Annabella was that sooner or later everything in the world bored her. 'Now, I want to hear,' she would soon be saying to Lairdman, 'every single thing since the moment you left the house.' And the poor man would begin a long history about catching a bus and passing through the entrance doors of his blockboard business, how he had said good morning to the typist and listened to the foreman's complaint concerning a reprehensible employee, how he'd eaten a doughnut with his eleven o'clock coffee, not as good a doughnut as he'd eaten the day before. Later, in a quarrel, she'd fling it all back at him: who on earth wanted to know about his doughnuts? she'd screech at him, her fingers splayed out in the air so that her freshly applied crimson nail varnish would evenly dry. She had a way of quarrelling when she was doing her nails, because she found the task irksome and needed some distraction. Yet she'd have felt half undressed if her fingernails weren't properly painted, or if her make-up wasn't right or her hair just as she wanted it.

'I'll be able to say,' Lairdman was stating with what appeared to be pride, 'that there wasn't an acrimonious word between us. She'll be pleased about that.'

Boland smiled, nodding agreeably. He couldn't imagine his wife being pleased since she so rarely was. He wondered what it was in Lairdman that attracted her. She'd said, when he'd asked her, that her lover was fun; he liked to go abroad, she'd said, he appreciated food and painting; he possessed what she called a 'devastating' sense of humour. She hadn't mentioned his sexual prowess, since it wasn't her habit to talk in that way. 'Will you be taking those cats?' Boland had inquired. 'I don't want them here.' Her lover would willingly supply a home for her Siamese cats, she had replied, both of which she called 'Ciao'. Boland wondered if his successor even knew of their existence.

'I wonder what became,' he said, 'of Roche and Dead Smith?'

He didn't know why he said it, why he couldn't have accepted that the business between them was over. He should have shaken hands with Lairdman and left it at that, perhaps saying there were no hard feelings. He would never have to see the man again; once in a while he would feel sorry for the memory of him.

'Dead Smith?' Lairdman said.

'Big eejit with a funny eye. There's a barrister called Roche now; I often wonder if that's the same fellow.'

'I don't think I remember either of them.'

'Roche used to go round in a pin-striped blue suit. He looked like one of the masters.'

Lairdman shook his head. 'I'll say cheerio, Fergus. Again, my gratitude.'

'They were the bright sparks who washed your hair in a lavatory bowl.'

Boland had said to himself over and over again that Lairdman was welcome to her. He looked ahead to an easy widower's life, the house she had filled with her perversities and falsehoods for the last twelve years as silent as a peaceful sleep. He would clear out the memories of her because naturally she wouldn't do that herself— the hoarded magazines, the empty medicine bottles, the clothes she had no further use for, the cosmetics she'd pitched into the corners of cupboards, the curtains and chair-covers clawed by her cats. He would get Molloy in to paint out the rooms. He would cook his own meals, and Mrs Coughlan would still come every morning. Mrs Coughlan wouldn't be exactly sorry to see the back of her, either.

'I don't know why,' Lairdman said, 'you keep going on about your schooldays.'

'Let me get you a decent drink before you go. Bring us two big ones,' he called out to the barman, who was listening to an anecdote the man in the gaberdine coat was retailing at the far end of the bar.

'No, really,' Lairdman protested. 'Really now.'

'Oh, go on, man. We're both in need of it.'

Lairdman had buttoned his black overcoat and drawn on a pair of black leather gloves. Finger by finger he drew one of the gloves off again. Boland could feel him thinking that, for the sake of the woman who loved him, he must humour the cuckold.

'It takes it out of you,' Boland said. 'An emotional thing like this. Good luck to you.'

They drank, Lairdman seeming awkward now because of what had been said. He looked a bit like a priest, Boland thought, the black attire and the way he wore it. He tried to imagine the pair of them abroad, sitting down together in a French restaurant, Lairdman being pernickety about a plate of food he didn't like the look of. It didn't make sense, all this stuff about a devastating sense of humour.

'I only mentioned the school,' Boland said, 'because it was the other thing we had in common.'

'As a matter of fact, I'm a governor up there now.'

'Ah, go on!'

'That's why I said we'd maybe send the children there.'

'Well, doesn't that beat the band!'

'I'm pleased myself. I'm pleased they asked me.'

'Sure, anyone would be.'

Stupid he might be, Boland thought, but he was cute as well, the way he'd managed not to make a comment on the Roche and Dead Smith business. Cuteness was the one thing you could never get away from in Dublin. Cute as weasels they were.

'You don't remember it?' he prompted.

'What's that?'

'The lavatory thing.'

'Look here, Boland—'

'I've offended you. I didn't mean that at all.'

'Of course you haven't offended me. It's just that I see no point in harping on things like that.'

'We'll talk of something else.'

'Actually, I'm a bit on the late side.'

The second glove was again drawn on, the buttons of the smooth black overcoat checked to see that all was well for the street. The glove was taken off again when Lairdman remembered there'd have to be a handshake.

'Thanks for everything,' he said.

For the second time, Boland surprised himself by being unable to leave well alone. He wondered if it was the whiskey; the long drive and then the whiskey on top of an empty stomach because of course there hadn't been anything in the house for his breakfast when he'd gone to look, not even a slice of bread. 'I'll come down and do you scrambled eggs and a few rashers,' she'd said the night before. 'You'll need something inside you before you set off.'

'I'm interested in what you say about sending your children there,' was what he heard himself saying. 'Would these be your and Annabella's children you have in mind?'

Lairdman looked at him as if he'd gone out of his senses. His narrow mouth gaped in bewilderment. Boland didn't know if he was trying to smile or if some kind of rictus had set in.

'What other children are there?' Lairdman shook his head, still perplexed. He held his hand out, but Boland did not take it.

'I thought those might be the children you had in mind,' he said.

'I don't follow what you're saying.'

'She can't have children, Lairdman.'

'Ah now, look here—'

'That's a medical fact. The unfortunate woman is incapable of mothering children.'

'I think you're drunk. One after another you've had. I thought it a moment ago when you got maudlin about your schooldays. Annabella's told me a thing or two, you know.'

'She hasn't told you about the cats she's going to spring on you. She hasn't told you she can't give birth. She hasn't told you she gets so bored her face turns white with fury. It's best not to be around then, Lairdman. Take my tip on that.'

'She's told me you can't stay sober. She's told me you've been warned off every racecourse in Ireland.'

'I don't go racing, Lairdman, and apart from occasions like this

I hardly drink at all. A lot less than our mutual friend, I can promise you that.'

'You have been unable to give Annabella children. She's sorry for you, she doesn't blame you.'

'Annabella was never sorry for anyone in her life.'

'Now look here, Boland—'

'Look nowhere, man. I've had twelve years of the woman. I'm obliging you by stepping aside. But there's no need for this talk of divorce, Lairdman, in England or anywhere else. I'm just telling you that. She'll come and live with you in your seven-room flat; she'll live in any house you care to buy, but if you wait till kingdom come you'll not find children trotting along. All you'll have is two Siamese cats clawing the skin off you.'

'You're being despicable, Boland.'

'I'm telling you the truth.'

'You seem to have forgotten that Annabella and myself have talked about all this. She knew you'd take it hard. She knew there'd be bitterness. Well, I understand that. I've said I'm sorry.'

'You're a mean little blockboard man, Lairdman. You belong with your head held down in a lavatory bowl. Were you wringing wet when they let go of you? I'd love to have seen it, Lairdman.'

'Will you keep your damn voice down? And will you stop trying to pick a quarrel? I came out this morning in good faith. I'm aware of the delicacy of the thing, and I'm not saying I've been a saint. But I'll not stand here and be insulted. And I'll not hear Annabella insulted.'

'I think Dead Smith became a vet.'

'I don't care what he became.'

Abruptly, Lairdman was gone. Boland didn't turn his head, or otherwise acknowledge his departure. He examined the row of bottles behind the bar, and in a moment he lit a fresh cigarette.

For half an hour he remained on his own where his usurper had left him. All he could think of was Lairdman as he remembered him, a boy who was pointed out because of what two bullies had done to him. The old cokeman, McArdle, used to laugh over the incident. Sometimes, when the classroom radiator wasn't hot enough, the boarders would go down to McArdle's cokehole and sit around his furnace. He'd tell them obscene stories, all of them to do with the matron and cook, or else he told them about Lairdman. The more Boland thought about it all the more clearly he remembered Lairdman: not much different in appearance, the same trap of a mouth, a propelling pencil and a fountain pen clipped into the pocket of his jacket. He had a bicycle, Boland could remember, a new one that had perhaps replaced an older one, a Golden Eagle. 'Oh, we met at a party Phyllis gave,' she had said, but there was no way of knowing how much truth there was in that, presumably none.

Boland ate his lunch in the dining-room of the hotel, among people he did not know, who gave the impression of lunching there regularly. He didn't have to say he'd take nothing to drink because the waitress didn't ask him. There was water in a glass jug on the table; he'd be all right for the journey home, he decided.

'The cod,' he ordered. 'Yes, I'll have the cod. And the cream of celery.'

He remembered a time when the thirteen boarders had smashed a window in an outhouse that no longer had a purpose. Most of the window-panes were broken already, the roof had long ago tumbled in, and one of the walls was so badly split that it had begun to disintegrate. It was forbidden for any boy to enter this small, crumbling building, and the boarders had not done so. They had stood twenty or so yards away throwing stones at the remaining window-panes, as they might have thrown stones at a cockshot. They had meant no harm, and did not realize that an outhouse which was so badly damaged already might be worthy of preservation. Ceremoniously the following morning the Belted Earl had taken his cane to them in the presence of the assembled day boys. Lairdman would have been watching, Boland reflected as he ate his soup: Lairdman might have brought it up just as he himself had brought up the other matter, but of course that wasn't Lairdman's way. Lairdman considered himself a sophisticate; even in the days of his Golden Eagle he would have considered himself that.

Boland crumbled the bread on his side plate, picking up bits of it between mouthfuls of soup. He saw himself, one day in the future, entering the silence of his house. He saw himself on a summer evening pushing open the french windows of the drawing-room and going out into the garden, strolling among its fuchsia bushes and apple trees. He'd known the house all his life; he'd actually been born in it. Opposite O'Connor Motors, it was the last one in the town, yellow-washed and ordinary, but a house he loved.

'Did you say the fish, sir?' the waitress inquired.

'Yes, I did.'

He'd been married in Dublin, she being the daughter of a Dublin wine merchant. The old man was still alive and so was her mother. 'You've taken on a handful,' the old man once had said, but he'd said it playfully because in those days Annabella had been a handful to delight in. What they thought of her now Boland had no idea.

'The plate's hot, sir,' the waitress warned.

'Thanks very much.'

People who'd known him in his childhood had been delighted when he brought her to live among them. They'd stopped him on the street and said he was lucky. They were happy for him: he'd come back from Dublin with a crown of jewels, which was how they saw it. And yet those same people would be delighted when she left. The terrible frustration that possessed her—the denial of children through some mischance within her—turned beauty into wanton eccentricity. It was that that had happened, nothing else.

Slowly he ate his cod, with parsley sauce and cabbage and potatoes. Nobody would mention it much; they'd know what had happened and they'd say to one another that one day, probably, he'd marry again. He wondered if he would. He'd spoken airily of divorce to Lairdman, but in truth he knew nothing of divorce in Ireland these days. A marriage should wither away, he somehow felt, it should rot and die; it didn't seem quite like a cancer, to be swiftly cut out.

He ordered apple tart and cream, and later coffee came. He was glad it was all over: the purpose of his visit to Dublin had been to set a seal on everything that had happened, and in the encounter that had taken place the seal had at some point been set. The air had been cleared, he had accepted the truth it had been necessary to hear from someone else besides his wife. When first she'd told him he'd wondered if she could possibly be making it all up, and he'd wondered it since. Even while he'd waited in Buswell's bar he'd said to himself he wouldn't be surprised if no one turned up.

On the way to the car park two tinker children begged from him. He knew it wasn't coppers they were after, but his wallet or whatever else they could get their fingers on. One held out a cardboard box, the other pressed close to him, with a rug folded over her hands. He'd seen the trick before; Dublin was like that now. 'Go on, along with you,' he ordered them as harshly as he could.

It was because there hadn't been enough for her to do: he thought that as he eased the car through the heavy city traffic. And from the very start she hadn't taken to provincial life. A childless woman in a provincial town had all the time in the world to study its limitations. She had changed the furniture around, and had chosen the wallpapers that her Siamese cats had later damaged. But she'd resisted bridge and tennis, and had deplored the absence of even a cinema café. He'd thought he'd understood; so well used to the limitations himself, he was nevertheless aware that the society he had plunged her into was hardly scintillating. He'd driven her as often as he could to Dublin, before she'd taken to going on her own to visit Phyllis. For years he'd known she wasn't happy, but until she told him he'd never suspected she'd become involved with a man.

He stopped in Mullingar and had a cup of tea. The Dublin evening papers had arrived before him. He read in the *Herald* that the Italian government had been successfully re-formed after the Achille Lauro incident; the dollar was slipping again; a meat-processing plant was to close in Cork. He dawdled over the paper, not wanting to go home. Lairdman would have telephoned her by now. 'Why don't you drive up this afternoon?' he might have said. Maybe she had been packing all day, knowing the encounter was only a formality. 'He won't stand in the way,' Lairdman would have said. 'He'll even supply grounds.' There'd be nothing to keep her, now that all three of them knew where they stood, and it was the kind of thing she'd do, pack up and go when she'd got him out of the way.

A coal fire was burning in the café. A rare welcome these days, he remarked to the woman who'd served him, and pulled a chair up close to it. 'I'd take another cup of tea,' he said.

The little white Volkswagen he'd bought her might be on the road to Dublin already. She wouldn't leave a note because she wouldn't consider it necessary. If the Volkswagen passed by now she would be puzzled at not meeting him on the road; she'd never notice his own car parked outside the café.

'Ah well, you'd need a fire,' the woman said, returning with his tea. 'A shocking foggy old month we're having.'

'I've known better certainly.'

He drove on after he'd had a third cup of tea, keeping an eye out for the Volkswagen. Would she greet him with a touch on the horn? Or would he greet her? He didn't know if he would. Better to wait for the moment.

But over the next fifty or so miles there was no sign of his wife's car. And of course, he told himself, there was no reason why there should be: it was pure conjecture that she'd depart that afternoon, and the amount she had to pack made it unlikely that she could manage to do so in a day. For the next few miles he speculated on how, otherwise, her departure would be. Would Lairdman drive down to assist her? That had not been agreed upon or even touched upon as a possibility: he would instantly put his foot down if it was suggested. Would Phyllis arrive to help her? He would naturally have no objection to that. Certainly, the more he thought about it, the less likely was it that she could be capable of completing the move on her own. She had a way of calling on other people when something difficult had to be undertaken. He imagined her sitting on the second step of the stairs, chattering on the telephone. 'Would you ever . . . ?' she had a way of beginning her demands and her requests.

His headlights caught the familiar sign, in English and Irish, indicating that the town which was his home was the next one. He turned the radio on. 'Dancing in the dark', a sensual female voice lilted, reminding him of the world he supposed his wife and Lairdman belonged to; the thrill of illicit love, tête-à-tête dancing, as the song implied. 'Poor Annabella', he said aloud, while the music still played. Poor girl, ever to have got herself married to the inheritor of a country-town bakery. Lucky, in all fairness, that cocky little Lairdman had turned up. The music continued, and he imagined them running towards one another along an empty street, like lovers in a film. He imagined their embrace, and then their shared smile before they embraced again. As the dull third party, not even a villain, he had no further part to play.

But as Boland reached the first few houses on this side of the town he knew that none of that was right. Not only had the white Volkswagen not conveyed her to Lairdman in his absence, it would not do so tomorrow or the next day, or next week. It would not do so next month, or after Christmas, or in February, or in the spring: it would not ever do so. It hadn't mattered reminding Lairdman of the ignominy he had suffered as a boy; it hadn't mattered reminding him that she was a liar, or insulting him by calling him mean. All that abuse was conventional in the circumstances, an expected element in the man-to-man confrontation, the courage for it engendered by an intake of John Jameson. Yet something had impelled him to go further: little men like Lairdman always wanted children. 'That's a total lie,' she'd have said already on the telephone, and Lairdman would have soothed her. But soothing wasn't going to be enough for either of them.

Boland turned the radio off. He drew the car up outside Donovan's public house and sat for a moment, swinging the keys between his thumb and forefinger before going in and ordering a bottle of Smithwick's with lime. At the bar he greeted men he knew and stood with them drinking, listening to talk of racehorses and politics. They drifted away when a few more drinks had been taken but Boland remained there for a long time, wondering why he hadn't been able to let Lairdman take her from him.

Events at Drimaghleen

Nothing as appalling had happened before at Drimaghleen; its people had never been as shocked. They'd had their share of distress, like any people; there were memories of dramatic occurrences; stories from a more distant past were told. In the 1880s a woman known as the Captain's wife had run away with a hunchbacked pedlar. In 1798 there'd been resistance in the hills and fighting in Drimaghleen itself. During the Troubles a local man had been executed in a field by the Black and Tans. But no story, and no long memory, could match the horror of the tragedy that awaited the people of Drimaghleen on 22 May 1985, a Wednesday morning.

The McDowds, that morning, awoke in their farmhouse and began the day as they always did, McDowd pulling on his shirt and trousers and lifting down a black overcoat from the pegs beside the kitchen door. He fastened it with a length of string which he kept in one of its pockets, found his socks in his gum-boots and went out with his two sheepdogs to drive the cows in for milking. His wife washed herself, put the kettle on the stove, and knocked on her daughter's door. 'Maureen!' she called. 'Come on now, Maureen!'

It was not unusual that Maureen failed to reply. Mrs McDowd reentered her bedroom and dressed herself. 'Get up out of that, Maureen!' she shouted, banging again on her daughter's door. 'Are you sick?' she inquired, puzzled now by the lack of movement from within the room: always at this second rousing Maureen yawned or spoke. 'Maureen!' she shouted again, and then opened the door.

McDowd, calling in the cattle, was aware that there had been something wrong in the yard as he'd passed through it, but an early-morning torpor hindered the progression of his thoughts when he endeavoured to establish what it was. His wife's voice shouting across the field at him, and his daughter's name used repeatedly in the information that was being inadequately conveyed to him, jolted him into an awareness that what had been wrong was that Maureen's bicycle had not been leaning against the kitchen window-sill. 'Maureen hasn't come back,' his wife repeated again when he was close enough to hear her. 'She's not been in her bed.'

The cows were milked because no matter what the reason for Maureen's absence they had to be. The breakfast was placed on the kitchen table because no good would come of not taking food. McDowd, in silence, ate with an appetite that was unaffected; his wife consumed less than usual. 'We will drive over,' he said when they had finished, anger thickening his voice.

She nodded. She'd known as soon as she'd seen the unused bed that they would have to do something. They could not just wait for a letter to arrive, or a telegram, or whatever it was their daughter had planned. They would drive over to the house where Lancy Butler lived with his mother, the house to which their daughter had cycled the evening before. They did not share the thought that possessed both of them: that their daughter had taken the law into her own hands and gone off with Lancy Butler, a spoilt and useless man.

McDowd was a tallish, spare man of sixty-two, his face almost gaunt, grey hair ragged on his head. His wife, two years younger, was thin also, with gnarled features and the hands of a woman who all her life had worked in the fields. They did not say much to one another, and never had; but they did not quarrel either. On the farm, discussion was rarely apt, there being no profit in it; it followed naturally that grounds for disagreement were limited. Five children had been born to the McDowds; Maureen was the youngest and the only one who had remained at home. Without a show of celebration, for that was not the family way, her twenty-fifth birthday had passed by a month ago.

'Put your decent trousers on,' Mrs McDowd urged. 'You can't go like that.'

'I'm all right the way I am.'

She knew he would not be persuaded and did not try, but instead hurried back to her bedroom to change her shoes. At least he wouldn't drive over in the overcoat with the string round it: that was only for getting the cows in from the field when the mornings were cold. He'd taken it off before he'd sat down to his breakfast and there would be no cause to put it on again. She covered up her own old skirt and jumper with her waterproof.

'The little bitch,' he said in the car, and she said nothing.

They both felt the same, anxious and cross at the same time, not wanting to believe the apparent truth. Their daughter had ungratefully deceived them: again in silence the thought was shared while he drove the four miles to the Butlers' house. When they turned off the tarred road into a lane, already passing between the Butlers' fields, they heard the dog barking. The window of the Volkswagen on Mrs McDowd's side wouldn't wind up, due to a defect that had developed a month ago: the shrill barking easily carried above the rattle of the engine.

That was that, they thought, listening to the dog. Maureen and Lancy had gone the night before, and Mrs Butler couldn't manage the cows on her own. No wonder the old dog was beside himself. Bitterly, McDowd called his daughter a bitch again, though only to himself. Lancy Butler, he thought, my God! Lancy Butler would lead her a dance, and lead her astray, and lead her down into the gutters of some town. He'd warned her a thousand times about Lancy Butler. He'd told her the kind of fool he was.

'His father was a decent man,' he said, breaking at last the long silence. 'Never touched a drop.'

'The old mother ruined him.'

It wouldn't last long, they both thought. Lancy Butler might marry her, or he might wriggle out of it. But however it turned out she'd be back in six months' time or at any rate a year's. There'd probably be a baby to bring up.

The car turned into the yard, and neither McDowd nor his wife immediately saw their daughter lying beside the pump. For the first

few moments of their arrival their attention was claimed by the
distressed dog, a black-and-white sheepdog like their own two. Dust
had risen from beneath the Volkswagen's wheels and was still thick
in the air as they stepped from the car. The dog was running wildly
across a corner of the yard, back and forth, and back and forth
again. The dog's gone mad, Mrs McDowd thought, something's
after affecting it. Then she saw her daughter's body lying by the
pump, and a yard or so away her daughter's bicycle lying on its
side, as if she had fallen from it. Beside the bicycle were two dead
rabbits.

'My God,' McDowd said, and his wife knew from his voice that
he hadn't seen his daughter yet but was looking at something else.
He had walked to another part of the yard, where the dog was. He
had gone there instinctively, to try to calm the animal.

She knelt down, whispering to Maureen, thinking in her confusion that her daughter had just this minute fallen off her bicycle.
But Maureen's face was as cold as stone, and her flesh had already
stiffened. Mrs McDowd screamed, and then she was aware that she
was lying down herself, clasping Maureen's dead body. A moment
later she was aware that her husband was weeping piteously, unable
to control himself, that he was kneeling down, his hands on the
body also.

Mrs McDowd did not remember rising to her feet, or finding
the energy and the will to do so. 'Don't go over there,' she heard
her husband saying to her, and saw him wiping at his eyes with
the arm of his jersey. But he didn't try to stop her when she went
to where the dog was; he remained on his knees beside their daughter, calling out to her between his sobs, asking her not to be dead.

The dog was crouched in a doorway, not barking any more. A
yard or so away Mrs Butler lay with one of her legs twisted under
her, blood on the ground already turned brown, a pool of it still
scarlet. Looking down at her, Mrs McDowd thought with abrupt
lucidity: Maureen did not fall off her bicycle. She went back to
where her daughter lay and behind the two tin barrels that stood
by the pump she saw the body of Lancy Butler, and on the ground

not far from it the shotgun that must have blown off Mrs Butler's face.

O'Kelly of the Garda arrived at a swift conclusion. Old Mrs Butler had been as adamant as the McDowds in her opposition to the match that her son and Maureen McDowd had planned for themselves. And there was more to it than that: Mrs Butler had been obsessively possessive, hiding from no one her determination that no other woman should ever take her son away from her. Lancy was her only child, the single one to survive years of miscarrying. His father had died when Lancy was two years old, leaving mother and child to lead a lonely life on a farm that was remote. O'Kelly knew that Mrs Butler had been reputed to be strange in the head, and given to furious jealousies where Lancy was concerned. In the kind of rage that people who'd known her were familiar with she had shot her son's sweetheart rather than suffer the theft of him. He had wrenched the shotgun from her and by accident or otherwise it had exploded. A weak man at the best of times, he had turned it upon himself rather than face the reality of what had happened. This deduction, borne out by the details in the yard, satisfied O'Kelly of the Garda; the people of Drimaghleen arrived themselves at the same conclusion. 'It was always trouble,' McDowd said on the day of the funerals. 'The minute she went out with Lancy Butler it was trouble written down for poor Maureen.'

Drimaghleen was a townland, with nothing to mark it except a crossroads that was known as Drimaghleen Crossroads. The modest farms that comprised it, each of thirty or so acres, were scattered among bogland, one separated from the next by several miles, as the McDowds' and the Butlers' were. The village of Kilmona was where the people of Drimaghleen went to Mass, and where they confessed to Father Sallins. The children of the farms went to school in the small town of Mountcroe, driven each morning in a yellow bus that drove them back to the end of their lanes or farm tracks in the afternoon. Milk churns were collected in much the same way by the creamery lorry. Bread and groceries were bought in the village; fresh meat in Mountcroe. When the men of Drimaghleen got drunk they did so in Mountcroe, never in the village, although often they took a few bottles of stout there, in the bar beside the grocery counter. Hardware and clothes were bought in Mountcroe, which had had a cinema called the Abbey Picture House until the advent of television closed it in the early 1960s. Drimaghleen, Kilmona and Mountcroe formed a world that bounded the lives of the people of the Drimaghleen farms. Rarely was there occasion to venture beyond it to the facilities of a town that was larger—unless the purpose happened to be a search for work or the first step on the way to exile.

The children of the McDowds, whose search for such work had taken them far from the townland, returned heartbroken for their sister's Mass. All four of them came, two with husbands, one with a wife, one on her own. The weddings which had taken place had been the last family occasions, two of them in Kilmona, the third in distant Skibbereen, the home of the girl whom the McDowds' son had married a year ago. That wedding was on their minds at Maureen's Mass—the long journey there had been in the Volkswagen, the night they had spent in Tierney's Hotel, the farewells the next day. Not in the wildest horror of a nightmare could any of the McDowds have guessed the nature of the occasion destined to bring them together next.

After the funeral the family returned to the farm. The younger McDowds had known of Maureen's and Lancy Butler's attachment, and of their parents' opposition to it. They had known as well of Mrs Butler's possessive affection for her son, having grown up with stories of this maternal eccentricity, and having witnessed Lancy himself, as a child and as a boy, affected by her indulgence. 'Oh, it can wait, Lancy, it can wait,' she would say a dozen times an hour, referring to some necessary chore on the farm. 'Ah, sure, we won't bother with school today,' she had said before that, when

Lancy had complained of a difficulty he was experiencing with the seven-times table or Brother Martin's twenty weekend spellings. The people of Drimaghleen used to wonder whether the farm or Lancy would suffer more in the end.

'What did she see in him?' Mrs McDowd mused sadly at the funeral meal. 'Will anyone ever tell me what she saw in him?'

They shook their heads. The cheeks of all of them were still smeared with the tears they had shed at the service. Conversation was difficult.

'We will never recover from it,' the father said, with finality in his voice. It was all that could be said, it was all they knew with certainty: for as long as the older McDowds remained in this farmhouse—which would be until their own deaths—the vicious, ugly tragedy would haunt them. They knew that if Maureen had been knocked from her bicycle by a passing motor-car they could have borne her death with greater fortitude; or if she had died of an illness, or been the victim of incurable disease. The knife that turned in their pain was their memory of the Butlers' farmyard, the barking dog running back and forth, the three still bodies. There was nothing but the waste of a life to contemplate, and the cruelty of chance—for why should it have been simple, pretty Maureen whose fate it was to become mixed up with so peculiar a couple as that mother and son? There were other girls in the neighbourhood—underhand girls and girls of doubtful character—who somehow more readily belonged with the Butlers: anyone would tell you that.

'Why don't you drive over and see us?' one of the daughters invited. 'Can't we persuade you?'

Her father stared into the table without trying to reply. It was unnecessary to say that a drive of such a distance could only be contemplated when there was a wedding or a funeral. Such journeys had not been undertaken during Maureen's lifetime, when she might have looked after the farm for a day; in no way could they be considered now. Mrs McDowd tried to smile, making an effort

to acknowledge the concern that had inspired the suggestion, but
no smile came.

Being of a nature that might interest strangers, the deaths were
reported in the newspapers. They were mentioned on the radio,
and on the television news. Then everything became quiet again at
Drimaghleen, and in the village and in the town. People wrote
letters to the McDowds, expressing their sorrow. People came to
see them but did not stay long. 'I am always there,' Father Sallins
said. 'Kilmona 23. You have only to summon me. Or call up at
the rectory.'

The McDowds didn't. They watched the summer going by, taking in their hay during the warm spell in June, keeping an eye on
the field of potatoes and the ripening barley. It began to rain more
than usual; they worried about the barley.

'Excuse me,' a man said in the yard one afternoon in October.
'Are you Mr McDowd?'

McDowd said he was, shouting at the dogs to behave themselves.
The stranger would be a traveller in fertilizers, he said to himself,
a replacement for Donoghue, who had been coming to the farm
for years. Then he realized that it was the wrong time of year for
Donoghue.

'Would it be possible to have a word, Mr McDowd?'

McDowd's scrawny features slowly puckered; slowly he frowned.
He lifted a hand and scratched at his grey, ragged hair, which was
a way he had when he wished to disguise bewilderment. Part of his
countryman's wiliness was that he preferred outsiders not to know,
or deduce, what was occurring in his mind.

'A word?' he said.

'Could we maybe step inside, sir?'

McDowd saw no reason to step inside his own house with this
man. The visitor was florid-faced, untidily dressed in dark corduroy
trousers and a gaberdine jacket. His hair was long and black, and
grew coarsely down the sides of his face in two brushlike panels.

He had a city voice; it wasn't difficult to guess he came from Dublin.

'What d'you want with me?'

'I was sorry to hear that thing about your daughter, Mr McDowd. That was a terrible business.'

'It's over and done with.'

'It is, sir. Over and done with.'

The red bonnet of a car edged its way into the yard. McDowd watched it, reminded of some cautious animal by the slow, creeping movement, the engine purring so lightly you could hardly hear it. When the car stopped by the milking shed nobody got out of it, but McDowd could see a figure wearing sunglasses at the wheel. This was a woman, with black hair also, smoking a cigarette.

'It could be to your advantage, Mr McDowd.'

'What could be? Does that car belong to you?'

'We drove down to see you, sir. That lady's a friend of mine, a colleague by the name of Hetty Fortune.'

The woman stepped out of the car. She was taller than the man, with a sombre face and blue trousers that matched her blue shirt. She dropped her cigarette on to the ground and carefully stubbed it out with the toe of her shoe. As slowly as she had driven the car she walked across the yard to where the two men were standing. The dogs growled at her, but she took no notice. 'I'm Hetty Fortune,' she said in an English accent.

'I didn't tell you my own name, Mr McDowd,' the man said. 'It's Jeremiah Tyler.'

'I hope Jeremiah has offered you our condolences, Mr McDowd. I hope both you and your wife will accept our deepest sympathy.'

'What do you want here?'

'We've been over at the Butlers' place, Mr McDowd. We spent a long time there. We've been talking to a few people. Could we talk to you, d'you think?'

'Are you the newspapers?'

'In a manner of speaking. Yes, in a manner of speaking we represent the media. And I'm perfectly sure,' the woman added hastily, 'you've had more than enough of all that. I believe you'll find what we have to say to you is different, Mr McDowd.'

'The wife and myself have nothing to say to the newspapers. We didn't say anything at the time, and we have nothing to say since. I have things to do about the place.'

'Mr McDowd, would you be good enough to give us five minutes of your time? Five minutes in your kitchen, talking to yourself and your wife? Would you give us an opportunity to explain?'

Attracted by the sound by voices, Mrs McDowd came out of the house. She stood in the doorway, not quite emerging from the kitchen porch, regarding the strangers even more distrustfully than her husband had. She didn't say anything when the woman approached her and held out a hand which she was obliged to shake.

'We are sorry to obtrude on your grief, Mrs McDowd. Mr Tyler and I have been keen to make that clear to your husband.'

Mrs McDowd did not acknowledge this. She didn't like the look of the sombre-faced woman or her unkempt companion. There was a seediness about him, a quality that city people seemed often to exude if they weren't smartly attired. The woman wasn't seedy but you could see she was insincere from the way her mouth was. You could hear the insincerity when she spoke.

'The full truth has not been established, Mrs McDowd. It is that we would like to discuss with you.'

'I've told you no,' McDowd said. 'I've told them to go away,' he said to his wife.

Mrs McDowd's eyes stared at the woman's sunglasses. She remained where she was, not quite coming into the yard. The man said:

'Would it break the ice if I took a snap? Would you mind that, sir? If I was to take a few snaps of yourself and the wife?'

He had spoken out of turn. A shadow of anger passed over the woman's face. The fingers of her left hand moved in an irritated wriggle. She said quickly:

'That's not necessary at this stage.'

'We've got to get the pictures, Hetty,' the man mumbled, hush-ing the words beneath his breath so that the McDowds wouldn't hear. But they guessed the nature of his protest, for it showed in his pink face. The woman snapped something at him.

'If you don't leave us alone we'll have to get the Guards,' McDowd said. 'You're trespassing on this land.'

'Is it fair on your daughter's memory that the truth should be hidden, Mr McDowd?'

'Another thing is, those dogs can be fierce if they want to be.'

'It isn't hidden,' Mrs McDowd said. 'We all know what happened. Detectives worked it out, but sure anyone could have told them.'

'No, Mrs McDowd, nothing was properly worked out at all. That's what I'm saying to you. The surface was scarcely disturbed. What seemed to be the truth wasn't.'

McDowd told his wife to lock the door. They would drive over to Mountcroe and get a Guard to come back with them. 'We don't want any truck with you,' he harshly informed their visitors. 'If the dogs eat the limbs off you after we've gone don't say it wasn't mentioned.'

Unmoved by these threats, her voice losing none of its confidence, the woman said that what was available was something in the region of three thousand pounds. 'For a conversation of brief duration you would naturally have to be correctly reimbursed. Already we have taken up your working time, and of course we're not happy about that. The photograph mentioned by Mr Tyler would naturally have the attachment of a fee. We're talking at the end of the day of something above a round three thousand.'

Afterwards the McDowds remembered that moment. They remembered the feeling they shared, that this was no kind of trick, that the money spoken of would be honestly paid. They remembered thinking that the sum was large, that they could do with thirty pounds never mind three thousand. Rain had destroyed the barley; they missed their daughter's help on the farm; the tragedy had aged and weakened them. If three thousand pounds could come out of it, they'd maybe think of selling up and buying a bungalow.

'Let them in,' McDowd said, and his wife led the way into the kitchen.

The scene of the mystery is repeated all over rural Ireland. From Cork to Cavan, from Roscommon to Rosslare you will come across small, tucked-away farms like the Butlers' and the McDowds'. Maureen McDowd had been gentle-natured and gentle-tempered. The sins of sloth and greed had not been hers; her parents called her a perfect daughter, close to a saint. A photograph, taken when Maureen McDowd was five, showed a smiling, freckled child; another showed her in her First Communion dress; a third, taken at the wedding of her brother, was of a healthy-looking girl, her face creased up in laughter, a cup of tea in her right hand. There was a photograph of her mother and father, standing in their kitchen. Italicized beneath it was the information that it had been taken by Jeremiah Tyler. *The Saint of Drimaghleen,* Hetty Fortune had written, *never once missed Mass in all her twenty-five years.*

The story was told in fashionably faded pictures. 'You know our Sunday supplement?' Hetty Fortune had said in the McDowds' kitchen, but they hadn't: newspapers from England had never played a part in their lives. They read the *Sunday Independent* themselves.

The Butlers' yard was brownly bleak in the pages of the supplement; the pump had acquired a quality not ordinarily noticed. A bicycle similar to Maureen's had been placed on the ground, a sheepdog similar to the Butlers' nosed about the doors of the cowshed. But the absence of the three bodies in the photographed yard, the dust still rising where the bicycle had fallen, the sniffing dog, lent the composition an eerie quality—horror conveyed without horror's presence. 'You used a local man?' the supplement's assistant editor inquired, and when informed that Jeremiah Tyler was a Dublin man he requested that a note be kept of the photographer's particulars.

The gardai—in particular Superintendent O'Kelly—saw only what was convenient to see. Of the three bodies that lay that morning in the

May sunshine they chose that of Lancy Butler to become the victim of their sluggish imagination. Mrs Butler, answering her notoriously uncontrollable jealousy, shot her son's sweetheart rather than have him marry her. Her son, so Superintendent O'Kelly infers from no circumstantial evidence whatsoever, wrenched the shotgun out of her hands and fired on her in furious confusion. He then, within seconds, took his own life. The shotgun bore the fingerprints of all three victims: what O'Kelly has signally failed to explain is why this should be so. Why should the Butlers' shotgun bear the fingerprints of Maureen McDowd? O'Kelly declares that 'in the natural course of events' Maureen McDowd would have handled the shotgun, being a frequent visitor to the farm. Frequent visitors, in our experience, do not, 'in the natural course of events' or otherwise, meddle with a household's firearms. The Superintendent hedges the issue because he is himself bewildered. The shotgun was used for keeping down rabbits, he states, knowing that the shotgun's previous deployment by the Butlers is neither here nor there. He mentions rabbits because he still can offer no reasonable explanation why Maureen McDowd should ever have handled the death weapon. The fingerprints of all three victims were blurred and 'difficult', and had been found on several different areas of the weapon. Take it or leave it is what the Superintendent is saying. And wearily he is saying: does it matter?

We maintain it does matter. We maintain that this extraordinary crime—following, as it does, hard on the heels of the renowned Kerry Babies mystery, and the Flynn case—has not been investigated, but callously shelved. The people of Drimaghleen will tell you everything that O'Kelly laboured over in his reports: the two accounts are identical. Everyone knows that Lancy Butler's mother was a sharp-tongued, possessive woman. Everyone knows that Lancy was a ne'er-do-well. Everyone knows that Maureen McDowd was a deeply religious girl. Naturally it was the mother who sought to end an intrusion she could not bear. Naturally it was slow, stupid Lancy who didn't pause to think what the consequences would be after he'd turned the gun on his mother. Naturally it was he who could think of no more imaginative

way out of his dilemma than to join the two women who had domi-
nated his life.

The scenario that neither O'Kelly nor the Butlers' neighbours paused
to consider is a vastly different one. A letter, apparently—and aston-
ishingly—overlooked by the police, was discovered behind the drawer
of a table which was once part of the furniture of Lancy Butler's bed-
room and which was sold in the general auction after the tragedy—
land, farmhouse and contents having by this time become the property
of Allied Irish Banks, who held the mortgage on the Butlers' possessions.
This letter, written by Maureen McDowd a week before the tragedy,
reads:

Dear Lancy, Unless she stops I can't see any chance of marrying
you. I want to, Lancy, but she never can let us alone. What would
it be like for me in your place, and if I didn't come to you where
would we be able to go because you know my father wouldn't
accept you here. She has ruined the chance we had, Lancy, she'll
never let go of you. I am always cycling over to face her insults and
the way she has of looking at me. I think we have reached the end
of it.

This being a direct admission by Maureen McDowd that the conclusion
of the romance had been arrived at, why would the perceptive Mrs
Butler—a woman who was said to 'know your thoughts before you
knew them yourself'—decide to kill Lancy's girl? And the more the
mental make-up of that old woman is dwelt upon the more absurd it
seems that she would have destroyed everything she had by committing
a wholly unnecessary murder. Mrs Butler was not the kind to act
blindly, in the fury of the moment. Her jealousy and the anger that
protected it smouldered cruelly within her, always present, never
varying.

But Maureen McDowd—young, impetuous, bitterly deprived of the
man she loved—a saint by nature and possessing a saint's fervour, on
that fatal evening made up for all the sins she had ever resisted. Hell

hath no fury like a woman scorned—except perhaps a woman unfairly defeated. The old woman turned the screw, aware that victory was in sight. The insults and 'the way of looking' became more open and more arrogant; Mrs Butler wanted Maureen McDowd out, she wanted her gone for ever, never to dare to return.

It is known that Lancy Butler found two rabbits in his snares that night. It is known that he and Maureen often made the rounds of the snares when she visited him in the evenings. He would ride her bicycle to the field where they were, Maureen sitting side-saddle on the carrier at the back. Lancy had no bicycle of his own. It is our deduction that the reason the shotgun bore Maureen's fingerprints is because they had gone on a shooting expedition as well and when they returned to the yard she was carrying both the shotgun and the snared rabbits. It is known that Maureen McDowd wept shortly before her death. In the fields, as they stalked their prey, Lancy comforted her but Maureen knew that never again would they walk here together, that never again would she come over to see him in the evening. The hatred his mother bore her, and Lancy's weakness, had combined to destroy what most of all she wanted. Mrs Butler was standing in the yard shouting her usual abuse and Maureen shot her. The rabbits fell to the ground as she jumped off the bicycle, and her unexpectedly sudden movement caused the bicycle itself, and Lancy on it, to turn over. He called out to her when it was too late, and she realized she could never have him now. She blamed him for never once standing up to his mother, for never making it easier. If she couldn't have this weak man whom she so passionately loved no one else would either. She shot her lover, knowing that within seconds she must take her own life too. And that, of course, she did.

There was more about Maureen. In the pages of the colour supplement Mrs McDowd said her daughter had been a helpful child. Her father said she'd been his special child. When she was small she used to go out with him to the fields, watching how he planted the seed-potatoes. Later on, she would carry out his tea to him, and later still she would assist with whatever task he was engaged in. Father Sallins gave it as his opinion that she had been specially chosen. A nun at the convent in Mountcroe remembered her with lasting affection.

O'Kelly fell prey to this local feeling. Whether they knew what they were doing or not, the people of Drimaghleen were protecting the memory of Maureen McDowd, and the Superintendent went along with the tide. She was a local girl of unblemished virtue, who had been 'specially chosen'. Had he publicly arrived at any other conclusion Superintendent O'Kelly might never safely have set foot in the neighbourhood of Drimaghleen again, nor the village of Kilmona, nor the town of Mountcroe. The Irish do not easily forgive the purloining of their latter-day saints.

'I wanted to tell you this stuff had been written,' Father Sallins said. 'I wanted it to be myself that informed you before you'd get a shock from hearing it elsewhere.'

He'd driven over specially. As soon as the story in the paper had been brought to his own notice he'd felt it his duty to sit down with the McDowds. In his own opinion, what had been printed was nearly as bad as the tragedy itself, his whole parish maligned, a police superintendent made out to be no better than the criminals he daily pursued. He'd read the thing through twice; he'd looked at the photographs in astonishment. Hetty Fortune and Jeremiah Tyler had come to see him, but he'd advised them against poking about in what was over and done with. He'd explained that people wanted to try to forget the explosion of violence that had so suddenly occurred in their midst, that he himself still prayed for the souls of the Butlers and Maureen McDowd. The woman had nodded her head, as though persuaded by what he said. 'I have the camera here, Father,' the man had remarked as they were leaving. 'Will I take a snap of you?' Father Sallins had stood by the fuchsias, seeing no harm in having his photograph taken. 'I'll send it down to you when it's developed,' the man said, but the photograph had never arrived. The first he saw of it was in the Sunday magazine, a poor likeness of himself, eyelids drooped as though he had drink taken, dark stubble on his chin.

'This is a terrible thing,' he said in the McDowds' kitchen, re-membering the photograph of that also: the cream-enamelled elec-tric cooker, the Holy Child on the green-painted dresser, beside the alarm clock and the stack of clothes-pegs, the floor carpeted for cosiness, the blue, formica-topped table, the radio, the television set. In the photograph the kitchen had acquired an extraneous qual-ity, just as the photograph of the Butlers' yard had. The harsh, ordinary colours, the soiled edges of the curtains, the chipped paint-work, seemed like part of a meticulous composition: the photograph was so much a picture that it invited questioning as a record.

'We never thought she was going to say that about Maureen,' Mrs McDowd said. 'It's lies, Father.'

'Of course it is, Mrs McDowd.'

'We all know what happened that night.'

'Of course we do.'

McDowd said nothing. They had taken the money. It was he who had said that the people should be allowed into the house. Three thousand, one hundred and fifty pounds was the sum the woman had written the cheque for, insisting that the extra money was owed.

'You never said she'd been specially chosen, Father?'

'Of course I didn't, Mrs McDowd.'

He'd heard that Superintendent O'Kelly had gone to see a solic-itor to inquire if he'd been libelled, and although he was told he probably had been he was advised that recourse in the courts would be costly and might not be successful. The simple explanation of what had happened at the Butlers' farm had been easy for the people of Drimaghleen and for the police to accept because they had known Mrs Butler and they had known her son. There'd been no mystery, there'd been no doubt.

'Will we say a prayer together?' the priest suggested.

They knelt, and when they rose again Mrs McDowd began to cry. Everyone would know about it, she said, as if the priest had neither prayed nor spoken. The story would get about and people would believe it. '*Disadvantaged people*', she quoted from the newspaper. She frowned, still sobbing, over the words. 'It says the Butlers were disadvantaged people. It says we are disadvantaged ourselves.'

'That's only the way that woman has of writing it down, Mrs McDowd. It doesn't mean much.'

'*These simple farm folk,*' Mrs McDowd read, '*of Europe's most western island form limited rural communities that all too often turn in on themselves.*'

'Don't pay attention,' Father Sallins advised.

'Does disadvantaged mean we're poor?'

'The way that woman would see it, Mrs McDowd.'

There was confusion now in Drimaghleen, in Kilmona and Mountcroe; and confusion, Father Sallins believed, was insidious. People had been separated from their instinct, and other newspaper articles would follow upon this one. More strangers would come. Father Sallins imagined a film being made about Maureen McDowd, and the mystery that had been created becoming a legend. The nature of Maureen McDowd would be argued over, books would be written because all of it was fascinating. For ever until they died her mother and her father would blame themselves for taking the money their poverty had been unable to turn away.

'The family'll see the pictures.'

'Don't upset yourself, Mrs McDowd.'

'No one ever said she was close to being a saint. That was never said, Father.'

'I know, I know.'

Mrs McDowd covered her face with her hands. Her thin shoulders heaved beneath the pain of her distress; sobs wrenched at her body. Too much had happened to her, the priest thought; it was too much for any mother that her murdered daughter should be accused of murder herself in order to give newspaper-readers something to think about. Her husband had turned away from the table she sat at. He stood with his back to her, looking out into the yard. In a low, exhausted voice he said:

'What kind of people are they?'

The priest slowly shook his head, unable to answer that, and in the kitchen that looked different in Jeremiah Tyler's photograph Mrs McDowd screamed. She sat at the blue-topped table with her lips drawn back from her teeth, one short, shrill scream following fast upon another. Father Sallins did not again attempt to comfort her. McDowd remained by the window.

Family Sins

A telegram arrived out of the blue. *Come for the weekend,* Hubert's message read, and I remember the excitement I felt because I valued his friendship more than anyone else's. I had no money for the train journey and had to raise the matter with my father. 'It's hard to come by these days,' my father said, giving me only what he could easily spare. I increased it playing rummy with McCaddy the courthouse clerk, who had a passion for the game.

It was the summer of 1946. Long warm days cast an unobtrusive spell, one following another in what seemed like orderly obedience. The train I took crept through a landscape that was just beginning to lose its verdancy but was not yet parched. The railway for the last few miles of the journey ran by the sea, which twinkled brilliantly, sunlight dancing on it.

'There's someone called Pamela,' Hubert said, greeting me in no other way. 'Probably I mightn't have mentioned her.'

We walked from Templemairt railway station, away from the sea, into a tangle of small suburban roads. Everywhere there were boarding-houses, cheaper than those by the promenade, Hubert said. Bookies' families stayed there, he said: Sans Souci, Freshlea House, Cois na Farraige. We climbed a hill and passed through iron gates into a garden that was also on a hill, steep rockeries on either side of a path with occasional steps in it. I could see the house above us, through hollyhocks and shrubs, a glass veranda stretching the length of its façade.

'Who's Pamela?'

'She spends the summers here. My cousin.'

We entered the house and a voice at once called out. 'Hubert, I should like to meet your friend.'

'Hell,' Hubert muttered. He led me into a small room, its burnt-brown blinds half drawn against the sun. An old woman sat at a piano, turning on the stool as we entered. She was dressed severely, in long, old-fashioned black clothes; her grey hair was swept up and neatly rolled. You could tell she had once been beautiful; and in the wrinkled tiredness of her face her eyes were still young.

'You are very welcome,' she said. 'Hubert does not often invite a friend.'

'It's nice of you to have me, Mrs Plunkett.'

The piano stool swivelled again. The first notes of a Strauss waltz were played. I picked my suitcase up and followed Hubert from the room. In the hall he threw his eyes upwards, but did not speak. Silently we mounted the stairs, and when we reached the first-floor landing a woman's voice called up from some lower part of the house: 'Hubert, don't tell me you forgot the honeycomb?'

'Oh, *God!*' Hubert muttered crossly. 'Leave your case. We'll have to go back for the damn thing.'

I placed my suitcase on the bed of the room we'd entered: a small cell of a place, masculine in character. Just before we left it Hubert said:

'My grandfather had a stroke. You won't be bothered with him. He doesn't come downstairs.'

On a table in the hall there was a dark-framed photograph of the man he spoke of, taken earlier in his lifetime: a stern, blade-like face with a tidy grey moustache, hair brushed into smooth wings on either side of a conventional parting, pince-nez, a watch-chain looping across a black waistcoat. At school Hubert had spoken a lot about his grandfather.

'That was Lily who was on about the honeycomb,' Hubert said as we descended the path between the rockeries. 'A kind of general maid I think you call her. They work the poor old thing to the bone.'

We passed out of the garden and walked back the way we'd come. Hubert talked about boys we'd been at school with, in particular Ossie Richpatrick and Gale and Furney. He'd had news of all three of them: Ossie Richpatrick had become a medical student, Gale had joined the British army, Furney was in a handkerchief business.

'The Dublin Handkerchief Company,' Hubert said. 'He wrote me a letter on their writing-paper.'

'Does he make the handkerchiefs? I can't see Furney making handkerchiefs.'

'He sells them actually.'

Ossie Richpatrick and Gale and Furney had left school the previous summer; Hubert and I more recently, only a matter of weeks ago. It was now August; in October I was, like Ossie Richpatrick, to become a student, though not of medicine. Hubert was uncertain about his future.

'This is the place,' he said. We passed through high wooden doors into what appeared to be a builder's yard. Bricks were stacked, lengths of plumber's piping were tied together with cord. In a shed there was a circular saw. 'This woman sells honey,' Hubert said.

He knocked on a half-open door and a moment later a woman arrived with a honeycomb already in her hand. 'I saw you turning in,' she said. 'How are you, Hubert?'

'I'm all right. Are you well yourself, Mrs Hanrahan?'

'I am of course, Hubert.'

She examined me with curiosity, but Hubert made no attempt to introduce me. He gave the woman some money and received the honeycomb in return. 'I picked that comb out for them. It's good rich honey.'

'You can tell by the look of it.'

'Is your grandmother well? Mr Plunkett no worse, is he?'

'Well, he's still ga-ga, Mrs Hanrahan. No worse than that.'

The woman had placed her shoulder against the doorjamb so that she could lean on it. You could see she wanted to go on talking, and I sensed that had I not been there Hubert would have remained a little longer. As we made our way through the yard he said: 'She lives in ignorance of Hanrahan's evil ways. He died a while back.'

Hubert didn't elaborate on Mr Hanrahan's evil ways, but suggested instead that we go down to the sea. He led the way to a sandy lane that twisted and turned behind small back gardens and came out eventually among sand dunes. He held the honeycomb by one side of its wooden frame. Wind would have blown sand into it, but the day was still, late-afternoon sunshine lightening an empty sky. We walked by the edge of the sea; there was hardly anyone about.

'What's your cousin like?'

'You'll see soon enough.'

Hubert had a face to which a faintly melancholy expression seemed naturally to belong. But when he laughed, or smiled, its bony landscape changed dramatically, delight illuminating every crevice, eyes sparkling like excited sapphires. Hair the colour of wheat was smoothly brushed, never untidy. 'Fancies himself a dandy, does he?' a disagreeable teacher of Greek and Latin had once remarked.

'I'm thinking of going to Africa,' he revealed when we'd turned and begun to make our way back to the house.

Hubert's mother and father had been killed in a car accident in England. 'The last thing that happened before the war,' Hubert used to say, regaling us at school with the story of the tragedy. On Saturday September 2nd, 1939, late at night, they had driven away from a roadhouse near Virginia Water and unfortunately had had a head-on collision with a lorry belonging to a travelling zoo. There'd been a cage full of apes on the back of the lorry, Hubert subsequently reported, which the impact had caused to become unfastened. He himself had been ten at the time, at a preparatory school in the suburbs of Oxford, and he told how the headmaster had broken the news to him, introducing it with references to courage and manliness. These had failed to prepare him for the death of his parents, because he'd imagined that what was coming next was the news that he would have to be sent home on the grounds that, yet again, the fees hadn't been paid. Already there had been the wireless announcement about the declaration of war, the whole school assembled to hear it. 'You will know no blacker day, Hubert,' the headmaster had asserted before releasing the more personal tidings. 'Take strength at least from that.'

We delivered the honeycomb to the kitchen. 'Lily,' Hubert said, by way of introducing the wiry little woman who was kneading bread on a baking board at the table. 'Mrs Hanrahan says it's good rich honey.'

She nodded in acknowledgement, and nodded a greeting at me. She asked me what kind of a journey I'd had and when I said it had been unremarkable she vouchsafed the information that she didn't like trains. 'I always said it to Hubert,' she recalled, 'when he was going back to school. I suffer on a train.'

'Have you a fag, Lily?' Hubert asked, and she indicated with a gesture of her head a packet of Player's on the dresser. 'I'll pay you back,' he promised. 'I'm taking two.'

'That's seven you owe the kitchen, mind, and I don't want money. You go and buy a packet after supper.'

'I was going to say, Lily, could you lend me a pound?' As he spoke he opened a green purse beside the Player's packet. 'Till Tuesday that would be.'

'It's always till Tuesday with you. You'd think the kitchen was made of Her Ladyships.'

'If Lily was a few years younger,' Hubert said, addressing me, 'I'd marry her tomorrow.'

He removed a pound note from the purse and smoothed it out on the surface of the dresser, examined the romantic countenance of Lady Lavery, raised it to his lips, and then carefully secreted the note in an inside pocket. 'We're going dancing tonight,' he said. 'Did you ever dance in the Four Provinces Ballroom, Lily?'

'Oh, don't be annoying me.'

We smoked in Hubert's room, a tidily kept place with Leonardo da Vinci's *Annunciation* on the wall between the windows. Hubert wound up a gramophone and then lay on his bed. I sat on the only chair. Frank Sinatra sang.

'They're trying to grow groundnuts in Africa,' Hubert said. 'I think I'd be interested in that.'

'What are groundnuts?'

'The groundnut is a nut they have an idea about. I think they'll pay my fare.'

He was vague about which African country he referred to, replying when I asked him that it didn't matter. There was another scheme he'd heard about, to do with supplying telephone-boxes, and a third one that involved teaching selected Africans the rudiments of hydraulic engineering. 'You have to go on a course yourself, naturally enough,' Hubert explained. 'Personally I favour the nuts.'

He turned the record over. Sinatra sang 'Begin the Beguine'. Hubert said:

'We can go in on the half-seven train. We'll have to try for a lift back. Don't dawdle in the dining-room.'

At school Hubert had been thought of as 'wild', a reputation he had to some extent inherited from his father's renown at the same school twenty-five years before. For his own part, it was not that he was constantly in breach of the rules, but rather that he tended to go his own way. Short of funds, which regularly he was, he had been known to sell his clothes. The suit of 'sober colouring' which we were permitted to wear on weekend exeats, and for Chapel on Sunday evenings, with either a school, House or Colours tie, he sold in a Dublin secondhand-clothes shop and, never known to go out on exeats himself, managed for Sunday Chapel with the black serge jacket and trousers that was our normal everyday wear. He sold his bicycle to Ossie Richpatrick for eleven shillings, and a suitcase for eightpence. 'I don't understand why that should be,' Hubert had a way of saying in class, voicing what the rest of us felt but didn't always have the courage to say. He didn't mind not understanding; he didn't mind arguing with the Chaplain about the existence of the Deity; he didn't mind leaving an entire meal untouched and afterwards being harangued by the duty prefect for what was considered to be a form of insolence. But, most of all, what marked Hubert with the characteristics of a personality that was unusual were the stories he repeated about his relationship with his grandfather, which was not a happy one. Mr Plunkett's strictures and appearance were endlessly laid before us, a figure emerging of a tetchy elder statesman, wing-collared and humourless, steeped in the Christian morality of the previous century. Mr Plunkett said grace at mealtimes, much as it was said at school, only continuing for longer; he talked importantly of the managerial position he had reached, after a lifetime of devotion and toil, in Guinness's brewery. 'Never himself touches a drop of the stuff, you understand. Having been an abstainer since the age of seven or something. A clerky figure even as a child.' Since Hubert's reports allowed Mrs Plunkett so slight a place in the household, and Lily none at all, his home life sounded spiky and rather cold. At the beginning of each term he was always the first to arrive back at school, and had once returned a week early, claiming to have misread the commencing date on the previous term's report.

'OK, let's go,' he said when a gong sounded, and we swiftly descended the stairs, Hubert setting the pace. I caught a brief glimpse of a door opening and of a girl. In the hall Hubert struck the gong again as he passed.

'No need for that,' his grandmother gently reprimanded in the dining-room. 'We are all present and correct.'

The girl smiled at me, so shyly that I was made to feel shy myself. In the absence of her husband Mrs Plunkett said grace while we stood with our hands resting on the backs of our chairs. 'We are quite a houseful now,' she chattily remarked as she sat down. 'Pamela, please pass that salad along to our visitor.'

'Yes, of course.'

Pamela blushed as she spoke, her eyes flittering for a moment in my direction. Hubert, silent beside me, was relishing her discomfiture: I knew that, I could feel it. He and I and his cousin were aware that we had not met; the old woman imagined we had.

'I hope you are a salad-eater.' Mrs Plunkett smiled at me. 'Hubert does not much go in for salad. I'm not sure why.'

'Because Hubert doesn't like the taste,' Hubert replied. 'Lettuce does not seem to him to taste at all. The skin of tomatoes catches in his throat. Chives hang about on his breath. Radishes are nasty little things. And so on.'

His cousin laughed. She was a pretty girl, with dark bobbed hair and blue eyes: I didn't, that evening, notice much else about her except that she was wearing a pale pink dress with white buttons down the front. She became even prettier when she smiled, a dimple appearing in one of her cheeks, her nose wrinkling in a way that became her.

'Well, that's most interesting,' Mrs Plunkett said, a little stiffly, when Hubert ceased to talk about his dislikes.

There was corned beef with the salad. Hubert buttered two slices of brown bread to make a sandwich of his, and all the time he was preparing this his grandmother watched him. She did so uncomfortably, in an odd, dutiful kind of way, and I received the impression that she would have preferred not to. It was what her husband would have done, I suddenly realized: as if guided by his silent presence in an upstairs room she was honourably obeying him, keeping faith with his wishes. Mustard was spread on the corned beef, pepper was sprinkled. Mrs Plunkett made no comment. The slow movements of Hubert's knife, a faint whispering under his breath of one of the songs Frank Sinatra had sung, contributed to the considerable unease of both Hubert's cousin and myself. Pamela reddened when she accidentally knocked the little silver spoon out of the salt cellar.

'You're not in a public house, Hubert,' Mrs Plunkett said when he lifted the sandwich to his mouth. 'Pamela, please pour the tea.'

Hubert ignored the reference to a public house. 'Don't dawdle,' he reminded me. 'If we miss the seven-thirty we'll have to cadge a lift and that takes ages.'

Pamela poured the tea. Mrs Plunkett cut her lettuce into fine shreds. She added salad cream, meticulously mixing everything up. She said eventually:

'Are you going in to Dublin?'

'We're going dancing,' Hubert said. 'The Four Provinces Ballroom in Harcourt Street. Music tonight by Ken Mackintosh.'

'I don't think I've heard of Mr Mackintosh.'

'Celebrity spot, the Inkspots.'

'Inkspots?'

'They sing songs.'

On a large round breadboard beside Mrs Plunkett there were several kinds of bread, which she cut very slowly with a battered breadsaw. On the table there was plum jam and raspberry jam, and the honeycomb we had bought from Mrs Hanrahan. There was a fruitcake and a coffee cake, biscuits and shortbread, and when we'd finished our corned beef Lily came in and added to this array a plate of éclairs. She lifted away the plates and dishes we'd finished with. Mrs Plunkett thanked her.

'Mrs Hanrahan said she picked that honeycomb out for you,' Hubert said.

'Well, that was most kind of her.'

'She's lonely since Hanrahan died. She'd talk the legs off you.'

'It's hard for the poor woman. A builder's widow.' Mrs Plunkett explained to me what I already knew. 'He fell off a roof six weeks ago.'

'As a matter of fact,' Hubert said, 'she's better off without him.'

'What on earth d'you mean, Hubert?'

'Hanrahan went after shop girls. Famous for it.'

'Don't speak so coarsely, Hubert.'

'Is Pam shocked? Are you shocked, Pam?'

'No, no, not at all.' Pamela swiftly replied before her grandmother could answer for her. She had reddened again in her confusion, but being flustered made her more vivacious and was not unattractive.

'Mr Hanrahan was a perfectly decent man,' Mrs Plunkett insisted. 'You're repeating tittle-tattle, Hubert.'

'There's a girl serves in Binchy's, another in Edwards' the cake shop. Hanrahan took both of them to the dunes. D'you remember Hanrahan, Pam?'

She shook her head.

'He painted the drain-pipes one time.'

'You'll need to hurry if you wish to catch the train,' Mrs Plunkett said. As she spoke she drew back the cuff of her sleeve to consult a wristwatch that had not been visible before. She nodded in agreement with the statement she'd just made. Addressing her granddaughter, she said:

'It doesn't matter if you don't finish.'

Doubtfully, Pamela half smiled at Mrs Plunkett. She began to say something, then changed her mind. Vaguely, she shook her head.

'Is Pamela going in to Dublin too?' Hubert said. 'Going to the flicks, Pamela?'

'Isn't she accompanying you? Don't you want to go dancing with the boys, Pamela?'

'No, no.' She shook her head, more vehemently than before. She was going to wash her hair, she said.

'But surely you'd like to go dancing, Pamela?'

Hubert stood up, half a piece of shortbread in one hand. He jerked his head at me, indicating that I should hurry. Pamela said again that she wanted to wash her hair.

'Jesus Christ!' Hubert murmured in the hall. He stifled laughter. 'I'm bloody certain,' he said as we hurried through the garden, 'she remembers Hanrahan. The man made a pass at her.'

In the train he told me when I asked that she was the child of his father's sister. 'She comes over every summer from some back-of-beyond rectory in Roscommon.' He was vague when I asked further questions, or else impatiently brushed them aside. 'Pam's dreary,' was all he said.

'She doesn't seem dreary to me.'

'The old man worships her. Like he did her mother by all accounts.'

In the Four Provinces Ballroom we met girls who were quite different from Hubert's cousin. Hubert said they came from the slums, though this could not have been true since they were fashionably dressed and had money for soft drinks and cigarettes. Their legs were painted—the liquid stockings of that time—and their features were emphasized with lipstick and mascara. But each one I danced with was either stunted or lumpy, and I kept thinking of Pamela's slim figure and her pretty face. Her lips, in particular, I remembered.

We danced to 'As Time Goes By' and 'Autumn Leaves' and 'Falling in Love with Love'. The Inkspots sang. One of the partners I danced with said: 'Your friend's very handsome, isn't he?'

In the end Hubert picked up two girls who were agreeable to being seen home when the evening came to an end.

Ken Mackintosh and his band began to pack away their instruments. We walked a little way along Harcourt Street and caught a number 11 bus. The girls were nurses. The one allocated to me, being bouncy and talkative, wanted to know what it was like living in a provincial town, as I did, and what my plans were for getting out of it. When I told her she said: 'Maybe I'll run into you when you're a student,' but her voice wasn't exactly loaded with pleasurable anticipation. She was wearing a thick, green woollen coat even though it was August. Her face was flat and pale, her lips garish beneath a fresh coating of lipstick. She had to get up at five o'clock every morning, she said, in order to get to the ward on time. The Sister was a tartar.

When we arrived at the girls' flat Hubert suggested that we might be offered a cup of tea, but the girls would permit us no further than the doorstep of the house. 'I thought we were away,' he murmured disconsolately. His father would have got in, he said. They'd have cooked a meal for his father, anything he wanted. We walked to where we hoped to get a lift to Templemairt. Two hours later a lorry driver picked us up.

The next day being a Saturday, Hubert and I went to Phoenix Park races. We missed breakfast and due to pressure of time we missed lunch also—and, in fact, the first race. 'The old man'll have been livid,' Hubert said. 'You understand he takes in what's going on?' Mrs Plunkett and Pamela would have sat waiting for us in the dining-room, he said, then Pamela would have been sent up to see if we were still asleep, and after that Mrs Plunkett would have gone up herself. 'They'll have asked Lily and she'll have told them we've hooked it to the races.' He neither laughed nor smiled, even though he seemed amused. Another two pounds had been borrowed from Lily before we left.

'He'll be livid because he'll think we should have taken Pam with us.'

'Why don't you like Pamela?'

Hubert didn't reply. He said instead: 'I'd love to have heard Hanrahan putting a proposition to her.'

At school all of it would have sounded different. We'd have laughed—I more than anyone—at the report of the lively builder attempting to seduce Hubert's cousin. And somehow it would have been funnier because this had occurred in his grandfather's house, his grandfather being the sort he was. We would have imagined the embarrassment of Hubert's cousin, and Hanrahan saying what harm was a little kiss. We would have imagined the old man oblivious of it all, and would have laughed because Hubert's cousin couldn't bring herself to say anything about it afterwards. Hubert told his stories well.

'He may not,' I said, 'have had a go at her.'

'He couldn't leave them alone, that man. I'm going for this Summer Rain thing.'

We stood in the crowd, examining the list of runners. Announcements were made over loudspeakers; all around us people were talking furiously. Men were in shirt-sleeves, women and girls in summer dresses. It was another sunny day.

'Paddy's Pride no good?' I said.

'Could be.' But we both put our bets on Summer Rain and to my surprise the horse won at nine to one. 'Let's have a drink,' Hubert said. Without asking me what I wanted he ordered stout at the bar.

We won again with Sarah's Cottage, lost with Monaghan Lad and King of Them All. We drank further bottles of stout. 'Take Gay Girl for a place,' a man who had dropped into conversation with us in the bar advised. We did so and were again successful. Between us we were now almost seventeen pounds richer than when we started. We watched the last race in high spirits, grasping glasses of stout and urging on a horse called Marino. We hadn't backed it; we hadn't backed anything because Hubert said he could tell our luck had come to an end. Marino didn't win.

'We'll have something to eat and then go to the pictures,' Hubert said.

The grass beneath our feet was littered with discarded race tickets and programmes. The bookmakers were dismantling their stands. Pale evening sunlight slanted over the drifting crowds; voices were more subdued than they had been. I kept thinking of Pamela in the house in Templemairt, of Mrs Plunkett saying grace again in the dining-room, the old man sensing that we weren't present for yet another meal.

'What about *The Moon and Sixpence*?' Hubert suggested, having bought an *Evening Herald* as we left the racecourse. 'George Sanders?'

We ordered two mixed grills at the cinema restaurant, and tea and cakes. We both bought packets of cigarettes. When *The Moon and Sixpence* came to an end we went to an ice-cream parlour and then we caught a Saturday-night bus that brought us almost as far as Templemairt. We walked the last bit, Hubert talking about Africa. Before we reached the town he said:

'He disowned my father, you know. When my father got involved with my mother that was the end of that. My mother was a barmaid, you understand.'

I nodded, having been informed of that before. Hubert said:

'I didn't know that old man existed until I was told after the funeral. He didn't even come to it.'

I didn't say it must have been awful, having both your parents killed at once. We'd often thought so at school and had said it when Hubert wasn't there. We'd often considered it must have affected him, perhaps made him the way he was—careless, it seemed, of what people thought of him.

'You should have heard him when he could talk, laying into me because he thinks I'm like my father. A chip off the old block is what he thinks. My father lived on his wits. A con man, you understand.'

Hubert had often told us this also. His father had briefly been a racing correspondent, had managed a night-club, had apparently worked in a bank. But none of these forays into the realm of employment had lasted long; each had been swiftly terminated, either on the grounds of erratic service or for liberties taken with funds. Hubert, at school, had made no bones about his father's reprehensible tendencies, nor about his mother's background. On the contrary, he had taken a certain pride in the fact that his father, in later life, had lived up to the reputation he had established when a schoolboy himself. The apes that had escaped from the circus cage at the time of the tragedy had chattered with delight, scampering over the wreckage. His father would have appreciated that, he said.

A weak crescent moon lightened the darkness as we walked towards Templemairt. The stars were out in force. No car passed us, but even if we'd been aware of headlights behind us I doubt that we'd have bothered to try for a lift. We smoked one cigarette after another, still exhilarated by our triumphant afternoon, and in the circumstances it seemed natural that Hubert should talk about his parents, who had spent a lot of time on racecourses.

'They were drunk, of course, when they crashed that car.'

It was not difficult to believe they were, but none the less I did not feel that hearty agreement was in order. I nodded briefly. I said:

'Were you born in England?'

'I believe in the back row of a cinema.'

I had never heard that before, but there was something about Hubert's honesty in other matters that prevented me from suspecting invention. The photograph of his grandfather in the hall was precisely as Mr Plunkett had so often been described, down to his eyebrows being almost a single horizontal line, and the celluloid collar of his shirt.

'When the lights went up she couldn't move. They had to send for a doctor, but before the ambulance arrived she popped me.'

We entered the house quietly and went to our rooms without further conversation. I had hoped that Pamela might still be up since it wasn't as late as last night. I had even prepared a scene that I felt could easily take place: Pamela in the hall as we closed the front door behind us, Pamela offering us tea in the kitchen and Hubert declining while I politely accepted.

'Pam, do you want to play tennis?'

She was as astonished as I was to hear this. A startled look came into her face. She stammered slightly when she replied.

'Three of us?' she said.

'We'll show you how three can play.'

Sunday lunch had already taken place, a somewhat silent occasion because Hubert and I were more than ever out of favour. Mrs Plunkett said quietly, but in the firm tones of one conveying a message as a matter of trust, that her husband had been disappointed because we hadn't accompanied Pamela and herself to church. I did my best to apologize; Hubert ignored the revelation. 'We won a fortune at the races,' he said, which helped matters as little as it would have had the old man been present.

'Tennis would be lovely,' Pamela said.

She added that she'd change. Hubert said he'd lend me a pair of tennis shoes.

A remarkable transformation appeared to have overtaken him, and for a moment I thought that the frosty lunchtime and his grandfather's reported distress had actually stirred his conscience. It then occurred to me that since there was nothing else to do on a Sunday afternoon, tennis with Pamela was better than being bored. I knew what he meant when he said we'd show her how three could play: on the tennis court Hubert belonged in a class far more exalted than my own, and often at school Ossie Richpatrick and I had together played against him and still not managed to win. It delighted me that Pamela and I were to be partners.

Hubert's tennis shoes didn't fit me perfectly, but I succeeded in getting them on to my feet. There was no suggestion that he and I should change our clothes, as Pamela had said she intended to. Hubert offered me a choice of several racquets and when I'd selected one we made our way to the tennis court at the back of the house. We raised the net, measured its height, and knocked up while we waited.

'I'm afraid we can't,' Pamela said.

She was wearing a white dress and tennis shoes and socks of the same pristine freshness. There was a white band in her hair and she was wearing sunglasses. She wasn't carrying her tennis racquet.

'Can't what?' Hubert said, stroking a ball over the net. 'Can't what, Pam?'

'We're not allowed to play tennis.'

'Who says we're not allowed to? What d'you mean, allowed?'

'Grandmother says we mustn't play tennis.'

'Why on earth not?'

'Because it's Sunday, because you haven't been to church.'

'Oh, don't be so bloody silly.'

'He asked her what we were doing. She had to tell him.'

'The idiotic old brute.'

'I don't want to play, Hubert.'

Hubert stalked away. I wound the net down. I was glad he hadn't insisted that he and I should play on our own.

'Don't be upset by it.' I spoke apologetically. I didn't know what else to say.

'There won't be a quarrel,' she reassured me, and in fact there wasn't. The raised voices of Hubert and his grandmother, which I thought we'd hear coming from the house, didn't materialize. Pamela went to change her dress. I took off Hubert's tennis shoes. In the drawing-room at teatime Mrs Plunkett said:

'Hubert's turned his face to the wall, has he?'

'Shall I call him?' Pamela offered.

'Hubert knows the hour of Sunday tea, my dear.'

Lily brought more hot water. She, too, seemed affected by what had occurred, her mouth tightly clamped. But I received the impression that the atmosphere in the drawing-room was one she was familiar with.

'A pity to turn one's face to the wall on such a lovely day,' Mrs Plunkett remarked.

Silence took over then and was not broken until Mrs Plunkett rose and left the room. Strauss began on the piano, tinkling faintly through the wall. Lily came in to collect the tea things.

'Perhaps we should go for a walk,' Pamela said.

We descended the stepped path between the rockeries and strolled past Hanrahan's yard. We turned into the sandy lane that led to the dunes and made our way on to the strand. We didn't refer to what had occurred.

'Are you still at school?' I asked.

'I left in July.'

'What are you going to do now?'

'I'm hoping to study botany.'

She was shyer than I'd thought. Her voice was reticent when she said she hoped to study botany, as if the vaunting of this ambition constituted a presumption.

'What are you going to do?'

I told her. I envied Hubert going to Africa, I said, becoming garrulous in case she was bored by silence. I mentioned the culti-vation of groundnuts.

'Africa?' she said. When she stopped she took me unawares and I had to walk back a pace or two. Too late, I realized I had inad-vertently disclosed a confidence.

'It's just an idea he has.'

I tried to change the subject, but she didn't seem to hear, or wasn't interested. I watched while she drew a pattern on the sand with the toe of her shoe. More slowly than before, she walked on again.

'I don't know why,' I said, 'we don't have a bathe.'

She didn't reply. Children were running into and out of the sea. Two men were paddling, with their trousers rolled up to their knees. A girl was sunbathing on a li-lo, both hands in the water, resisting the tide that would have carried her away from the shore.

'My bathing-dress is in the house,' Pamela said at last. 'I could get it if you like.'

'Would *you* like?'

She shrugged. Perhaps not, she said, and I wondered if she was thinking that bathing, as much as tennis, might be frowned upon as a breach of the Sabbath.

'I don't think, actually,' she said, 'that Hubert will ever go to Africa.'

Lily stood beside my deck-chair, a bunch of mint she'd picked in one hand. I hadn't known what else to do, since Hubert had not come out of his room, so I'd wandered about the garden and had eventually found the deck-chair on a triangle of grass in a corner. 'I'm going to read for a while,' Pamela had said when we returned from our walk.

'It's understandable they never had to be so severe with Pamela,' Lily said. 'On account of her mother being sensible in her life. Different from Hubert's father.'

I guessed she was talking to me like this because she'd noticed I was bewildered. The pettiness I had witnessed in my friend was a shock more than a surprise. Affected by it, I'd even wondered as I'd walked with Pamela back from the strand if I'd been invited to the house in order to become an instrument in her isolation. I'd dismissed the thought as a ridiculous flight of fancy: now I was not so sure.

'It's understandable, Hubert being bad to her. When you think about it, it's understandable.'

Lily passed on, taking with her the slight scent of mint that had begun to waft towards me because she'd crushed a leaf or two. 'He tried to beat me with a walking-stick,' Hubert had reported at school, and I imagined the apprehension Lily hinted at—the father of the son who'd gone to the bad determined that history should not be repeated, the mother anxious and agreeing.

'I was looking for you,' Hubert said, sitting down on the grass beside me. 'Why don't we go down to the hotel?'

I looked at him, his lean face in profile. I remembered Pamela drawing the pattern on the sand, her silence the only intimation of her love. When had an intonation or a glance first betrayed it to him? I wondered.

Hubert pushed himself to his feet and we sauntered off to the lounge-bar of the hotel beside the railway station. Without asking me what I would like, Hubert ordered gin and orange. The tennis we hadn't played wasn't mentioned, nor did I say that Pamela and I had walked on the strand.

'No need to go tomorrow,' Hubert said. 'Stay on a bit.'

'I said I'd be back.'

'Send them a wire.'

'I don't want to over-stay, Hubert. It's good of your grandmother to have me.'

'That girl stays for three months.'

I'd never drunk gin before. The orange made it pleasantly sweet, with only a slight aftertaste. I liked it better than stout.

'My father's drink,' Hubert said. 'My mother preferred gimlets. A gimlet,' he added, 'is gin with lime in it. They drank an awful lot, you understand.'

He confided to me that he intended to slip away to England himself. He was softening Lily up, he said, with the intention of borrowing a hundred pounds from her. He knew she had it because she never spent a penny; a hundred pounds would last him for ages, while he found out more about the prospects in Africa.

'I'll pay her back. I'd never not.'

'Yes, of course.'

'Anything would be better than the Dublin Handkerchief Company. Imagine being in the Dublin Handkerchief Company when you were fifty years of age! A lifetime of people blowing their noses!'

We sat there, talking about school, remembering the time Fitzherbert had dressed himself up in the kind of woman's clothes he considered suitable for a streetwalker and demanded an interview with Farquie, the senior languages master; and the time the Kingsmill brothers had introduced a laxative into the High Table soup; and when Prunty and Tatchett had appropriated a visiting rugby team's clothes while they were in the showers. We recalled the days of our first term: how Hubert and I had occupied beds next to one another in the junior dormitory, how Miss Fanning, the common-room secretary, had been kind to us, thinking we were homesick.

'One *pour la route*,' Hubert said.

He held the man who served us in conversation, describing the same mixture of gin and orangeade as he'd had it once in some other bar. There had been iced sugar clinging to the rim of the glass; delicious, he said. The man just stared at him.

'I'll fix it up with Lily tonight,' Hubert said on the way back to the house. 'If she can't manage the hundred I'd settle for fifty.'

We were still talking loudly as we mounted the stepped path between the rockeries, and as we passed through the hall. In the dining-room Mrs Plunkett and Pamela had clearly been seated at the table for some time. When we entered the old woman rose without commenting on our lateness and repeated the grace she had already said. A weary expression froze Hubert's features while he waited for her voice to cease.

'We were down in the hotel,' he said when it did, 'drinking gin and orange. Have you ever wandered into the hotel, Pam?'

She shook her head, her attention appearing to be occupied with the chicken leg on her plate. Hubert said the hotel had a pleasant little lounge-bar, which wasn't the description I'd have chosen myself. A rendezvous for the discriminating, he said, even if one encountered difficulty there when it came to a correctly concocted gin and orange. He was pretending to be drunker than he was.

'A rather dirty place, Dowd's Hotel,' Mrs Plunkett interposed, echoing what I knew would have been her husband's view.

'Hanrahan used to drink there,' Hubert continued. 'Many's the time I saw him with a woman in the corner. I've forgotten if you said you remembered the late Hanrahan, Pam?'

She said she didn't. Mrs Plunkett held out her cup and saucer for more tea. Pamela poured it.

'Hanrahan painted the drain-pipes,' Hubert said. 'D'you remember that time, Pam?'

She shook her head. I wanted to tell him to stop. I wanted to remind him that he had already asked his cousin if she remembered Hanrahan painting the drain-pipes, to point out that it wasn't she who had caused the difficulty that afternoon, that it wasn't she who had made us stand there while grace was said again.

'I'm surprised you don't,' Hubert said. 'I'm really very surprised, Pam.'

Mrs Plunkett didn't understand the conversation. She smiled kindly at me, and briefly indicated dishes I might like to help myself to. She lifted a forkful of cold chicken to her mouth.

'It's only that he mentioned you once in Dowd's,' Hubert said. He laughed, his eyes sparkling, as if with delight. 'He asked how you were getting on one time. A very friendly man.'

Pamela turned away from the table, but she couldn't hide what she wished to hide and she couldn't control her emotions. Her cheeks were blazing now. She sobbed, and then she pushed her chair back and hurried from the room.

'What have you said to her?' Mrs Plunkett asked in astonishment.

I could not sleep that night. I kept thinking about Pamela, unhappy in her bedroom, and Hubert in his. I imagined Hubert's father and Pamela's mother, children in the house also, the bad son, the good daughter. I imagined the distress suffered in the house when Hubert's father was accused of some small theft at school, which Hubert said he had been. I imagined the misdemeanour forgotten, a new leaf turned, and some time later the miscreant dunned by a debt collector for a sum he could not pay. Letters came to the house from England, pleading for assistance, retailing details of hardship due to misfortune. When I closed my eyes, half dreaming though I was not yet asleep, Mrs Plunkett wept, as Pamela had. She dreaded the letters, she sobbed; for a day or two she was able to forget and

then another letter came. 'I will write a cheque': the man I had not
seen spoke blankly, taking a cheque-book from his pocket and, at
the breakfast table, writing it immediately.

I opened my eyes; I murmured Pamela's name. 'Pamela,' I whispered
because repeating it made her face more vivid in my mind. I might have
told her that Hubert, at school, had been sought out and admired more
than any other boy because he was not ordinary, that he'd been
attractive and different in all sorts of ways. I might have begged her
not to hate the memory of him when she ceased to love him.

I fell asleep. We played tennis and Hubert easily beat us. A car
lay on its side, headlights beaming on the apes that scampered from
the broken cage. On the bloody grass of the roadside verge the two
dead faces still smiled. 'You will know no blacker day,' the voice of
a schoolmaster promised.

In the morning, after breakfast, I packed my suitcase while
Hubert sat smoking a cigarette in silence. I said goodbye to Lily in
the kitchen, and to Mrs Plunkett. Pamela was in the hall when we
passed through it.

'Goodbye,' she said. At breakfast she had seemed to have recovered her composure. She smiled at me now, saying she was sorry I
was going.

'Goodbye, Pamela.'

Hubert stood by the open hall door, not looking at her, gazing
out into the sunlit garden. On the way to the railway station we
talked again about incidents at school. He mentioned the two
nurses we'd accompanied to their doorstep and the luck we'd had
at the races. 'A pity we wouldn't have time for a gin and orange,'
he said as we passed the hotel.

On the slow train, close at first to the sea and then moving into the
landscape that was just beginning to seem parched because of the
heatwave, I knew that I would never see Hubert again. A friendship
had come to an end because when a little more time went by he would
be ashamed, knowing I would not easily forget how he had made his
cousin a casualty of the war with his grandfather. There would always
be an awkwardness now, and the memory of Hubert at home.

The Piano Tuner's Wives

Violet married the piano tuner when he was a young man. Belle married him when he was old.

There was a little more to it than that, because in choosing Violet to be his wife the piano tuner had rejected Belle, which was something everyone remembered when the second wedding was announced. 'Well, she got the ruins of him anyway,' a farmer of the neighbourhood remarked, speaking without vindictiveness, stating a fact as he saw it. Others saw it similarly, though most of them would have put the matter differently.

The piano tuner's hair was white and one of his knees became more arthritic with each damp winter that passed. He had once been svelte but was no longer so, and he was blinder than on the day he married Violet—a Thursday in 1951, June 7th. The shadows he lived among now had less shape and less density than those of 1951.

'I will,' he responded in the small Protestant church of St Colman, standing almost exactly as he had stood on that other afternoon. And Belle, in her fifty-ninth year, repeated the words her one-time rival had spoken before this altar also. A decent interval had elapsed; no one in the church considered that the memory of Violet had not been honoured, that her passing had not been distressfully mourned. '. . . and with all my worldly goods I thee endow,' the piano tuner stated, while his new wife thought she would like to be standing beside him in white instead of suitable wine-red. She had not attended the first wedding, although she had been invited. She'd kept herself occupied that day, whitewashing the chicken shed, but even so she'd wept. And tears or not, she was more beautiful—and younger by almost five years—than the bride who so vividly occupied her thoughts as she battled with her jealousy. Yet he had preferred Violet—or the prospect of the house that would one day become hers, Belle told herself bitterly in the chicken shed, and the little bit of money there was, an easement in a blind man's existence. How understandable, she was reminded later on, whenever she saw Violet guiding him as they walked, whenever she thought of Violet making everything work for him, giving him a life. Well, so could she have.

As they left the church the music was by Bach, the organ played by someone else today, for usually it was his task. Groups formed in the small graveyard that was scattered around the small grey building, where the piano tuner's father and mother were buried, with ancestors on his father's side from previous generations. There would be tea and a few drinks for any of the wedding guests who cared to make the journey to the house, two miles away, but some said goodbye now, wishing the pair happiness. The piano tuner shook hands that were familiar to him, seeing in his mental eye faces that his first wife had described for him. It was the depth of summer, as in 1951, the sun warm on his forehead and his cheeks, and on his body through the heavy wedding clothes. All his life he had known this graveyard, had first felt the letters on the stones as a child, spelling out to his mother the names of his father's family. He and Violet had not had children themselves, though they'd have liked them. He was her child, it had been said, a statement that was an irritation for Belle whenever she heard it. She would have given him children, of that she felt certain.

'I'm due to visit you next month,' the old bridegroom reminded a woman whose hand still lay in his, the owner of a Steinway, the only one among all the pianos he tuned. She played it beautifully. He asked her to whenever he tuned it, assuring her that to hear was fee enough. But she always insisted on paying what was owing.

'Monday the third I think it is.'

'Yes, it is, Julia.'

She called him Mr Dromgould: he had a way about him that did not encourage familiarity in others. Often when people spoke of him he was referred to as the piano tuner, this reminder of his profession reflecting the respect accorded to the possessor of a gift. Owen Francis Dromgould his full name was.

'Well, we had a good day for it,' the new young clergyman of the parish remarked. 'They said maybe showers but sure they got it wrong.'

'The sky—?'

'Oh, cloudless, Mr Dromgould, cloudless.'

'Well, that's nice. And you'll come on over to the house, I hope?'

'He must, of course,' Belle pressed, then hurried through the gathering in the graveyard to reiterate the invitation, for she was determined to have a party.

Some time later, when the new marriage had settled into a routine, people wondered if the piano tuner would begin to think about retiring. With a bad knee, and being sightless in old age, he would readily have been forgiven in the houses and the convents and the school halls where he applied his skill. Leisure was his due, the good fortune of company as his years slipped by no more than he deserved. But when, occasionally, this was put to him by the loquacious or the inquisitive he denied that anything of the kind was in his thoughts, that he considered only the visitation of death as bringing any kind of end. The truth was, he would be lost without his work, without his travelling about, his arrival every six months or so in one of the small towns to which he had offered his services for so long. No, no, he promised, they'd still see the white Vauxhall turning in at a farm gate or parked for half an hour in a convent play-yard, or drawn up on a verge while he ate his lunch-time sandwiches, his tea poured out of a Thermos by his wife.

It was Violet who had brought most of this activity about. When they married he was still living with his mother in the gate-lodge of Barnagorm House. He had begun to tune pianos—the two in Barnagorm House, another in the town of Barnagorm, and one in a farmhouse he walked to four miles away. In those days he was a charity because he was blind, was now and again asked to repair the sea-grass seats of stools or chairs, which was an ability he had acquired, or to play at some function or other the violin his mother had bought him in his childhood. But when Violet married him she changed his life. She moved into the gate-lodge, she and his mother not always agreeing but managing to live together none the less. She possessed a car, which meant she could drive him to wherever she discovered a piano, usually long neglected. She drove to houses as far away as forty miles. She fixed his charges, taking the consumption of petrol and wear and tear to the car into account. Efficiently, she kept an address book and marked in a diary the date of each next tuning. She recorded a considerable improvement in earnings, and saw that there was more to be made from the playing of the violin than had hitherto been realized: Country-and-Western evenings in lonely public houses, the crossroads platform dances of summer—a practice that in 1951 had not entirely died out. Owen Dromgould delighted in his violin and would play it anywhere, for profit or not. But Violet was keen on the profit.

So the first marriage busily progressed, and when eventually Violet inherited her father's house she took her husband to live there. Once a farmhouse, it was no longer so, the possession of the land that gave it this title having long ago been lost through the fondness for strong drink that for generations had dogged the family but had not reached Violet herself.

'Now, tell me what's there,' her husband requested often in their early years, and Violet told him about the house she had brought him to, remotely situated on the edge of the mountains that were blue in certain lights, standing back a bit from a bend in a lane. She described the nooks in the rooms, the wooden window shutters he could hear her pulling over and latching when wind from the east caused a draught that disturbed the fire in the room once called the parlour. She described the pattern of the carpet on the single flight of stairs, the blue-and-white porcelain knobs of the kitchen cupboards, the front door that was never opened. He loved to listen. His mother, who had never entirely come to terms with his affliction, had been impatient. His father, a stableman at Barnagorm

House who'd died after a fall, he had never known. 'Lean as a greyhound,' Violet described his father from a photograph that remained.

She conjured up the big, cold hall of Barnagorm House. 'What we walk around on the way to the stairs is a table with a peacock on it. An enormous silvery bird with bits of coloured glass set in the splay of its wings to represent the splendour of the feathers. Greens and blues,' she said when he asked the colour, and yes, she was certain it was only glass, not jewels, because once, when he was doing his best with the badly flawed grand in the drawingroom, she had been told that. The stairs were on a curve, he knew from going up and down them so often to the Chappell in the nursery. The first landing was dark as a tunnel, Violet said, with two sofas, one at each end, and rows of unsmiling portraits half lost in the shadows of the walls.

'We're passing Doocey's now,' Violet would say. 'Father Feely's getting petrol at the pumps.' Esso it was at Doocey's, and he knew how the word was written because he'd asked and had been told. Two different colours were employed; the shape of the design had been compared with shapes he could feel. He saw, through Violet's eyes, the gaunt façade of the McKirdys' house on the outskirts of Oghill. He saw the pallid face of the stationer in Kiliath. He saw his mother's eyes closed in death, her hands crossed on her breast. He saw the mountains, blue on some days, misted away to grey on others. 'A primrose isn't flamboyant,' Violet said. 'More like straw or country butter, with a spot of colour in the middle.' And he would nod, and know. Soft blue like smoke, she said about the mountains; the spot in the middle more orange than red. He knew no more about smoke than what she had told him also, but he could tell those sounds. He knew what red was, he insisted, because of the sound; orange because you could taste it. He could see red in the Esso sign and the orange spot in the primrose. 'Straw' and 'country butter' helped him, and when Violet called Mr Whitten gnarled it was enough. A certain Mother Superior was austere. Anna Craigie was fanciful about the eyes. Thomas in the sawmills was a streel. Bat Conlon had the forehead of the Merricks' retriever, which was stroked every time the Merricks' Broadwood was attended to.

Between one woman and the next, the piano tuner had managed without anyone, fetched by the possessors of pianos and driven to their houses, assisted in his shopping and his housekeeping. He felt he had become a nuisance to people, and knew that Violet would not have wanted that. Nor would she have wanted the business she built up for him to be neglected because she was no longer there. She was proud that he played the organ in St Colman's Church. 'Don't ever stop doing that,' she whispered some time before she whispered her last few words, and so he went alone to the church. It was on a Sunday, when two years almost had passed, that the romance with Belle began.

Since the time of her rejection Belle had been unable to shake off her jealousy, resentful because she had looks and Violet hadn't, bitter because it seemed to her that the punishment of blindness was a punishment for her too. For what else but a punishment could you call the dark the sightless lived in? And what else but a punishment was it that darkness should be thrown over her beauty? Yet there had been no sin to punish and they would have been a handsome couple, she and Owen Dromgould. An act of grace it would have been, her beauty given to a man who did not know that it was there.

It was because her misfortune did not cease to nag at her that Belle remained unmarried. She assisted her father first and then her brother in the family shop, making out tickets for the clocks and watches that were left in for repair, noting the details for the engraving of sports trophies. She served behind the single counter, the Christmas season her busy time, glassware and weather indicators the most popular wedding gifts, cigarette lighters and inexpensive jewellery for lesser occasions. In time, clocks and watches required only the fitting of a battery, and so the gift side of the business was expanded. But while that time passed there was no man in the town who lived up to the one who had been taken from her.

Belle had been born above the shop, and when house and shop became her brother's she continued to live there. Her brother's children were born, but there was still room for her, and her position in the shop itself was not usurped. It was she who kept the chickens at the back, who always had been in charge of them, given the responsibility on her tenth birthday: that, too, continued. That she lived with a disappointment had long ago become part of her, had made her what she was for her nieces and her nephew. It was in her eyes, some people noted, even lent her beauty a quality that enhanced it. When the romance began with the man who had once rejected her, her brother and his wife considered she was making a mistake, but did not say so, only laughingly asked if she intended taking the chickens with her.

That Sunday they stood talking in the graveyard when the handful of other parishioners had gone. 'Come and I'll show you the graves,' he said, and led the way, knowing exactly where he was going, stepping on to the grass and feeling the first gravestone with his fingers. His grandmother, he said, on his father's side, and for a moment Belle wanted to feel the incised letters herself instead of looking at them. They both knew, as they moved among the graves, that the parishioners who'd gone home were very much aware of the two who had been left behind. On Sundays, ever since Violet's death, he had walked to and from his house, unless it happened to be raining, in which case the man who drove old Mrs Purtill to church took him home also. 'Would you like a walk, Belle?' he asked when he had shown her his family graves. She said she would.

Belle didn't take the chickens with her when she became a wife. She said she'd had enough of chickens. Afterwards she regretted that, because every time she did anything in the house that had been Violet's she felt it had been done by Violet before her. When she cut up meat for a stew, standing with the light falling on the board that Violet had used, and on the knife, she felt herself a follower. She diced carrots, hoping that Violet had sliced them. She bought new wooden spoons because Violet's had shrivelled away so. She painted the upright rails of the banisters. She painted the inside of the front door that was never opened. She disposed of the stacks of women's magazines, years old, that she found in an upstairs cupboard. She threw away a frying-pan because she considered it unhygienic. She ordered new vinyl for the kitchen floor. But she kept the flowerbeds at the back weeded in case anyone coming to the house might say she was letting the place become run-down.

There was always this dichotomy: what to keep up, what to change. Was she giving in to Violet when she tended her flowerbeds? Was she giving in to pettiness when she threw away a frying-pan and three wooden spoons? Whatever Belle did she afterwards doubted herself. The dumpy figure of Violet, grey-haired as she had been in the end, her eyes gone small in the plumpness of her face, seemed irritatingly to command. And the unseeing husband they shared, softly playing his violin in one room or another, did not know that his first wife had dressed badly, did not know she had thickened and become sloppy, did not know she had been an unclean cook. That Belle was the one who was alive, that she was offered all a man's affection, that she plundered his other woman's possessions and occupied her bedroom and drove her car, should have been enough. It should have been everything, but as time went on it seemed to Belle to be scarcely anything at all. He had become set in ways that had been allowed and hallowed in a marriage of nearly forty years: that was what was always there.

A year after the wedding, as the couple sat one lunchtime in the car which Belle had drawn into the gateway to a field, he said:

'You'd tell me if it was too much for you?'

'Too much, Owen?'

'Driving all over the county. Having to get me in and out. Having to sit there listening.'

'It's not too much.'

'You're good the way you've patience.'

'I don't think I'm good at all.'

'I knew you were in church that Sunday. I could smell the perfume you had on. Even at the organ I could smell it.'

'I'll never forget that Sunday.'

'I loved you when you let me show you the graves.'

'I loved you before that.'

'I don't want to tire you out, with all the traipsing about after pianos. I could let it go, you know.'

He would do that for her, her thought was as he spoke. He wasn't much for a woman, he had said another time: a blind man moving on towards the end of his days. He confessed that when first he wanted to marry her he hadn't put it to her for more than two months, knowing better than she what she'd be letting herself in for if she said yes. 'What's that Belle look like these days?' he had asked Violet a few years ago, and Violet hadn't answered at first. Then apparently she'd said: 'Belle still looks a girl.'

'I wouldn't want you to stop your work. Not ever, Owen.'

'You're all heart, my love. Don't say you're not good.'

'It gets me out and about too, you know. More than ever in my life. Down all those avenues to houses I didn't know were there. Towns I've never been to. People I never knew. It was restricted before.'

The word slipped out, but it didn't matter. He did not reply that he understood about restriction, for that was not his style. When they were getting to know one another, after that Sunday by the church, he said he'd often thought of her in her brother's jeweller's shop, wrapping up what was purchased there, as she had wrapped for him the watch he bought for one of Violet's birthdays. He'd thought of her putting up the grilles over the windows in the evenings and locking the shop door, and then going upstairs to sit with her brother's family. When they were married she told him more: how most of the days of her life had been spent, only her chickens her own. 'Smart in her clothes,' Violet had added when she said the woman he'd rejected still looked a girl.

There hadn't been any kind of honeymoon, but a few months

after he had wondered if travelling about was too much for her he took Belle away to a seaside resort where he and Violet had many times spent a week. They stayed in the same boarding-house, the Sans Souci, and walked on the long, empty strand and in lanes where larks scuttered in and out of the fuchsia, and on the cliffs. They drank in Malley's public house. They lay in autumn sunshine on the dunes.

'You're good to have thought of it.' Belle smiled at him, pleased because he wanted her to be happy.

'Set us up for the winter, Belle.'

She knew it wasn't easy for him. They had come to this place because he knew no other; he was aware before they set out of the complication that might develop in his emotions when they arrived. She had seen that in his face, a stoicism that was there for her. Privately, he bore the guilt of betrayal, stirred up by the smell of the sea and seaweed. The voices in the boarding-house were the voices Violet had heard. For Violet, too, the scent of honeysuckle had lingered into October. It was Violet who first said a week in the autumn sun would set them up for the winter: that showed in him, also, a moment after he spoke the words.

'I'll tell you what we'll do,' he said. 'When we're back we'll get you the television, Belle.'

'Oh, but you—'

'You'd tell me.'

They were walking near the lighthouse on the cape when he said that. He would have offered the television to Violet, but Violet must have said she wouldn't be bothered with the thing. It would never be turned on, she had probably argued; you only got silliness on it anyway.

'You're good to me,' Belle said instead.

'Ah no, no.'

When they were close enough to the lighthouse he called out and a man called back from a window. 'Hold on a minute,' the man said, and by the time he opened the door he must have guessed that the wife he'd known had died. 'You'll take a drop?' he offered when they were inside, when the death and the remarriage had been mentioned. Whiskey was poured, and Belle felt that the three glasses lifted in salutation were an honouring of her, although this was not said. It rained on the way back to the boarding-house, the last evening of the holiday.

'Nice for the winter,' he said as she drove the next day through rain that didn't cease. 'The television.'

When it came, it was installed in the small room that once was called the parlour, next to the kitchen. This was where mostly they sat, where the radio was. A fortnight after the arrival of the television set Belle acquired a small black sheepdog that a farmer didn't want because it was afraid of sheep. This dog became hers and was always called hers. She fed it and looked after it. She got it used to travelling with them in the car. She gave it a new name, Maggie, which it answered to in time.

But even with the dog and the television, with additions and disposals in the house, with being so sincerely assured that she was loved, with being told she was good, nothing changed for Belle. The woman who for so long had taken her husband's arm, who had guided him into rooms of houses where he coaxed pianos back to life, still claimed existence. Not as a tiresome ghost, some unforgiving spectre uncertainly there, but as if some part of her had been left in the man she'd loved.

Sensitive in ways that other people weren't, Owen Dromgould continued to sense his second wife's unease. She knew he did. It was why he had offered to give up his work, why he'd taken her to Violet's seashore and borne there the guilt of his betrayal, why there was a television set now, and a sheepdog. He had guessed why she'd re-covered the kitchen floor. Proudly, he had raised his glass to her in the company of a man who had known Violet. Proudly, he had sat with her in the dining-room of the boarding-house and in Malley's public house.

Belle made herself remember all that. She made herself see the bottle of John Jameson taken from a cupboard in the lighthouse, and hear the boarding-house voices. He understood, he did his best to comfort her; his affection was in everything he did. But Violet would have told him which leaves were on the turn. Violet would have reported that the tide was going out or coming in. Too late Belle realized that. Violet had been his blind man's vision. Violet had left her no room to breathe.

One day, coming away from the house that was the most distant they visited, the first time Belle had been there, he said:

'Did you ever see a room as sombre as that one? Is it the holy pictures that do it?'

Belle backed the car and straightened it, then edged it through a gateway that, thirty years ago, hadn't been made wide enough.

'Sombre?' she said on a lane like a riverbed, steering around the potholes as best she could.

'We used wonder could it be they didn't want anything colourful in the way of a wallpaper in case it wasn't respectful to the pictures.'

Belle didn't comment on that. She eased the Vauxhall out on to the tarred road and drove in silence over a stretch of bogland. Vividly she saw the holy pictures in the room where Mrs Grenaghan's piano was: Virgin and Child, Sacred Heart, St Catherine with her lily, the Virgin on her own, Jesus in glory. They hung against nondescript brown; there were statues on the mantelpiece and on a corner shelf. Mrs Grenaghan had brought tea and biscuits to that small, melancholy room, speaking in a hushed tone as if the holiness demanded that.

'What pictures?' Belle asked, not turning her head, although she might have, for there was no other traffic and the bog road was straight.

'Aren't the pictures still in there? Holy pictures all over the place?'

'They must have taken them down.'

'What's there then?'

Belle went a little faster. She said a fox had come from nowhere, over to the left. It was standing still, she said, the way foxes do.

'You want to pull up and watch him, Belle?'

'No. No, he's moved on now. Was it Mrs Grenaghan's daughter who played that piano?'

'Oh, it was. And she hasn't seen that girl in years. We used say the holy pictures maybe drove her away. What's on the walls now?'

'A striped paper.' And Belle added: 'There's a photograph of the daughter on the mantelpiece.'

Some time later, on another day, when he referred to one of the sisters at the convent in Meena as having cheeks as flushed as an eating apple, Belle said that that nun was chalky white these days, her face pulled down and sunken. 'She has an illness so,' he said.

Suddenly more confident, not caring what people thought, Belle rooted out Violet's plants from the flowerbeds at the back, and grassed the flowerbeds over. She told her husband of a change at Doocey's garage: Texaco sold instead of Esso. She described the Texaco logo, the big red star and how the letters of the word were arranged. She avoided stopping at Doocey's in case a conversation took place there, in case Doocey were asked if Esso had let him down, or what. 'Well, no, I wouldn't call it silvery exactly,' Belle said about the peacock in the hall of Barnagorm house. 'If they cleaned it up I'd say it's brass underneath.' Upstairs, the sofas at each end of the landing had new loose covers, bunches of different-coloured chrysanthemums on them. 'Well no, not *lean,* I wouldn't call him that,' Belle said with the photograph of her husband's father in her hand. 'A sturdy face, I'd say.' A schoolteacher whose teeth were once described as gusty had false teeth now, less of a mouthful, her smile sedate. Time had apparently drenched the bright white of the McKirdys' façade, almost a grey you'd call it. 'Forget-me-not blue,' Belle said one day, speaking of the mountains that were blue when the weather brought that colour out. 'You'd hardly credit it.' And it was never again said in the piano tuner's house that the blue of the mountains was the subtle blue of smoke.

Owen Dromgould had run his fingers over the bark of trees. He could tell the difference in the outline of their leaves; he could tell the thorns of gorse and bramble. He knew birds from their song, dogs from their bark, cats from the touch of them on his legs. There were the letters on the gravestones, the stops of the organ, his violin. He could see red, berries on holly and cotoneaster. He could smell lavender and thyme.

All that could not be taken from him. And it didn't matter if, overnight, the colour had worn off the kitchen knobs. It didn't matter if the china light-shade in the kitchen had a crack he hadn't heard about before. What mattered was damage done to something as fragile as a dream.

The wife he had first chosen had dressed drably: from silence and inflexions—more than from words—he learned that now. Her grey hair straggled to her shoulders, her back was a little humped. He poked his way about, and they were two old people when they went out on their rounds, older than they were in their ageless happiness. She wouldn't have hurt a fly, she wasn't a person you could be jealous of, yet of course it was hard on a new wife to be haunted by happiness, to be challenged by the simplicities there had been. He had given himself to two women; he hadn't withdrawn himself from the first, he didn't from the second.

Each house that contained a piano brought forth its contradictions. The pearls old Mrs Purtill wore were opals, the pallid skin of the stationer in Kiliath was freckled, the two lines of oaks above Oghill were surely beeches? 'Of course, of course,' Owen Dromgould agreed, since it was fair that he should do so. Belle could not be blamed for making her claim, and claims could not be made without damage or destruction. Belle would win in the end because the living always do. And that seemed fair also, since Violet had won in the beginning and had had the better years.

Honeymoon in Tramore

They stayed in a boarding-house, St Agnes's, run by a Mrs Hurley. 'You have it written all over you!' this woman said when she opened the door to them. She eyed a speck of confetti on the lapel of his navy-blue suit and then glanced briefly at the rounding of Kitty's stomach. It was the summer of 1948, a warm afternoon in July.

Mrs Hurley was a middle-aged landlady in a brown coat, who apologized for the wellington boots she was wearing: she'd been brushing down the yard. Her fingernails were enamelled a vivid shade of pink, her hair was contained by a tidy blue hairnet which partially disguised an arrangement of pins and curling papers. They would be very happy in St Agnes's, she said; they'd have the place to themselves because there was no one else stopping in the house at the moment. When they were carrying their two suitcases upstairs she said that marriage was a God-given institution and added that her husband went to Mass every morning of his life, on his way to work with the county council. 'Your tea'll be on the table at six on the dot,' she said.

On their own, they embraced. He put his hand under his wife's skirt and felt for the warm flesh at the top of her stockings. 'Jesus, you're terrible,' she murmured thickly at him, as she had on the bus when he'd pressed himself close against her. She was sweating because of her condition and the July heat. Her face was sticky with perspiration, and small patches of it had developed on her dress, beneath each armpit. 'Jesus,' she whispered again. 'Oh Jesus, go easy now.'

He didn't want to go easy. They were free of the farm, and of her father and her aunt and her Uncle Ned Cauley. He had a right to his desires.

'That woman'll be listening,' she whispered in the same slurred voice, but it didn't matter if the woman was listening. It didn't even matter if the woman opened the door and walked in. The bed made creaking sounds when she wriggled away from him, saying again that he was terrible, giggling as she said it. The bedroom smelt of flies, as if the windows hadn't been opened for a long time. 'God, you're great, Kitty,' he said, his own voice thickening also.

He was thirty-three, Kitty two years older. At fifteen he had been taken from the orphans' home in Cork by Kitty's father and her Uncle Ned Cauley. The two men had let it be known that they could do with a young fellow on the farm, and Father Doran, who was their parish priest at that time, had made inquiries of Father Lyhane at the orphans' home on their behalf. 'Davy Toome's a good lad,' Father Lyhane had said, and a few weeks later, after the recommendation had been passed on to the farmers and after Father Doran had been assured that the candidate would be strong enough for farm-work, a label with that name on it had been attached to the boy and he'd been forwarded by train. 'And did you never do farm-work before?' Kitty's Uncle Ned Cauley had asked, sitting beside him in the cart as they slowly progressed on the road from the railway junction. But Davy had never even seen fields with corn in them before, let alone taken part in farm-work. 'I'm thinking,' said Kitty's uncle, who'd spent an hour in Doolin's public house at the railway junction, 'that it could be we bought a pig in a poke.' He said it again in the kitchen when they arrived, while his wife and his brother-in-law were examining Davy, silently agreeing that he was not as strong as the priest had claimed. 'Will you for God's sake take off that label!' the woman said to him, and then, in a gentler voice, asked him about his name. She'd never heard of Toome before, she said, so he told them that his name had been given to him when the orphans' home had taken him in as an infant, that there'd been a priest connected with it then who'd had an interest in naming the orphans. His first name was in memory of St David. Toome meant a burial mound. 'Is he right in the head?' he afterwards heard Kitty's father asking his brother-in-law and her uncle replying that you wouldn't know, the way he was talking about burial mounds.

'Will you come on now, for heaven's sake!' Kitty rebuked him in the bedroom at St Agnes's. 'And let me take off my hat.'

She pushed him away from her and told him to open the window. It was she who had chosen Tramore for the weekend of their honeymoon, saying she'd heard it was lovely, with a sandy little beach. Kitty knew what she wanted, her aunt used to say, and you couldn't budge her when she made up her mind. 'Would you accompany me to Cork?' she had suggested one day four months ago. 'I'm a stranger to the city, Davy.' He hadn't been back to Cork since he'd come to the farm, and he didn't really know his way around it; but it turned out that Kitty had never been there at all. 'We'll fix it to go on a Saturday,' she said, and on the bus he felt proud to be sitting there with her, a big handsome girl, the daughter of his employer: he hoped that on the streets they'd maybe meet someone from the orphans' home. She'd looked out the window most of the time, not saying very much to him, her round face pink with excitement. She was good-looking in a way he admired, better-looking than any of the other girls at Mass, or the tinker girls whom he'd caught once stealing turnips from the field, who'd shouted over a hedge at him that their sister would marry him. Her hair was very fine and very black, like a dark mist encircling her face. He'd heard her aunt calling her sullen, but he'd never noticed that himself, even though sometimes a blankness came into her face and stayed there till she roused herself. Her three brothers had all been born with something wrong with them and had died in childhood, before he had come to the farm. Nobody mentioned them; he hadn't even known about her brothers until one of the men who came to help with the harvest referred to them in passing. Her mother had died giving birth to the last of them.

'Are you OK, pet?' Kitty said, putting lipstick on at the dressing-table. 'Isn't it great we're on our own?'

He leaned against the window-frame, looking at her, seeing her in the looking-glass as well. She had to go to see a Mr Minogue, she'd said eventually on the bus, a chemist in McHenry Street.

'Great,' he said from the window.

'Can you hear the sea there?'

He shook his head. They'd found the chemist's shop, having had to ask for directions to McHenry Street. If her mother was alive she'd have accompanied her, she said all of a sudden, and then she said she couldn't go into the chemist's shop alone. Her voice became different. Her legs wouldn't have taken her, she said, and then she told him she was in trouble. Her aunt had found out about the chemist, she said, only she'd refused to accompany her. 'Take Toome to show you the way,' her aunt had said.

'Will we go down, pet?'

He moved to where she stood by the dressing-table but when he put his arms around her she said sharply that she didn't want to get messed up again. She'd spilt powder on the glass top of the dressing-table, the same peach shade that was on her cheeks. She'd put on perfume he could smell, a strong sweet smell that made him want to try again to put his arms around her. But already she had crossed the room to the door. She opened it and he followed her downstairs.

'I've done you black puddings,' Mrs Hurley said in the dining-room, placing before them plates of fried sausages and fried eggs and slices of the delicacy she spoke of.

'God, I love black pudding,' Kitty said, and he passed her his because as a boy in the orphans' home he had developed a revulsion for this dark composition of pig's blood and entrails. The table they sat at was empty of other guests, as Mrs Hurley had promised. He smiled at his bride across it. On the way downstairs she had kept repeating that this would be their first meal as husband and wife. She attached importance to the fact. She'd said it again as they sat down. Through the wooden hatch that opened into the kitchen the voice of Mrs Hurley could be heard raised in abuse, speaking about a greyhound.

'Are you hungry, pet?'

He wasn't; he shook his head.

'D'you know what it is,' Kitty said, cutting into a soda farl, 'I could eat the head off of a horse.'

A low mumble of protest had begun in the kitchen, which he guessed must emanate from Mrs Hurley's husband. 'Errah, have a pick of sense, will you?' the landlady stridently interrupted. 'Would any animal in its sane mind keep getting into a cement mixer?'

Kitty giggled. She'd nearly died, she said, when Mrs Kilfedder gave her a kiss at the wedding. 'One thing about Kilfedder,' she added, 'he keeps his hands to himself.'

At that moment a man in shirtsleeves entered the dining-room. He greeted them and introduced himself as Mr Hurley. He inquired if they'd like another pot of tea, already seizing the metal teapot and moving towards the hatch with it. They'd find St Agnes's restful, he said, no children for miles around. The hatch opened and Mrs Hurley's freshly rouged face appeared. She had removed her hairnet, and the hair it had controlled, now seen to be a shade of henna, fluffed elaborately about her head. 'Have they butter enough?' she demanded of her husband, in the same uncompromising tone she had employed when protesting about the activities of the greyhound. 'It's good country butter,' she shouted at her guests. 'Fresh as a daisy.'

'We have plenty,' Kitty replied. 'It's good butter all right, Mrs Hurley.'

The teapot was handed back through the hatch and placed on the table. 'There's a big attraction in Tramore tonight,' Mr Hurley said. 'Have you ever heard tell of the Carmodys?'

When they said they hadn't he told them that the Carmodys ran a Wall of Death that was reputed to be great entertainment. She had never seen a Wall of Death yet, Kitty said when he'd gone. 'D'you like the sausages, pet?'

He nodded, holding his cup out for tea. Under the table the calves of their legs were pressed together.

'Coddy Donnegan wanted to take me once, only I said I couldn't watch it.'

'Maybe we wouldn't bother in that case.'

'I'd watch anything with yourself, Davy. Maybe we'd walk down by the sea as well.'

He nodded again and she leaned forward to say she was feeling fine, a reference to the fact that she had recently been subject to bouts of sickness in her stomach. They'd have a few drinks after the Wall of Death and the walk, she suggested, in case it wouldn't look good, coming back to the bedroom too soon. She winked and nudged him with her knee. Under the table he put his hand on her lightly stockinged leg. 'Oh Jesus, lay off now,' she whispered.

It wasn't Coddy Donnegan, she'd told him in McHenry Street, standing outside the chemist's shop. She'd never been in love with Coddy Donnegan. She'd never been in love until the other thing happened, until there was a man taking her hand in a way Coddy Donnegan wouldn't do in a million years—a cousin of Father Tolan's, who was destined himself for the priesthood. He'd been about in the parish for the summer holidays; she'd have put down her life for him, she said. 'He'd marry me if he knew, Davy. He'd give up the priesthood, only I'd never tell him.'

They finished the meal Mrs Hurley had prepared for them. 'I'll just go upstairs a minute,' she said. 'I won't be a tick, pet.'

Waiting in the hall, Davy examined the pictures on the walls. A light burned beneath the Virgin and Child; there were reproductions of Victorian paintings, one of a match-seller, another of a shawled woman with a basket of lavender. He turned away from them, and the face of the chemist crept into his recollection: the jaw dark, the chin pimpled beneath a raw shave, eyes magnified behind heavily lensed spectacles, cheeks as pale as the white coat he wore. 'Come in,' Mr Minogue had welcomed them that day, knowing what they wanted although nothing had been said yet. It was the afternoon when his shop was closed, and he led them through the stillness of it into a room at the back, where there were no chairs to sit on, only a table with a rubber sheet on it. 'I take a grave risk,' Mr Minogue announced without preamble, his un-smiling countenance reflecting eloquently the gravity he spoke of. 'The assistance I offer you in your distress is offered for humani-tarian reasons only. But the risk must be covered, you understand that? It is not of my own volition that I charge a fee.' While he spoke he did not remove his bulbously magnified eyes from their faces, revolving his stare in a circle around each, sliding it from one to the other. 'You may know the fee?' he said, and when Kitty placed the money before him his grey, closely barbered head bowed over the notes he counted. 'Yes, this is correct,' he said, speaking directly to Davy, clearly assuming him to be the father of the un-wanted child and the source of the fee. He placed the notes in a wallet he'd taken out of the back pocket of his trousers, and jerked his head at Davy, indicating that he should return to the shop and wait there. But before Davy could do so both he and the abortionist were taken by surprise because without any warning whatsoever Kitty cried out that she couldn't do it. She would burn in hell for it, she shrieked in sudden, shrill, unexpected emotion; she could never confess it, there was no penance she could be given. 'I'd rather die as I stand, sir,' she said to Mr Minogue, and gave way to tears. They flooded on her flushed, round cheeks; the humane abortionist stood arrested, one hand still in the back pocket of his trousers. 'Hail Mary, Mother of God!' Kitty cried, shrill again. 'Sweet Mother, don't abandon me!' The money was handed back, no fur-ther word was spoken. Mr Minogue removed his white coat and led the way to the door of his shop, glancing before he opened it around the edge of an advertisement for liver salts pasted to its glass. The street was empty. As there had been no salutation, so there was no farewell.

'Are we right so?' Kitty said, descending the stairs.

He opened the hall door and they stepped out into the evening. It was warm and quiet on the terraced cul-de-sac, in which St Agnes's was the last house. They still couldn't hear the sea and Kitty said the waves wouldn't be big in that case. 'I'm sorry,' she'd said outside the chemist's shop, still sobbing, and then they'd walked for ages through the streets, before having a cup of tea in a café. She was calm by that time; it had never for a second occurred to her that she couldn't do it, she said, but the sin when she'd handed Mr Minogue the money had been like something alive in the room with them. 'I swear to God, Davy.' He'd said he understood, but in fact he didn't. He was confused because there was so much to take in—her being in trouble, the purpose of their journey being revealed, and then the episode with Mr Minogue. He was the man on the farm, the labourer who worked in the yard and the fields: it had been strange enough being asked to go to Cork with her. In the café, after she'd drunk two cups of tea, she said she was better. She ate a bun with currants in it, but he couldn't eat anything himself. Then he brought her to the orphans' home just to look at the outside of. 'God, Davy, what am I going to do?' she suddenly cried when they were standing there, as suddenly as she'd said in the back room of the chemist's that she couldn't go through with it.

'It's down at the strand,' a man told them when they asked about the Wall of Death. He pointed out the way, and soon they heard the music that accompanied it and the roar of the motor-cycle's engine. '. . . *to see again the moonlight over Clara*', moaned a tenor voice, robbed of its mellifluous quality by the scratching of a gramophone needle. '. . . *and to see the sun going down on Galway Bay*'. They paid the admission charge and climbed up rickety stairs, like a ladder, that led to the top of the circular wooden wall. A platform ran around the circumference, with a balustrade to prevent the jostling audience from falling into the pit below. 'God, it's great,' Kitty shouted above the noise, and Davy gave her arm a squeeze. A small, wizened man in red gaiters and black leather clothes, with a spotted red neckerchief, mounted the quivering motor-cycle that stood on its pedestal in the centre of the pit. He pushed it forward and ran it on to the incline at the bottom of the wall, gradually easing it on to the wall itself. Each circle he made increased the angle of his machine until in the end, close to the balustrade over which the audience leaned, he and his motor-cycle were horizontal. The timbers of the wall and of the platform shuddered, the roar of the engine was deafening. Waving above his head, the performer descended, the same circular motion in reverse. The audience clapped and threw coins into the pit. 'Are you OK?' Davy shouted, for in the excitement Kitty had closed her eyes. In the pit the motor-cycle was returned to its stand. The man bowed his gratitude for the money that still lay on the ground, and then threw out an arm in a sudden, dramatic gesture. He was joined immediately by a woman, dressed in red-and-black clothing also, who climbed on to the pillion of his motor-cycle and when it reached the centre of the wall clambered on to his back. She stood on his shoulders, with his spotted neckerchief streaming from between her teeth. Kitty screamed and closed her eyes again. More coins were thrown.

'Is she his wife, Davy?' Kitty asked as they walked away.

'I'd say she was.'

'Wouldn't it be shocking if she came off?'

'I'd say she wouldn't.'

'God, I love the smell of the sea, Davy.'

If she hadn't been wearing stockings she'd have paddled, she said, and he told her about a time they'd been taken from the orphans' home to the seaside at Courtmacsherry. He continued to tell her about this while they walked back to the town and went in search of a public house. They found one that was as quiet as St Agnes's, a murky place that Kitty said was cosy. Two elderly men sat at the counter, steadily drinking, not conversing. The publican was shifting sacks of meal in the grocery that adjoined the bar. Davy called out to him, ordering bottles of stout.

'Was it terrible in the orphans' home?' Kitty asked when he'd carried them to the table she was sitting at. 'Did you hate it the whole time?'

He said he hadn't. It hadn't been bad; he'd never known anywhere else until he came to the farm. 'Jeez, it looks like a prison,' she'd said that day, looking up at the orphans' home from the street.

'It's terrible, though, no family to turn to,' she said now. 'I have the half of it myself, with no mother.'

'You get used to the way it is.'

A week after their visit to Cork her aunt said to him in the yard
that Kitty would marry him if he asked her. Her aunt stood there
in the early-morning sunlight, a heavily made woman who was
always dressed in black. She more than anyone, more than her
husband or her brother or Kitty herself, knew that ever since he'd
arrived at the farm with a label on him he'd had a notion of Kitty.
The aunt was the sharpest of them, her eyes as black as her clothes,
always watchful. She had noticed him looking at Kitty across the
table when they all sat down to their dinner; he'd never been able
to help looking at her, and it embarrassed him every time her aunt
caught him. Did she guess that he lay in bed at night imagining
Kitty's lips on his own, and the lovely white softness of her? They
would have the farm between them was what she omitted to say in
the yard because it was not necessary to say it: Kitty would inherit
the farm since there was no one else, and if he married her he
would no longer be the hired man, with the worst of the work
always reserved for him. 'I'll ask her so,' he said, and because of
the day there had been in Cork it was easier to pluck up the courage. Before that, Kitty had always ordered him about in the way
her father and her uncle did when they all worked together at
certain seasons, making hay or lifting the potatoes. He had never
disliked her for it, any more than he'd ever felt he had a right to
resent Coddy Donnegan's rusty old Vauxhall arriving in the yard
and Coddy Donnegan waiting in it, and the way he'd push open
a door of the car when he heard the sound of her heels tip-tapping
across the concrete. Father Tolan's cousin had never come near the
farm; all that was a mystery.

'Would there be anything to eat in here, pet? Would they have
biscuits?'

At the bar he ordered two more bottles of stout and inquired if
biscuits could be supplied. The publican said he had ginger-snaps
and went to the grocery to weigh out half a pound.

'Oh, great,' Kitty said. She crumbled one in her mouth. He

poured out the stout. The day before her aunt had made her suggestion in the yard he had noticed Kitty going up to Coddy Donnegan after Mass, and Coddy Donnegan had turned away from her
as if they'd had a quarrel, which was understandable in view of her
friendship with Father Tolan's cousin. After that, Coddy Donnegan's Vauxhall never again drove up to the farm.

'We'll never forget our honeymoon,' Kitty said. 'I wish we had
a camera. I'd love to take snaps of Tramore.'

He knew what she meant. For the rest of their lives they'd be at
the farm, milking every morning and evening, taking the churns
down to the creamery, ploughing and sowing and ditching. No
matter how you fixed it there was never enough time, except for
the couple of hours you took to go to Mass. He always rode to
Mass on his bicycle, and on Sunday afternoons he rode over to
Doolin's at the old railway junction, where no trains came any
more. A new road passed by Doolin's now and on Sunday afternoons there would always be bicycles propped up against its window, and the same dozen or so faces inside. 'I hear you're marrying
in,' one of the men said to him on the Sunday after Kitty agreed.
'More power to your elbow, Davy!' No one was displeased at his
good fortune, in Doolin's or anywhere else. Father Tolan came up
to the farm specially and walked down to the mangold field to
shake his hand and to congratulate him. Even Ned Cauley, who
rarely had a good word to say on any subject, wagged his head at
him in an approving way.

'I love the taste of ginger-snaps and stout,' Kitty said. 'Did you
know ginger-snaps were my favourite?'

'They're all the man had.'

Suddenly she asked him if he was happy. She repeated the question, putting it differently, asking him if he was contented in himself. He said he was.

'Will you ever forget the day we went to Cork, Davy?'

From her voice, he thought she was maybe getting drunk, that
her condition made the stout go to her head. She was looking at

him, giggling. She leaned closer to him and said that on the bus that day she'd thought to herself she wouldn't mind being married to him.

'You were good to me that day, Davy, d'you know that?'

'I always had a notion of you, Kitty.'

'I never noticed it till that day, pet. That was the first time I knew it.'

He went to the bar for two further bottles of stout. He had wondered if the men in Doolin's knew the state she was in, and if they imagined he was the man involved. The same applied where her father and her uncle were concerned, and Father Tolan. He didn't know if there'd been talk or not.

'Didn't it work out OK, in the end?' she said when he returned with the stout. She asked if there were any more biscuits and he went back to buy another quarter pound. When he returned to where they sat she said:

'Were you ever jealous of Coddy, pet?'

He nodded, pouring his stout from the bottle, and she laughed because she'd made him feel awkward. He looked away, wishing she hadn't brought up Coddy Donnegan. Then he turned and clumsily attempted to kiss her on the lips, but found them gritty with biscuit crumbs.

'Oh, Coddy's the right romantic! It was maybe ten or eleven times he said would we get married.'

He frowned, feeling that something wasn't quite right, yet for the moment uncertain as to what it was.

'Did I tell you poor Coddy cried?' she said. 'The day I told him I was marrying yourself?'

After that the conversation became confused. Kitty again mentioned her surprise when Mrs Kilfedder had embraced her at the wedding. She counted up the wedding guests, and said it must have been the biggest wedding for a long time. Her father had had to sell two bullocks to pay for it. 'Did you see the cut of old Feehy, without a collar or tie?' She went through all the guests then, commenting or their dress and wondering why other women hadn't embraced her. 'Will we take back a few bottles?' she suggested, nudging him and winking. 'Hey!' she called out to the publican. 'Put a dozen stout in a bag for us, Mister.'

When Davy had paid for them they left the public house, Kitty talking about a girl called Rose she'd been at the national school with, wondering where she was now. She hung on to his arm; he listened vaguely. Turning into the cul-de-sac, they met Mr Hurley exercising a greyhound, a dejected animal which in the course of conversation Mr Hurley said was worth a fortune. 'Is it the one that gets into the cement mixer?' Kitty asked, and Mr Hurley explained that the greyhound only got into the cement mixer the odd time.

Kitty laughed shrilly. The trouble with a habit like that, she pointed out, was that the creature might get turned into concrete. 'Will you take a stout, Mr Hurley? We brought home a few bottles.'

Mr Hurley instantly fell into step with them and when they arrived at the house he led them round to the back, incarcerating the greyhound in a shed on the way. 'Sit down on a chair,' he said in the kitchen and his wife produced glasses, saying it was unusual to have guests bringing drink back to St Agnes's, but where was the harm in it? 'Good luck!' said Mr Hurley.

Details of the Wall of Death were given, and details of the wedding. The unexpected embrace of Mrs Kilfedder was retailed, and reference made to Kitty's father singing 'Lily of Laguna' and to old Feehy without his collar or tie. 'Poor Coddy Donnegan hadn't the heart to attend,' Kitty said. 'He's a fellow from the slaughterhouse, Mrs Hurley. I went out with poor Coddy for three years.'

'They take it hard,' agreed Mrs Hurley.

'He cried, poor Coddy.'

'I had a similar case myself. A fellow by the name of O'Gorman.'

'A chancer,' said Mr Hurley beneath his breath. 'A real oiler.'

'O'Gorman could have charmed the leaves off the trees. I heard him called the handsomest man in Tramore.'

'The story is told,' Mr Hurley said in the same low voice, 'that he fecked a crucifix off a nun.'

' "Well, I'll never marry now," was what poor Coddy came out with when I told him. "I'll keep myself by for you, Kitty." '

'Where'd the point be in that, though?' Mrs Hurley interposed. 'Is poor Coddy a bit slow?'

'It's only his way of putting the thing, Mrs Hurley.'

The dozen bottles took an hour to drink, during which time Mr Hurley gave Davy a number of racing tips. He talked about famous greyhounds he had known or had even had a hand in the breeding of, but Davy was more interested in what the two women were discussing and was unable to prevent himself from listening. He heard Kitty saying the husband she'd married would do anything for you. He watched her leaning closer to Mrs Hurley and heard her referring to the cousin of Father Tolan. 'Errah, go on, are you serious?' Mrs Hurley exclaimed, glancing across at him, and he guessed at once what she'd been told—that the lapse of the priest's cousin had determined him in his vocation, that God had gained in the end.

'Held back all summer,' Mr Hurley continued. 'Put every penny in your pocket on him.'

Davy promised he would, although he had never in his life backed a horse and hadn't heard what the one Mr Hurley recommended was called. Kitty stood up and was swaying back and forth, her eyes blearily staring. 'I don't know should I have eaten the ginger e m ered uneasily, but Mrs Hurley said a ginger-snap never did anyone any harm. Mr Hurley was talking about another horse, and Davy kept nodding.

'You're a good man,' the landlady whispered as he went by her. He had one arm around Kitty, holding her up. He shook his head, silently disclaiming the goodness Mrs Hurley imbued him with.

'Are you all right?' he asked Kitty on the stairs, and she didn't reply until they were in the bedroom, when she said she wasn't. He lifted the china jug out of the basin on the wash-stand and after she had finished being sick he carried the basin across the landing to the lavatory.

'God, I'm sorry, pet,' she managed to say before she fell asleep, lying across the bed.

Even though she couldn't hear him, he said it didn't matter. It had never occurred to him before that a cousin of Father Tolan's who came to the parish for his holidays must have attended Mass on Sundays, yet he had never seen him there. Nor had he ever heard anyone else but Kitty mention him. She had painted a picture of a saintly young man who had since become a priest, and in her befuddled state she'd wanted Mrs Hurley to know about him too. She had wanted Mrs Hurley to know that it wasn't anything crude that had occurred, like going with Coddy Donnegan in the back of a bloodstained Vauxhall.

'It's all right, Kitty.' He spoke aloud, sitting beside her on the bed, looking down into her face. In the bedroom there was the rancid smell of her vomit; her breath as he pulled the dress over her head was cloyed with it. Again he looked down into her face, understanding why she had told the lies. When she'd approached Coddy Donnegan after Mass that day he'd probably retorted that she'd let herself get into that condition in order to catch him.

Davy stood up and slowly took his clothes off. He was lucky that she had gone with Coddy Donnegan because if she hadn't she wouldn't now be sleeping on their honeymoon bed. Once more he looked down into her face: for eighteen years she had seemed like a queen to him and now, miraculously, he had the right to kiss her. He straightened her slackened body, moving her arms and legs until she was lying comfortably. Slowly he pulled the bed-clothes up and turned the light out; then he lay beside her and caressed her in the darkness. He had come to the farm with a label round his neck; he had come out of nowhere, from rooms and corridors that were as bleakly anonymous as the orphan home's foundling inmates. He had been known as her father's hired man, but now he would be known as her husband. That was how people would refer to him, and in the end it wouldn't matter when she talked about Coddy Donnegan, or lowered her voice to mention the priest's cousin. It was natural that she should do so since she had gained less than he had from their marriage.

Lost Ground

On the afternoon of September 14th 1989, a Thursday, Milton Leeson was addressed by a woman in his father's upper orchard. He was surprised. If the woman had been stealing the apples she could easily have dodged out of sight around the slope of the hill when she heard his footfall. Instead, she came forward to greet him, a lean-faced woman with straight black hair that seemed too young for her wasted features. Milton had never seen her before.

Afterwards he remembered that her coat, which did not seem entirely clean, was a shade of dark blue, even black. At her throat there was a scarf of some kind. She wasn't carrying anything. If she'd been stealing the apples she might have left whatever contained her takings behind the upper orchard's single growth of brambles, only yards from where she stood.

The woman came close to Milton, smiling at him with her eyes and parted lips. He asked her what she wanted; he asked her what she was doing in the orchard, but she didn't reply. In spite of her benign expression he thought for a moment she was mad and intended to attack him. Instead, the smile on her lips increased and she raised her arms as if inviting him to step into her embrace. When Milton did not do so the woman came closer still. Her hands were slender, her fingers as frail as twigs. She kissed him and then turned and walked away.

Afterwards Milton recalled very thin calves beneath the hem of her dark coat, and narrow shoulders, and the luxuriant black hair that seemed more than ever not to belong. When she'd kissed him her lips hadn't been moist like his mother's. They'd been dry as a bone, the touch of them so light he had scarcely felt it.

———

'Well?' Mr Leeson enquired that evening in the farmhouse kitchen.

Milton shook his head. In the upper orchard the Cox's were always the first to ripen. Nobody expected them to be ready as soon as this, but just occasionally, after a sunny summer, the first of the crop could catch you out. Due to his encounter with the stranger, he had forgotten to see if an apple came off easily when he twisted it on the branch. But he had noticed that not many had fallen, and guessed he was safe in intimating that the crop was better left for a while yet. Shyness prevented him from reporting that there'd been a woman in the orchard; if she hadn't come close to him, if she hadn't touched his lips with hers, it would have been different.

Milton was not yet sixteen. He was chunky, like his father and his brothers, one of them much older, the other still a child. The good looks of the family had gone into the two girls, which Mrs Leeson privately gave thanks for, believing that otherwise neither would have married well.

'They look laden from the lane,' Mr Leeson said, smearing butter on half a slice of bread cut from the loaf. Mr Leeson had small eyes and a square face that gave an impression of determination. Sparse grey hair relieved the tanned dome of his head, more abundant in a closely cropped growth around his ears and the back of his neck.

'They're laden all right,' Milton said.

The Leesons' kitchen was low-ceilinged, with a flagged floor and pale blue walls. It was a rambling, rectangular room, an illusion of greater spaciousness created by the removal of the doors from two wall-cupboards on either side of a recess that for almost fifty years had held the same badly stained Esse cooker. Sink and draining-boards, with further cupboards, lined the wall opposite, beneath narrow windows. An oak table, matching the proportions of the room, dominated its centre. There was a television set on a corner shelf, to the right of the Esse. Beside the door that led to the yard a wooden settee with cushions on it, and a high-backed chair, were placed to take advantage of the heat from the Esse while viewing the television screen. Five unpainted chairs were arranged around the table, four of them now occupied by the Leesons.

Generations of the family had sat in this kitchen, ever since 1809, when a Leeson had married into a household without sons. The house, four-square and slated, with a porch that added little to its appeal, had been rebuilt in 1931, when its walls were discovered to be defective. The services of a reputable local builder being considered adequate for the modifications, no architect had been employed. Nearly sixty years later, with a ragged front garden separating it from a lane that was used mainly by the Leesons, the house still stood white and slated, no tendrils of creeper softening its spare usefulness. At the back, farm buildings with red corrugated roofs and breeze-block walls were clustered around a concrete yard; fields and orchards were on either side of the lane. For three-quarters of a mile in any direction this was Leeson territory, a tiny fraction of County Armagh. The yard was well kept, the land well tended, both reflecting the hard-working Protestant family the Leesons were.

'There's more, Milton.'

His mother offered him salad and another slice of cold bacon. She had fried the remains of the champ they'd had in the middle of the day: potatoes mashed with butter and spring onions now had a crispy brown crust. She dolloped a spoonful on to Milton's plate beside the bacon and passed the plate back to him.

'Thanks,' Milton said, for gratitude was always expressed around this table. He watched his mother cutting up a slice of bacon for his younger brother, Stewart, who was the only other child of the family still at home. Milton's sister Addy had married the Reverend Herbert Cutcheon a year ago; his other sister was in Leicester, married also. His brother Garfield was a butcher's assistant in Belfast.

'Finish it up.' Mrs Leeson scooped the remains of the champ and spooned it on to her husband's plate. She was a small, delicately made woman with sharp blue eyes and naturally wavy hair that retained in places the reddish-brown of her girlhood. The good looks of her daughters had once been hers also and were not yet entirely dispelled.

Having paused while the others were served—that, too, being a tradition in the family—Milton began to eat again. He liked the champ best when it was fried. You could warm it in the oven or in a saucepan, but it wasn't the same. He liked crispness in his food—fingers of a soda farl fried, the spicy skin of a milk pudding, fried champ. His mother always remembered that. Milton sometimes thought his mother knew everything about him, and he didn't mind: it made him fond of her that she bothered. He felt affection for her when she sat by the Esse on winter's evenings or by the open back door in summer, sewing and darning. She never read the paper and only glanced up at the television occasionally. His father read the paper from cover to cover and never missed the television News. When Milton was younger he'd been afraid of his father, although he'd since realized that you knew where you were with him, which came from the experience of working with him in the fields and the orchards. 'He's fair,' Mrs Leeson used to repeat when Milton was younger. 'Always remember that.'

Milton was the family's hope, now that Garfield had gone to Belfast. Questioned by his father three years ago, Garfield had revealed that if he inherited the farm and the orchards he would sell them. Garfield was urban by inclination; his ambition during his growing-up was to find his feet in Belfast and to remain there. Stewart was a mongol.

'We'll fix a day for the upper orchard,' his father said. 'I'll fix with Gladdy about the boxes.'

That night Milton dreamed it was Esme Dunshea who had come to the upper orchard. Slowly she took off her dark coat, and then a green dress. She stood beneath an apple tree, skimpy underclothes revealing skin as white as flour. Once he and Billie Carew had followed his sisters and Esme Dunshea when they went to bathe in the stream that ran along the bottom of the orchards. In his dream

Esme Dunshea turned and walked away, but to Milton's disappointment she was fully dressed again.

The next morning that dream quickly faded to nothing, but the encounter with the stranger remained with Milton, and was as vivid as the reality had been. Every detail of the woman's appearance clung tightly to some part of his consciousness—the black hair, the frail fingers outstretched, her coat and her scarf.

On the evening of that day, during the meal at the kitchen table, Milton's father asked him to cut the bramble patch in the upper orchard. He meant the next morning, but Milton went at once. He stood among the trees in the twilight, knowing he was not there at his father's behest but because he knew the woman would arrive. She entered the upper orchard by the gate that led to the lane and called down to where he was. He could hear her perfectly, although her voice was no more than a whisper.

'I am St Rosa,' the woman said.

She walked down the slope toward him, and he saw that she was dressed in the same clothes. She came close to him and placed her lips on his.

'That is holy,' she whispered.

She moved away. She turned to face him again before she left the orchard, pausing by the gate to the lane.

'Don't be afraid,' she said, 'when the moment comes. There is too much fear.'

Milton had the distinct impression that the woman wasn't alive.

Milton's sister Hazel wrote every December, folding the pages of the year's news inside her Christmas card. Two children whom their grandparents had never seen had been born to her in Leicester. Not once since her wedding had Hazel been back to County Armagh.

We drove to Avignon the first day even though it meant being up half the night. The children couldn't have been better, I think the excitement exhausted them.

On the third Sunday in December the letter was on the mantelpiece of what the household had always called the back room, a room used only on Sundays in winter, when the rest of the year's stuffiness was disguised by the smoke from a coal fire. Milton's sister Addy and Herbert Cutcheon were present on the third Sunday in December, and Garfield was visiting for the weekend. Stewart sat on his own Sunday chair, grimacing to himself. Four o'clock tea with sandwiches, apple-pie and cakes, was taken on winter Sundays, a meal otherwise dispensed with.

'They went travelling to France,' Mr Leeson stated flatly, his tone betraying the disappointment he felt concerning his older daughter's annual holiday.

'France?' Narrow-jawed and beaky, head cocked out inquisitively, the Reverend Herbert Cutcheon dutifully imbued his repetition of the word with a note of surprised disdain. It was he who had conducted Hazel's wedding, who had delivered a private homily to the bride and bridegroom three days before the ceremony, who had said that at any time they could turn to him.

'See for yourself.' Mr Leeson inclined his tanned pate toward the mantelpiece. 'Have you read Hazel's letter, Addy?'

Addy said she had, not adding that she'd been envious of the journey to Avignon. Once a year she and Herbert and the children went for a week to Portrush, to a boarding-house with reduced rates for clergy.

'France,' her husband repeated. 'You'd wonder at that.'

'Aye, you would,' her father agreed.

Milton's eyes moved from face to face as each person spoke. There was fatigue in Addy's prettiness now, a tiredness in the skin even, although she was only twenty-seven. His father's features were impassive, nothing reflecting the shadow of resentment in his voice. A thought glittered in Herbert Cutcheon's pale brown eyes and was accompanied by a private nod: Milton guessed he was saying to himself it was his duty to write to Hazel on this matter. The clergyman had written to Hazel before: Milton had heard Addy saying so in the kitchen.

'I think Hazel explained in the letter,' Mrs Leeson put in. 'They'll

come one of these years,' she added, although she, more than anyone, knew they wouldn't. Hazel had washed her hands of the place.

'Sure, they will,' Garfield said.

Garfield was drunk. Milton watched him risking his observation,
his lips drawn loosely back in a thick smile. Specks of foam lingered
on the top of the beer can he held, around the triangular opening.
He'd been drinking Heineken all afternoon. Mr Leeson drank only
once a year, on the occasion of the July celebration; Herbert Cutcheon was teetotal. But neither disapproved of Garfield's tippling
when he came back for the weekend, because that was Garfield's
way and if you raised an objection you wouldn't see him for dust.

Catching Milton's eye on him, Garfield winked. He was not
entirely the reason why Hazel would not return, but he contributed
to it. For in Belfast Garfield was more than just a butcher's assistant.
Garfield had a role among the Protestant paramilitaries, being what
he himself called a 'hard-man volunteer' in an organization intent
on avenging the atrocities of the other side. The tit-for-tat murders
spawned by that same hard-man mentality, the endless celebration
of a glorious past on one side and the picking over of ancient rights
on the other, the reluctance to forgive: all this was what Hazel had
run away from. 'Only talk,' Mrs Leeson confidently dismissed Garfield's reports of his activities as, recalling that he had always been
a boaster. Mr Leeson did not comment.

'Hi!' Stewart suddenly exclaimed in the back room, the way he
often did. 'Hi! Hi!' he shouted, his head bent sideways to his shoulder, his mouth flopping open, eyes beginning to roll.

'Behave yourself, Stewart,' Mrs Leeson sternly commanded. 'Stop
it now.'

Stewart took no notice. He completed his effort at communi-
cation, his fat body becoming awkward on the chair. Then the
tension left him and he was quiet. *Give Stewart a hug from all of
us,* Hazel's letter said.

Addy collected her husband's cup and her father's. More tea was
poured. Mrs Leeson cut more cake.

'Now, pet.' She broke a slice into portions for Stewart. 'Good boy now.'

Milton wondered what they'd say if he mentioned the woman in the orchard, if he casually said that on the fourteenth of September, and again on the fifteenth, a woman who called herself St Rosa had appeared to him among the apple trees of the upper orchard. It wouldn't have been necessary to say he'd dreamed about her also; the dream was just an ordinary thing, a dream he might have had about any woman or girl. 'Her hair was strange,' he might have said.

But Milton, who had kept the whole matter to himself, continued to do so. Later that evening, alone in the back room with Garfield, he listened while his brother hinted at his city exploits, which he always did when he'd been drinking. Milton watched the damp lips sloppily opening and closing, the thick smile flashing between statements about punishment meted out and premises raided, youths taken in for questioning, warnings issued. There was always a way to complete the picture, Garfield liked to repeat, and would tell about some Catholic going home in the rain and being given a lift he didn't want to accept. Disposal completed the picture, you could call it that: you could say he was in the disposal business. When the phone rang in the middle of the night he always knew at once. No different from dealing with the side of a cow, a professional activity. Garfield always stopped before he came to the end of his tales; even when he'd had a few he left things to the imagination.

Every summer Mr Leeson gave the six-acre field for the July celebration—a loyal honouring, yet again renewed, of King William's famous victory over Papist James in 1690. Bowler-hatted and sashed, the men assembled there on the twelfth of the month, their drums and flutes echoing over the Leeson lands. At midday there was the long march to the village, Mr Leeson himself prominent among the marchers. He kept a dark serge suit specially for Sundays and the July celebration, as his father and his grandfather had. Before Garfield had gone to Belfast he'd marched also, the best on the flute for miles around. Milton marched, but didn't play an instrument because he was tone-deaf.

Men who had not met each other since the celebration last year came to the six-acre field in July. Mr Leeson's elderly Uncle Willie came, and Leeson cousins and relatives by marriage. Milton and his friend Billie Carew were among the younger contingent. It pleased Mr Leeson and the other men of his age that boys made up the numbers, that there was no falling away, new faces every year. The Reverend Cutcheon gave an address before the celebration began.

With the drums booming and the flutes skilfully establishing the familiar tunes, the marchers swung off through the iron gate of the field, out on to the lane, later turning into the narrow main road. Their stride was jaunty, even that of Mr Leeson's Uncle Willie and that of Old Knipe, who was eighty-four. Chins were raised, umbrellas carried as rifles might be. Pride was everywhere on these faces; in the measured step and the music's beat, in the swing of the arms and the firm grip of the umbrellas. No shoe was unpolished, no dark suit unironed. The men of this neighbourhood, by long tradition, renewed their Protestant loyalty and belief through sartorial display.

Milton's salt-and-pepper jacket and trousers had been let down at the cuffs. This showed, but only on close scrutiny—a band of lighter cloth and a second band, less noticeable because it had faded, where the cuffs had been extended in the past. His mother had said, only this morning, that that was that, what material remained could not be further adjusted. But she doubted that Milton would grow any more, so the suit as it was should last for many years yet. While she spoke Milton felt guilty, as many times he had during the ten months that had passed since his experience in the upper orchard. It seemed wrong that his mother, who knew everything about him, even that he wouldn't grow any more, shouldn't have been confided in, yet he hadn't been able to do it. Some instinct assured him that the woman would not return. There was no need for her to return, Milton's feeling was, although he did not know where the feeling came from: he would have found it awkward, explaining all that to his mother. Each of the seasons that had passed since September had been suffused by the memory of the woman. That autumn had been warm, its shortening days mellow with sunshine until the rain came in November. She had been with him in the sunshine and the rain, and in the bitter cold that came with January. On a day when the frost remained, to be frozen again at nightfall, he had walked along the slope of the upper orchard and looked back at the long line of his footsteps on the whitened grass, for a moment surprised that hers weren't there, miraculously, also. When the first primroses decorated the dry, warm banks of the orchards he found himself thinking that these familiar flowers were different this year because he was different himself and saw them in some different way. When summer came the memory of the woman was more intense.

'They'll draw in,' a man near the head of the march predicted as two cars advanced upon the marchers. Obediently the cars pressed into a gateway to make room, their engines turned off, honouring the music. Women and children in the cars waved and saluted; a baby was held up, its small paw waggled in greeting. 'Does your heart good, that,' one of the men remarked.

The day was warm. White clouds were stationary, as if pasted on to the vast dome of blue. It was nearly always fine for the July celebration, a fact that did not pass unnoticed in the neighbourhood, taken to be a sign. Milton associated the day with sweat on his back and in his armpits and on his thighs, his shirt stuck to him in patches that later became damply cold. As he marched now the sun was hot on the back of his neck. 'I wonder will we see the Kissane girl?' Billie Carew speculated beside him.

The Kissane girl lived in one of the houses they passed. She and her two younger sisters usually came out to watch. Her father and her uncles and her brother George were on the march. She was the best-looking girl in the neighbourhood now that Milton's sisters were getting on a bit. She had glasses, which she took off when she went dancing at the Cuchulainn Inn. She had her hair done regularly and took pains to get her eyeshadow right; she matched the shade of her lipstick to her dress. There wasn't a better pair of legs in Ulster, Billie Carew claimed.

'Oh, God!' he muttered when the marchers rounded a bend and there she was with her two young sisters. She had taken her glasses off and was wearing a dress that was mainly pink, flowers like roses on it. When they drew nearer, her white sandals could be seen. 'Oh, God!' Billie Carew exclaimed again, and Milton guessed he was undressing the Kissane girl, the way they used to undress girls in church. One of the girl's sisters had a Union Jack, which she waved.

Milton experienced no excitement. Last year he, too, had undressed the Kissane girl, which hadn't been much different from undressing Esme Dunshea in church. The Kissane girl was older than Esme Dunshea, and older than himself and Billie Carew by five or six years. She worked in the chicken factory.

'D'you know who she looks like?' Billie Carew said. 'Ingrid Bergman.'

'Ingrid Bergman's dead.'

Busy with his thoughts, Billie Carew didn't reply. He had a thing about Ingrid Bergman. Whenever *Casablanca* was shown on the television nothing would get him out of the house. For the purpose he put her to it didn't matter that she was dead.

'God, man!' Billie Carew muttered, and Milton could tell from the urgency of his intonation that the last of the Kissane girl's garments had been removed.

At ten to one the marchers reached the green corrugated-iron sheds of McCourt's Hardware and Agricultural Supplies. They passed a roadside water pump and the first four cottages of the village. They were in Catholic country now: no one was about, no face appeared at a window. The village was a single wide street, at one end Vogan's stores and public house, at the other Tiernan's grocery and filling station, where newspapers could be obtained.

Next door was O'Hanlon's public house and then the road widened, so that cars could turn in front of the Church of the Holy Rosary and the school. The houses of the village were colour-washed different colours, green and pink and blue. They were modest houses, none of more than two storeys.

As the marchers melodiously advanced upon the blank stare of so many windows, the stride of the men acquired an extra fervour. Arms were swung with fresh intent, jaws were more firmly set. The men passed the Church of the Holy Rosary, then halted abruptly. There was a moment of natural disarray as ranks were broken so that the march might be reversed. The Reverend Herbert Cutcheon's voice briefly intoned, a few glances were directed at, and over, the nearby church. Then the march returned the way it had come, the music different, as though a variation were the hidden villagers' due. At the corrugated sheds of McCourt's Hardware and Agricultural Supplies the men swung off to the left, marching back to Mr Leeson's field by another route.

The picnic was the reward for duty done, faith kept. Bottles appeared. There were sandwiches, chicken legs, sliced beef and ham, potato crisps and tomatoes. The men urinated in twos, against a hedge that never suffered from its annual acidic dousing—this, too, was said to be a sign. Jackets were thrown off, bowler hats thrown down, sashes temporarily laid aside. News was exchanged; the details of a funeral or a wedding passed on; prices for livestock deplored. The Reverend Herbert Cutcheon passed among the men who sat easily on the grass, greeting those from outside his parish whom he hadn't managed to greet already, enquiring after womenfolk. By five o'clock necks and faces were redder than they had earlier been, hair less tidy, beads of perspiration catching the slanting sunlight. There was euphoria in the field, some drunkenness, and an occasional awareness of the presence of God.

'Are you sick?' Billie Carew asked Milton. 'What's up with you?'

Milton didn't answer. He was maybe sick, he thought. He was

sick or going round the bend. Since he had woken up this morning she had been there, but not as before, not as a tranquil presence. Since he'd woken she had been agitating and nagging at him.

'I'm OK,' he said.

He couldn't tell Billie Carew any more than he could tell his mother, or anyone in the family, yet all the time on the march he had felt himself being pressed to tell, all the time in the deadened village while the music played, when they turned and marched back again and the tune was different. Now, at the picnic, he felt himself being pressed more than ever.

'You're bloody not OK,' Billie Carew said.

Milton looked at him and found himself thinking that Billie Carew would be eating food in this field when he was as old as Old Knipe. Billie Carew with his acne and his teeth would be satisfied for life when he got the Kissane girl's knickers off. 'Here,' Billie Carew said, offering him his half-bottle of Bushmills.

'I want to tell you something,' Milton said, finding the Reverend Herbert Cutcheon at the hedge where the urinating took place.

'Tell away, Milton.' The clergyman's edgy face was warm with the pleasure the day had brought. He adjusted his trousers. Another day to remember, he said.

'I was out in the orchards a while back,' Milton said. 'September it was. I was seeing how the apples were doing when a woman came in the top gate.'

'A woman?'

'The next day she was there again. She said she was St Rosa.'

'What d'you mean, St Rosa, Milton?'

The Reverend Cutcheon had halted in his stroll back to the assembled men. He stood still, frowning at the grass by his feet. Then he lifted his head and Milton saw bewilderment, and astonishment, in his opaque brown eyes.

'What d'you mean, St Rosa?' he repeated.

Milton told him, and then confessed that the woman had kissed him twice on the lips, a holy kiss, as she'd called it.

'No kiss is holy, boy. Now, listen to me, Milton. Listen to this carefully, boy.'

A young fellow would have certain thoughts, the Reverend Cutcheon explained. It was the way of things that a young fellow could become confused, owing to the age he was and the changes that had taken place in his body. He reminded Milton that he'd left school, that he was on the way to manhood. The journey to manhood could have a stumble or two in it, he explained, and it wasn't without temptation. One day Milton would inherit the farm and the orchards, since Garfield had surrendered all claim to them. That was something he needed to prepare himself for. Milton's mother was goodness itself, his father would do anything for you. If a neighbour had a broken fence while he was laid up in bed, his father would be the first to see to it. His mother had brought up four fine children, and it was God's way that the fifth was afflicted. God's grace could turn affliction into a gift: poor Stewart, you might say, but you only had to look at him to realize you were glad Stewart had been given life.

'We had a great day today, Milton, we had an enjoyable day. We stood up for the people we are. That's what you have to think of.'

In a companionable way the clergyman's arm was placed around Milton's shoulders. He'd put the thing neatly, the gesture suggested. He'd been taken aback but had risen to the occasion.

'She won't leave me alone,' Milton said.

Just beginning to move forward, the Reverend Cutcheon halted again. His arm slipped from Milton's shoulders. In a low voice he said:

'She keeps bothering you in the orchards, does she?'

Milton explained. He said the woman had been agitating him all day, since the moment he awoke. It was because of that that he'd had to tell someone, because she was pressing him to.

'Don't tell anyone else, Milton. Don't tell a single soul. It's said now between the two of us and it's safe with myself. Not even Addy will hear the like of this.'

Milton nodded. The Reverend Cutcheon said:

'Don't distress your mother and your father, son, with talk of a woman who was on about holiness and the saints.' He paused, then spoke with emphasis, and quietly. 'Your mother and father wouldn't rest easy for the balance of their days.' He paused again. 'There are no better people than your mother and father, Milton.'

'Who was St Rosa?'

Again the Reverend Cutcheon checked his desire to rejoin the men who were picnicking on the grass. Again he lowered his voice.

'Did she ask you for money? After she touched you did she ask you for money?'

'Money?'

'There are women like that, boy.'

Milton knew what he meant. He and Billie Carew had many a time talked about them. You saw them on television, flamboyantly dressed on city streets. Billie Carew said they hung about railway stations, that your best bet was a railway station if you were after one. Milton's mother, once catching a glimpse of these street-traders on the television, designated them 'Catholic strumpets'. Billie Carew said you'd have to go careful with them in case you'd catch a disease. Milton had never heard of such women in the neighbourhood.

'She wasn't like that,' he said.

'You'd get a travelling woman going by and maybe she'd be thinking you had a coin or two on you. Do you understand what I'm saying to you, Milton?'

'Yes.'

'Get rid of the episode. Put it out of your mind.'

'I was only wondering about what she said in relation to a saint.'

'It's typical she'd say a thing like that.'

Milton hesitated. 'I thought she wasn't alive,' he said.

Mr Leeson's Uncle Willie used to preach. He had preached in the towns until he was too old for it, until he began to lose the thread of what he was saying. Milton had heard him. He and Garfield and his sisters had been brought to hear Uncle Willie in his heyday, a bible clenched in his right hand, gesturing with it and quoting from it. Sometimes he spoke of what happened in Rome, facts he knew to be true: how the Pope drank himself into a stupor and had to have the sheets of his bed changed twice in a night, how the Pope's own mother was among the women who came and went in the papal ante-rooms.

Men still preached in the towns, at street corners or anywhere that might attract a crowd, but the preachers were fewer than they had been in the heyday of Mr Leeson's Uncle Willie because the popularity of television kept people in at nights, and because people were in more of a hurry. But during the days that followed the July celebration Milton remembered his great-uncle's eloquence. He remembered the words he had used and the way he could bring in a quotation, and the way he was so certain. Often he had laid down that a form of cleansing was called for, that vileness could be exorcized by withering it out of existence.

The Reverend Cutcheon had been more temperate in his advice, even if what he'd said amounted to much the same thing: if you ignored what happened it wouldn't be there any more. But on the days that followed the July celebration Milton found it increasingly impossible to do so. With a certainty that reminded him of his great-uncle's he became convinced beyond all doubt that he was not meant to be silent. Somewhere in him there was the uncontrollable urge that he should not be. He asked his mother why the old man had begun to preach, and she replied that it was because he had to.

Father Mulhall didn't know what to say.

To begin with, he couldn't remember who St Rosa had been, even if he ever knew. Added to which, there was the fact that it wasn't always plain what the Protestant boy was trying to tell him. The boy stammered rapidly through his account, beginning sentences again because he realized his meaning had slipped away, speaking more slowly the second time but softening his voice to a pitch that made it almost inaudible. The whole thing didn't make sense.

'Wait now till we have a look,' Father Mulhall was obliged to offer in the end. He'd said at first that he would make some investigations about this saint, but the boy didn't seem satisfied with that. 'Sit down,' he invited in his living-room, and went to look for *Butler's Lives of the Saints*.

Father Mulhall was fifty-nine, a tall, wiry man, prematurely white-haired. Two sheepdogs accompanied him when he went to find the relevant volume. They settled down again, at his feet, when he returned. The room was cold, hardly furnished at all, the carpet so thin you could feel the boards.

'There's the Blessed Roseline of Villeneuve,' Father Mulhall said, turning over the pages. 'And the Blessed Rose Venerini. Or there's St Rose of Lima. Or St Rosalia. Or Rose of Viterbo.'

'I think it's that one. Only she definitely said Rosa.'

'Could you have fallen asleep? Was it a hot day?'

'It wasn't a dream I had.'

'Was it late in the day? Could you have been confused by the shadows?'

'It was late the second time. The first time it was the afternoon.'

'Why did you come to me?'

'Because you'd know about a saint.'

Father Mulhall heard how the woman who'd called herself St Rosa wouldn't let the boy alone, how she'd come on stronger and stronger as the day of the July celebration approached, and so strong on the day itself that he knew he wasn't meant to be silent, the boy said.

'About what though?'

'About her giving me the holy kiss.'

The explanation could be that the boy was touched. There was another boy in that family who wasn't the full shilling either.

'Wouldn't you try getting advice from your own clergyman? Isn't Mr Cutcheon your brother-in-law?'

'He told me to pretend it hadn't happened.'

The priest didn't say anything. He listened while he was told how the presence of the saint was something clinging to you, how neither her features nor the clothes she'd worn had faded in any way whatsoever. When the boy closed his eyes he could apparently see her more clearly than he could see any member of his family, or anyone he could think of.

'I only wanted to know who she was. Is that place in France?'

'Viterbo is in Italy actually.'

One of the sheepdogs had crept on to the priest's feet and settled down to sleep. The other was asleep already. Father Mulhall said:

'Do you feel all right in yourself otherwise?'

'She said not to be afraid. She was on about fear.' Milton paused. 'I can still feel her saying things.'

'I would talk to your own clergyman, son. Have a word with your brother-in-law.'

'She wasn't alive, that woman.'

Father Mulhall did not respond to that. He led Milton to the hall-door of his house. He had been affronted by the visit, but he didn't let it show. Why should a saint of his Church appear to a Protestant boy in a neighbourhood that was overwhelmingly Catholic, when there were so many Catholics to choose from? Was it not enough that that march should occur every twelfth of July, that farmers from miles away should bang their way through the village just to show what was what, strutting in their get-up? Was that not enough without claiming the saints as well? On the twelfth of July they closed the village down, they kept people inside. Their noisy presence was a reminder that beyond this small, immediate neighbourhood there was a strength from which they drew their own. This boy's father would give you the time of day if he met you on the road, he'd even lean on a gate and talk to you, but once your back was turned he'd come out with his statements. The son who'd gone to Belfast would salute you and maybe afterwards laugh because he'd saluted a priest. It was widely repeated that Garfield Leeson belonged in the ganglands of the Protestant back streets, that his butcher's skills came in handy when a job had to be done.

'I thought she might be foreign,' Milton said. 'I don't know how I'd know that.'

Two scarlet dots appeared in Father Mulhall's scrawny cheeks. His anger was more difficult to disguise now; he didn't trust himself to speak. In silence Milton was shown out of the house.

When he returned to his living-room Father Mulhall turned on the television and sat watching it with a glass of whiskey, his sheep-dogs settling down to sleep again. 'Now, that's amazing!' a chat-show host exclaimed, leading the applause for a performer who balanced a woman on the end of his finger. Father Mulhall wondered how it was done, his absorption greater than it would have been had he not been visited by the Protestant boy.

Mr Leeson finished rubbing his plate clean with a fragment of loaf bread, soaking into it what remained of bacon fat and small pieces of black pudding. Milton said:

'She walked in off the lane.'

Not fully comprehending, Mr Leeson said the odd person came after the apples. Not often, but you knew what they were like. You couldn't put an orchard under lock and key.

'Don't worry about it, son.'

Mrs Leeson shook her head. It wasn't like that, she explained; that wasn't what Milton was saying. The colour had gone from Mrs Leeson's face. What Milton was saying was that a Papist saint had spoken to him in the orchards.

'An apparition,' she said.

Mr Leeson's small eyes regarded his son evenly. Stewart put his side plate on top of the plate he'd eaten his fry from, with his knife and fork on top of that, the way he had been taught. He made his belching noise and to his surprise was not reprimanded.

'I asked Father Mulhall who St Rosa was.'

Mrs Leeson's hand flew to her mouth. For a moment she thought she'd scream. Mr Leeson said:

'What are you on about, boy?'

'I have to tell people.'

Stewart tried to speak, gurgling out a request to carry his two plates and his knife and fork to the sink. He'd been taught that also, and was always obedient. But tonight no one heeded him.

'Are you saying you went to the priest?' Mr Leeson asked.

'You didn't go into his house, Milton?'

Mrs Leeson watched, incredulous, while Milton nodded. He said Herbert Cutcheon had told him to keep silent, but in the end he couldn't. He explained that on the day of the march he had told his brother-in-law when they were both standing at the hedge, and later he had gone into Father Mulhall's house. He'd sat down while the priest looked the saint up in a book.

'Does anyone know you went into the priest's house, Milton?' Mrs Leeson leaned across the table, staring at him with widened eyes that didn't blink. 'Did anyone see you?'

'I don't know.'

Mr Leeson pointed to where Milton should stand, then rose from the table and struck him on the side of the face with his open palm. He did it again. Stewart whimpered, and became agitated.

'Put them in the sink, Stewart,' Mrs Leeson said.

The dishes clattered into the sink, and the tap was turned on as Stewart washed his hands. The side of Milton's face was inflamed, a trickle of blood came from his nose.

Herbert Cutcheon's assurance that what he'd heard in his father-in-law's field would not be passed on to his wife was duly honoured. But when he was approached on the same subject a second time he realized that continued suppression was pointless. After a Sunday-afternoon visit to his in-laws' farmhouse, when Mr Leeson had gone off to see to the milking and Addy and her mother were reaching down pots of last year's plum jam for Addy to take back to the rectory, Milton had followed him to the yard. As he drove the four miles back to the rectory, the clergyman repeated to Addy the conversation that had taken place.

'You mean he wants to *preach?*' Frowning in astonishment, Addy half shook her head, her disbelief undisguised.

He nodded. Milton had mentioned Mr Leeson's Uncle Willie. He'd said he wouldn't have texts or scriptures, nothing like that.

'It's not Milton,' Addy protested, this time shaking her head more firmly.

'I know it's not.'

He told her then about her brother's revelations on the day of the July celebration. He explained he hadn't done so before because he considered he had made her brother see sense, and these matters were better not referred to.

'Heavens above!' Addy cried, her lower jaw slackened in fresh amazement. The man she had married was not given to the kind of crack that involved lighthearted deception, or indeed any kind of crack at all. Herbert's virtues lay in other directions, well beyond the realm of jest. Even so, Addy emphasized her bewilderment by stirring doubt into her disbelief. 'You're not serious surely?'

He nodded without taking his eyes from the road. Neither of them knew of the visit to the priest or of the scene in the kitchen that had ended in a moment of violence. Addy's parents, in turn believing that Milton had been made to see sense by his father's spirited response, and sharing Herbert Cutcheon's view that such matters were best left unaired, had remained silent also.

'Is Milton away in the head?' Addy whispered.

'He's not himself certainly. No way he's himself.'

'He never showed an interest in preaching.'

'D'you know what he said to me just now in the yard?'

But Addy was still thinking about the woman her brother claimed to have conversed with. Her imagination had stuck there, on the slope of her father's upper orchard, a Catholic woman standing among the trees.

'Dudgeon McDavie,' Herbert Cutcheon went on. 'He mentioned that man.'

Nonplussed all over again, Addy frowned. Dudgeon McDavie was a man who'd been found shot dead by the roadside near Loughgall. Addy remembered her father coming into the kitchen and saying they'd shot poor Dudgeon. She'd been seven at the time;

Garfield had been four, Hazel a year older; Milton and Stewart hadn't been born. 'Did he ever do a minute's harm?' she remembered her father saying. 'Did he ever so much as raise his voice?' Her father and Dudgeon McDavie had been schooled together; they'd marched together many a time. Then Dudgeon McDavie had moved out of the neighbourhood, to take up a position as a quantity surveyor. Addy couldn't remember ever having seen him, although from the conversation that had ensued between her mother and her father at the time of his death it was apparent that he had been to the farmhouse many a time. 'Blew half poor Dudgeon's skull off': her father's voice, leaden and grey, echoed as she remembered. 'Poor Dudgeon's brains all over the tarmac.' Her father had attended the funeral, full honours because Dudgeon McDavie had had a hand in keeping law and order, part-time in the UDR. A few weeks later two youths from Loughgall were set upon and punished, although they vehemently declared their innocence.

'Dudgeon McDavie's only hearsay for Milton,' Addy pointed out, and her husband said he realized that.

Drawing up in front of the rectory, a low brick building with metal-framed windows, he said he had wondered about going in search of Mr Leeson when Milton had come out with all that in the yard. But Milton had hung about by the car, making the whole thing even more difficult.

'Did the woman refer to Dudgeon McDavie?' Addy asked. 'Is that it?'

'I don't know if she did. To tell you the truth, Addy, you wouldn't know where you were once Milton gets on to this stuff. For one thing, he said to me the woman wasn't alive.'

In the rectory Addy telephoned. 'I'll ring you back,' her mother said and did so twenty minutes later, when Milton was not within earshot. In the ensuing conversation what information they possessed was shared: the revelations made on the day of the July celebration, what had later been said in the kitchen and an hour ago in the yard.

'Dudgeon McDavie,' Mrs Leeson reported quietly to her husband as soon as she replaced the receiver. 'The latest thing is he's on to Herbert about Dudgeon McDavie.'

Milton rode his bicycle one Saturday afternoon to the first of the towns in which he wished to preach. In a car park two small girls, sucking sweets, listened to him. He explained about St Rosa of Viterbo. He felt he was a listener too, that his voice came from somewhere outside himself—from St Rosa, he explained to the two small girls. He heard himself saying that his sister Hazel refused to return to the province. He heard himself describing the silent village, and the drums and the flutes that brought music to it, and the suit his father wore on the day of the celebration. St Rosa could mourn Dudgeon McDavie, he explained, a Protestant man from Loughgall who'd been murdered ages ago. St Rosa could forgive the brutish soldiers and their masked adversaries, one or other of them responsible for the shattered motor-cars and shrouded bodies that came and went on the television screen. Father Mulhall had been furious, Milton said in the car park, you could see it in his eyes: he'd been furious because a Protestant boy was sitting down in his house. St Rosa of Viterbo had given him her holy kiss, he said: you could tell that Father Mulhall considered that impossible.

The following Saturday Milton cycled to another town, a little further away, and on the subsequent Saturday he preached in a third town. He did not think of it as preaching, more just telling people about his experience. It was what he had to do, he explained, and he noticed that when people began to listen they usually didn't go away. Shoppers paused, old men out for a walk passed the time in his company, leaning against a shop window or the wall of a public lavatory. Once or twice in an afternoon someone was abusive.

On the fourth Saturday Mr Leeson and Herbert Cutcheon arrived in Mr Leeson's Ford Granada and hustled Milton into it. No one spoke a word on the journey back.

'Shame?' Milton said when his mother employed the word.

'On all of us, Milton.'

In church people regarded him suspiciously, and he noticed that Addy sometimes couldn't stop staring at him. When he smiled at Esme Dunshea she didn't smile back; Billie Carew avoided him. His father insisted that in no circumstances whatsoever should he ever again preach about a woman in the orchards. Milton began to explain that he must, that he had been given the task.

'No,' his father said.

'That's the end of it, Milton,' his mother said. She hated it even more than his father did, a woman kissing him on the lips.

The next Saturday afternoon they locked him into the bedroom he shared with Stewart, releasing him at six o'clock. But on Sunday morning he rode away again, and had again to be searched for on the streets of towns. After that, greater care was taken. Stewart was moved out of the bedroom and the following weekend Milton remained under duress there, the door unlocked so that he could go to the lavatory, his meals carried up to him by his mother, who said nothing when she placed the tray on a chest of drawers. Milton expected that on Monday morning everything would be normal again, that his punishment would then have run its course. But this was not so. He was released to work beside his father, clearing out a ditch, and all day there were never more than a couple of yards between them. In the evening he was returned to the bedroom. The door was again secured, and so it always was after that.

On winter Sundays when his sister Addy and the Reverend Cutcheon came to sit in the back room he remained upstairs. He no longer accompanied the family to church. When Garfield came from Belfast at a weekend he refused to carry food to the bedroom, although Milton often heard their mother requesting him to. For a long time now Garfield had not addressed him or sought his company.

When Milton did the milking his father didn't keep so close to him. He put a padlock on the yard gate and busied himself with some task or other in one of the sheds, or else kept an eye on the yard from the kitchen. On two Saturday afternoons Milton climbed out of the bedroom window and set off on his bicycle, later to be pursued. Then one day when he returned from the orchards with his father he found that Jimmy Logan had been to the farmhouse to put bars on his bedroom window. His bicycle was no longer in the turf shed; he caught a glimpse of it tied on to the boot of the Ford Granada and deduced that it was being taken to be sold. His mother unearthed an old folding card-table, since it was a better height for eating off than the chest of drawers. Milton knew that people had been told he had become affected in the head, but he could tell from his mother's demeanour that not even this could exorcize the shame he had brought on the family.

When the day of the July celebration came again Milton remained in his bedroom. Before he left the house his father led him to the lavatory and waited outside it in order to lead him back again. His father didn't say anything. He didn't say it was the day of the July celebration, but Milton could tell it was, because he was wearing his special suit. Milton watched the car drawing out of the yard and then heard his mother chatting to Stewart in the kitchen, saying something about sitting in the sun. He imagined the men gathering in the field, the clergyman's blessing, the drums strapped on, ranks formed. As usual, the day was fine; from his bedroom window he could see there wasn't a cloud in the sky.

It wasn't easy to pass the time. Milton had never been much of a one for reading, had never read a book from cover to cover. Sometimes when his mother brought his food she left him the weekly newspaper and he read about the towns it gave news of, and the different rural neighbourhoods, one of which was his own. He listened to his transistor. His mother collected all the jigsaw puzzles she could find, some of which had been in the farmhouse since Hazel and Garfield were children, others of a simple nature bought specially for Stewart. She left him a pack of cards, with only the three of diamonds missing, and a cardboard box containing scraps of wool and a spool with tacks in it that had been Addy's French-knitting outfit.

On the day of the celebration he couldn't face, yet again, completing the jigsaw of Windsor Castle or the Battle of Britain, or playing patience with the three of diamonds drawn on the back of an envelope, or listening all day to cheery disc-jockeys. He practised preaching, all the time seeing the woman in the orchard instead of the sallow features of Jesus or a cantankerous-looking God, white-haired and bearded, frowning through the clouds.

From time to time he looked at his watch and on each occasion established the point the march had reached. The Kissane girl and her sisters waved. Cars drew courteously in to allow the celebration to pass by. McCourt's Hardware and Agricultural Supplies was closed, the village street was empty. Beyond the school and the Church of the Holy Rosary the march halted, then returned the way it had come, only making a change when it reached McCourt's again, swinging off to the left.

Mrs Leeson unlocked the door and handed in a tray, and Milton imagined the chicken legs and the sandwiches in the field, bottles coming out, the men standing in a row by the hedge. 'No doubt about it,' his father said. 'Dr Gibney's seen cases like it before.' A nutcase, his father intimated without employing the term, but when he was out of hearing one of the men muttered that he knew for a fact Dr Gibney hadn't been asked for an opinion. In the field the shame that was spoken about spread from his father to the men themselves.

Milton tumbled out on the card-table the jigsaw pieces of a jungle scene and slowly turned them right side up. He didn't know any more what would happen if they opened the door and freed him. He didn't know if he would try to walk to the towns, if he'd feel again the pressure to do so or if everything was over, if he'd been cleansed, as his father's old uncle would have said. Slowly he found the shape of a chimpanzee among the branches of a tree. He wished he were in the field, taking the half-bottle from Billie Carew.

He wished he could feel the sun on his face and feel the ache going out of his legs after the march.

He completed the top left-hand corner of the jungle scene, adding brightly coloured birds to the tree with the chimpanzees in it. The voices of his mother and Stewart floated up to him from the yard, the incoherent growling of his brother, his mother soothing. From where he sat he saw them when they moved into view, Stewart lumbering, his mother holding his hand. They passed out of the yard, through the gate that was padlocked when he did the milking. Often they walked down to the stream on a warm afternoon.

Again he practised preaching. He spoke of his father ashamed in the field, and the silent windows of the village. He explained that he had been called to go among people, bearing witness on a Saturday afternoon. He spoke of fear. It was that that was most important of all. Fear was the weapon of the gunmen and the soldiers, fear quietened the village. In fear his sister had abandoned the province that was her home. Fearful, his brother disposed of the unwanted dead.

Later Milton found the two back legs of an elephant and slipped the piece that contained them into place. He wondered if he would finish the jigsaw or if it would remain on the mildewed baize of the card-table with most of its middle part missing. He hadn't understood why the story of Dudgeon McDavie had occurred to him as a story he must tell. It had always been there; he'd heard it dozens of times; yet it seemed a different kind of story when he thought about the woman in the orchard, when over and over again he watched her coming towards him, and when she spoke about fear.

He found another piece of the elephant's grey bulk. In the distance he could hear the sound of a car. He paid it no attention, not even when the engine throbbed with a different tone, indicating that the car had drawn up by the yard gate. The gate rattled in a familiar way, and Milton went to his window then. A yellow Vauxhall moved into the yard.

He watched while a door opened and a man he had never seen

before stepped out from the driver's seat. The engine was switched off. The man stretched himself. Then Garfield stepped out too.

'It took a death to get you back,' her father said.

On the drive from the airport Hazel did not reply. She was twenty-six, two years younger than Addy, small and dark-haired, as Addy was, too. Ever since the day she had married, since her exile had begun, the truth had not existed between her and these people she had left behind. The present occasion was not a time for prevarication, not a time for pretence, yet already she could feel both all around her. Another death in a procession of deaths had occurred; this time close to all of them. Each death that came was close to someone, within some family: she'd said that years ago, saying it only once, not arguing because none of them wanted to have a conversation like that.

Mr Leeson slowed as they approached the village of Glenavy, then halted to allow two elderly women to cross the street. They waved their thanks, and he waved back. Eventually he said:

'Herbert's been good.'

Again Hazel did not respond. 'God took him for a purpose,' she imagined Herbert Cutcheon comforting her mother. 'God has a job for him.'

'How's Addy?'

Her sister was naturally distressed also, she was told. The shock was still there, still raw in all of them.

'That stands to reason.'

They slid into a thin stream of traffic on the motorway, Mr Leeson not accelerating much. He said:

'I have to tell you what it was with Milton before we get home.'

'Was it the Provos? Was Milton involved in some way?'

'Don't call them the Provos, Hazel. Don't give them any kind of title. They're not worthy of a title.'

'You have to call them something.'

'It wasn't them. There was no reason why it should have been.'

Hazel, who had only been told that her brother had died violently—shot by intruders when he was alone in the house—heard how Milton had insisted he'd received a supernatural visitation from a woman. She heard how he had believed the woman was the ghost of a Catholic saint, how he had gone to the priest for information, how he had begun street-corner preaching.

'He said things people didn't like?' she suggested, ignoring the more incredible aspect of this information.

'We had to keep him in. I kept him by me when we worked, Garfield wouldn't address him.'

'You kept him in?'

'Poor Milton was away in the head, Hazel. He'd be all right for a while, maybe for weeks, longer even. Then suddenly he'd start about the woman in the orchard. He wanted to travel the six counties preaching about her. He told me that. He wanted to stand up in every town he came to and tell his tale. He brought poor Dudgeon McDavie into it.'

'What d'you mean, you kept him in?'

'We sometimes had to lock his bedroom door. Milton didn't know what he was doing, girl. We had to get rid of his bicycle, but even so he'd have walked. A couple of times on a Saturday he set off to walk, and myself and Herbert had to get him back.'

'My God!'

'You can't put stuff like that in a letter. You can't blame anyone for not writing that down for you. Your mother didn't want to. "What've you said to Hazel?" I asked her one time and she said, "Nothing," so we left it.'

'Milton went mad and no one told me?'

'Poor Milton did, Hazel.'

Hazel endeavoured to order the confusion of her thoughts. Pictures formed: of the key turned in the bedroom door; of the household as it had apparently become, her parents' two remaining children a double burden—Stewart's mongol blankness, Milton's gibberish. 'Milton's been shot,' she had said to her husband after the telephone call, shocked that Milton had apparently become involved, as Garfield was, drawn into it no doubt by Garfield. Ever since, that assumption had remained.

They left the motorway, bypassed Craigavon, then again made their way on smaller roads. This is home, Hazel found herself reflecting in that familiar landscape, the reminder seeming alien among thoughts that were less tranquil. Yet in spite of the reason for her visit, in spite of the upsetting muddle of facts she'd been presented with on this journey, she wanted to indulge the moment, to close her eyes and let herself believe that it was a pleasure of some kind to be back where she belonged. Soon they would come to Drumfin, then Anderson's Crossroads. They would pass the Cuchulainn Inn, and turn before reaching the village. Everything would be familiar then, every house and cottage, trees and gateways, her father's orchards.

'Take it easy with your mother,' he said. 'She cries a lot.'

'Who was it shot Milton?'

'There's no one has claimed who it was. The main concern's your mother.'

Hazel didn't say anything, but when her father began to speak again she interrupted him.

'What about the police?'

'Finmoth's keeping an open mind.'

The car passed the Kissanes' house, pink and respectable, delphiniums in its small front garden. Next came the ruined cowshed in the middle of Malone's field, three of its stone walls standing, the fourth tumbled down, its disintegrating roof mellow with rust. Then came the orchards, and the tarred gate through which you could see the stream, steeply below.

Her father turned the car into the yard of the farmhouse. One of the dogs barked, scampering back and forth, wagging his tail as he always did when the car returned.

'Well, there we are.' With an effort Mr Leeson endeavoured to extend a welcome. 'You'd recognize the old place still!'

In the kitchen her mother embraced her. Her mother had a

shrunken look; a hollowness about her eyes, and shallow cheeks that exposed the shape of bones beneath the flesh. A hand grasped at one of Hazel's and clutched it tightly, as if in a plea for protection. Mr Leeson carried Hazel's suitcase upstairs.

'Sit down.' With her free hand Hazel pulled a chair out from the table and gently eased her mother toward it. Her brother grinned across the kitchen at her.

'Oh, Stewart!'

She kissed him, hugging his awkward body. Pimples disfigured his big forehead, his spiky short hair tore uncomfortably at her cheek.

'We should have seen,' Mrs Leeson whispered. 'We should have known.'

'You couldn't. Of course you couldn't.'

'He had a dream or something. That's all he was on about.'

Hazel remembered the dreams she'd had herself at Milton's age, half-dreams because sometimes she was awake—close your eyes and you could make Mick Jagger smile at you, or hear the music of U2 or The Damage. 'Paul Hogan had his arms round me,' Addy giggled once. Then you began going out with someone and everything was different.

'Yet how would he know about a saint?' her mother whispered. 'Where'd he get the name from?'

Hazel didn't know. It would have come into his head, she said to herself, but didn't repeat the observation aloud. In spite of what she said, her mother didn't want to think about it. Maybe it was easier for her mother, too, to believe her son had been away in the head, or maybe it made it worse. You wouldn't know that, you couldn't tell from her voice or from her face.

'Don't let it weigh on you,' she begged. 'Don't make it worse for yourself.'

Later Addy and Herbert Cutcheon were in the kitchen. Addy made tea and tumbled biscuits on to a plate. Herbert Cutcheon was solemn, Addy subdued. Like her father, Hazel sensed, both of them were worried about her mother. Being worried about her mother was the practical aspect of the grief that was shared, an avenue of escape from it, a distraction that was permitted. Oblivious to all emotion, Stewart reached out for a biscuit with pink marshmallow in it, his squat fingers and bitten nails ugly for an instant against the soft prettiness.

'He'll get the best funeral the Church can give him,' Herbert Cutcheon promised.

Garfield stood a little away from them, with a black tie in place and his shoes black also, not the trainers he normally wore. Looking at him across the open grave, Hazel suddenly knew. In ignorance she had greeted him an hour ago in the farmhouse; they had stood together in the church; she had watched while he stepped forward to bear the coffin. Now, in the bleak churchyard, those images were illuminated differently. The shame had been exorcized, silence silently agreed upon.

'I will keep my mouth as it were with a bridle,' Herbert Cutcheon proclaimed, his voice heavy with the churchiness that was discarded as soon as his professional duties ceased, never apparent on a Sunday afternoon in the back room of the farmhouse. 'Forasmuch as it hath pleased Almighty God.'

Earth was thrown on to the coffin. *'Our Father, who art in heaven,'* Herbert Cutcheon suitably declared, and Hazel watched Garfield's lips, in unison with Addy's and their parents'. Stewart was there too, now and again making a noise. Mrs Leeson held a handkerchief to her face, clinging on to her husband in sudden bright sunshine. *'And forgive us our trespasses.'* Garfield mouthed the words too.

With bitter calmness, Hazel allowed the facts to settle into place. Milton had been told not to. He had been told, even by Garfield himself, that you had fancies when you were fifteen. He had been told that talk about a Catholic saint was like the Catholics claiming one of their idolatrous statues had been seen to move. But in spite of all that was said to him Milton had disobeyed. 'Your bodies a living sacrifice,' Hazel's Great-Uncle Willie used to thunder, steadfast in his certainty. Prominent among the mourners, the old man's granite features displayed no emotion now.

'Amen,' Herbert Cutcheon prompted, and the mourners murmured and Mrs Leeson sobbed. Hazel moved closer to her, as Addy did, receiving her from their father's care. All of them knew, Hazel's thoughts ran on: her father knew, and her mother, and Addy, and Herbert Cutcheon. It was known in every house in the neighbourhood; it was known in certain Belfast bars and clubs, where Garfield's hard-man reputation had been threatened, and then enhanced.

'It's all right, Mother,' Addy whispered as the three women turned from the grave, but Hazel did not attempt to soothe her mother's distress because she knew she could not. Her mother would go to her own grave with the scalding agony of what had happened still alive within her; her father would be reminded of the day of the occurrence on all the July marches remaining to him. The family would not ever talk about the day, but through their pain they would tell themselves that Milton's death was the way things were, the way things had to be: that was their single consolation. Lost ground had been regained.

August Saturday

'You don't remember me,' the man said.

His tone suggested a statement, not a question, but Grania did remember him. She had recognized him immediately, his face smiling above the glass he held. He was a man she had believed she would never see again. For sixteen years—since the summer of 1972—she had tried not to think about him, and for the most part had succeeded.

'Yes, I do remember you,' she said. 'Of course.'

A slice of lemon floated on the surface of what she guessed was gin and tonic; there were cubes of ice and the little bubbles that came from tonic when it was freshly poured. It wouldn't be tonic on its own; it hadn't been the other time. 'I've drunk a bit too much,' he'd said.

'I used to wonder,' he went on now, 'if ever we'd meet again. The kind of thing you wonder when you can't sleep.'

'I didn't think we would.'

'I know. But it doesn't matter, does it?'

'Of course not.'

She wondered why he had come back. She wondered how long he intended to stay. He'd be staying with the Prendergasts, she supposed, as he had been before. For sixteen years she had avoided the road on which the avenue that led to the Prendergasts' house was, the curve of the green iron railings on either side of the open gates, the unoccupied gate-lodge.

'You weren't aware that Hetty Prendergast died?' he said.

'No, I wasn't.'

'Well, she did. Two days ago.'

The conversation took place in the bar of the Tara Hotel, where

Grania and her husband, Desmond, dined once a month with other couples from the tennis club—an arrangement devised by the husbands so that the wives, just for a change, wouldn't have to cook.

'You don't mind my talking to you?' the man said. 'I'm on my own again.'

'Of course I don't.'

'When I was told about the death I came on over. I've just come in from the house to have a meal with the Quiltys.'

'Tonight, you mean?'

'When they turn up.'

Quilty was a solicitor. He and his wife, Helen, belonged to the tennis club and were usually present at the monthly dinners in the Rhett Butler Room of the Tara Hotel. The death of old Hetty Prendergast had clearly caught them unawares, and Grania could imagine Helen Quilty sulkily refusing to cancel a long-booked babysitter in order to remain at home to cook a meal for the stranger who had arrived from England, with whom her husband presumably had business to discuss. 'We'll take him with us,' Quilty would have said in his soothing voice, and Helen would have calmed down, as she always did when she got her way.

'Still playing tennis, Grania?'

'Pretty badly.'

'You've hardly aged, you know.'

This was so patently a lie that it wasn't worth protesting about. After the funeral of the old woman he would go away. He hadn't arrived for the other funeral, that of Mr Prendergast, which had taken place nearly ten years ago, and there wouldn't be another one because there was no other Prendergast left to die. She wondered what would happen to the house and to the couple who had looked after the old woman, driving in every Friday to shop for her. She didn't ask. She said:

'A group of us have dinner here now and again, the Quiltys too. I don't know if they told you that.'

'You mean tonight?'

'Yes.'

'No, that wasn't said.'

He smiled at her. He sipped a little gin. He had a long face, high cheekbones, greying hair brushed straight back from a sallow forehead. His blue-green eyes were steady, almost staring because he didn't blink much. She remembered the eyes particularly, now that she was again being scrutinized by them. She remembered asking who he was and being told a sort of nephew of the Prendergasts, an Englishman.

'I've often wondered about the tennis club, Grania.'

'It hasn't changed. Except that we've become the older generation.'

Desmond came up then and she introduced her companion, reminding Desmond that he'd met him before. She stumbled when she had to give him a name because she'd never known what it was. 'Prendergast,' she mumbled vaguely, not sure if he was called Prendergast or not. She'd never known that.

'Hetty died, I hear,' Desmond said.

'So I've been telling your wife. I've come over to do my stuff.'

'Well, of course.'

'The Quiltys have invited me to your dinner do.'

'You're very welcome.'

Desmond had a squashed pink face and receding hair that had years ago been sandy. As soon as he put his clothes on they became crumpled, no matter how carefully Grania ironed them. He was a man who never lost his temper, slow-moving except on a tennis court, where he was surprisingly subtle and cunning, quite unlike the person he otherwise was.

Grania moved away. Mavis Duddy insisted she owed her a drink from last time and led her to the bar, where she ordered two more Martinis. 'Who was that?' she asked, and Grania replied that the grey-haired man was someone from England, related to the Prendergasts, she wasn't entirely certain about his name. He'd come to the tennis club once, she said, an occasion when Mavis hadn't been there. 'Over for old Hetty's funeral, is he?' Mavis said and, accepting the drink, Grania agreed that was so.

They were a set in the small town; since the time they'd been teenagers the tennis club had been the pivot of their social lives. In winter some of them played bridge or golf, others chose not to. But all of them on summer afternoons and evenings looked in at the tennis club even if, like Francie MacGuinness and the Haddons, they didn't play much any more. They shared memories, and likes and dislikes, that had to do with the tennis club; there were photographs that once in a blue moon were sentimentally mulled over; friendships had grown closer or apart. Billy MacGuinness had always been the same, determinedly a winner at fourteen and determinedly a winner at forty-five. Francie, who'd married him when it had seemed that he might marry Trish, was a winner also: Trish had made do with Tom Crosbie. There'd been quarrels at the tennis club: a great row in 1961 when Desmond's father had wanted to raise money for a hard court and resigned in a huff when no one agreed; and nearly ten years later there had been the quarrel between Laverty and Dr Timothy Sweeney which had resulted in both their resignations, all to do with a dispute about a roller. There were jealousies and gossip, occasionally both envy and resentment. The years had been less kind to some while favouring others; the children born to the couples of the tennis club were often compared, though rarely openly, in terms of achievement or promise. Tea was taken, supplied by the wives, on Saturday afternoons from May to September. The men supplied drinks on that one day of the week also, and even washed up the glasses. The children of the tennis club tasted their first cocktails there, Billy MacGuinness's White Ladies and Sidecars.

A handful of the tennis-club wives were best friends, and had been since their convent days: Grania and Mavis, Francie, Helen, Trish. They trusted one another, doing so more easily now than they had when they'd been at the convent together or in the days when each of them might possibly have married one of the others' husbands. They told one another most things, confessing their errors and their blunders; they comforted and were a solace, jollying away feelings of inadequacy or guilt. Trish had worried at the convent because her breasts wouldn't grow, Helen because her face was scrawny and her lips too thin. Francie had almost died when a lorry had knocked her off her bicycle. Mavis had agonized for months before she said yes to Martin Duddy. As girls, they had united in their criticism of girls outside their circle; as wives they had not changed.

'I heard about that guy,' Mavis said. 'So that's what he looks like.'

That August Saturday in 1972 he'd come to the tennis club on a bicycle, in whites he had borrowed at the house where he was staying, a racquet tied with string to the crossbar. He'd told Grania afterwards that Hetty Prendergast had looked the whites out for him and had lent him the racquet as well. Hetty had mentioned the tennis club, to which she and her husband had years ago belonged themselves. 'Of course a different kind of lot these days,' she'd said. 'Like everywhere.' He'd pushed the bicycle through the gate and stood there watching a doubles game, not yet untying his racquet. 'Who on earth's that?' someone had said, and Grania approached him after about a quarter of an hour, since she was at that time the club's secretary and vaguely felt it to be her duty.

Sipping the Martini Mavis had claimed to owe her, Grania remembered the sudden turning of his profile in her direction when she spoke and then his smile. Nothing of what she subsequently planned had entered her head then; she would have been stunned by even the faintest inkling of it. 'I'm awfully sorry,' he'd said. 'I'm barging in.'

Grania had been twenty-seven then, married to Desmond for almost eight years. Now she was forty-three, and her cool brown eyes still strikingly complemented the lips that Desmond had once confessed he'd wanted to kiss ever since she was twelve. Her dark hair had been in plaits at twelve, later had been fashionably long, and now was short. She wasn't tall and had always wished she was, but at least she didn't have to slim. She hadn't become a mother yet, that Saturday afternoon when the stranger arrived at the tennis club. But she was happy, and in love with Desmond.

'Aisling's going out with some chartered accountant,' Mavis said, speaking about her daughter. 'Martin's hopping mad.'

The Quiltys arrived. Grania watched while they joined Desmond and their dinner guest. Desmond moved to the bar to buy them drinks. Quilty—a small man who reminded Grania of a monkey —lit a cigarette. Politely, Grania transferred her attention to her friend. Why should Martin be angry? she asked, genuinely not knowing. She could tell from Mavis's tone of voice that she was not displeased herself.

'Because he's nine years older. We had a letter from Aisling this morning. Martin's talking about going up to have it out with her.'

'That might make it worse, actually.'

'If he mentions it will you tell him that? He listens to you, you know.'

Grania said she would. She knew Martin Duddy would mention it, since he always seemed to want to talk to her about things that upset him. Once upon a time, just before she'd become engaged to Desmond, he'd tried to persuade her he loved her.

'They earn a fortune,' Mavis said. 'Chartered accountants.'

Soon after that they all began to move into the Rhett Butler Room. Grania could just remember the time when the hotel had been called O'Hara's Commercial, in the days of Mr and Mrs O'Hara. It wasn't all that long ago that their sons, giving the place another face-lift as soon as they inherited it, had decided to change the name to the Tara and to give the previously numbered bedrooms titles such as 'Ashley's' and 'Melanie's'. The bar was known as Scarlett's Lounge. There were regular discos in Belle's Place.

'Who's that fellow with the Quiltys?' Francie MacGuinness asked, and Grania told her.

'He's come back for Hetty Prendergast's funeral.'

'God, I didn't know she died.'

As always, several tables had been pushed together to form a single long one in the centre of the dining-room. At it, the couples who'd been drinking in the bar sat as they wished: there was no formality. Una Carty-Carroll, Trish Crosbie's sister, was unmarried but was usually partnered on these Saturday occasions by the surveyor from the waterworks. This was so tonight. At one end of the table a place remained unoccupied: Angela, outside the circle of best friends, as Una Carty-Carroll and Mary Ann Haddon were, invariably came late. In a distant corner of the Rhett Butler Room one other couple were dining. Another table, recently occupied, was being tidied.

'I think it's Monday,' Grania said when Francie asked her when the funeral was.

She hoped he'd go away again immediately. That other Saturday he'd said he found it appallingly dull at the Prendergasts', a call of duty, no reason in the world why he should ever return. His reassurances had in a way been neither here nor there at the time, but afterwards of course she'd recalled them. Afterwards, many times, she'd strained to establish every single word of the conversation they'd had.

'D'you remember poor old Hetty,' Francie said, 'coming in to the club for a cup of tea once? Ages ago.'

'Yes, I remember her.'

A small woman, they remembered, a frail look about her face. There was another occasion Francie recalled: when the old woman became agitated because one of Wm. Cole's meal lorries had backed into her Morris Minor. 'I thought she'd passed on years ago,' Francie said.

They separated. Helen was sitting next to him, Grania noticed, Quilty on his other side. Presumably they'd talk over whatever business there was, so that he wouldn't have to delay once the funeral had taken place.

'How're you doing, dear?' Martin Duddy said, occupying the chair on her left. Desmond was on her right; he nearly always chose to sit next to her.

'I'm all right,' she replied. 'Are you OK, Martin?'

'Far from it, as a matter of fact.' He twisted backwards and stretched an arm out, preventing the waitress who was attempting to pass by from doing so. 'Bring me a Crested Ten, will you?

Aisling's in the family way,' he muttered into Grania's ear. 'Jesus Christ, Grania!'

He was an architect, responsible for the least attractive bungalows in the county, possibly in the province. He and Mavis had once spent a protracted winter holiday in Spain, the time he'd been endeavouring to find himself. He hadn't done so, but that period of his life had ever since influenced the local landscape. Also, people said, his lavatories didn't work as well as they might have.

'Do you mean it, Martin? Are you sure?'

'Some elderly Mr Bloody. I'll wring his damn neck for him.'

He was drunk to the extent that failing to listen to him wouldn't matter. No opportunity for comment would be offered. The advice sought, the plea for understanding, would not properly register in the brain that set in motion the requests. It was extremely unlikely that Aisling was pregnant.

'Old Hetty left him the house,' Desmond said on her other side. 'He's going to live in it. Nora,' he called out to the waitress, 'I need to order the wine.'

Martin Duddy gripped her elbow, demanding the return of her attention. His face came close to hers: the small, snub nose, the tightly bunched, heated cheeks, droplets of perspiration on forehead and chin. Grania looked away. Across the table, Mavis was better-looking than her husband in all sorts of ways, her lips prettily parted as she listened to whatever it was Billy MacGuinness was telling her about, her blue eyes sparkling with Saturday-evening vivacity. Francie was listening to the surveyor. Mary Ann Haddon was nervously playing with her fork, the way she did when she felt she was being ignored: she had a complex about her looks, which were not her strong point. Helen Quilty was talking to the man who'd come back for the funeral, her wide mouth swiftly opening and closing. Francie, who'd given up smoking a fortnight ago, lit a cigarette. Billy MacGuinness's round face crinkled with sudden laughter. Mavis laughed also.

The waitress hurried away with Desmond's wine order. Light caught one lens of Mary Ann's glasses. 'Oh, I don't *believe* you!'

Francie cried, her voice for a single instant shrill above the buzz of conversation. The man who'd come back to attend the old woman's funeral still listened politely. Trish—the smallest, most demure of the wives—kept nodding while Kevy Haddon spoke in his dry voice, his features drily matching it.

There were other faces in the Rhett Butler Room, those of Clark Gable and Vivien Leigh reproduced on mirrored glass with bevelled edges, huge images that also included the shoulders of the film stars, the *décolletage* of one, the frilled evening shirt of the other. Clark Gable was subtly allowed the greater impact; in Scarlett's Lounge, together on a single mirror, the two appeared to be engaged in argument, he crossly pouting from a distance, she imperious in close-up.

'This man here, you mean?' Grania said to her husband when there was an opportunity. She knew he did; there was no one else he could mean. She didn't want to think about it, yet it had to be confirmed. She wanted to delay the knowledge, yet just as much she had to know quickly.

'So he's been saying,' Desmond said. 'You know, I'd forgotten who he was when you introduced us.'

'But what on earth does he want to come and live in that awful old house for?'

'He's on his uppers apparently.'

Often they talked together on these Saturday occasions, in much the same way as they did in their own kitchen while she finished cooking the dinner and he laid the table. In the kitchen they talked about people they'd run into during the day, the same people once a week or so, rarely strangers. When his father retired almost twenty years ago, Desmond had taken over the management of the town's laundry and later had inherited it. The Tara Hotel was his second most important customer, the Hospital of St Bernadette of Lourdes being his first. He brought back to Grania reports of demands for higher wages, and the domestic confidences of his staff. In return she passed on gossip, which both of them delighted in.

'How's Judith?' Martin Duddy inquired, finger and thumb again tightening on her elbow. 'No Mr Bloody yet?'

'Judith's still at the convent, remember.'

'You never know these days.'

'I think you've got it wrong about Aisling being pregnant.'

'I pray to God I have, dear.'

Desmond said he intended to go to Hetty Prendergast's funeral, but she saw no reason why she should go herself. Desmond went to lots of funerals, often of people she didn't know, business acquaintances who'd lived miles away. Going to funerals was different when there was a business reason, not that the Prendergasts had ever made much use of the laundry.

'I have a soft spot for Judith,' Martin Duddy said. 'She's getting to be a lovely girl.'

It was difficult to agree without sounding smug, yet it seemed disloyal to her daughter to deny what was claimed for her. Grania shrugged, a gesture that was vague enough to indicate whatever her companion wished to make of it. There was no one on Martin Duddy's other side because the table ended there. Angela, widow of a German businessman, had just sat down in the empty place opposite him. The most glamorous of all the wives, tall and slim, her hair the colour of very pale sand, Angela was said to be on the look-out for a second marriage. Her husband had settled in the neighbourhood after the war and had successfully begun a cheese-and-pâté business, supplying restaurants and hotels all over the country. With a flair he had cultivated in her, Angela ran it now. 'How's Martin?' She smiled seductively across the table, the way she'd smiled at men even in her husband's lifetime. Martin Duddy said he was all right, but Grania knew that only a desultory conversation would begin between the two because Martin Duddy didn't like Angela for some reason, or else was alarmed by her.

'Judith always has a word for you,' he said. 'Rare, God knows, in a young person these days.'

'Who's that?' Angela leaned forward, her eyes indicating the stranger.

She was told, and Grania watched her remembering him. Angela had been pregnant with the third of her sons that August afternoon. 'Uncomfortably warm,' she now recalled, nodding in recollection.

Martin Duddy displayed no interest. He'd been at the club that afternoon and he remembered the arrival of the stranger, but an irritated expression passed over his tightly made face while Grania and Angela agreed about the details of the afternoon in question: he resented the interruption and wished to return to the subject of daughters.

'What I'm endeavouring to get at, Grania, is what would you say if Judith came back with some fellow old enough to be her father?'

'Mavis didn't say Aisling's friend was as old as that.'

'Aisling wrote us a letter, Grania. There are lines to read between.'

'Well, naturally I'd prefer Judith to marry someone of her own age. But of course it all depends on the man.'

'D'you find a daughter easy, Grania? There's no one thinks more of Aisling than myself. The fonder you are the more worry there is. Would you say that was right, Grania?'

'Probably.'

'You're lucky in Judith, though. She has a great way with her.'

Angela was talking to Tom Crosbie about dairy products. The Crosbies were an example of a marriage in which there was a considerable age difference, yet it appeared not to have had an adverse effect. Trish had had four children, two girls and two boys; they were a happy, jolly family, even though when Trish married it had been widely assumed that she was not in love, was if anything still yearning after Billy MacGuinness. It was even rumoured that Trish had married for money, since Tom Crosbie owned Boyd Motors, the main Ford franchise in the neighbourhood. Trish's family had once been well-to-do but had somehow become penurious.

'What's Judith going to do for herself? Nursing, is it, Grania?'

'If it is she's never mentioned it.'

'I only thought it might be.'

'There's talk about college. She's not bad at languages.'

'Don't send her to Dublin, dear. Keep the girl by you. D'you hear what I'm saying, Desmond?' Martin Duddy raised his voice, shouting across Grania. He began all over again, saying he had a soft spot for Judith, explaining about the letter that had arrived from Aisling. Grania changed places with him. 'Martin's had a few,' Angela said.

'He's upset about Aisling. She's going out with an older man.'

She shouldn't have said it with Tom Crosbie sitting there. She made a face to herself and leaned across the table to tell him he was looking perky. As soon as she'd spoken she felt she'd made matters worse, that her remark could be taken to imply he was looking young for his years.

'There's a new place,' Angela said when Grania asked her about her dress. ' "Pursestrings". D'you know it?'

Ever since she'd become a widow Angela had gone to Dublin to buy something during the week before each Saturday dinner. Angela liked to be first, though often Francie ran her close. Mavis tried to keep up with them but couldn't quite. Grania sometimes tried too; Helen didn't mind what she wore.

'Is Desmond going to the funeral?' Tom Crosbie asked in his agreeable way—perhaps, Grania thought, to show that no offence had been taken.

'Yes, he is.'

'Desmond's very good.'

That was true. Desmond was good. He'd been the pick of the tennis club when she'd picked him herself, the pick of the town. Looking round the table—at Tom Crosbie's bald head and Kevy Haddon's joylessness, at the simian lines of Quilty's cheeks and Billy MacGuinness's tendency to glow, Martin Duddy's knotted features—she was aware that, on top of everything else, Desmond had worn better than any of them. He had acquired authority in middle age; the reticence of his youth had remained, but time had displayed that he was more often right than wrong, and his opinion was sought in a way it once had not been. Desmond was quietly obliging, a quality more appreciated in middle age than in youth. Mavis had called him a dear when he was still a bachelor.

They ate their prawn cocktails. The voices became louder. For a moment Grania's eye was held by the man who had said, at first, that she didn't remember him. A look was exchanged and persisted for a moment. Did he suspect that she had learnt already of his intention to live in the Prendergasts' house? Would he have told her himself if they hadn't been interrupted by Desmond?

'Hetty was a nice old thing,' Angela said. 'I feel I'd like to attend her funeral myself.'

She glanced again in the direction of the stranger. Tom Crosbie began to talk about a court case that was causing interest. Martin Duddy got up and ambled out of the dining-room, and Desmond moved to where he'd been sitting so that he was next to his wife again. The waitresses were collecting the prawn-cocktail glasses. 'Martin's being a bore about this Aisling business,' Desmond said.

'Desmond, did Prendergast mention being married now?'

He looked down the table, and across it. He shook his head. 'He hasn't the look of being married. Another thing is, I have a feeling he's called something else.'

'Angela says she's going to the funeral.'

One of the waitresses brought round plates of grilled salmon, the other offered vegetables. Martin Duddy returned with a glass of something he'd picked up in the bar, whiskey on ice it looked like. He sat between Desmond and Una Carty-Carroll, not seeming to notice that it wasn't where he'd been sitting before.

Mavis's back was reflected in the Rhett Butler mirror, the V of her black dress plunging deeply down her spine. Her movements, and those of Billy MacGuinness next to her, danced over the features of Clark Gable.

'He might suit Angela,' Desmond said. 'You never know.'

That August afternoon Billy MacGuinness, who was a doctor, had been called away from the club, some complication with a confinement. 'Damned woman,' he'd grumbled unfeelingly, predicting an all-night job. 'Come back to the house, Francie,' Grania had invited when the tennis came to an end, and it was then that Desmond had noticed the young man attaching his tennis racquet to the crossbar of his bicycle and had issued the same invitation. Desmond had said he'd drive him back to the Prendergasts' when they'd all had something to eat, and together they lifted his bicycle on to the boot of the car. 'I've something to confess,' Francie had said in the kitchen, cutting the rinds off rashers of bacon, and Grania knew what it would be because 'I've something to confess' was a kind of joke among the wives, a time-honoured way of announcing pregnancy. 'You're *not!*' Grania cried, disguising envy. 'Oh, Francie, how grand!' Desmond brought them drinks, but Francie didn't tell him, as Grania had guessed she wouldn't. 'February,' Francie said. 'Billy says it should be February.'

Billy telephoned while they were still in the kitchen, guessing where Francie was when there'd been no reply from his own number. He'd be late, as he'd predicted. 'Francie's pregnant,' Grania told Desmond while Francie was still on the phone. 'Don't tell her I said.'

In the sitting-room they had a few more drinks while in the kitchen the bacon cooked on a glimmer of heat. All of them were still in their tennis clothes and nobody was in a hurry. Francie wasn't because of the empty evening in front of her. Grania and Desmond weren't because they'd nothing to do that evening. The young man who was staying with the Prendergasts was like a schoolboy prolonging his leave. The sipping of their gin, the idle conversation—the young man told about the town and the tennis club, told who Angela was, and which the Duddys were: all of it took on the pleasurable feeling of a party happening by chance. Desmond picked up the telephone and rang the Crosbies but Trish said they wouldn't be able to get a babysitter or else of course they'd come over, love to. Eventually Desmond beat up eggs to scramble and Grania fried potato cakes and soda bread. 'We're none of us sober,' Desmond said, offering a choice of white or red wine as they sat down to eat. Eartha Kitt sang 'Just an Old-fashioned Girl'.

In the Rhett Butler Room Grania heard the tune again. '. . . and an old-fashioned millionaire', lisped the cool, sensuous voice, each emphasis strangely accented. They'd danced to it among the furniture of the sitting-room, Francie and the young man mostly, she and Desmond. 'I'm sorry, darling,' Desmond whispered, but she shook her head, refusing to concede that blame came into it. If it did, she might as well say she was sorry herself. 'I have to get back,' Francie said. 'Cook something for Billy.' Desmond said he'd drop her off on his way to the Prendergasts, but then he changed the record to 'Love Grows', and fell asleep as soon as the music began.

Francie didn't want a lift. She wanted to walk because the air would do her good. 'D'you trust me?' Grania asked the young man, and he laughed and said he'd have to because he didn't have a lamp on his bicycle. She'd hardly spoken to him, had been less aware of him than of Desmond's apparent liking of him. With strangers Desmond was often like that. 'What do you do?' she asked in the car, suddenly shy in spite of all the gin and wine there'd been. He'd held her rather close when he'd danced with her, but she'd noticed he'd held Francie close too. Francie had kissed him goodbye. 'Well, actually I've been working in a pub,' he said. 'Before that I made toast in the Marine Hotel in Bournemouth.'

She drove slowly, with extreme caution, through the narrow streets of the town. The public houses were closing; gaggles of men loitered near each, smoking or just standing. Youths thronged the pavement outside the Palm Grove fish-and-chip shop. Beyond the last of its lamp-posts the town straggled away to nothing, solitary cottages and bungalows gave way to fields. 'I haven't been to this house before,' Grania said in a silence that had developed. Her companion had vouchsafed no further information about himself beyond the reference to a pub and making toast in Bournemouth. 'They'll be in bed,' he said now. 'They go to bed at nine.'

The headlights picked out trunks of trees on the avenue, then urns, and steps leading up to a hall door. White wooden shutters flanked the downstairs windows, the paint peeling, as it was on the iron balustrade of the steps. All of it was swiftly there, then lost: the car lights isolated a rose-bed and a seat on a lawn. 'I won't be a minute,' he said, 'unshackling this bike.'

She turned the lights off. The last of the August day hadn't quite gone; a warm duskiness was scented with honeysuckle she could not see when she stepped out of the car. 'You've been awfully good to me,' he said, unknotting the strings that held the bicycle in place. 'You and Desmond.'

In the Rhett Butler Room, now rowdy with laughter and raised voices, she didn't want to look at him again, and yet she couldn't help herself: waiting for her were the unblinking eyes, the hair brushed back from the sallow forehead, the high cheekbones. Angela would stand at the graveside and afterwards would offer him sympathy. Quilty would be there, Helen wouldn't bother. 'I'd say we all need a drink': Grania could imagine Angela saying that, including Desmond in the invitation, gathering the three men around her. In the dark the bicycle had been wheeled away and propped against the steps. 'Come in for a minute,' he'd said, and she'd begun to protest that it was late, even though it wasn't. 'Oh, don't be silly,' he'd said.

She remembered in the garish hotel dining-room, the flash of his smile in the gloom, and how she'd felt his unblinking eyes caressing her. He reached out for her hand, and in a moment they were in a hall, the electric light turned on, a grandfather clock ticking at the bottom of the stairs. There was a hallstand, and square cream-and-terracotta tiles, brown engravings framed in oak, fish in glass cases. 'I shall offer you a nightcap,' he whispered, leading her into a flagged passage and then into a cavernous kitchen. 'Tullamore Dew is what they have,' he murmured. 'Give every man his dew.' She knew what he intended. She'd known it before they'd turned in at the avenue gates; she'd felt it in the car between them. He poured their drinks and then he kissed her, taking her into his arms as though that were simply a variation of their dancing together. 'Dearest,' he murmured, surprising her: she hadn't guessed that he intended, also, the delicacy of endearments.

Did she, before the car turned in at the avenue gates, decide herself what was to happen? Or was it later, even while still protesting that it was late? Or when he reached up to the high shelf of the dresser for the bottle? At some point she had said to herself: I am going to do this. She knew she had because the words still echoed. 'How extraordinary!' he murmured in the kitchen, all his talk as soft as that now. 'How extraordinary to find you at a tennis club in Ireland!' Her own arms held him to her; yet for some reason she didn't want to see his face, not that she found it unattractive.

The empty glasses laid down on the kitchen table, stairs without a carpet, a chest of drawers on a landing, towels in a pile on a chair, the door of his bedroom closing behind them: remembered images were like details from a dream. For a moment the light went on in his room: a pink china jug stood in a basin on a wash-stand, there was a wardrobe, a cigarette packet on the dressing-table, the shirt and trousers he'd changed from into his tennis clothes were thrown on to the floor. Then the light was extinguished and again he embraced her, his fingers already unbuttoning her tennis dress, which no one but Desmond had ever done in that particular way. Before her marriage she'd been kissed, twice, by Billy MacGuinness, and once by a boy who'd left the neighbourhood and gone to Canada. As all the tennis-club wives were when they married, she'd been a virgin. 'Oh God, Grania!' she heard him whispering, and her thoughts became worries when she lay, naked, on the covers of his bed. Her father's face was vivid in her mind, disposing of her with distaste. 'No, don't do that, dear,' her mother used to say, smacking with her tongue when Grania picked a scab on her knee or made a pattern on the raked gravel with a stick.

In the kitchen they ate raspberries and cream. She asked him again about himself but he hardly responded, questioning her instead and successfully extracting answers. The raspberries were delicious; he put a punnet on the seat beside the driving seat in the car. They were for Desmond, but he didn't say so. 'Don't feel awkward,' he said. 'I'm going back on Monday.'

A hare ran in front of the car on the avenue, bewildered by the lights. People would guess, she thought; they would see a solitary shadow in the car and they would know. It did not occur to her that if her expedition to the Prendergasts' house had been as innocent as its original purpose the people who observed her return would still have seen what they saw now. In fact, the streets were quite deserted when she came to them.

'God, I'm sorry,' Desmond said, sitting up on the sofa, his white clothes rumpled, the texture of a cushion-cover on his cheek, his hair untidy. She smiled, not trusting herself to speak or even to laugh, as in other circumstances she might have. She put the raspberries in the refrigerator and had a bath.

In the Rhett Butler Room they began to change places in the usual way, after the Black Forest gâteau. She sat by Francie and Mavis. 'Good for Aisling,' Francie insisted when Mavis described the chartered accountant; he did not seem old at all. 'I'll have it out with Martin when we get back,' Mavis said. 'There's no chance whatsoever she's been naughty. I can assure you I'd be the first to know.' They lowered their voices to remark on Angela's interest in the stranger. 'The house would suit her rightly,' Mavis said.

All the rooms would be done up. The slatted shutters that flanked the windows would be repainted, and the balustrade by the steps. There'd be new curtains and carpets; a gardener would be employed. Angela had never cared for the house her well-to-do husband had built her, and since his death had made no secret of the fact.

'I'll never forget that night, Grania.' Francie giggled, embarrassedly groping for a cigarette. 'Dancing with your man and Desmond going to sleep. Wasn't it the same night I told you Maureen was on the way?'

'Yes, it was.'

The three women talked of other matters. That week in the town an elderly clerk had been accused of embezzlement. Mavis observed that the surveyor from the waterworks was limbering up to propose to Una Carty-Carroll. 'And doesn't she know it!' Francie said. Grania laughed.

Sometimes she'd wondered if he was still working in a pub and told herself that of course he wouldn't be, that he'd have married and settled down ages ago. But when she saw him tonight she'd guessed immediately that he hadn't. She wasn't surprised when Desmond had said he was on his uppers. 'I am going to do this': the echo of her resolve came back to her as she sat there. 'I am going to do this because I want a child.'

'God, I'm exhausted,' Mavis said. 'Is it age or what?'

'Oh, it's age, it's age.' Francie sighed, stubbing out her cigarette. 'Damn things,' she muttered.

Mavis reached for the packet and flicked it across the table. 'Present for you, Kevy,' she said, but Francie pleaded with her eyes and he flicked it back again. Grania smiled because they'd have noticed if she didn't.

In the intervening years he would never have wondered about a child being born. But if Angela married him he would think about it; being close by would cause him to. He would wonder, and in the middle of a night, while he lay beside Angela in bed, it would be borne in upon him that Desmond and Grania had one child only. Grania considered that: the untidiness of someone else knowing, her secret shared. There'd been perpetually, every instant of the day it sometimes seemed, the longing to share—with Desmond and with her friends, with the child that had been born. But this was different.

The evening came to an end. Cars were started in the yard of the hotel; there were warnings of ice on the roads. 'Good-night, Grania,' the man who'd come for the funeral said. She buckled herself into her seat-belt. Desmond backed and then crawled forward into West Main Street. 'You're quiet,' he said, and immediately she began to talk about the possibility of Una Carty-Carroll being proposed to in case he connected her silence with the presence of the stranger. 'As a matter of fact,' he said when that subject was exhausted, 'I met that fellow of Aisling's once. He's only thirty-five.' She opened the garage door and he drove the car in. The air was refreshingly cold, sharper than it had been in the yard of the hotel.

They locked their house. Grania put things ready for the morning. It was a relief that a babysitter was no longer necessary, that she didn't have to wait with just a trace of anxiety while Desmond drove someone home. He'd gone upstairs and she knew that he'd done so in order to press open Judith's door and glance in at her while she slept. Whenever they came in at night he did that.

At the sink Grania poured glasses of water for him and for herself, and carried them upstairs. When she had placed them on either side of their bed she, too, went to look in at her daughter—a mass of brown hair untidy on the pillow, eyes lightly closed. 'I might play golf tomorrow,' Desmond said, settling his trousers into his electric press. Almost as soon as he'd clambered into bed he fell asleep. She switched out his bedside light and went downstairs.

Alone in the kitchen, sitting over a cup of tea, she returned again to the August Saturday. Two of Trish's children had already been born then, and two of Mavis's, and Helen's first. 'I wouldn't be surprised,' Billy MacGuinness had said, 'if Angela doesn't drop this one in a deck-chair.' Mary Ann Haddon had just started her second. Older children were sitting on the clubhouse steps.

Grania forced her thoughts through all the rest of it, through the party that had happened by chance, the headlights picking out the rose-bed. She savoured easily the solitude she had disguised during the years that had passed since then, the secret that had seemed so safe. In the quiet kitchen, when she had been over this familiar ground, she felt herself again possessed by the confusion that had come like a fog when she'd seen tonight the father of her child. Then slowly it lifted: she was incapable of regret.

Kathleen's Field

'I'm after a field of land, sir.'

Hagerty's tone was modest to the bank agent, careful and cautious. He was aware that Mr Ensor would know what was coming next. He was aware that he constituted a risk, a word Mr Ensor had used a couple of times when endeavouring to discuss the overdraft Hagerty already had with the bank.

'I was wondering, sir . . .' His voice trailed away when Mr Ensor's head began to shake. He'd like to say yes, the bank agent assured him. He would say yes this very instant, only what use would it be when Head Office wouldn't agree? 'They're bad times, Mr Hagerty.'

It was a Monday morning in 1948. Leaning on the counter, his right hand still grasping the stick he'd used to drive three bullocks the seven miles from his farm, Hagerty agreed that the times were as bad as ever he'd known them. He'd brought the bullocks in to see if he could get a price for them, but he hadn't been successful. All the way on his journey he'd been thinking about the field old Lally had spent his lifetime carting the rocks out of. The widow the old man had left behind had sold the nineteen acres on the other side of the hill, but the last of her fields was awkwardly placed for anyone except Hagerty. They both knew it would be convenient for him to have it; they both knew there'd be almost as much profit in that single pasture as there was in all the land he possessed already. Gently sloping, naturally drained, it was free of weeds and thistles, and the grass it grew would do you good to look at. Old Lally had known its value from the moment he'd inherited it. He had kept it ditched, with its gates and stone walls always cared for.

And for miles around, no one had ever cleared away rocks like old Lally had.

'I'd help you if I could, Mr Hagerty,' the bank agent assured him. 'Only there's still a fair bit owing.'

'I know there is, sir.'

Every December Hagerty walked into the bank with a plucked turkey as a seasonal statement of gratitude: the overdraft had undramatically continued for seventeen years. It was less than it had been, but Hagerty was no longer young and he might yet be written off as a bad debt. He hadn't had much hope when he'd raised the subject of the field he coveted.

'I'm sorry, Mr Hagerty,' the bank agent said, stretching his hand across the width of the counter. 'I know that field well. I know you could make something of it, but there you are.'

'Ah well, you gave it your consideration, sir.'

He said it because it was his way to make matters easier for a man who had lent him money in the past: Hagerty was a humble man. He had a tired look about him, his spare figure stooped from the shoulders, a black hat always on his head. He hadn't removed it in the bank, nor did he in Shaughnessy's Provisions and Bar, where he sat in a corner by himself, with a bottle of stout to console him. He had left the bullocks in Cronin's yard in order to free himself for his business in the bank, and since Cronin made a small charge for this fair-day service he'd thought he might as well take full advantage of it by delaying a little longer.

He reflected as he drank that he hardly needed the bank agent's reminder about the times being bad. Seven of his ten children had emigrated, four to Canada and America, the three others to England. Kathleen, the youngest, now sixteen, was left, with Biddy, who wasn't herself, and Con, who would inherit the farm. But without the Lallys' field it wouldn't be easy for Con to keep going. Sooner or later he would want to marry the McKrill girl, and there'd always have to be a home for Biddy on the farm, and for a while at least an elderly mother and father would have to be accommodated also. Sometimes one or other of the exiled children sent back a cheque and Hagerty never objected to accepting it. But none of them could afford the price of a field, and he wasn't going to ask them. Nor would Con accept these little presents when his time came to take over the farm entirely, for how could the oldest brother be beholden like that in the prime of his life? It wasn't the same for Hagerty himself: he'd been barefoot on the farm as a child, which was when his humility had been learned.

'Are you keeping yourself well, Mr Hagerty?' Mrs Shaughnessy inquired, crossing the small bar to where he sat. She'd been busy with customers on the grocery side since soon after he'd come in; she'd drawn the cork out of his bottle, apologizing for her busyness when she gave it to him to pour himself.

'I am,' he said. 'And are you, Mrs Shaughnessy?'

'I have the winter rheumatism again. But thank God it's not severe.'

Mrs Shaughnessy was a tall, big-shouldered woman whom he remembered as a girl before she'd married into the shop. She wore a bit of makeup, and her clothes were more colourful than his wife's, although they were hidden now by her green shop overall. She had been flighty as a girl, so he remembered hearing, but in no way could you describe her as that in her late middle age; 'well-to-do' was the description that everything about Mrs Shaughnessy insisted upon.

'I was wanting to ask you, Mr Hagerty. I'm on the look-out for a country girl to assist me in the house. If they're any good they're like gold dust these days. Would you know of a country girl out your way?'

Hagerty began to shake his head and was at once reminded of the bank agent shaking his. It was then, while he was still actually engaged in that motion, that he recalled a fact which previously had been of no interest to him: Mrs Shaughnessy's husband lent people money. Mr Shaughnessy was a considerable businessman. As well as the Provisions and Bar, he owned a barber's shop and was an agent for the Property & Life Insurance Company; he had funds to spare. Hagerty had heard of people mortgaging an area of their land with Mr Shaughnessy, or maybe the farmhouse itself, and as a consequence being able to buy machinery or stock. He'd never yet heard of any unfairness or sharp practice on the part of Mr Shaughnessy after the deal had been agreed upon and had gone into operation.

'Haven't you a daughter yourself, Mr Hagerty? Pardon me now if I'm guilty of a presumption, but I always say if you don't ask you won't know. Haven't you a daughter not long left the nuns?'

Kathleen's round, open features came into his mind, momentarily softening his own. His youngest daughter was inclined to plumpness, but her wide, uncomplicated smile often radiated moments of prettiness in her face. She had always been his favourite, although Biddy, of course, had a special place also.

'No, she's not long left the convent.'

Her face slipped away, darkening to nothing in his imagination. He thought again of the Lallys' field, the curving shape of it like a tea-cloth thrown over a bush to dry. A stream ran among the few little ash trees at the bottom, the morning sun lingered on the heart of it.

'I'd never have another girl unless I knew the family, Mr Hagerty. Or unless she'd be vouched for by someone the like of yourself.'

'Are you thinking of Kathleen, Mrs Shaughnessy?'

'Well, I am. I'll be truthful with you, I am.'

At that moment someone rapped with a coin on the counter of the grocery and Mrs Shaughnessy hurried away. If Kathleen came to work in the house above the Provisions and Bar, he might be able to bring up the possibility of a mortgage. And the grass was so rich in the field that it wouldn't be too many years before a mortgage could be paid off. Con would be left secure, Biddy would be provided for.

Hagerty savoured a slow mouthful of stout. He didn't want Kathleen to go to England. *I can get her fixed up,* her sister, Mary Florence, had written in a letter not long ago. 'I'd rather Kilburn than Chicago,' he'd heard Kathleen herself saying to Con, and at the time he'd been relieved because Kilburn was nearer. Only Biddy would always be with them, for you couldn't count on Con not being tempted by Kilburn or Chicago the way things were at the present time. 'Sure, what choice have we in any of it?' their mother had said, but enough of them had gone, he'd thought. His father had struggled for the farm and he'd struggled for it himself.

'God, the cheek of some people!' Mrs Shaughnessy exclaimed, reentering the bar. 'Tinned pears and ham, and her book unpaid since January! Would you credit that, Mr Hagerty?'

He wagged his head in an appropriate manner, denoting amazement. He'd been thinking over what she'd put to him, he said. There was no girl out his way who might be suitable, only his own Kathleen. 'You were right enough to mention Kathleen, Mrs Shaughnessy.' The nuns had never been displeased with her, he said as well.

'Of course, she would be raw, Mr Hagerty. I'd have to train every inch of her. Well, I have experience in that, all right. You train them, Mr Hagerty, and the next thing is they go off to get married. There's no sign of that, is there?'

'Ah, no, no.'

'You'd maybe spend a year training them and then they'd be off. Sure, where's the sense in it? I often wonder I bother.'

'Kathleen wouldn't go running off, no fear of that, Mrs Shaughnessy.'

'It's best to know the family. It's best to know a father like yourself.'

As Mrs Shaughnessy spoke, her husband appeared behind the bar. He was a medium-sized man, with grey hair brushed into spikes, and a map of broken veins dictating a warm redness in his complexion. He wore a collar and tie, which Mr Hagerty did not, and the waistcoat and trousers of a dark-blue suit. He carried a number of papers in his right hand and a packet of Sweet Afton cigarettes in his left. He spread the papers out on the bar and, having lit a cigarette, proceeded to scrutinize them. While he listened to Mrs Shaughnessy's further exposition of her theme, Hagerty was unable to take his eyes off him.

'You get in a country girl and you wouldn't know was she clean or maybe would she take things. We had a queer one once, she used eat a raw onion. You'd go into the kitchen and she'd be at it. "What are you chewing, Kitty?" you might say to her politely. And she'd open her mouth and you'd see the onion in it.'

'Kathleen wouldn't eat onions.'

'Ah, I'm not saying she would. Des, will you bring Mr Hagerty another bottle of stout? He has a girl for us.'

Looking up from his papers but keeping a finger in place on them, her husband asked her what she was talking about.

'Kathleen Hagerty would come in and assist me, Des.'

Mr Shaughnessy asked who Kathleen Hagerty was, and when it was revealed that her father was sitting in the bar with a bottle of stout, and in need of another one, he bundled his papers into a pocket and drew the corks from two further bottles. His wife winked at Hagerty. He liked to have a maid about the house, she said. He pretended he didn't, but he liked the style of it.

All the way back to the farm, driving home the bullocks, Hagerty reflected on that stroke of luck. In poor spirits he'd turned into Shaughnessy's, it being the nearest public house to the bank. If he hadn't done so, and if Mrs Shaughnessy hadn't mentioned her domestic needs, and if her husband hadn't come in when he had, there wouldn't have been one bit of good news to carry back. 'I'm after a field of land,' he'd said to Mr Shaughnessy, making no bones about it. They'd both listened to him, Mrs Shaughnessy only going away once, to pour herself half a glass of sherry. They'd understood immediately the thing about the field being valuable to him because of its position. 'Doesn't it sound a grand bit of land, Des?' Mrs Shaughnessy had remarked with enthusiasm. 'With a good hot sun on it?' He'd revealed the price old Lally's widow was asking; he'd laid every fact he knew down before them.

In the end, on top of four bottles of stout, he was poured a glass of Paddy, and then Mrs Shaughnessy made him a spreadable-cheese sandwich. He would send Kathleen in, he promised, and after that it would be up to Mrs Shaughnessy. 'But, sure, I think we'll do business,' she'd confidently predicted.

Biddy would see him coming, he said to himself as he urged the bullocks on. She'd see the bullocks and she'd run back into the house to say they hadn't been sold. There'd be long faces then, but he'd take it easy when he entered the kitchen and reached out for his tea. A bad old fair it had been, he'd report, which was nothing only the truth, and he'd go through the offers that had been made to him. He'd go through his conversation with Mr Ensor and then explain how he'd gone into Shaughnessy's to rest himself before the journey home.

On the road ahead he saw Biddy waving at him and then doing what he'd known she'd do: hurrying back to precede him with the news. As he murmured the words of a thanksgiving, his youngest daughter again filled Hagerty's mind. The day Kathleen was born it had rained from dawn till dusk. People said that was lucky for the family of an infant, and it might be they were right.

Kathleen was led from room to room and felt alarmed. She had never experienced a carpet beneath her feet before. There were boards or linoleum in the farmhouse, and linoleum in the Reverend Mother's room at the convent. She found the papered walls startling: flowers cascaded in the corners, and ran in a narrow band around the room, close to the ceiling. 'I see you admiring the frieze,' Mrs Shaughnessy said. 'I had the house redone a year ago.' She paused and then laughed, amused by the wonder in Kathleen's face. 'Those little borders,' she said. 'I think they call them friezes these days.'

When Mrs Shaughnessy laughed her chin became long and smooth, and the skin tightened on her forehead. Her very white false teeth—which Kathleen was later to learn she referred to as her 'delf'—shifted slightly behind her reddened lips. The laugh was a sedate whisper that quickly exhausted itself.

'You're a good riser, are you, Kathleen?'

'I'm used to getting up, ma'am.'

Always say ma'am, the Reverend Mother had adjured, for Kathleen had been summoned when it was known that Mrs Shaughnessy was interested in training her as a maid. The Reverend Mother liked to have a word with any girl who'd been to the convent when the question of local employment arose, or if emigration was mooted. The Reverend Mother liked to satisfy herself that a girl's future promised to be what she would herself have chosen for the girl; and she liked to point out certain hazards, feeling it her duty to do so. The Friday fast was not observed in Protestant households, where there would also be an absence of sacred reminders. Conditions met with after emigration left even more to be desired.

'Now, this would be your own room, Kathleen,' Mrs Shaughnessy said, leading her into a small bedroom at the top of the house. There was a white china wash-basin with a jug standing in it, and a bed with a mattress on it, and a cupboard. The stand the basin and the jug were on was painted white, and so was the cupboard. A net curtain covered the bottom half of a window and at the top there was a brown blind like the ones in the Reverend Mother's room. There wasn't a carpet on the floor and there wasn't linoleum either; but a rug stretched on the boards by the bed, and Kathleen couldn't help imagining her bare feet stepping on to its softness first thing every morning.

'There'll be the two uniforms the last girl had,' Mrs Shaughnessy said. 'They'd easily fit, although I'd say you were bigger on the chest. You wouldn't be be familiar with a uniform, Kathleen?'

'I didn't have one at the convent, ma'am.'

'You'll soon get used to the dresses.'

That was the first intimation that Mrs Shaughnessy considered her suitable for the post. The dresses were hanging in the cupboard, she said. There were sheets and blankets in the hot press.

'I'd rather call you Kitty,' Mrs Shaughnessy said. 'If you wouldn't object. The last girl was Kitty, and so was another we had.'

Kathleen said that was all right. She hadn't been called Kitty at the convent, and wasn't at home because it was the pet name of her eldest sister.

'Well, that's great,' Mrs Shaughnessy said, the tone of her voice implying that the arrangement had already been made.

'I was never better pleased with you,' her father said when Kathleen returned home. 'You're a great little girl.'

When she'd packed some of her clothes into a suitcase that Mary Florence had left behind after a visit one time, he said it was hardly like going away at all because she was only going seven miles. She'd return every Sunday afternoon; it wasn't like Kilburn or Chicago. She sat beside him on the cart and he explained that the Shaughnessys had been generous to a degree. The wages he had agreed with them would be held back and set against the debt: it was that that made the whole thing possible, reducing his monthly repayments to a figure he was confident he could manage, even with the bank overdraft. 'It isn't everyone would agree to the convenience of that, Kathleen.'

She said she understood. There was a new sprightliness about her father; the fatigue in his face had given way to an excited pleasure. His gratitude to the Shaughnessys, and her mother's gratitude, had made the farmhouse a different place during the last couple of weeks. Biddy and Con had been affected by it, and so had Kathleen, even though she had no idea what life would be like in the house above the Shaughnessys' Provisions and Bar. Mrs Shaughnessy had not outlined her duties beyond saying that every night when she went up to bed she should carry with her the alarm clock from the kitchen dresser, and carry it down again every morning. The most important thing of all appeared to be that she should rise promptly from her bed.

'You'll listen well to what Mrs Shaughnessy says,' her father begged her. 'You'll attend properly to all the work, Kathleen?'

'I will of course.'

'It'll be great seeing you on Sundays, girl.'

'It'll be great coming home.'

A bicycle, left behind also by Mary Florence, lay in the back of the cart. Kathleen had wanted to tie the suitcase on to the carrier and cycle in herself with it, but her father wouldn't let her. It was dangerous, he said; a suitcase attached like that could easily unbalance you.

'Kathleen's field is what we call it,' her father said on their journey together, and added after a moment: 'They're decent people, Kathleen. You're going to a decent house.'

'Oh, I know, I know.'

But after only half a day there Kathleen wished she was back in the farmhouse. She knew at once how much she was going to miss the comfort of the kitchen she had known all her life, and the room along the passage she shared with Biddy, where Mary Florence had slept also, and the dogs nosing up to her in the yard. She knew how much she would miss Con, and her father and her mother, and how she'd miss looking after Biddy.

'Now, I'll show you how to set a table,' Mrs Shaughnessy said. 'Listen to this carefully, Kitty.'

Cork mats were put down on the tablecloth so that the heat of the dishes wouldn't penetrate to the polished surface beneath. Small plates were placed on the left of each mat, to put the skins of potatoes on. A knife and a fork were arranged on each side of the mats and a spoon and a fork across the top. The pepper and salt were placed so that Mr Shaughnessy could easily reach them. Serving spoons were placed by the bigger mats in the middle. The breakfast table was set the night before, with the cups upside down on the saucers so that they wouldn't catch the dust when the ashes were taken from the fireplace.

'Can you cut kindling, Kitty? I'll show you how to do it with the little hatchet.'

She showed her, as well, how to sweep the carpet on the stairs with a stiff hand-brush, and how to use the dust-pan. She explained that every mantelpiece in the house had to be dusted every morning, and all the places where grime would gather. She showed her where saucepans and dishes were kept, and instructed her in how to light the range, the first task of the day. The backyard required brushing once a week, on Saturday between four o'clock and five. And every morning after breakfast water had to be pumped from the tank in the yard, fifteen minutes' work with the hand lever.

'That's the W.C. you'd use, Kitty,' Mrs Shaughnessy indicated, leading her to a privy in another part of the backyard. 'The maids always use this one.'

The dresses of the uniforms didn't fit. She looked at herself in the blue one and then in the black. The mirror on the dressing-table was tarnished, but she could tell that neither uniform enhanced her in any way whatsoever. She looked as fat as a fool, she thought, with the hems all crooked, and the sleeves too tight on her forearms. 'Oh now, that's really very good,' Mrs Shaughnessy said when Kathleen emerged from her bedroom in the black one. She demonstrated how the bodice of the apron was kept in place and how the afternoon cap should be worn.

'Is your father fit?' Mr Shaughnessy inquired when he came upstairs for his six o'clock tea.

'He is, sir.' Suddenly Kathleen had to choke back tears because without any warning the reference to her father had made her want to cry.

'He was shook the day I saw him,' Mr Shaughnessy said, 'on account he couldn't sell the bullocks.'

'He's all right now, sir.'

The Shaughnessys' son reappeared then too, a narrow-faced youth who hadn't addressed her when he'd arrived in the dining-room in the middle of the day and didn't address her now. There were just the three of them, two younger children having grown up and gone away. During the day Mrs Shaughnessy had often referred to her other son and her daughter, the son in business in Limerick, the daughter married to a county surveyor. The narrow-faced son would inherit the businesses, she'd said, the barber's shop and the Provisions and Bar, maybe even the insurances. With a bout of wretchedness, Kathleen was reminded of Con inheriting the farm. Before that he'd marry Angie McKrill, who wouldn't hesitate to accept him now that the farm was improved.

Kathleen finished laying the table and went back to the kitchen, where Mrs Shaughnessy was frying rashers and eggs and slices of soda bread. When they were ready she scooped them on to three plates and Kathleen carried the tray, with a teapot on it as well, into the dining-room. Her instructions were to return to the kitchen when she'd done so and to fry her own rasher and eggs, and soda bread if she wanted it. 'I don't know will we make much of that one,' she heard Mrs Shaughnessy saying as she closed the dining-room door.

That night she lay awake in the strange bed, not wanting to sleep because sleep would too swiftly bring the morning, and another day like the day there'd been. She couldn't stay here: she'd say that on Sunday. If they knew what it was like they wouldn't want her to. She sobbed, thinking again of the warm kitchen she had left behind, the sheepdogs lying by the fire and Biddy turning the wheel of the bellows, the only household task she could do. She thought of her mother and father sitting at the table as they always did, her mother knitting, her father pondering, with his hat still on his head. If they could see her in the dresses they'd understand. If they could see her standing there pumping up the water they'd surely be sorry for the way she felt. 'I haven't the time to tell you twice, Kitty,' Mrs Shaughnessy said over and over again, her long, painted face not smiling in the least way whatsoever. If anything was broken, she'd said, the cost of it would have to be stopped out of the wages, and she'd spoken as though the wages would actually change hands. In Kathleen's dreams Mrs Shaughnessy kept laughing, her chin going long and smooth and her large white teeth moving in her mouth. The dresses belonged to one of the King of England's daughters, she explained, which was why they didn't fit. And then Mary Florence came into the kitchen and said she was just back from Kilburn with a pair of shoes that belonged to someone else. The price of them could be stopped out of the wages, she suggested, and Mrs Shaughnessy agreed.

When Kathleen opened her eyes, roused by the alarm clock at half past six, she didn't know where she was. Then one after another the details of the previous day impinged on her waking consciousness: the cork mats, the shed where the kindling was cut, the narrow face of the Shaughnessys' son, the greasy doorknobs in the kitchen, the impatience in Mrs Shaughnessy's voice. The reality was worse than the confusion of her dreams, and there was nothing magical about the softness of the rug beneath her bare feet: she didn't even notice it. She lifted her night-dress over her head and for a moment caught a glimpse of her nakedness in the tarnished looking-glass— plumply rounded thighs and knees, the dimple in her stomach. She drew on stockings and underclothes, feeling even more lost than she had when she'd tried not to go to sleep. She knelt by her bed, and when she'd offered her usual prayers she asked that she might be taken away from the Shaughnessys' house. She asked that her father would understand when she told him.

'The master's waiting on his breakfast, Kitty.'

'I lit the range the minute I was down, ma'am.'

'If you don't get it going by twenty to seven it won't be hot in time. I told you that yesterday. Didn't you pull the dampers out?'

'The paper wouldn't catch, ma'am.'

'If the paper wouldn't catch you'll have used a damp bit. Or maybe paper out of a magazine. You can't light a fire with paper out of a magazine, Kitty.'

'If I'd had a drop of paraffin, ma'am—'

'My God, are you mad, child?'

'At home we'd throw on a half cup of paraffin if the fire was slow, ma'am.'

'Never bring paraffin near the range. If the master heard you he'd jump out of his skin.'

'I only thought it would hurry it, ma'am.'

'Set the alarm for six if you're going to be slow with the fire. If the breakfast's not on the table by a quarter to eight he'll raise the roof. Have you the plates in the bottom oven?'

When Kathleen opened the door of the bottom oven a black

kitten darted out, scratching the back of her hand in its agitation.

'Great God Almighty!' exclaimed Mrs Shaughnessy. 'Are you trying to roast the poor cat?'

'I didn't know it was in there, ma'am.'

'You lit the fire with the poor creature inside there! What were you thinking of to do that, Kitty?'

'I didn't know, ma'am—'

'Always look in the two ovens before you light the range, child. Didn't you hear me telling you?'

After breakfast, when Kathleen went into the dining-room to clear the table, Mrs Shaughnessy was telling her son about the kitten in the oven. 'Haven't they brains like turnips?' she said, even though Kathleen was in the room. The son released a half-hearted smile, but when Kathleen asked him if he'd finished with the jam he didn't reply. 'Try and speak a bit more clearly, Kitty,' Mrs Shaughnessy said later. 'It's not everyone can understand a country accent.'

The day was similar to the day before except that at eleven o'clock Mrs Shaughnessy said:

'Go upstairs and take off your cap. Put on your coat and go down the street to Crawley's. A half pound of round steak, and suet. Take the book off the dresser. He'll know who you are when he sees it.'

So far, that was the pleasantest chore she had been asked to do. She had to wait in the shop because there were two other people before her, both of whom held the butcher in conversation. 'I know your father,' Mr Crawley said when he'd asked her name, and he held her in conversation also, wanting to know if her father was in good health and asking about her brothers and sisters. He'd heard about the buying of the Lallys' field. She was the last uniformed maid in the town, he said, now that Nellie Broderick at Maclure's had had to give up because of her legs.

'Are you mad?' Mrs Shaughnessy shouted at her on her return. 'I should be down in the shop and not waiting to put that meat on. Didn't I tell you yesterday not to be loitering in the mornings?'

'I'm sorry, ma'am, only Mr Crawley—'

'Go down to the shop and tell the master I'm delayed over cooking the dinner and can you assist him for ten minutes.'

But when Kathleen appeared in the grocery Mr Shaughnessy asked her if she'd got lost. The son was weighing sugar into grey paper bags and tying string round each of them. A murmur of voices came from the bar.

'Mrs Shaughnessy is delayed over cooking the dinner,' Kathleen said. 'She was thinking I could assist you for ten minutes.'

'Well, that's a good one!' Mr Shaughnessy threw back his head, exploding into laughter. A little shower of spittle damped Kathleen's face. The son gave his half-hearted smile. 'Can you make a spill, Kitty? D'you know what I mean by a spill?' Mr Shaughnessy demonstrated with a piece of brown paper on the counter. Kathleen shook her head. 'Would you know what to charge for a quarter pound of tea, Kitty? Can you weigh out sugar, Kitty? Go back to the missus, will you, and tell her to have sense.'

In the kitchen Kathleen put it differently, simply saying that Mr Shaughnessy hadn't required her services. 'Bring a scuttle of coal up to the dining-room,' Mrs Shaughnessy commanded. 'And get out the mustard. Can you make up mustard?'

Kathleen had never tasted mustard in her life; she had heard of it but did not precisely know what it was. She began to say she wasn't sure about making some, but even before she spoke Mrs Shaughnessy sighed and told her to wash down the front steps instead.

'I don't want to go back there,' Kathleen said on Sunday. 'I can't understand what she says to me. It's lonesome the entire time.'

Her mother was sympathetic, but even so she shook her head. 'There's people I used to know,' she said. 'People placed like ourselves whose farms failed on them. They're walking the roads now, no better than tinkers. I have ten children, Kathleen, and seven are gone from me. There's five of them I'll maybe never see again. It's that you have to think of, pet.'

'I cried the first night. I was that lonesome when I got into bed.'

'But isn't it a clean room you're in, pet? And aren't you given food to eat that's better than you'd get here? And don't the dresses she supplies save us an expense again? Wouldn't you think of all that, pet?'

A bargain had been struck, her mother also reminded her, and a bargain was a bargain. Biddy said it sounded great, going out into the town for messages. She'd give anything to see a house like that, Biddy said, with the coal fires and a stairs.

'I'd say they were well pleased with you,' Kathleen's father said when he came in from the yard later on. 'You'd have been back here inside a day if they weren't.'

She'd done her best, she thought as she rode away from the farmhouse on Mary Florence's bicycle; if she'd done everything badly she would have obtained her release. She wept because she wouldn't see Biddy and Con and her father and mother for another week. She dreaded the return to the desolate bedroom which her mother had reminded her was clean, and the kitchen where there was no one to keep her company in the evenings. She felt as if she could not bear it, more counting of the days until Sunday and when Sunday came the few hours passing so swiftly. But she knew, by now, that she would remain in the Shaughnessys' house for as long as was necessary.

'I must have you back by half six, Kitty,' Mrs Shaughnessy said when she saw her. 'It's closer to seven now.'

Kathleen said she was sorry. She'd had to stop to pump the back tyre of her bicycle, she said, although in fact this was not true: what she'd stopped for was to wipe away the signs of her crying and to blow her nose. In the short time she had been part of Mrs Shaughnessy's household she had developed the habit of making excuses, and of obscuring her inadequacies beneath lies that were easier than the truth.

'Fry the bread like I showed you, Kitty. Get it brown on both sides. The master likes it crisp.'

There was something Mr Shaughnessy liked also, which Kathleen discovered when seven of her free Sunday afternoons had gone by.

She was dusting the dining-room mantelpiece one morning when he came and stood very close to her. She thought she was in his way, and moved out of it, but a week or so later he stood close to her again, his breath warm on her cheek. When it happened the third time she felt herself blushing.

It was in this manner that Mr Shaughnessy rather than his wife came to occupy, for Kathleen, the central role in the household. The narrow-faced son remained as he had been since the day of her arrival, a dour presence, contributing little in the way of conversation and never revealing the fruits of his brooding silence. Mrs Shaughnessy, having instructed, had apparently played out the part she'd set herself. She came into the kitchen at midday to cook meat and potatoes and one of the milk puddings her husband was addicted to, but otherwise the kitchen was Kathleen's province now and it was she who was responsible for the frying of the food for breakfast and for the six o'clock tea. Mrs Shaughnessy preferred to be in the shop. She enjoyed the social side of that, she told Kathleen; and she enjoyed the occasional half glass of sherry in the bar. 'That's me all over, Kitty. I never took to housework.' She was more amiable in her manner, and confessed that she always found training a country girl an exhausting and irksome task and might therefore have been a little impatient. 'Kitty's settled in grand,' she informed Kathleen's father when he looked into the bar one fairday to make a mortgage payment. He'd been delighted to hear that, he told Kathleen the following Sunday.

Mr Shaughnessy never said anything when he came to stand close to her, although on other occasions he addressed her pleasantly enough, even complimenting her on her frying. He had an easy way with him, quite different from his son's. He was more like his two other children, the married daughter and the son who was in Limerick, both of whom Kathleen had met when they had returned to the house for an uncle's funeral. He occasionally repeated a joke he'd been told, and Mrs Shaughnessy would laugh, her chin becoming lengthy and the skin tightening on her forehead. On the occasion of the uncle's funeral his other son and his daughter laughed at the jokes also, but the son who'd remained at home only smiled. 'Wait till I tell you this one, Kitty,' he'd sometimes say, alone with her in the dining-room. He would tell her something Bob Crowe, who ran the barber's shop for him, had heard from a customer, making the most of the anecdote in a way that suggested he was anxious to entertain her. His manner and his tone of voice denied that it had ever been necessary for him to stand close to her, or else that his practice of doing so had been erased from his memory.

But the scarlet complexion of Mr Shaughnessy's face and the spiky grey hair, the odour of cigarette smoke that emanated from his clothes, could not be so easily forgotten by Kathleen. She no longer wept from loneliness in her bedroom, yet she was aware that the behaviour of Mr Shaughnessy lent the feeling of isolation an extra, vivid dimension, for in the farmhouse kitchen on Sundays the behaviour could not be mentioned.

Every evening Kathleen sat by the range, thinking about it. The black kitten that had darted out of the oven on her second morning had grown into a cat and sat blinking beside her chair. The alarm clock ticked loudly on the dresser. Was it something she should confess? Was it a sin to be as silent as she was when he came to stand beside her? Was it a sin to be unable to find the courage to tell him to leave her alone? Once, in the village where the convent was, another girl in her class had pointed out a boy who was loitering with some other boys by the sign-post. That boy was always trying to kiss you, the girl said; he would follow you about the place, whispering to you. But although Kathleen often went home alone the boy never came near her. He wasn't a bad-looking boy, she'd thought, she wouldn't have minded much. She'd wondered if she'd mind the boys her sisters had complained about, who tried to kiss you when they were dancing with you. Pests, her sisters had called them, but Kathleen thought it was nice that they wanted to.

Mr Shaughnessy was different. When he stood close to her his breathing would become loud and unsteady. He always moved away quite quickly, when she wasn't expecting him to. He walked off, never looking back, soundlessly almost.

Then one day, when Mrs Shaughnessy was buying a new skirt and the son was in the shop, he came into the kitchen, where she was scrubbing the draining boards. He came straight to where she was, as if between them there was some understanding that he should do so. He stood in a slightly different position from usual, behind her rather than at her side, and she felt for the first time his hands passing over her clothes.

'Mr Shaughnessy!' she whispered. 'Mr Shaughnessy, now.'

He took no notice. Some part of his face was touching her hair. The rhythm of his breathing changed.

'Mr Shaughnessy, I don't like it.'

He seemed not to hear her; she sensed that his eyes were closed. As suddenly, and as quickly as always, he went away.

'Well, Bob Crowe told me a queer one this evening,' he said that same evening, while she was placing their plates of fried food in front of them in the dining-room. 'It seems there's a woman asleep in Clery's shop window above in Dublin.'

His wife expressed disbelief. Bob Crowe would tell you anything, she said.

'In a hypnotic trance, it seems. Advertising Odearest Mattresses.'

'Ah, go on now! He's pulling your leg, Des.'

'Not a bit of him. She'll stop there a week, it seems. The Guards have to move the crowds on.'

Kathleen closed the dining-room door behind her. He had turned to look at her when he'd said there was a woman asleep in Clery's window, in an effort to include her in what he was retailing. His eyes had betrayed nothing of their surreptitious relationship, but Kathleen hadn't been able to meet them.

'We ploughed the field,' her father said the following Sunday. 'I've never turned up earth as good.'

She almost told him then. She longed to so much she could hardly prevent herself. She longed to let her tears come and to hear his voice consoling her. When she was a child she'd loved that.

'You're a great girl,' he said.

Mr Shaughnessy took to attending an earlier Mass than his wife and son, and when they were out at theirs he would come into the kitchen. When she hid in her bedroom he followed her there. She'd have locked herself in the outside W.C. if there'd been a latch on the door.

'Well, Kitty and myself were quiet enough here,' he'd say in the dining-room later on, when the three of them were eating their midday dinner. She couldn't understand how he could bring himself to speak like that, or how he could so hungrily eat his food, as though nothing had occurred. She couldn't understand how he could act normally with his son or with his other children when they came on a visit. It was extraordinary to hear Mrs Shaughnessy humming her songs about the house and calling him by his Christian name.

'The Kenny girl's getting married,' Mrs Shaughnessy said on one of these mealtime occasions. 'Tyson from the hardware.'

'I didn't know she was doing a line with him.'

'Oh, that's been going on a long time.'

'Is it the middle girl? The one with the peroxide?'

'Enid she's called.'

'I wonder Bob Crowe didn't hear that. There's not much Bob misses.'

'I never thought much of Tyson. But, sure, maybe they're well matched.'

'Did you hear that, Kitty? Enid Kenny's getting married. Don't go taking ideas from her.' He laughed, and Mrs Shaughnessy laughed, and the son smiled. There wasn't much chance of that, Kathleen thought. 'Are you going dancing tonight?' Mr Crawley often asked her on a Friday, and she would reply that she might, but she never did because it wasn't easy to go alone. In the shops and at Mass no one displayed any interest in her whatsoever, no one eyed her the way Mary Florence had been eyed, and she supposed it was because her looks weren't up to much. But they were good enough for Mr Shaughnessy, with his quivering breath and his face in her hair. Bitterly, she dwelt on that; bitterly, she imagined herself turning on him in the dining-room, accusing him to his wife and son.

'Did you forget to sweep the yard this week?' Mrs Shaughnessy asked her. 'Only it's looking poor.'

She explained that the wind had blown in papers and debris from a knocked-over dustbin. She'd sweep it again, she said.

'I hate a dirty backyard, Kitty.'

Was this why the other girls had left, she wondered, the girls whom Mrs Shaughnessy had trained, and who'd then gone off? Those girls, whoever they were, would see her, or would know about her. They'd imagine her in one uniform or the other, obedient to him because she enjoyed his attentions. That was how they'd think of her.

'Leave me alone, sir,' she said when she saw him approaching her the next time, but he took no notice. She could see him guessing she wouldn't scream.

'Please, sir,' she said. 'Please, sir. I don't like it.'

But after a time she ceased to make any protestation and remained as silent as she had been at first. Twelve years or maybe fourteen, she said to herself, lying awake in her bedroom: as long as that, or longer. In her two different uniforms she would continue to be the outward sign of Mrs Shaughnessy's well-to-do status, and her ordinary looks would continue to attract the attentions of a grey-haired man. Because of the field, the nature of the farm her father had once been barefoot on would change. 'Kathleen's field,' her father would often repeat, and her mother would say again that a bargain was a bargain.

FOR THE BEST IN PAPERBACKS, LOOK FOR THE

In every corner of the world, on every subject under the sun, Penguin represents quality and variety—the very best in publishing today.

For complete information about books available from Penguin—including Puffins, Penguin Classics, and Arkana—and how to order them, write to us at the appropriate address below. Please note that for copyright reasons the selection of books varies from country to country.

In the United Kingdom: Please write to *Dept. JC, Penguin Books Ltd, FREEPOST, West Drayton, Middlesex UB7 0BR.*

If you have any difficulty in obtaining a title, please send your order with the correct money, plus ten percent for postage and packaging, to *P.O. Box No. 11, West Drayton, Middlesex UB7 0BR*

In the United States: Please write to *Consumer Sales, Penguin USA, P.O. Box 999, Dept. 17109, Bergenfield, New Jersey 07621-0120.* VISA and MasterCard holders call 1-800-253-6476 to order all Penguin titles

In Canada: Please write to *Penguin Books Canada Ltd, 10 Alcorn Avenue, Suite 300, Toronto, Ontario M4V 3B2*

In Australia: Please write to *Penguin Books Australia Ltd, P.O. Box 257, Ringwood, Victoria 3134*

In New Zealand: Please write to *Penguin Books (NZ) Ltd, Private Bag 102902, North Shore Mail Centre, Auckland 10*

In India: Please write to *Penguin Books India Pvt Ltd, 706 Eros Apartments, 56 Nehru Place, New Delhi 110 019*

In the Netherlands: Please write to *Penguin Books Netherlands bv, Postbus 3507, NL-1001 AH Amsterdam*

In Germany: Please write to *Penguin Books Deutschland GmbH, Metzlerstrasse 26, 60594 Frankfurt am Main*

In Spain: Please write to *Penguin Books S.A., Bravo Murillo 19, 1° B, 28015 Madrid*

In Italy: Please write to *Penguin Italia s.r.l., Via Felice Casati 20, I-20124 Milano*

In France: Please write to *Penguin France S.A., 17 rue Lejeune, F–31000 Toulouse*

In Japan: Please write to *Penguin Books Japan, Ishikiribashi Building, 2–5–4, Suido, Bunkyo-ku, Tokyo 112*

In Greece: Please write to *Penguin Hellas Ltd, Dimocritou 3, GR–106 71 Athens*

In South Africa: Please write to *Longman Penguin Southern Africa (Pty) Ltd, Private Bag X08, Bertsham 2013*